EVERYMAN,
I WILL GO WITH THEE,
AND BE THY GUIDE,
IN THY MOST NEED
TO GO BY THY SIDE

MARGUERITE DURAS

THE LOVER

WARTIME NOTEBOOKS

PRACTICALITIES

WITH AN INTRODUCTION BY
RACHEL KUSHNER

EVERYMAN'S LIBRARY
Alfred A. Knopf   New York   London   Toronto
380

THIS IS A BORZOI BOOK
PUBLISHED BY ALFRED A. KNOPF

First included in Everyman's Library, 2018

The Lover
Translation copyright © 1985 by Random House, Inc. and William Collins
Sons & Co. Ltd.
Originally published in France as *L'Amant* by Les Editions de Minuit
Copyright © Les Editions de Minuit, 1984
First published in Great Britain by William Collins Sons & Co. Ltd., London,
and in the United States by Pantheon Books, a division of Random House,
Inc., New York, in 1985

Wartime Notebooks
© 2006 by P.O.L. éditeur/Imec éditeur
English translation © 2008 by The New Press
'Wartime Notebooks' initially published in France as the first part of *Cahiers de
la guerre et autres textes* by Editions P.O.L/IMEC, Paris, 2006
Published in the United States by The New Press, New York, 2008
Reprinted by arrangement with The New Press

Practicalities
Copyright © 1987 by P.O.L. éditeur
English translation copyright © 1990 by William Collins
La Vie matérielle first published in France by P.O.L, 1987
First published in Great Britain as *Practicalities*, 1990
English translation published in the USA by arrangement with
Grove Atlantic, Inc.

Introduction Copyright © 2018 by Rachel Kushner
Bibliography and Chronology Copyright © 2018 by Everyman's Library
Typography by Peter B. Willberg

All rights reserved. Published in the United States by Alfred A. Knopf, a
division of Penguin Random House LLC, New York, and in Canada by
Penguin Random House Canada Limited, Toronto. Distributed by Penguin
Random House LLC, New York. Published in the United Kingdom by
Everyman's Library, 50 Albemarle Street, London W1S 4DB and
distributed by Penguin Random House UK, 20 Vauxhall Bridge Road,
London SW1V 2SA.

www.randomhouse/everymans
www.everymanslibrary.co.uk

ISBN 978-1-101-90793-1 (US)
978-1-84159-380-7 (UK)

A CIP catalogue reference for this book is available from the British Library

Book design by Barbara de Wilde and Carol Devine Carson
Typeset in the UK by Input Data Services Ltd, Somerset.
Printed and bound in Germany by GGP Media GmbH, Pössneck

CONTENTS

INTRODUCTION

Duras with an S

Marguerite wasn't always Duras. She was born Donnadieu, but with the publication of her first novel, *Les impudents*, in 1943, she went from Donnadieu to Duras and stayed that way. She chose, as her alias, the village of her father's origins, distancing herself from her family, and binding herself to the emanations of that place name, which is pronounced with a regionally southern preference for a sibilant 's.' The village of Duras is in Lot-et-Garonne, an area south of the Dordogne and just north of Gascony. The language of Gascon, from which this practice of a spoken 's' derives, is not considered chic. More educated French people not from the region might be tempted to opt for a silent 's' with a proper name. In English, one hears a lot of Duraaah – especially from Francophiles. Duras herself said Durasss, and that's the correct, if unrefined, way to say it.

Proust, whom Duras admired a great deal and reread habitually, modeled the compelling and ridiculous Baron de Charlus on Robert de Montesquiou, of Gascony. Some argue that on account of Montesquiou's origins, Charlus should be pronounced Charlusss. In *Sodom and Gomorrah* Proust himself makes quite a bit of fun of the issue of pronunciations, and how they signify class and tact, and specifically, the matter of an 's,' of guessing if it's silent or sibilant. Madame de Cambremer-Legrandin experiences a kind of rapture the first time she hears a proper name *without* the sibilant 's' – Uzai instead of Uzès, and suddenly the silent 's,' 'a suppression that had stupefied her the day before, but which it now seemed to her so vulgar not to know,' becomes the proof, and apotheosis, of a lifetime of good breeding and 'smartness.'

So vulgar not to know, and yet what Proust is really saying is that it's equally vulgar to be so conscious of elite significations, even as he was entranced by the world of them. Madame de Cambremer-Legrandin is, after all, a mere bourgeois who elevated her station through marriage, and her self-conscious, snobbish silent 's' will never change that, and can only ever be a kind of striving, made touchingly comical in *Sodom and Gomorrah*. Duras is something else. No tricks, full 's.' Maybe, in part, her late life and notorious habit of referring to herself in the third person was a reminder to say it the humble way, Durasss. Or maybe it was just an element of what some labeled her narcissism, which seems like a superficial way to reject a genius. Duras was consumed with herself, true enough, but almost as if under a spell. Certain people experience their own lives very strongly. Regardless, there is a consistent quality, a kind of earthy simplicity, in all of her novels, films, plays, screenplays, notebooks, and in the dreamily precise oral 'telling' of *La Vie matérielle*, which is a master index of Durassianisms, of 's'-ness: lines that function on boldness and ease, which is to say, without pretension.

> 'There is one thing I'm good at, and that's looking at the sea.'
> 'When a woman drinks it's as if an animal were drinking, or a child.'
> 'Alcohol is a substitute for pleasure though it doesn't replace it.'
> 'A life is no small matter.'

Her assertions have the base facticity of soil and stones, even if one doesn't always agree with them. In *La Vie matérielle* she is particularly hard on men, her homophobia appearing to get worse as her life fused into a fraught and complicated autumn–spring intimacy with Yann Andréa, who was gay.

La Vie matérielle was translated as *Practicalities* by Barbara Bray, but might be more felicitously titled 'material life,' or 'everyday life.' The book began as recordings of Duras speaking to her son's friend Jérôme Beaujour. After the recordings were transcribed, there was much reworking and cutting and reformulating by Duras. In terms of categories, the book is unique, but all of Duras's writing is novelistic in its breadth and profundity, and all of it can be poured from one flask to another, from play to novel to film, without altering its Durassness. In part, this is because speech and writing are in some sense the same thing with Duras. When she talks, she is both feature in *Madame Dodin* but made their first appearances in the posthumously published *Wartime Notebooks*. The moments of truth in her work are elemental and felt, not synthetic or abstruse. She told Delphine Seyrig she might give up writing and open a service station for trucks along the highway. Meanwhile she was much loved and admired by many twentieth-century intellectuals, such as Jacques Lacan and Maurice Blanchot, both of whom wrote about her work ('I never understood much of him,' she said of Lacan). Samuel Beckett credited hearing her radio play of *The Square* as a significant moment in his own creative life. She had what both Beckett and the filmmaker Alain Resnais marveled over and admired as 'tone.' Durassian. Everything she made was marked by it, and the distinct quality of that tone is certainly what led to the accusation, true enough, that she was at risk sometimes, and inadvertently, of self-caricature. But every writer aspires to have some margin of original power, a patterning and order that comes to them as a gift bestowed, and is sent to no one else. If Duras wasn't so lucky, if she wasn't such a natural writer, her critics would have no object for their envy, their policing of excess, as well as the inverse – a suspicion of her restrained economy with words.

*

At the end of *La Vie matérielle*, she describes an encounter with an imaginary man, a hallucination, as if this man is perfectly real and he is: he is part of her fictive universe, the primal scenes she spent her life rendering, and reworking, telling, and then telling again. A lot of things happened to Marguerite Duras. She lost a child while giving birth, and in that experience lost God and gained unwanted knowledge of death. Her husband Robert Antelme was deported to Dachau, came back, but weighing eighty pounds. Duras worked for the Occupation, and later joined the Resistance, then the Communist Party. Was expelled from the Communist Party but remained a Marxist. Conducted televized interviews with both President François Mitterrand and Jean-Luc Godard. Aspects of her life are legends, like the destitute poverty of her childhood in Indochina. In some writings, her mother's ailment is madness.

In others, menopause. Or financial ruin. Sometimes, the mother's madness is her strength. Maybe these are not contradictions. The erotic charge between her and the older Chinese lover in Saigon seems like art, scenes that bloomed on paper. Things happened to Duras 'that she never experienced,' as she put it. The story of her life did not exist, she said. The novel of her life – yes. She obsessively read Proust, Conrad, and Ecclesiastes. She pursued a poetic absorption in the sacred and secret. She may have engendered a trend called autofiction, but she dismissed trends, and more importantly, she was adamant that the genre of autobiography was base, degraded. The same applied to 'essayistic' writing. She resisted the anti-novel rhetoric of the practitioners of the *nouveau roman*, whom she called 'businessmen.' Literature was her interest, *that* kind of truth.

Even her earliest works, from the notebooks, evince her gift for fiction. None of it reads like a diary, even when the experiences are ones we know are close to her biography. Much of it is in the third person, as if she were already controlling the levers of character, and the entries include crafted dialogue, artful gaps, compression. 'At one time,' she writes of childhood, 'we used to feast on the pickled flesh of young crocodiles, but in the end we tired of everything.' In an early draft of *The Sea Wall*, the sea, 'making itself at home, would come in and scorch the crops.' In an unpublished story called 'Théodora,' a knack for insinuating authorial intrusion, metafictional, but not distancing, is already present: 'Her eyes are green and shining, her dress is red. That's the situation.' In the early drafts from the notebooks of *The War*, she powerfully conveys the chaos of waiting to learn of her husband's fate in a concentration camp. 'I know everything you can know,' she writes, 'when you know nothing.' A woman waits to get news of her daughter, chattering that she's had new taps put on her daughter's shoes, but then blurts that her daughter has probably been gassed. 'With her stiff leg,' the mother says, 'they'll have gassed her.'

In a section about losing a baby, a nurse says, 'When they're that little we burn them.' The piece ends, 'People who believe in God have become complete strangers to me.'

The notebooks are full of that tone, that 's': high stakes, and brute experience.

*

By the time she wrote *The Lover*, Duras was seventy years old. The book, some may forget, begins with a man telling her he prefers her face 'as it is now. Ravaged.' But she was, according to men I've spoken to who knew her, devastatingly sexy, even in her advanced age. My surprise makes one of these men, the film director Barbet Schroeder, laugh. It suggests a hopeless ignorance of the force of Duras. Does it matter that she was sexy? In a sense, yes, because it allowed her to feed her insatiable need, so her biographers report, for erotic attention, and to understand her way around desire, which is to say, around writing. *The Lover* begins with that comment about her ravaged face and then corrects for the ravaging of age by presenting childhood, and memories, as ideals that continue to glow through the haze of history. *The Lover* is not an autobiography, but it was received as disclosure. Duras became a huge star. Readers were eager to wade in to a steamy vision of a colonial childhood and to presume it was her life. As a novel it is no more conventional than her others, but in its vivid compactness, the way it marbles and integrates the close and distant sensations and memories of a single life, one mind, it is a kind of artistic zenith.

The girl in the novel, never named, the 'I' and the 'she,' is 'a little white tart,' dressed in 'clown's hat and lamé shoes,' wearing a millionaire's diamond. The millionaire is a handsome Chinese landowner who takes her to a secret apartment in Cholon, the Chinese quarter of Saigon. Their liaison is forbidden, since he's not a white, but all the better; a forbidden love is more urgent.

The first instance of a lover appears in the *Wartime Notebooks*. He's called Léo, and he's not Chinese, but Vietnamese. He is ugly, scarred, and repulsive to her, but because of his wealth, and the pressure of her family, the young Duras pursues a relationship. She speaks of his 'profound stupidity'; he is 'truly pathetic' (how all suitors seem, whose affections are not requited). At one point Léo kisses her, and she's revolted. The scene is described almost like a rape.

In *The Lover*, the young girl has transformed into a pleasure doll. The lover bathes her, dries her, carries her to the bed. She's worshipped and adored and enjoys it, as power and as sensual rapture, and the reader feels the author's pleasure in this too. The child prostitute is gloriously self-possessed; her humiliations are society's hang-ups, not her own, and they only make her shine brighter, for the author and reader, both, who collude in whoring her out. It's the 'good' whoring, not the bad whoring – which may or may not have taken place, but either way, came first. Later, Duras said the depiction in *The Lover* was her actual childhood, but those who knew her best suggest she had begun to confuse her fiction with reality. The affair in the novel is a 'structure,' as Lacan might say, a triangle of narrator, child, and lover. Even Alain Vircondelet, the most credulous of her three biographers, calls the story a legend she invented, which, 'having ripened during her whole life, finally became true.' In *La Vie matérielle* she offers a corrective that seems only further embellishment: she says the lover didn't actually dry her after he bathed her with jars of water, but set her down on the bed *still wet*.

Rain water. Bath water. Rice paddies flooded by the Pacific: these are reflecting pools of an internal universe. Later, Duras poured the volume from *The Lover* into a new jar, *The North China Lover*, a new telling. But *The Lover*, a wisp of a book you can read in an afternoon, is the primal scene around which other myths and reveries all revolve.

Alcoholic, woman, writer: these identity-acts, the one who drinks, who lives as woman, who writes, seem to relate, all three, to a more fundamental, primordial action: the production of fiction, even when that fiction is somehow rooted in memory, the return to a childhood scene. If we associate fiction with writing, what about with women? With drinkers?

The scene in *La Vie matérielle* when Duras encounters the man who does not speak and cannot hear her, was no mere daydream, but a full-blown hallucination brought on by delirium tremens from alcohol withdrawal. The man wears a black overcoat. She wonders if maybe he is there to remind her of 'some immemorial connection' that has been cut but had been her '*raison d'être*' ever since she was born. She calls him a 'master apparition.' He's been in her house for a fortnight, looking at her, unaware she can't understand him, and unwavering in his plea, whatever it is. This man is distinct from the imagery in her novels. He's something else – a nightmare, in which a lifetime of expression, of finding a way to speak, fell on deaf ears.

The hallucination broke. When the man finally left, she wept for a long time. Three years later, she found a way to speak of him, to Jérôme Beaujour. Probably she even embellished the account a little, who knows, but in any case, how do you straighten the facts of a phantasm?

Rachel Kushner

RACHEL KUSHNER is the author of a collection of short fiction, *The Strange Case of Rachel K*, and two novels, *The Flamethrowers*, and *Telex from Cuba*, both of which were finalists for the National Book Award.

CHRONOLOGY

DATE	AUTHOR'S LIFE	LITERARY CONTEXT
1914	Born Marguerite Donnadieu, 4 April, in Gia Dinh (a suburb of Saigon), in Cochinchina (part of French Indochina, now Vietnam). Father Henri (a maths teacher), mother Marie Obscur (*née* Legrand) had both been married before. When Marguerite six months old, mother rushed back to France with numerous serious maladies.	Gide: *The Cellars of the Vatican.* Joyce: *Dubliners.*
1915	Mother returns to Saigon, but father falls ill and hospitalized in Marseille, then unable to return to Indochina because enlisted in French army.	Conrad: *Victory.* Ford: *The Good Soldier.* Woolf: *The Voyage Out.* Romain Rolland: Nobel Prize.
1916	Father returns to Saigon after (temporarily) being invalided out of army.	Joyce: *A Portrait of the Artist as a Young Man.* Kafka: *Metamorphosis.*
1917	Father appointed director of primary education, Hanoi.	Barbusse: *Under Fire.* Pirandello: *Right You are (if you think so).*
1918		Apollinaire: *Calligrammes.* Cather: *My Ántonia.* Tzara: *Dada Manifesto.*
1919		Gide: *The Pastoral Symphony.*
1920	Family moves to large house in Phnom Penh as result of father's promotion.	Colette: *Chéri.* Duhamel: *Midnight Confession.* Fitzgerald: *This Side of Paradise.* Lawrence: *Women in Love.* Mansfield: *Bliss and Other Stories.* Wharton: *The Age of Innocence.*
1921	Mother appointed headmistress of Norodom school. Father again repatriated, gravely ill, dies in Lot-et-Garonne, 4 December.	Pirandello: *Six Characters in Search of an Author.* Zamyatin: *We.* Anatole France: Nobel Prize.
1922	Mother takes family (Marguerite and two brothers, Pierre and	Colette: *Claudine's House.* Eliot: *The Waste Land.*

Austrian Archduke Franz Ferdinand and his wife assassinated in Sarajevo (28 June). Allies, championing Serb independence (threatened by Austria), drawn into First World War.

Lusitania sunk by German submarine.

Einstein's general theory of relativity published. First Battle of Somme (July–November).

February and October Revolutions in Russia; civil war begins. US joins First World War. Mutinies in French army. Battle of Passchendaele. Balfour Declaration on Palestine. Duchamps' *Fountain*. Freud: *Introduction to Psychoanalysis*.
Armistice (Allies and Germany) signed 11 November.

Versailles Peace Treaty. France regains Alsace and Lorraine.
French Socialists split at congress in Tours; French Communist Party (SFIC) founded. League of Nations founded.

Britain attempts to lower German war reparations; France resists. Famine in Russia. Paris attracts intellectuals and artists such as Picasso, Man Ray, Stravinsky, Beckett, Joyce, and 'Lost Generation' of American writers (Hemingway, Pound, Fitzgerald etc.).

Russia becomes USSR. Mussolini marches on Rome. Tutankhamun's tomb discovered.

DATE	AUTHOR'S LIFE	LITERARY CONTEXT
1922 *cont.*	Paul) to France, attempts to inherit Le Platier (Lot-et-Garonne).	Fitzgerald: *The Beautiful and the Damned.* Joyce: *Ulysses.* Woolf: *Jacob's Room.*
1923	Marguerite forms deep attachment for French country life.	Svevo: *Confessions of Zeno.*
1924	Mother takes family back to Saigon, but is posted to Phnom Penh, back to Norodom school. In December, she is posted up-country, to Vinh Long, Cochinchina.	Forster: *A Passage to India.* Mann: *The Magic Mountain.* Breton's Surrealist Manifesto.
1925	Mother becomes subject to bouts of depression, brothers (especially the violent Pierre) viewed as delinquents.	Dreiser: *An American Tragedy.* Fitzgerald: *The Great Gatsby.* Gide: *The Counterfeiters.* Kafka: *The Trial.* Woolf: *Mrs Dalloway.*
1926	Pierre repatriated. Mother sells house in Hanoi.	Aragon: *Paris Peasant.* Hemingway: *The Sun Also Rises.* Kafka: *The Castle.*
1927	Mother continues to request grant of land on Pacific in order to grow rice.	Desnos: *Liberty or Love!* Hesse: *Steppenwolf.* Mauriac: *Thérèse Desqueyroux.* Proust: *In Search of Lost Time* (posthumously published in full). Woolf: *To the Lighthouse.*
1928	Mother takes up post as headmistress of girls' school in Sadec. Nicknamed 'Madame Dieu'. Also takes possession of rice-growing concession (Prey-Nop) on Gulf of Siam, south-western Cambodia.	Brecht: *The Threepenny Opera.* Breton: *Nadja.* Colette: *Break of Day.* Hall: *The Well of Loneliness.* Lawrence: *Lady Chatterley's Lover.* Woolf: *Orlando.*
1929	Pierre, back from France, brings discord and violence to household. Rice-growing concession proves disastrous, ruins family. Marguerite sent to lycée Chasseloup-Laubat, Saigon.	Cocteau: *Les Enfants Terribles.* Faulkner: *The Sound and the Fury.* Woolf: *A Room of One's Own.*
1930	Marguerite lodges with 'Mademoiselle C.' ('la Bardet' in short story 'Boa'), begins two-year affair immortalized in *The Lover.*	Baum: *Grand Hotel.* Lawrence: *The Virgin and the Gypsy.* Musil: *The Man without Qualities.*

CHRONOLOGY

French PM Poincaré sends troops into Ruhr after Germany again defaults on reparations. Failure of Hitler's Munich *putsch*.
Poincaré loses power to coalition of the left, the Cartel des Gauches. French financial crisis. Death of Lenin.

Locarno Pact confirms Franco-German frontier, French troops leave Ruhr. First Surrealist exhibition, Galerie Pierre, Paris. Hitler publishes *Mein Kampf*.

Poincaré leads Union Nationale government, stabilizes French economy. Germany admitted to League of Nations. Trotsky dismissed from Politburo, USSR.
Far-right Croix-de-feu league founded. Lindbergh flies across Atlantic. *The Jazz Singer* first 'talkie'.

Devaluation of franc to fifth of its value. Kellogg-Briand Pact, outlawing war, accepted by Germany. Stalin becomes *de facto* dictator, USSR.

Ho Chi Minh founds Vietnamese Communist Party in Hong Kong. Poincaré retires. Young Plan requires Allies to evacuate Rhineland by June 1930. Collectivization begins in USSR; millions killed, sent to exile or concentration camps. Wall Street crash.

Construction of Maginot line begun. Amy Johnson flies from London to Australia. Gandhi begins Indian civil disobedience campaign.

MARGUERITE DURAS

DATE	AUTHOR'S LIFE	LITERARY CONTEXT
1930 *cont.*		Némirovsky: *The Ball.* Rhys: *After Leaving* *Mr Mackenzie.*
1931	Family returns briefly to France, living at Le Platier and visiting Paris.	Beckett: *Proust.* Faulkner: *Sanctuary.* Saint-Exupéry: *Night Flight.* Woolf: *The Waves.*
1932	Family returns to Saigon, lives in house in rue Testard. Mother teaches at local school; Marguerite returns to lycée Chasseloup-Laubat to take second baccalaureate.	Broch: *The Sleepwalkers.* Céline: *Journey to the End of the Night.* Faulkner: *Light in August.* Huxley: *Brave New World.*
1933	Marguerite returns to Marseille, travels to Paris, refuses to live with Pierre, moves in to boarding house behind the Bon Marché.	Lorca: *Blood Wedding.* Malraux: *Man's Fate.* Orwell: *Down and Out in Paris and London.* Stein: *The Autobiography of Alice B. Toklas.* White: *Frost in May.*
1934	Marguerite studies at faculty of law, rue Saint-Jacques.	Beckett: *More Pricks than Kicks.* Chevallier: *Clochemerle.* Cocteau: *The Infernal Machine.* Dinesen: *Seven Gothic Tales.* Fitzgerald: *Tender is the Night.* H. Roth: *Call It Sleep.*
1935	Meets Jean Lagrolet, fellow student, who shares her love of literature, and helps her discover the theatre.	Eliot: *Murder in the Cathedral.* Isherwood: *Mr Norris Changes Trains.* Malraux: *Days of Wrath.*
1936	Forges firm bond with Georges Beauchamp and Robert Antelme ('the most important man to me personally and to others'), two friends of Jean Lagrolet's.	Bernanos: *The Diary of a Country Priest.* Cain: *Double Indemnity.* Faulkner: *Absalom, Absalom!* Huxley: *Eyeless in Gaza.* Lehmann: *The Weather in the Streets.*
1937	Leaves Lagrolet for Antelme, and lives emancipated, independent life in Paris.	Hemingway: *To Have and Have Not.* Hurston: *Their Eyes were Watching God.* Woolf: *The Years.*
1938	Antelme enlists in French army. Marguerite joins Colonial Office as an 'assistant'.	Bowen: *The Death of the Heart.* Connolly: *Enemies of Promise.* Nabokov: *The Gift.* Queneau: *Children of Clay.* Sartre: *Nausea.*

CHRONOLOGY

Depression in France. Germany suspends payment of war reparations. Britain abandons Gold Standard.

French president Doumer assassinated. Famine in Ukraine. Roosevelt elected US president.

Radical Daladier French PM. Growth of Fascist movement in France. Hitler becomes German Chancellor, proclaims Third Reich and leaves League of Nations.

Stavisky Affair (financial scandal) implicates leading Radicals. Anti-Fascist General Strike in France. Daladier resigns, replaced by Doumerge. Hitler becomes Führer, commences German rearmament. Stalin places national security under NKVD control; Kirov murdered.

Short-lived premiership of Laval. Left-wing parties unite, forming Front Populaire. French-Soviet mutual assistance pact. Mussolini invades Abyssinia. Nuremberg Laws (Germany) debar Jews from public life. Stalin begins purges, liquidating millions.
Front Populaire wins French election; Communists refuse to participate in government. Léon Blum PM, embarks on programme of social reform. Spanish Civil War. Hitler marches into demilitarized Rhineland. Abdication crisis in UK.

French unemployment high; Blum's cabinet falls. Paris hosts exposition universelle. Germans attack Guernica in Basque region, inspiring Picasso's eponymous painting.

Front Populaire disintegrates, Daladier becomes PM. Hitler sends troops into Austria and part of Czechoslovakia, but is appeased by Britain and France via the Munich Agreement. Kristallnacht sees German Jews systematically terrorized.

DATE	AUTHOR'S LIFE	LITERARY CONTEXT
1939	Works for intercolonial department of information, tasked with writing book praising the virtues of colonial empire (*L'Empire français*). Marries Antelme 23 September.	Green: *Party Going.* Isherwood: *Goodbye to Berlin.* Joyce: *Finnegans Wake.* Sarraute: *Tropisms.* Steinbeck: *The Grapes of Wrath.*
1940	*L'Empire français* published 25 April. Marguerite leaves for Tours, then for Brive, but returns to Paris (September), where she resigns from Colonial Office.	Chandler: *Farewell, My Lovely.* Hemingway: *For Whom the Bell Tolls.* Koestler: *Darkness at Noon.* McCullers: *The Heart is a Lonely Hunter.*
1941	Living in rue Saint-Benoît with Antelme, Marguerite begins first novel, initially entitled *La famille Taneran*. Meets Raymond Queneau.	Anouilh: *Eurydice.* Brecht: *Mother Courage and Her Children.* Cain: *Mildred Pierce.* Némirovsky writes *Suite Française* (to 1942).
1942	Has stillborn child. Joins Book Organization Office (July), in charge of readers' reports. Begins affair with Dionys Mascolo. Brother Paul dies (December).	Anouilh: *Antigone.* Camus: *The Outsider.* Queneau: *Pierrot mon ami.*
1943	Publishes first novel, now called *Les Impudents* (Plon), under name of Duras. Brother Pierre plagues her in Paris, but she supports him. Joins Resistance.	Genet: *Our Lady of the Flowers.* Hesse: *The Glass Bead Game.* Peyrefitte: *Particular Friendships.* Saint-Exupéry: *The Little Prince.* Sartre: *The Flies.*
1944	Antelme arrested, sparking events described in *La Douleur* etc. Mascolo edits *Combat*, thanks to Albert Camus, then edits FFI (Forces françaises de l'intérieur) newspaper *Libres*, for which Marguerite works, also assisting with interrogations (see 'Albert of the Capitals'). Publishes *La Vie tranquille* (Gallimard).	Colette: *Gigi.* Jackson: *The Lost Weekend.* Sartre: *Huis Clos.*
1945	Settles back into liberated Parisian life with the returned Antelme and Mascolo, embracing Communism and	Beauvoir: *The Blood of Others.* Green: *Loving.* Orwell: *Animal Farm.* Sartre: *The Age of Reason.*

CHRONOLOGY

DATE	AUTHOR'S LIFE	LITERARY CONTEXT
1945 *cont.*	eschewing revenge. Founds publishing house, Cité universelle.	Smart: *By Grand Central Station I Sat Down and Wept.*
1946	Goes to Dordogne on her own to sort out feelings regarding Antelme and Mascolo. Becomes secretary of Communist cell 722, but has increasing doubts about Party.	Kazantzakis: *Zorba the Greek.* McCullers: *Member of the Wedding.* Peake: *Titus Groan.* Vian: *I Spit on Your Graves.*
1947	Son Jean born, 30 June. Divorces Antelme. Gives up writing *Théodora.*	Anouilh: *Invitation to the Castle.* Camus: *The Plague.* Genet: *The Maids.* Levi: *If This is a Man.* Lowry: *Under the Volcano.* Mann: *Doctor Faustus.* Queneau: *Exercises in Style.* Vian: *Froth on the Daydream.*
1948	Goes alone with son to Brittany. Ideological arguments (about Stalinism, Yugoslavia, Czechoslovakia etc.) rage in rue Saint-Benoît.	Bowen: *The Heat of the Day.* Faulkner: *Intruder in the Dust.*
1949	Marguerite, Mascolo and Antelme expelled from Communist Party.	Algren: *The Man with the Golden Arm.* Beauvoir: *The Second Sex.* Bowles: *The Sheltering Sky.* Orwell: *Nineteen Eighty-Four.* William Faulkner: Nobel Prize.
1950	Expulsion from Party confirmed. Publishes *Un barrage contre le Pacifique* [*The Sea Wall*] (Gallimard), shortlisted for the Prix Goncourt.	Bataille: *L'Abbé C.* Grossman: *Stalingrad.* Highsmith: *Strangers on a Train.* Lessing: *The Grass is Singing.*
1951	Starts brief relationship with Jacques-Laurent Bost.	Beckett: *Molloy.* Camus: *The Rebel.* Salinger: *The Catcher in the Rye.* Yourcenar: *Memoirs of Hadrian.*
1952	Publishes *Le marin de Gibraltar* [*The Sailor from Gibraltar*] (Gallimard).	Anouilh: *The Lark.* Frank: *Diary of a Young Girl.* O'Connor: *Wise Blood.* Steinbeck: *East of Eden.* François Mauriac: Nobel Prize.
1953	Publishes *Les petits chevaux de Tarquinia* [*The Little Horses of Tarquinia*] (Gallimard).	Baldwin: *Go Tell It on the Mountain.* Beckett: *Waiting for Godot.*

CHRONOLOGY

Nuremberg Trials. USSR extends influence over Eastern Europe, beginning Cold War. Churchill's 'Iron Curtain' speech. Fourth Republic in France, Socialist Félix Gouin president. French troops attack Viet Minh in Haiphong, sparking war of resistance to colonial power (Indochina War, to 1954).

Marshall Plan promises US aid for European recovery. Independence and partition of India. Rebellion against French rule, Madagascar.

USSR blockades East Berlin. Communist coup in Czechoslovakia. Jewish State of Israel founded. Gandhi assassinated. Apartheid introduced in South Africa. UN General Assembly adopts Universal Declaration of Human Rights.

North Atlantic Treaty signed. Germany divided into East and West. Communists win Chinese Civil War.

Korean War. China invades Tibet. Democratic Republic of Vietnam recognized by China and USSR.

Treaty of Paris establishes European Coal and Steel Community.

Eisenhower elected US president. First contraceptive pills available.

End of Korean War. Stalin dies. Tito president of Yugoslavia. European Court of Human Rights set up. Structure of DNA described by Watson and Crick.

DATE	AUTHOR'S LIFE	LITERARY CONTEXT
1953 *cont.*		Bellow: *The Adventures of Augie March*. Miller: *The Crucible*. Robbe-Grillet: *The Erasers*.
1954	Publishes short-story collection, *Des journées entières dans les arbres* [*Whole Days in the Trees*] (Gallimard), portraying her mother, currently living on the Loire.	Beauvoir: *The Mandarins*. Réage: *The Story of O*. Sagan: *Bonjour Tristesse*. Ernest Hemingway: Nobel Prize.
1955	Publishes short story/philosophical tale *Le square* (Gallimard). Signs petition against war in North Africa, along with fellow members of the Committee of Intellectuals Against the Pursuit of the War in Algeria.	Miller: *A View from the Bridge*. Nabokov: *Lolita*. Robbe-Grillet: *The Voyeur*. Williams: *Cat on a Hot Tin Roof*.
1956	Continues agitating against Algerian war. Drifts apart from Mascolo. *Le square* performed at the Studio des Champs-Elysées.	Baldwin: *Giovanni's Room*. Camus: *The Fall*. O'Neill: *Long Day's Journey into Night*. Sagan: *A Certain Smile*.
1957	Has passionate affair with Gérard Jarlot. Mother dies.	Butor: *Second Thoughts*. Durrell: *Justine*. Kerouac: *On the Road*. Nabokov: *Pnin*. Pasternak: *Doctor Zhivago*. Albert Camus: Nobel Prize.
1958	Publishes *Moderato cantabile* (Editions de Minuit), championed by Robbe-Grillet. Becomes one of only two female contributors to dissenting magazine *Le 14 Juillet*. Writes weekly articles for *France-Observateur* on books or social life.	Achebe: *Things Fall Apart*. Beckett: *The Unnamable*, *Krapp's Last Tape*. Genet: *The Blacks*.
1959	Publishes *Les viaducs de la Seine-et-Oise*, study of celebrated murder case. Buys house in Neauphle-le-Château. Writes screenplay of *Hiroshima mon amour* (Resnais).	Anouilh: *Becket*. Burroughs: *Naked Lunch*. Grossman: *Life and Fate*. Queneau: *Zazie in the Metro*. P. Roth: *Goodbye, Columbus*. Spark: *Memento Mori*.
1960	Elected to judge panel of prix Médicis. Publishes *Dix heures et demie de soir en été* [*Ten-Thirty on*	Céline: *North*. Durrell: *Clea*. Simon: *The Flanders Road*.

CHRONOLOGY

French defeat in Vietnam at battle of Dien Bien Phu; peace talks in Geneva; French withdrawal; Vietnam divided into North and South. Algerian War of Independence. Nasser comes to power in Egypt.

Warsaw Pact formed (USSR and several Eastern European countries).

French colonial rule ends, Tunisia and Morocco. USSR invades Hungary; Khrushchev denounces Stalin. Suez crisis.

European Economic Community founded (France, Belgium, Italy, Luxembourg, the Netherlands, West Germany). USSR launches Sputnik. Beginning of Communist insurgency in South Vietnam.

Fourth Republic falls, result of Algerian crisis. De Gaulle returns, strengthened, to power (Fifth Republic).

Castro takes power, Cuba. Resnais and Truffaut spearhead 'New Wave' cinema in France.

France conducts nuclear weapons tests, Algeria. Kennedy elected US president. Sharpeville massacre, South Africa; African National Congress (ANC) outlawed.

DATE	AUTHOR'S LIFE	LITERARY CONTEXT
1960 *cont.*	*a Summer Night*] and screenplay of *Hiroshima mon amour* (Gallimard).	Updike: *Rabbit, Run.*
1961	Her adaptation (with Antelme) of James's *The Aspern Papers* staged.	Beckett: *Happy Days.* Heller: *Catch-22.* Murdoch: *A Severed Head.* Spark: *The Prime of Miss Jean Brodie.* Yates: *Revolutionary Road.*
1962	Adaptation (with James Lord) of James's 'The Beast in the Jungle' staged. Drafts *L'homme assis dans le couloir* [*The Man Sitting in the Corridor*].	Baldwin: *Another Country.* Bassani: *The Garden of the Finzi-Continis.* Lessing: *The Golden Notebook.* Nabokov: *Pale Fire.* Solzhenitsyn: *One Day in the Life of Ivan Denisovich.*
1963	Finishes *Le ravissement de Lol V. Stein* [*The Ravishing of Lol Stein*] (Gallimard, 1964).	Grass: *Dog Years.* Kadare: *The General of the Dead Army.* Pagnol: *The Water of the Hills.* Plath: *The Bell Jar.* Spark: *The Girls of Slender Means.*
1964	Works on staging *Whole Days in the Trees*, meets actress Madeleine Renaud, who plays Marguerite's mother.	Bellow: *Herzog.* Nabokov: *The Defense.* Selby: *Last Exit to Brooklyn.* Jean-Paul Sartre: Nobel Prize.
1965	*Les eaux et les forêts* staged, théâtre Mouffetard. *La Musica* also staged. *Le vice-consul* published (Gallimard).	Drabble: *The Millstone.* Infante: *Three Trapped Tigers.* Levi: *The Truce.* Mailer: *An American Dream.* Plath: *Ariel.* Sagan: *La Chamade.*
1966	*Le vice-consol* badly reviewed. Marguerite decides to enter film world; shooting begins of *La Musica*. Scripts *La Voleuse* [*The Thief*]. Jarlot dies.	Capote: *In Cold Blood.* Endo: *Silence.* Rhys: *Wide Sargasso Sea.*
1967	Special envoy at Cannes Film Festival (May). Publishes *L'amante anglaise* [*The English Mistress*] (Gallimard).	Beauvoir: *The Woman Destroyed.* Kavan: *Ice.* Kundera: *The Joke.* Márquez: *One Hundred Years of Solitude.* Tournier: *Friday.*

CHRONOLOGY

Algerian demonstrators killed by Paris police. Berlin Wall erected. Yuri Gagarin (USSR) first man in space. Bay of Pigs invasion.

Algeria wins independence from France. Cuban missile crisis. Number of US military advisers in South Vietnam rises to 12,000.

De Gaulle vetoes British entry into EEC. Kennedy assassinated. Civil Rights march, Washington. Viet Cong (Communist guerrillas operating in South Vietnam) defeat South Vietnamese army; President Diem of South Vietnam overthrown in US-backed coup.

US Civil Rights Act (outlaws segregation in schools, public places, employment). Martin Luther King: Nobel Peace Prize. Nelson Mandela jailed for life, South Africa.

De Gaulle re-elected. Algiers police break up pro-Ben Bella demonstrations. US bombing in Vietnam begins, Marines deployed (March).

Mao's Cultural Revolution launched (China). Race riots across US. Michel Foucault: *The Order of Things*.

Arab-Israeli Six-Day War. De Gaulle visits Canada. First heart transplant operation.

DATE	AUTHOR'S LIFE	LITERARY CONTEXT
1968	Joins May protests, writes street slogans for protesters, continues theatre work.	Bowen: *Eva Trout.* Modiano: *La Place de l'étoile.* Updike: *Couples.* Vidal: *Myra Breckinridge.*
1969	Publishes *Détruire dit-elle* [*Destroy, She Said*] (Editions de Minuit).	Atwood: *The Edible Woman.* Perec: *A Void.* Roth: *Portnoy's Complaint.* Vonnegut: *Slaughterhouse Five.*
1970	Publishes *Abahn Sabana David* (Gallimard), her most obscure book.	Barthelme: *City Life.* Davies: *Fifth Business.*
1971	Publishes *L'amour* (Gallimard), but considering words 'dangerous', moves more into film.	Selby: *The Room.* Updike: *Rabbit Redux.*
1972	Films *Nathalie Granger* with family and close friends at Neauphle.	Beckett: *Not I.* Calvino: *Invisible Cities.*
1973	Films *Woman of the Ganges.*	Kundera: *Life is Elsewhere.* Pynchon: *Gravity's Rainbow.*
1974	Films *India Song*, her most popular movie.	Böll: *The Lost Honour of Katharina Blum.* Heller: *Something Happened.* Jong: *Fear of Flying.*
1975		Bellow: *Humboldt's Gift.* Bernhard: *Correction.* Perec: *W, or The Memory of Childhood.*
1976	Releases *Son nom de Venise dans Calcutta désert*, her favourite film.	Barthelme: *Amateurs.* Beckett: *Footfalls.*
1977	Releases *Vera Baxter* and *Le camion*, latter screened at Cannes. *L'Eden Cinéma*, a dramatic rewriting of *The Sea Wall*, opens at the théâtre d'Orsay.	Coover: *The Public Burning.* French: *The Women's Room.* Herr: *Dispatches.* Morrison: *Song of Solomon.*
1978	Begins shooting *Le navire night.*	Bernhard: *Yes.* Irving: *The World According to Garp.* Modiano: *Missing Person.* Perec: *Life: A User's Manual.* Selby: *Requiem for a Dream.*
1979	Publishes *Le navire night* as a novel, along with *Césarée* and *Les mains négatives* (Mercure de France). Writes *Aurélia Steiner* cycle, then films it.	Carter: *The Bloody Chamber and Other Stories.* Calvino: *If on a Winter's Night a Traveller.* Mailer: *The Executioner's Song.*

CHRONOLOGY

DATE	AUTHOR'S LIFE	LITERARY CONTEXT
1979 *cont.*		Roth: *The Ghost Writer.*
		Styron: *Sophie's Choice.*
1980	Alcohol and anti-depressant use triggers fainting fits and results in two months in hospital. Writes column for *Libération.* Publishes *Vera Baxter* (Albatros), *L'homme assis dans le couloir* (drafted 1962) and *L'Eté 80* [*Summer 1980*] (Editions de Minuit).	Bowen: *Collected Stories.* Eco: *The Name of the Rose.* Robinson: *Housekeeping.* Toole: *A Confederacy of Dunces.*
1981	Enters relationship with Yann Andréa. Publishes *Agatha,* about incest (Editions de Minuit) and *Outside* (Albin Michel).	Robbe-Grillet: *Djinn.* Rushdie: *Midnight's Children.* Thomas: *The White Hotel.* Yourcenar: *Anna, Soror.*
1982	Publishes *L'homme atlantique* [The *Atlantic Man*], *Savannah Bay* and *La maladie de la mort* [*The Malady of Death*] (Editions de Minuit). Goes into detox programme (cirrhosis).	Allende: *The House of the Spirits.* Keneally: *Schindler's Ark.* Pinget: *Monsieur Songe.* Walker: *The Color Purple.*
1983	Sparked by childhood photographs, begins writing *L'amant* [*The Lover*].	Bernhard: *The Loser.* Sarraute: *Childhood.*
1984	*The Lover,* her most famous novel, published; wins Prix Goncourt.	Brookner: *Hotel du Lac.* Kundera: *The Unbearable Lightness of Being.*
1985	*La Musica 2* staged. Publishes *La douleur* [*The War*] (POL). Film, *Les Enfants,* screened at Cannes.	Atwood: *The Handmaid's Tale.* Márquez: *Love in the Time of Cholera.* Tyler: *The Accidental Tourist.*
1986	Receives Ritz-Paris-Hemingway Prize ($50,000). Publishes *Les yeux bleus cheveux noirs* [*Blue Eyes, Black Hair*] and *La pute de la côte normande* [*The Slut of the Normandy Coast*] (Editions de Minuit).	Ford: *The Sportswriter.* Munro: *The Progress of Love.* Redonnet: *Hotel Splendid.* Tournier: *The Golden Droplet.*
1987	Publishes *La vie matérielle* [*Practicalities*] (POL) and *Emily L.* (Editions de Minuit).	Auster: *The Locked Room.* Lively: *Moon Tiger.* Morrison: *Beloved.* Murakami: *Norwegian Wood.* Wolfe: *The Bonfire of the Vanities.*
1988	Again admitted to hospital (breathing difficulties).	Eco: *Foucault's Pendulum.* Harris: *The Silence of the Lambs.* Rushdie: *The Satanic Verses.*

CHRONOLOGY

HISTORICAL EVENTS

Solidarity movement starts strikes in Poland. Reagan elected US president.

Mitterrand elected French president. Sadat assassinated (Egypt). Martial law declared in Poland. AIDS cases first reported, UK and US.

Falklands War.

US invasion of Grenada. Reagan announces 'Star Wars' initiative.

Indira Gandhi assassinated (India).

Gorbachev becomes General Secretary, USSR.

Chirac becomes French PM. Gorbachev–Reagan summit. US bombs Tripoli. State of Emergency (South Africa). Chernobyl nuclear power station accident.

'Black Monday' stock market crash worldwide.

Mitterrand re-elected. George Bush US president. USSR withdraws from Afghanistan. Stephen Hawking: *A Brief History of Time.*

DATE	AUTHOR'S LIFE	LITERARY CONTEXT
1989	Emerges from coma.	Tournier: *Midnight Love Feast*.
1990	Publishes *La pluie d'été* [*Summer Rain*] (POL).	Munro: *Friend of My Youth*. Pamuk: *The Black Book*.
1991	Publishes *L'amant de la Chine du nord* [*The North China Lover*] (Gallimard).	Smiley: *A Thousand Acres*.
1992	Jean-Jacques Annaud's film of *The Lover* released. Publishes *Yann Andréa Steiner* (Gallimard).	Byatt: *Angels and Insects*. Ondaatje: *The English Patient*. Sebald: *The Emigrants*. Winterson: *Written on the Body*.
1993	Publishes *Ecrire* [*Writing*] (Gallimard).	Lambrichs: *Hannah's Diary*. Proulx: *The Shipping News*. Shields: *The Stone Diaries*.
1994	Holes up in rue Saint-Benoît with Yann.	Munro: *Open Secrets*. Redonnet: *Nevermore*.
1995	Publishes *C'est tout* [*No More*] (POL).	Modiano: *Out of the Dark*.
1996	Dies 3 March.	Atwood: *Alias Grace*. Gallant: *Selected Stories*.

CHRONOLOGY

HISTORICAL EVENTS

Communism collapses in Eastern Europe. Berlin Wall falls; democratic elections, USSR. Tiananmen Square Massacre (China). Apartheid begins dismantling process (South Africa). Worldwide Web invented by Tim Berners-Lee.
Reunification of Germany. Lech Walesa president of Poland; Boris Yeltsin of Russian republic.
EEC becomes European Union after Maastricht Treaty. Gulf War breaks out. USSR, Warsaw Pact dissolved. War in the former Yugoslavia.

France signs Maastricht Treaty. Bill Clinton US president.

Arafat and Rabin sign Palestinian–Israeli peace agreement.

Mandela forms ANC government (South Africa).

Chirac elected French president. France condemned for nuclear tests in Pacific. Rabin assassinated (Israel). Jean Baudrillard: *The Gulf War Did Not Take Place.*
Clinton re-elected (US).

SELECT BIBLIOGRAPHY

LAURE ADLER, *Marguerite Duras: A Life*, translated by Anne-Marie Glasheen, Victor Gollancz, London, 2000; University of Chicago Press, Chicago, 2000.

ALAIN VIRCONDELET, *Duras: A Biography*, translated by Thomas Buckley, Dalkey Archive Press, Normal, Illinois, 1994.

JEAN VALLIERS, *C'était Marguerite Duras: 1914–1996*, Libraire générale française, Paris, 2014 (not available in English, but a crucial contribution to the works available on her life).

THE LOVER

TRANSLATED BY BARBARA BRAY

For Bruno Nuytten

ONE DAY, I was already old, in the entrance of a public place a man came up to me. He introduced himself and said: 'I've known you for years. Everyone says you were beautiful when you were young, but I want to tell you I think you're more beautiful now than then. Rather than your face as a young woman, I prefer your face as it is now. Ravaged.'

I often think of the image only I can see now, and of which I've never spoken. It's always there, in the same silence, amazing. It's the only image of myself I like, the only one in which I recognize myself, in which I delight.

Very early in my life it was too late. It was already too late when I was eighteen. Between eighteen and twenty-five my face took off in a new direction. I grew old at eighteen. I don't know if it's the same for everyone. I've never asked. But I believe I've heard of the way time can suddenly accelerate on people when they're going through even the most youthful and highly esteemed stages of life. My ageing was very sudden. I saw it spread over my features one by one, changing the relationship between them, making the eyes larger, the expression sadder, the mouth more final, leaving great creases in the forehead. But instead of being dismayed I watched this process with the same sort of interest I might have taken in the reading of a book. And I knew I was right, that one day it would slow down and take its normal course. The people who knew me at seventeen, when I went to France, were surprised when they saw me again two years later, at nineteen. And I've kept it ever since, the new face I had then. It has been my face. It's got older still, of course, but less, comparatively, than it would otherwise have done. It's scored with deep, dry wrinkles, the skin is cracked. But my face hasn't collapsed, as some with fine features have done. It's kept the same contours, but its substance has been laid waste. I have a face laid waste.

So, I'm fifteen and a half.

It's on a ferry crossing the Mekong river.

The image lasts all the way across.

I'm fifteen and a half, there are no seasons in that part of the world, we have just the one season, hot, monotonous, we're in the long hot girdle of the earth, with no spring, no renewal.

I'm at a state boarding school in Saigon. I eat and sleep there, but I go to classes at the French high school. My mother's a teacher and wants her girl to have a secondary education. 'You have to go to high school.' What was enough for her is not enough for her daughter. High school and then a good degree in mathematics. That was what had been dinned into me ever since I started school. It never crossed my mind I might escape the mathematics degree, I was glad to give her that hope. Every day I saw her planning her own and her children's future. There came a time when she couldn't plan anything very grand for her sons any more, so she planned other futures, makeshift ones, but they too served their purpose, they blocked in the time that lay ahead. I remember my younger brother's courses in book-keeping. From the Universal Correspondence School – every year, every level. You have to catch up, my mother used to say. It would last for three days, never four. Never. We'd drop the Universal School whenever my mother was posted to another place. And begin again in the next. My mother kept it up for ten years. It wasn't any good. My younger brother became an accountant's clerk in Saigon. There was no technical school in the colonies; we owed my elder brother's departure for France to that. He stayed in France for several years to study at the technical school. But he didn't keep it up. My mother must have known. But she had no choice, he had to be got away from the other two children.

For several years he was no longer part of the family. It was while he was away that my mother bought the land, the concession. A terrible business, but for us, the children who were left, not so terrible as the presence of the killer would have been, the child-killer of the night, of the night of the hunter.

I've often been told it was because of spending all one's childhood in too strong a sun. But I've never believed it. I've also been told it was because being poor made us brood. But no, that wasn't it. Children like little old men because of chronic hunger, yes. But us, no, we weren't hungry. We were white children, we were ashamed, we sold our furniture but we weren't hungry, we had a houseboy and we ate. Sometimes, admittedly, we ate garbage, storks, baby crocodiles, but the garbage was cooked and served by a houseboy, and sometimes we refused it, too, we indulged in the luxury of declining to eat. No, something occurred when I was eighteen to make this face happen. It must have been at night. I was afraid of myself, afraid of God. In the daylight I was less afraid, and death seemed less important. But it haunted me all the time. I wanted to kill – my older brother, I wanted to kill him, to get the better of him for once, just once, and see him die. I wanted to do it to remove from my mother's sight the object of her love, that son of hers, to punish her for loving him so much, so badly, and above all – as I told myself, too – to save my younger brother, my younger brother, my child, save him from the living life of that elder brother superimposed on his own, from that black veil over the light, from the law which was decreed and represented by the elder brother, a human being, and yet which was an animal law, filling every moment of every day of the younger brother's life with fear, a fear that one day reached his heart and killed him.

I've written a good deal about the members of my family, but then they were still alive, my mother and my brothers. And I skirted around them, skirted around all these things without really tackling them.

The story of my life doesn't exist. Does not exist. There's never any centre to it. No path, no line. There are great spaces where you pretend there used to be someone, but it's not true, there was no one. The story of one small part of my youth I've already written, more or less – I mean, enough to give a glimpse of it. Of this part, I mean, the part about the crossing of the river. What I'm doing now is both different and the same. Before, I spoke of clear periods, those on which the light fell. Now I'm talking about the hidden stretches of that same youth, of certain facts, feelings, events that I buried. I started to write in surroundings that drove me to reticence. Writing, for those people, was still something moral. Nowadays it often seems writing is nothing at all. Sometimes I realize that if writing isn't, all things, all contraries confounded, a quest for vanity and void, it's nothing. That if it's not, each time, all things confounded into one through some inexpressible essence, then writing is nothing but advertisement. But usually I have no opinion, I can see that all options are open now, that there seem to be no more barriers, that writing seems at a loss for somewhere to hide, to be written, to be read. That its basic unseemliness is no longer accepted. But at that point I stop thinking about it.

Now I see that when I was very young, eighteen, fifteen, I already had a face that foretold the one I acquired through drink in middle age. Drink accomplished what God did not. It also served to kill me; to kill. I acquired that drinker's face before I drank. Drink only confirmed it. The space for it existed in me. I knew it the same as other people, but, strangely, in advance. Just as the space existed in me for desire. At the age of fifteen I had the face of pleasure, and yet I had no knowledge of pleasure. There was no mistaking that face. Even my mother must have seen it. My brothers did. That was how everything started for me – with that flagrant, exhausted face, those rings round the eyes, in advance of time and experience.

I'm fifteen and a half. Crossing the river. Going back to Saigon I feel I'm going on a journey, especially when I take the bus, and this morning I've taken the bus from Sadec, where my mother's the headmistress of the girls' school. It's the end of some school vacation, I forget which. I've spent it in the little house provided with my mother's job. And today I'm going back to Saigon, to the boarding school. The native bus left from the market place in Sadec. As usual my mother came to see me off, and put me in the care of the driver. She always puts me in the care of the Saigon bus drivers, in case there's an accident, or a fire, or a rape, or an attack by pirates, or a fatal mishap on the ferry. As usual the driver had me sit near him in the front, in the section reserved for white passengers.

I think it was during this journey that the image became detached, removed from all the rest. It might have existed, a photograph might have been taken, just like any other, some-where else, in other circumstances. But it wasn't. The subject was too slight. Who would have thought of such a thing? The photograph could only have been taken if someone could have known in advance how important it was to be in my life, that event, that crossing of the river. But, while it was happening, no one even knew of its existence. Except God. And that's why – it couldn't have been otherwise – the image doesn't exist. It was omitted. Forgotten. It never was detached or removed from all the rest. And it's to this, this failure to have been created, that the image owes its virtue: the virtue of representing, of being the creator of, an absolute.

So it's during the crossing of a branch of the Mekong, on the ferry that plies between Vinh Long and Sadec in the great plain of mud and rice in southern Cochin-China. The Plain of the Birds.

I get off the bus. I go over to the rails. I look at the river. My mother sometimes tells me that never in my whole life shall I ever again see rivers as beautiful and big and wild as these, the Mekong and its tributaries going down to the sea, the great regions of water soon to disappear into the caves of ocean. In the surrounding flatness stretching as far as the eye can see, the rivers flow as fast as if the earth sloped downwards.

I always get off the bus when we reach the ferry, even at night, because I'm always afraid, afraid the cables might break and we might be swept out to sea. In the terrible current I watch my last moments. The current's so strong it could carry every-thing away – rocks, a cathedral, a city. There's a storm blowing inside the water. A wind raging.

I'm wearing a dress of real silk, but it's threadbare, almost trans-parent. It used to belong to my mother. One day she decided the colour was too bright for her and she gave it to me. It's a sleeveless dress with a very low neck. It's the sepia colour real silk takes on with wear. It's a dress I remember. I think it suits me. I'm wearing a leather belt with it, perhaps a belt belonging to one of my brothers. I can't remember the shoes I used to wear in those days, only certain dresses. Most of the time I wore canvas sandals, no stockings. I'm speaking of the time before the high school in Saigon. Since then, of course, I've always worn shoes. This particular day I must be wearing the famous pair of gold lamé high heels. I can't see any others

I could have been wearing, so I'm wearing them. Bargains, final reductions bought for me by my mother. I'm wearing these gold lamé shoes to school. Going to school in evening shoes decorated with little *diamanté* flowers. I insist on wearing them. I don't like myself in any others, and to this day I still like myself in them. These high heels are the first in my life, they're beautiful, they've eclipsed all the shoes that went before, the flat ones, for playing and running about, made of white canvas.

It's not the shoes, though, that make the girl look so strangely, so weirdly dressed. No, it's the fact that she's wearing a man's flat-brimmed hat, a brownish-pink fedora with a broad black ribbon.

The crucial ambiguity of the image lies in the hat.

How I came by it I've forgotten. I can't think who could have given it to me. It must have been my mother who bought it for me, because I asked her. The one thing certain is that it was another markdown, another final reduction. But why was it bought? No woman, no girl wore a man's fedora in that colony then. No native woman either. What must have happened is, I try it on just for fun, look at myself in the shopkeeper's glass, and see that there, beneath the man's hat, the thin awkward shape, the inadequacy of childhood, has turned into something else. Has ceased to be a harsh, inescapable imposition of nature. Has become, on the contrary, a provoking choice of nature, a choice of the mind. Suddenly it's deliberate. Suddenly I see myself as another, as another would be seen, outside myself, available to all, available to all eyes, in circulation for cities, journeys, desire. I take the hat, and am never parted from it. Having got it, this hat that all by itself makes me whole, I wear it all the time. With the shoes it must have been much the same, but after the hat. They contradict the hat, as the hat contradicts the puny body, so they're right for me. I wear them all the time too, go everywhere in these shoes, this hat, out of doors, in all weathers, on every occasion. And to town.

I found a photograph of my son when he was twenty. He's in California with his friends, Erika and Elizabeth Lennard. He's thin, so thin you'd think he was a white Ugandan too. His smile strikes me as arrogant, derisive. He's trying to assume the warped image of a young drifter. That's how he likes to see himself, poor, with that poor boy's look, that attitude of someone young and gaunt. It's this photograph that comes closest to the one never taken of the girl on the ferry.

The one who bought the flat-brimmed pink hat with the broad black ribbon was her, the woman in another photograph, my mother. I recognize her better in that than in more recent photos. It's the courtyard of a house by the Small Lake in Hanoi. We're together, she and us, her children. I'm four years old. My mother's in the middle of the picture. I recognize the awkward way she holds herself, the way she doesn't smile, the way she waits for the photo to be over and done with. By her drawn face, by a certain untidiness in her dress, by her drowsy expression, I can tell it's hot, that she's tired, that she's bored. But it's by the way we're dressed, us children, all anyhow, that I recognize a mood my mother sometimes used to fall into, and of which already, at the age we were in the photo, we knew the warning signs – the way she'd suddenly be unable to wash us, dress us, or sometimes even feed us.

Every day my mother experienced this deep despondency about living. Sometimes it lasted, sometimes it would vanish with the dark. I had the luck to have a mother desperate with a despair so unalloyed that sometimes even life's happiness, at its most poignant, couldn't quite make her forget it. What I'll never know is what kind of practical considerations made her leave us like that, every day. This time, perhaps, it's the foolish thing she's just done, the house she's just bought – the one in the photograph – which we absolutely didn't need, and at a time when my father was already very ill, not far from death, only a few months. Or has she just learned she's got the same illness he is going to die of? The dates are right. What I don't know, and she can't have known either, is what kind of considerations they were that haunted her and made that dejection rise up before her. Was it the death, already at hand, of my father? Or the dying of the light? Doubts about her marriage? About her husband? About her children? Or about all these appurtenances in general?

It happened every day. Of that I'm sure. It must have come on quite suddenly. At a given moment every day the despair would make its appearance. And then would follow in inability to go on, or sleep, or sometimes nothing, or sometimes, instead, the buying of houses, the removals, or sometimes the moodiness, just the moodiness, the dejection. Or sometimes she'd be like a queen, give anything she was asked for, take anything she was offered, that house by the Small Lake, for absolutely no reason, my father already dying, or the flat-brimmed hat, because the girl had set her heart on it, or the same thing with the gold lamé shoes. Or else nothing, or just sleep, die.

I've never seen any of those films where American Indian women wear the same kind of flat-brimmed hat, with their hair in braids hanging down in front. That day I have braids too, not put up as usual, but not the same as theirs either. I too have a couple of long braids hanging down in front like those women in the films I've never seen, but mine are the braids of a child. Ever since I've had the hat, I've stopped putting my hair up so that I can wear it. For some time I've scraped my hair back to try to make it flat, so that people can't see it. Every night I comb and braid it before I go to bed, as my mother taught me. My hair's heavy, soft, burdensome, a coppery mass that comes down to my waist. People often say it's my prettiest feature, and I take that to mean I'm not pretty. I had this remarkable hair cut off when I was twenty-three, in Paris, five years after I left my mother. I said: 'Cut it off.' And he did. All at once, a clean sweep, I felt the cold scissors on the skin of my neck. It fell on the floor. They asked me if I wanted to keep it, they'd wrap it up for me to take away. I said no. After that people didn't say I had pretty hair any more, I mean not as much as they used to, before. Afterwards they'd just say, 'She's got nice eyes. And her smile's not unattractive.'

On the ferry, look, I've still got my hair. Fifteen and a half. I'm using make-up already. I use Crème Tokalon, and try to camouflage the freckles on my cheeks, under the eyes. On top of the Crème Tokalon I put natural-colour powder – Houbigant. The powder's my mother's, she wears it to go to government receptions. That day I've got lipstick on too, dark red, cherry, as the fashion was then. I don't know where I got that, perhaps Hélène Lagonelle stole it for me from her mother, I forget. I'm not wearing perfume. My mother makes do with Palmolive and eau de Cologne.

On the ferry, beside the bus, there's a big black limousine with a chauffeur in white cotton livery. Yes, it's the big funereal car that's in my books. It's a Morris-Léon Bollée. The black Lancia at the French embassy in Calcutta hasn't yet made its entrance on the literary scene.

Between drivers and employers there are still sliding panels. There are still tip-up seats. A car's still as big as a bedroom.

Inside the limousine there's a very elegant man looking at me. He's not a white man. He's wearing European clothes – the light tussore suit of the Saigon bankers. He's looking at me.

I'm used to people looking at me. People do look at white women in the colonies; and at twelve-year-old white girls. For the past three years white men, too, have been looking at me in the streets, and my mother's men friends have been kindly asking me to have tea with them while their wives are out playing tennis at the Sporting Club.

I could get it wrong, could think I'm beautiful like women who really are beautiful, like women who are looked at, just because people really do look at me a lot. I know it's not a question of beauty, though, but of something else, for example, yes, something else – mind, for example. What I want to seem I do seem, beautiful too if that's what people want me to be. Beautiful or pretty, pretty for the family for example, for the family no more than that. I can become anything anyone wants me to be. And believe it. Believe I'm charming too. And when I believe it, and it becomes true for anyone seeing me who wants me to be according to his taste, I know that too. And so I can be deliberately charming even though I'm haunted by the killing of my brother. In that death, just one accomplice, my mother. I use the word charming as people used to use it in relation to me, in relation to children.

I already know a thing or two. I know it's not clothes that make women beautiful or otherwise, nor beauty care, nor expensive creams, nor the distinction or costliness of their finery. I know the problem lies elsewhere. I don't know where. I only know it isn't where women think. I look at the women in the streets of Saigon, and up-country. Some of them are very beautiful, very white, they take enormous care of their beauty here, especially up-country. They don't do anything, just save themselves up, save themselves up for Europe, for lovers, holidays in Italy, the long six-months' leaves every three years, when at last they'll be able to talk about what it's like here, this peculiar colonial existence, the

marvellous domestic service provided by the houseboys, the
vegetation, the dances, the white villas, big enough to get lost
in, occupied by officials in distant outposts. They wait, these
women. They dress just for the sake of dressing. They look at
themselves. In the shade of their villas, they look at themselves
for later on, they dream of romance, they already have huge
wardrobes full of more dresses than they know what to do
with, added together one by one like time, like the long days
of waiting. Some of them go mad. Some are deserted for a
young maid who keeps her mouth shut. Ditched. You can
hear the word hit them, hear the sound of the blow. Some kill
themselves.

This self-betrayal of women always struck me as a mistake,
an error.

You didn't have to attract desire. Either it was in the woman
who aroused it or it didn't exist. Either it was there at first
glance or else it had never been. It was instant knowledge of
sexual relationship or it was nothing. That too I knew before
I experienced it.

Hélène Lagonelle was the only one who escaped the law of
error. She was backward, a child still.

For a long time I've had no dresses of my own. My dresses are
all a sort of sack, made out of old dresses of my mother's which
themselves are all a sort of sack. Except for those my mother
has made for me by Dô. She's the housekeeper who'll never
leave my mother even when she goes back to France, even
when my elder brother tries to rape her in the house that goes
with my mother's job in Sadec, even when her wages stop
being paid. Dô was brought up by the nuns, she can embroider
and do pleats, she can sew by hand as people haven't sewed by
hand for centuries, with hair-fine needles. As she can embroider, my mother has her embroider sheets. As she can do
pleats, my mother has her make me dresses with pleats, dresses

with flounces, I wear them as if they were sacks, they're frumpish, childish, two sets of pleats in front and a Peter Pan collar, with a gored skirt or panels cut on the cross to make them look 'professional'. I wear these dresses as if they were sacks, with belts that take away their shape and make them timeless.

Fifteen and a half. The body's thin, undersized almost, childish breasts still, red and pale pink make-up. And then the clothes, the clothes that might make people laugh, but don't. I can see it's all there. All there, but nothing yet done. I can see it in the eyes, all there already in the eyes. I want to write. I've already told my mother: That's what I want to do – write. No answer the first time. Then she asks: Write what? I say: Books, novels. She says grimly: When you've got your maths degree you can write if you like, it won't be anything to do with me then. She's against it, it's not worthy, it's not real work, it's nonsense. Later she said: A childish idea.

The girl in the felt hat is in the muddy light of the river, alone on the deck of the ferry, leaning on the rails. The hat makes the whole scene pink. It's the only colour. In the misty sun of the river, the sun of the hot season, the banks have faded away, the river seems to reach to the horizon. It flows quietly, without a sound, like the blood in the body. No wind but that in the water. The engine of the ferry's the only sound, a rickety old engine with burned-out rods. From time to time, in faint bursts, the sound of voices. And the barking of dogs, coming from all directions, from beyond the mist, from all the villages. The girl has known the ferry-man since she was a child. He smiles at her and asks after her mother the headmistress, Madame la Directrice. He says he often sees her cross over at night, says she often goes to the concession in Cambodia. Her mother's well, says the girl. All around the ferry is the river, it's brimful, its moving waters sweep through, never mixing with, the stagnant waters of the rice-fields. The river's picked up all it's met with since Tonle Sap and the Cambodian forest. It carries everything along, straw huts, forests, burned-out fires, dead birds, dead dogs, drowned tigers and buffaloes, drowned men, bait, islands of water hyacinths all stuck together. Everything flows towards the Pacific, no time for anything to sink, all is swept along by the deep and head-long storm of the inner current, suspended on the surface of the river's strength.

I answered that what I wanted more than anything else in the world was to write, nothing else but that, nothing. Jealous. She's jealous. No answer, just a quick glance immediately averted, a slight shrug, unforgettable. I'll be the first to leave. There are still a few years to wait before she loses me, loses this one of her children. For the sons there's nothing to fear. But this one, she knows, one day she'll go, she'll manage to escape. Top in French. The headmaster of the high school tells her, your daughter's top in French, Madame. My mother says nothing, nothing, she's cross because it's not her sons who are top in French. The beast, my mother, my love, asks: What about maths? Answer: Not yet, but it will come. My mother asks: When? Answer: When she makes up her mind to it, Madame.

My mother, my love, her incredible ungainliness, with her cotton stockings darned by Dô, in the tropics she still thinks you have to wear stockings to be a lady, a headmistress, her dreadful shapeless dresses, mended by Dô, she's still straight out of her Picardy farm full of female cousins, thinks you ought to wear everything till it's worn out, that you have to be deserving, her shoes, her shoes are down-at-heel, she walks awkwardly, painfully, her hair's drawn back tight into a bun like a Chinese woman's, we're ashamed of her, I'm ashamed of her in the street outside the school, when she drives up to the school in her old Citroën B12 everyone looks, but she,

she doesn't notice anything, ever, she ought to be locked up, beaten, killed. She looks at me and says: Perhaps you'll escape. Day and night, this obsession. It's not that you have to achieve anything, it's that you have to get away from where you are.

When my mother emerges, comes out of her despair, she sees the man's hat and the gold lamé shoes. She asks what's it all about. I say nothing. She looks at me, is pleased, smiles. Not bad, she says, they quite suit you, make a change. She doesn't ask if it's she who bought them, she knows she did. She knows she's capable of it, that sometimes, those times I've mentioned, you can get anything you like out of her, she can't refuse us anything. I say: Don't worry, they weren't expensive. She asks where. I say it was in the rue Catinat, marked-down mark-downs. She looks at me with some fellow-feeling. She must think it's a good sign, this show of imagination, the way the girl's thought of dressing like this. She not only accepts this buffoonery, this unseemliness, she, sober as a widow, dressed in dark colours like an unfrocked nun, she not only accepts it, she likes it.

The link with poverty's there in the man's hat too, for money's got to be brought in, got to be brought in somehow. All around her are wildernesses, wastes. The sons are wilder-nesses, they'll never do anything. The salt land's a wilderness too, the money's lost for good, it's all over. The only thing left is this girl, she's growing up, perhaps one day she'll find out how to bring in some money. That's why, though she doesn't know it, that's why the mother lets the girl go out dressed like a child prostitute. And that's why the child already knows how to divert the interest people take in her to the interest she takes in money. That makes her mother smile.

Her mother won't stop her when she tries to make money. The child will say: I asked him for five hundred piastres so that we can go back to France. Her mother will say: Good, that's what we'll need to set ourselves up in Paris, we'll be able to manage, she'll say, with five hundred piastres. The child knows what she's doing is what the mother would have chosen for her to do, if she'd dared, if she'd had the strength, if the pain of her thoughts hadn't been there every day, wearing her out.

In the books I've written about my childhood I can't remember, suddenly, what I left out, what I said. I think I wrote about our love for our mother, but I don't know if I wrote about how we hated her too, or about our love for one another, and our terrible hatred too, in that common family history of ruin and death which was ours whatever happened, in love or in hate, and which I still can't understand however hard I try, which is still beyond my reach, hidden in the very depths of my flesh, blind as a new-born child. It's the area on whose brink silence begins. What happens there is silence, the slow travail of my whole life. I'm still there, watching those possessed children, as far away from the mystery now as I was then. I've never written, though I thought I wrote, never loved, though I thought I loved, never done anything but wait outside the closed door.

When I'm on the Mekong ferry, the day of the black limousine, my mother hasn't yet given up the concession with the dyke. Every so often, still, we make the journey, at night, as before, still all three of us, to spend a few days there. We stay on the verandah of the bungalow, facing the mountains of Siam. Then we go home again. There's nothing she can do there, but she goes. My younger brother and I are beside her on the verandah overlooking the forest. We're too old now, we don't go bathing in the river any more, we don't go hunting black panther in the marshes in the estuary any more, or into the forest, or into the villages in the pepper plantations. Everything has grown up all around us. There are no more children, either on the buffaloes or anywhere else. We too have become strange, and the same sluggishness that has overtaken my mother has overtaken us too. We've learned nothing, watching the forest, waiting, weeping. The lower part of the land is lost for good and all, the servants work the patches higher up, we let them keep the paddy for themselves, they stay on without wages, making use of the stout straw huts my mother had built. They love us as if we were members of their own family, they act as if they were looking after the bungalow for us, and they do look after it. All the cheap crockery's still there. The roof, rotted by the endless rain, goes on disintegrating. But the furniture's kept polished. And the shape of the bungalow stands out clear as a diagram, visible from the road. The doors are opened every day to let the wind through and dry out the wood. And shut every night against stray dogs and smugglers from the mountains.

So you see it wasn't in the bar at Réam, as I wrote, that I met the rich man with the black limousine, it was after we left the concession, two or three years after, on the ferry, the day I'm telling you about, in that light of haze and heat.

It's a year and a half after that meeting that my mother takes us back to France. She'll sell all her furniture. Then go one last time to the dyke. She'll sit on the verandah facing the setting sun, look towards Siam one last time as she never will again, not even when she leaves France again, changes her mind again and comes back once more to Indo-China and retires to Saigon. Never again will she go and see that mountain, that green and yellow sky above that forest.

Yes, I tell you, when she was already quite old she did it again. She opened a French language school, the Nouvelle Ecole Française, which made enough for her to help me with my studies and to provide for her elder son as long as she lived.

*   *   *

My younger brother died in three days, of bronchial pneumonia. His heart gave out. It was then that I left my mother. It was during the Japanese occupation. Everything came to an end that day. I never asked her any more questions about our childhood, about herself. She died, for me, of my younger brother's death. So did my elder brother. I never got over the horror they inspired in me then. They don't mean anything to me any more. I don't know any more about them since that day. I don't even know how she managed to pay off her debts to the *chettys*, the Indian moneylenders. One day they stopped coming. I can see them now. They're sitting in the little parlour in Sadec wearing white sarongs, they sit there without saying a word, for months, years. My mother can be heard weeping and insulting them, she's in her room and won't come out, she calls out to them to leave her alone, they're deaf, calm, smiling, they stay where they are. And then one day, gone. They're dead now, my mother and my two brothers. For memories too it's too late. Now I don't love them any more. I don't remember if I ever did. I've left them. In my head I no longer have the scent of her skin, nor in my eyes the colour of her eyes. I can't remember her voice, except sometimes when it grew soft with the weariness of evening. Her laughter I can't hear any more – neither her laughter nor her cries. It's over, I don't remember. That's why I can write about her so easily now, so long, so fully. She's become just something you write without difficulty, cursive writing.

She must have stayed on in Saigon from 1932 until 1949. It was in December 1942 that my younger brother died. She couldn't move any more. She stayed on – to be near the grave, she said. Then finally she came back to France. My son was two years old when we met again. It was too late for us to be reunited. We knew it at first glance. There was nothing left to reunite. Except for the elder son, all the rest was over. She went to live, and die, in the department of Loir-et-Cher, in the sham Louis XIV chateau. She lived there with Dô. She was still afraid at night. She bought a gun. Dô kept watch in the attics on the top floor. She also bought a place for her elder son near Amboise. With woods. He cut them down. Then went and gambled the money away in a baccarat club in Paris. The woods were lost in one night. The point at which my memory suddenly softens, and perhaps my brother brings tears to my eyes, is after the loss of the money from the woods. I know he's found lying in his car in Montparnasse, outside the Coupole, and that he wants to die. After that, I forget. What she did, my mother, with that chateau of hers, is simply unimaginable, still all for the sake of the elder son, the child of fifty incapable of earning any money. She buys some electric incubators and instals them in the main drawing-room. Suddenly she's got six hundred chicks, forty square metres of them. But she made a mistake with the infra-red rays, and none of the chicks can eat, all six hundred of them have beaks that don't meet or won't close, they all starve to death and she gives up. I came to the chateau while the chicks were hatching, there were great rejoicings. Afterwards the stench of the dead chicks and their food was so awful I couldn't eat in my mother's chateau without throwing up.

She died between Dô and him she called her child, in her big bedroom on the first floor, where during heavy frosts she used to put the sheep to sleep, five or six sheep all around her bed, for several winters, her last.

It's there, in that last house, the one on the Loire, when she finally gives up her ceaseless to-ing and fro-ing, that I see the madness clearly for the first time. I see my mother is clearly mad. I see that Dô and my brother have always had access to that madness. But that I, no, I've never seen it before. Never seen my mother in the state of being mad. Which she was.

From birth. In the blood. She wasn't ill with it, for her it was like health, flanked by Dô and her elder son. No one else but they realized. She always had lots of friends, she kept the same friends for years and years and was always making new ones, often very young, among the officials from up-country, or later on among the people in Touraine, where there were some who'd retired from the French colonies. She always had people around her, all her life, because of what they called her lively intelligence, her cheerfulness, and her peerless, indefatigable poise.

I don't know who took the photo with the despair. The one in the courtyard of the house in Hanoi. Perhaps my father, one last time. A few months later he'd be sent back to France because of his health. Before that he'd go to a new job, in Phnom Penh. He was only there a few weeks. He died in less than a year. My mother wouldn't go back with him to France, she stayed where she was, stuck there. In Phnom Penh. In the fine house overlooking the Mekong, once the palace of the king of Cambodia, in the midst of those terrifying grounds, acres of them, where my mother's afraid. At night she makes us afraid too. All four of us sleep in the same bed. She says she's afraid of the dark. It's in this house she'll hear of my father's death. She'll know about it before the telegram comes, the night before, because of a sign only she saw and could understand, because of the bird that called in the middle of the night, frightened and lost in the office in the north front of the palace, my father's office. It's there, too, a few days after her husband's death, that my mother finds herself face to face with her own father. She switches the light on. There he is, standing by the table in the big octagonal drawing-room. Looking at her. I remember a shriek, a call. She woke us up, told us what had happened, how he was dressed, in his Sunday best, grey, how he stood, how he looked at her, straight at her. She said: I wasn't afraid. She ran towards the vanished image. Both of them died on the day and at the time of the bird or the image. Hence, no doubt, our admiration for our mother's knowledge, about everything, including all that had to do with death.

The elegant man has got out of the limousine and is smoking an English cigarette. He looks at the girl in the man's fedora and the gold shoes. He slowly comes over to her. He's obviously nervous. He doesn't smile to begin with. To begin with he offers her a cigarette. His hand's trembling. There's the difference of race, he's not white, he has to get the better of it, that's why he's trembling. She says she doesn't smoke, no thanks. She doesn't say anything else, doesn't say Leave me alone. So he's less afraid. He tells her he must be dreaming. She doesn't answer. There's no point in answering, what would she say? She waits. So he asks, But where did you spring from? She says she's the daughter of the headmistress of the girls' school in Sadec. He thinks for a moment, then says he's heard of the lady, her mother, of her bad luck with the concession they say she bought in Cambodia, is that right? Yes, that's right.

He says again how strange it is to see her on this ferry. So early in the morning, a pretty girl like that, you don't realize, it's very surprising, a white girl on a native bus.

He says the hat suits her, suits her extremely well, that it's very . . . original . . . a man's hat, and why not? She's so pretty she can do anything she likes.

She looks at him. Asks him who he is. He says he's just back from Paris where he was a student, that he lives in Sadec too, on this same river, the big house with the big terraces with blue tiled balustrades. She asks him what he is. He says he's Chinese, that his family's from North China, from Fushun. Will you allow me to drive you where you want to go in Saigon? She says she will. He tells the chauffeur to get the girl's luggage off the bus and put it in the black car.

Chinese. He belongs to the small group of financiers of

Chinese origin who own all the working-class housing in the colony. He's the one who was crossing the Mekong that day in the direction of Saigon.

She gets into the black car. The door shuts. A barely discernible distress suddenly seizes her, a weariness, the light over the river dims, but only slightly. Everywhere, too, there's a very slight deafness, or fog.

Never again shall I travel in a native bus. From now on I'll have a limousine to take me to the high school and back from there to the boarding school. I shall dine in the most elegant places in town. And I'll always have regrets for everything I do, everything I've gained, everything I've lost, good and bad, the bus, the bus driver I used to laugh with, the old women chewing betel in the back seats, the children on the luggage racks, the family in Sadec, the awfulness of the family in Sadec, its inspired silence.

He talked. Said he missed Paris, the marvellous girls there, the riotous living, the binges, ooh là là, the Coupole, the Rotonde, personally I prefer the Rotonde, the night-clubs, the 'wonderful' life he'd led for two years. She listened, watching out for anything to do with his wealth, for indications as to how many millions he had. He went on. His own mother was dead, he was an only child. All he had left was his father, the one who owned the money. But you know how it is, for the last ten years he's been sitting staring at the river, glued to his opium pipe, he manages his money from his little iron cot. She says she sees.

He won't let his son marry the little white whore from Sadec.

The image starts long before he's come up to the white child by the rails, it starts when he got out of the black car, when he began to approach her, and when she knew, knew he was afraid.

From the first moment she knows more or less, knows he's at her mercy. And therefore that others beside him may be at her mercy too if the occasion arises. She knows something else too, that the time has now probably come when she can no longer escape certain duties towards herself. And that her mother will know nothing of this, nor her brothers. She knows this now too. As soon as she got into the black car she knew: she's excluded from the family for the first time and for ever. From now on they will no longer know what becomes of her. Whether she's taken away from them, carried off, wounded, spoiled, they will no longer know. Neither her mother nor her brothers. That is their fate henceforth. It's already enough to make you weep, here in the black limousine.

Now the child will have to reckon only with this man, the first, the one who introduced himself on the ferry.

It happened very quickly that day, a Thursday. He'd come every day to pick her up at the high school and drive her back to the boarding school. Then one Thursday afternoon, the weekly half-holiday, he came to the boarding school and drove off with her in the black car.

It's in Cholon. Opposite the boulevards linking the Chinese part of the city to the centre of Saigon, the great American-style streets full of trams, rickshaws and buses. It's early in the afternoon. She's got out of the compulsory outing with the other girls.

It's a native housing estate to the south of the city. His place is modern, hastily furnished from the look of it, with furniture supposed to be ultra-modern. He says: I didn't choose the furniture. It's dark in the studio, but she doesn't ask him to open the shutters. She doesn't feel anything in particular, no hate, no repugnance either, so probably it's already desire. But she doesn't know it. She agreed to come as soon as he asked her the previous evening. She's where she has to be, placed here. She feels a tinge of fear. It's as if this must be not only what she expects, but also what had to happen especially to her. She pays close attention to externals, to the light, to the noise of the city in which the room is immersed. He's trembling. At first he looks at her as though he expects her to speak, but she doesn't. So he doesn't do anything either, doesn't undress her, says he loves her madly, says it very softly. Then is silent. She doesn't answer. She could say she doesn't love him. She says nothing. Suddenly, all at once, she knows, knows that he doesn't understand her, that he never will, that he lacks the power to understand such perverseness. And that he can never move fast enough to catch her. It's up to her to know. And she does. Because of his ignorance she suddenly knows: she was attracted to him already on the ferry. She was attracted to him. It depended on her alone.

She says: I'd rather you didn't love me. But if you do, I'd like you to do as you usually do with women. He looks at her in horror, asks, Is that what you want? She says it is. He's started to suffer here in this room, for the first time, he's no longer lying about it. He says he knows already she'll never love him. She lets him say it. At first she says she doesn't know. Then she lets him say it.

He says he's lonely, horribly lonely because of this love he feels for her. She says she's lonely too. She doesn't say why. He says: You've come here with me as you might have gone anywhere with anyone. She says she can't say, so far she's never gone into a bedroom with anyone. She tells him she doesn't want him to talk, what she wants is for him to do as he usually does with the women he brings to his flat. She begs him to do that.

*　*　*

He's torn off the dress, he throws it down. He's torn off her little white cotton panties and carries her over like that, naked, to the bed. And there he turns away and weeps. And she, slow, patient, draws him to her and starts to undress him. With her eyes shut. Slowly. He makes as if to help her. She tells him to keep still. Let me do it. She says she wants to do it. And she does. Undresses him. When she tells him to, he moves his body in the bed, but carefully, gently, as if not to wake her.

The skin's sumptuously soft. The body. The body's thin, lacking in strength, in muscle, he may have been ill, may be convalescent, he's hairless, nothing masculine about him but his sex, he's weak, probably a helpless prey to insult, vulnerable. She doesn't look him in the face. Doesn't look at him at all. She touches him. Touches the softness of his sex, his skin, caresses his goldenness, the strange novelty. He moans, weeps. In dreadful love.

And, weeping, he makes love. At first, pain. And then the pain is possessed in its turn, changed, slowly drawn away, borne towards pleasure, clasped to it.

The sea, formless, simply beyond compare.

Already, on the ferry, in advance, the image owed something to this moment.

The image of the woman in darned stockings has crossed the room, and at last she emerges as a child. The sons knew it already. But not the daughter, yet. They'd never talk about the mother among themselves, about the knowledge of her which they both shared and which separated them from her: the final, decisive knowledge that their mother was a child.

Their mother never knew pleasure.

I didn't know you bled. He asks me if it hurt, I say no, he says he's glad.

He wipes the blood away, washes me. I watch him. Little by little he comes back, becomes desirable again. I wonder how I had the strength to go against my mother's prohibition. So calmly, with such determination. How I managed to follow my ideas to their 'logical conclusion'.

We look at each other. He puts his arms around me. Asks me why I came here. I say I had to, it was a sort of obligation. It's the first time we've talked. I tell him I have two brothers. That we haven't any money. All gone. He knows my elder brother, has met him in the local opium dens. I say my brother steals from my mother to go there, steals from the servants, and that sometimes the keepers of the dens come and demand money from my mother. I tell him about the dykes. I tell him my mother will die, it can't go on like this. That my mother's approaching death, too, must be connected with what's happened to me today.

I notice that I desire him.

He feels sorry for me, but I say no, I'm not to be pitied, no one is, except my mother. He says: You only came because I'm rich. I say that's how I desire him, with his money, that when I first saw him he was already in his car, in his money, so I can't say what I'd have done if he'd been different. He says: I wish I could take you away, go away with you. I say I couldn't leave my mother yet without dying of grief. He says he certainly hasn't been lucky with me, but he'll give me some money anyway, don't worry. He's lain down again. Again we're silent.

The noise of the city is very loud, in recollection it's like the sound-track of a film turned up too high, deafening. I remember clearly, the room's dark, we don't speak, it's surrounded by the continuous din of the city, caught up in the city, swept along with it. There are no panes in the windows, just shutters and blinds. On the blinds you can see the shadows of people going by in the sunlight on the sidewalks. Great crowds of them always. The shadows are divided into strips by the slats of the shutters. The clatter of wooden clogs is ear-splitting, the voices strident, Chinese is a language that's shouted the way I always imagine desert languages are, it's a language that's incredibly foreign.

Outside it's the end of the day, you can tell by the sound of the voices, the sound of more and more passers-by, more and more miscellaneous. It's a city of pleasure that reaches its peak at night. And night is beginning now, with the setting sun.

The bed's separated from the city by those slatted shutters, that cotton blind. There's nothing solid separating us from other people. They don't know of our existence. We glimpse something of theirs, the sum of their voices, of their movements, like the intermittent hoot of a siren, mournful, dim.

Whiffs of burnt sugar drift into the room, the smell of roasted peanuts, Chinese soups, roast meat, herbs, jasmin, dust, incense, charcoal fires, they carry fire about in baskets here, it's sold in the street, the smell of the city is the smell of the villages up-country, of the forest.

I suddenly saw him in a black bath-robe. He was sitting drinking a whisky, smoking.

He said I'd been asleep, he'd taken a shower. I'd fallen asleep almost unawares. He'd switched on a lamp on a low table.

He's a man of habit – I suddenly think of him – he must come to this room quite often, he's a man who must make love a lot, a man who's afraid, he must make love a lot to fight against fear. I tell him I like the idea of his having many women, the idea of my being one of them, indistinguishable. We look at each other. He understands what I've just said. Our expressions are suddenly changed, false, caught in evil and death.

I tell him to come over to me, tell him he must possess me again. He comes over. He smells pleasantly of English cigarettes, expensive perfume, honey, his skin has taken on the scent of silk, the fruity smell of silk tussore, the smell of gold, he's desirable. I tell him of this desire. He tells me to wait a while. Talks to me, says he knew right away, when we were crossing the river, that I'd be like this after my first lover, that I'd love love, he says he knows now I'll deceive him and deceive all the men I'm ever with. He says as for him he's been the cause of his own unhappiness. I'm pleased with all he's foretold, and say so. He becomes rough, desperate, he throws himself on me, devours the childish breasts, shouts, insults. I close my eyes on the intense pleasure. I think: He's used to it, this is his occupation in life, love, nothing else. His hands are expert, marvellous, perfect. I'm very lucky, obviously, it's as if it were his profession, as if unwittingly he knew exactly what to do and what to say. He calls me a whore, a slut, he says I'm his only love, and that's what he ought to say, and what you do say when you just let things say themselves, when you let the body alone, to seek and find and take what it likes, and then everything is right, and nothing's wasted, the waste's covered over and all is swept away in the torrent, in the force of desire.

The sound of the city's so near, so close, you can hear it brushing against the wood of the shutters. It sounds as if they're all going through the room. I caress his body amid the sound, the passers-by. The sea, the immensity, gathering, receding, returning.

I asked him to do it again and again. Do it to me. And he did, did it in the unctuousness of blood. And it really was unto death. It has been unto death.

He lit a cigarette and gave it to me. And very quietly, close to my lips, he talked to me.

And I talked to him too, very quietly.

Because he doesn't know for himself, I say it for him, in his stead. Because he doesn't know he carries within him a supreme elegance, I say it for him.

* * *

Now evening comes. He tells me I'll remember this afternoon all my life, even when I've forgotten his face and name. I wonder if I'll remember the house. He says: Take a good look at it. I do. I say it's like everywhere else. He says yes, yes, it's always the same.

I can still see the face, and I do remember the name. I see the whitewashed walls still, the canvas blind between us and the oven outside, the other door, arched, leading to the other room and to an open garden – the plants are dead from the heat – surrounded by blue balustrades like those at the big villa in Sadec with its tiers of terraces overlooking the Mekong.

It's a place of distress, shipwrecked. He asks me to tell him what I'm thinking about. I say I'm thinking about my mother, she'll kill me if she finds out the truth. I see he's making an effort, then he says it, says he understands what my mother means, this dishonour, he says. He says he himself couldn't bear the thought if it were a question of marriage. I look at him. He looks back, apologizes, proudly. He says: I'm a Chinese. We smile at each other. I ask him if it's usual to be sad, as we are. He says it's because we've made love in the daytime, with the heat at its height. He says it's always terrible after. He smiles. Says: Whether people love one another or not, it's always terrible. Says it'll pass as soon as it gets dark. I say he's wrong, it's not just because it was in the daytime, I feel a sadness I expected and which comes only from myself. I say I've always been sad. That I can see the same sadness in photos of myself when I was small. That today, recognizing it as the sadness I've always had, I could almost call it by my own name, it's so like me. Today I tell him it's a comfort, this sadness, a comfort to have fallen at last into a misfortune my mother's always predicted for me when she shrieks in the desert of her life. I say: I don't quite understand what she says, but I know this room's what I was expecting. I speak without waiting for an answer. I tell him my mother shouts out what she believes

like the messengers of God. She shouts that you shouldn't
expect anything, ever, either from anybody else or from any
government or from any God. He watches me speak, doesn't
take his eyes off me, watches my lips, I'm naked, he caresses
me, perhaps he's not listening, I don't know. I say I don't
regard my present misfortune as a personal matter. I tell him
how it was just so difficult to get food and clothes, to live, in
short, on nothing but my mother's salary. I'm finding it more
and more difficult to speak. He says: How did you all manage?
I say we lived out of doors, poverty had knocked down the
walls of the family and we were all left outside, each one fend-
ing for himself. Shameless, that's what we were. That's how
I came to be here with you. He is on me, engulfed again. We
stay like that, riveted, moaning amid the din of the still external city. We can still hear it. And then we don't hear it any
more.

Kisses on the body bring tears. Almost like a consolation. At
home I don't cry. But that day in that room, tears console both
for the past and for the future. I tell him one day I'll leave my
mother, one day even for my mother I'll have no love left.
I weep. He lays his head on me and weeps to see me weep.
I tell him that when I was a child my mother's unhappiness
took the place of dreams. My dreams were of my mother,
never of Christmas trees, always just her, a mother either flayed
by poverty or distraught and muttering in the wilderness,
either searching for food or endlessly telling what's happened
to her, Marie Legrand from Roubaix, telling of her innocence, her savings, her hope.

Through the shutters evening has come. The noise has got
louder. It's more penetrating, less muffled. The livid red street
lights are lit.

We've left the flat. I've put on the man's hat with the black
ribbon again, the gold shoes, the dark lipstick, the silk dress.

I've grown older. I suddenly know it. He sees, says: You're tired.

On the sidewalk the crowd, going in all directions, slow or fast, forcing its way, mangy as stray dogs, blind as beggars, a Chinese crowd, I can still see it now in pictures of present prosperity, in the way they go along together without any sign of impatience, in the way they are alone in a crowd, without happiness, it seems, without sadness, without curiosity, going along without seeming to, without meaning to, just going this way rather than that, alone and in the crowd, never alone even by themselves, always alone even in the crowd.

We go to one of those Chinese restaurants on several floors, they occupy whole buildings, they're as big as department stores, or barracks, they look out over the city from balconies and terraces. The noise that comes from these buildings is inconceivable in Europe, the noise of orders yelled out by the waiters, then taken up and yelled out by the kitchens. No one ever merely speaks. On the terraces there are Chinese orchestras. We go up to the quietest floor, the Europeans' floor, the menus are the same but there's less yelling. There are fans, and heavy draperies to deaden the noise.

I ask him to tell me about his father's money, how he got rich. He says it bores him to talk about money, but if I insist he'll tell me what he knows about his father's wealth. It all began in Cholon, with the housing estates for natives. He built three hundred of these 'compartments', cheap semi-detached dwellings, let out for rent. Owns several streets. Speaks French with a rather affected Paris accent, talks money with perfect ease. He used to own some apartment blocks, but sold them to buy building land south of Cholon. Some rice-fields in Sadec were sold too, the son thinks. I ask about epidemics. Say I've seen whole streets of native compartments closed off from one day to the next, the doors and windows nailed up, because of an epidemic of plague. He says there's not so much of it here, the rats are exterminated much more often than up-country. All of a sudden he starts telling me the tale about the compartments. They cost much less than either apartment blocks or detached houses, and meet the needs of working-class areas much better than separate dwellings. The people here like living close together, especially the poor, who come from the country and like living out of doors too, on the street. And you must try not to destroy the habits of the poor. His father's just built a whole series of compartments with covered balconies overlooking the street. This makes the streets very light and agreeable. People spend the whole day on these out-side balconies. Sleep there too when it's very hot. I say I'd have liked to live on an outside balcony myself, when I was small it was my ideal, to sleep out of doors.

Suddenly I have a pain. Very slight, almost imperceptible. It's my heart-beat, shifted into the fresh keen wound he's made in me, he, the one who's talking to me, the one who also made the afternoon's pleasure. I don't hear what he's say-ing, I've stopped listening. He sees, stops. I tell him to go on. He does. I listen again. He says he thinks about Paris a lot. He thinks I'm very different from the girls in Paris, not nearly so nice. I say the compartments can't be as profitable as all that. He doesn't answer.

Throughout our affair, for a year and a half, we'd talk like this, never about ourselves. From the first we knew we couldn't possibly have any future in common, so we'd never speak of the future, we'd talk about day-to-day events, evenly, hitting the ball back and forth.

I tell him his visit to France was fatal. He agrees. Says he bought everything in Paris, his women, his acquaintances, his ideas. He's twelve years older than I, and this scares him. I lis-ten to the way he speaks, makes mistakes, makes love even – with a sort of theatricality at once contrived and sincere.

I tell him I'm going to introduce him to my family. He wants to run away. I laugh.

He can only express his feelings through parody. I discover he hasn't the strength to love me in opposition to his father, to possess me, take me away. He often weeps because he can't find the strength to love beyond fear. His heroism is me, his cravenness is his father's money.

Whenever I mention my brothers he's overcome by this fear, as if unmasked. He thinks my people all expect a proposal of marriage. He knows he's lost, done for already in my family's eyes, that for them he can only become more lost, and as a result lose me.

He says he went to study at a business school in Paris, he tells the truth at last, says he didn't do any work and his father stopped his allowance, sent him his return ticket and he had to leave. This retreat is his tragedy. He didn't finish the course at the business school. He says he hopes to finish it here by correspondence.

The meetings with the family began with the big meals in Cholon. When my mother and brothers come to Saigon I tell him he has to invite them to the expensive Chinese restaurants they don't know, have never been to before.

These evenings are all the same. My brothers gorge themselves without saying a word to him. They don't look at him either. They can't. They're incapable of it. If they could, if they could make the effort to see him, they'd be capable of studying, of observing the elementary rules of society. During these meals my mother's the only one who speaks, she doesn't say much, especially the first few times, just a few comments about the dishes as they arrive, the exorbitant price, then silence. He, the first couple of times, plunges in and tries to tell the story of his adventures in Paris, but in vain. It's as if he hadn't spoken, as if nobody had heard. His attempt founders in silence. My brothers go on gorging. They gorge as I've never seen anyone else gorge, anywhere.

He pays. He counts out the money. Puts it in the saucer. Everyone watches. The first time, I remember, he lays out seventy-seven piastres. My mother nearly shrieks with laughter. We get up to leave. No one says thank you. No one ever says thank you for the excellent dinner, or hallo, or goodbye, or how are you, no one ever says anything to anyone.

My brothers never will say a word to him, it's as if he were invisible to them, as if for them he weren't solid enough to be perceived, seen or heard. This is because he adores me, but it's taken for granted I don't love him, that I'm with him for the money, that I can't love him, it's impossible, that he could take any sort of treatment from me and still go on loving me. This is because he's a Chinese, because he's not a white man. The way my elder brother treats my lover, not speaking to him, ignoring him, stems from such absolute conviction it acts as a model. We all treat my lover as he does. I myself never speak to him in their presence. When my family's there I'm never supposed to address a single word to him. Except, yes, except to give him a message. For example, after dinner, when my brothers tell me they want to go to the Fountain to dance and drink, I'm the one who has to tell him. At first he pretends he hasn't heard. And I, according to my elder brother's strategy, I'm not supposed to repeat what I've just said, not supposed to ask again, because that would be wrong, I'd be admitting he has a grievance. Quietly, as if between ourselves, he says he'd like to be alone with me for a while. He says it to end the agony. Then I'm still not supposed to catch what he says properly, one more treachery, as if by what he said he meant to object, to complain of my elder brother's behaviour. So I'm still not supposed to answer him. But he goes on, says, is bold enough to say: Your mother's tired, look at her. And our mother does get drowsy after those fabulous Chinese dinners in Cholon. But I still don't answer. It's then I hear my brother's voice. He says something short, sharp and final. My mother used to say, He's the one who speaks best out of all the three.

After he's spoken, my brother waits. Everything comes to a halt. I recognize my lover's fear, it's the same as my younger brother's. He gives in. We go to the Fountain. My mother too. At the Fountain she goes to sleep.

In my elder brother's presence he ceases to be my lover. He doesn't cease to exist, but he's no longer anything to me. He becomes a burnt-out shell. My desire obeys my elder brother, rejects my lover. Every time I see them together I think I can never bear the sight again. My lover's denied in just that weak body, just that weakness which transports me with pleasure. In my brother's presence he becomes an unmentionable outrage, a cause of shame who ought to be kept out of sight. I can't fight my brother's silent commands. I can when it concerns my younger brother. But when it concerns my lover I'm powerless against myself. Thinking about it now brings back the hypocrisy to my face, the absent-minded expression of someone who stares into space, who has other things to think about, but who just the same, as the slightly clenched jaws show, suffers and is exasperated at having to put up with this indignity just for the sake of eating well, in an expensive restaurant, which ought to be something quite normal. And surrounding the memory is the ghastly glow of the night of the hunter. It gives off a strident note of alarm, like the cry of a child.

No one speaks to him at the Fountain, either.

We all order Martells and Perrier. My brothers drink theirs straight off and order the same again. My mother and I give them ours. My brothers are soon drunk. But they still don't speak to him. Instead they start finding fault. Especially my younger brother. He complains that the place is depressing and there aren't any hostesses. There aren't many people at the Fountain on a weekday. I dance with him, with my younger brother. I don't dance with my elder brother, I've never danced with him. I was always held back by a sense of danger, of the sinister attraction he exerted on everyone, a disturbing sense of the nearness of our bodies.

We were strikingly alike, especially in the face.

The Chinese from Cholon speaks to me, he's on the brink of tears, he says: What have I done to them? I tell him not to worry, it's always like that, even among ourselves, no matter what the circumstances.

I'll explain when we are together again in the apartment. I tell him my elder brother's cold insulting violence is there whatever happens to us, whatever comes our way. His first impulse is always to kill, to wipe out, to hold sway over life, to scorn, to hunt, to make suffer. I tell him not to be afraid. He's got nothing to be afraid of. Because the only person my elder brother's afraid of, who, strangely, makes him nervous, is me.

Never a hallo, a good evening, a happy New Year. Never a thank you. Never any talk. Never any need to talk. Everything always silent, distant. It's a family of stone, petrified so deeply it's impenetrable. Every day we try to kill one another, to kill. Not only do we not talk to one another, we don't even look at one another. When you're being looked at you can't look. To look is to feel curious, to be interested, to lower yourself. No one you look at is worth it. Looking is always demeaning. The word conversation is banished. I think that's what best conveys the shame and the pride. Every sort of community, whether of the family or otherwise, is hateful to us, degrading. We're united in a fundamental shame at having to live. It's here we are at the heart of our common fate, the fact that all three of us are our mother's children, the children of a candid creature murdered by society. We're on the side of the society which has reduced her to despair. Because of what's been done to our mother, so amiable, so trusting, we hate life, we hate ourselves.

*   *   *

My mother didn't foresee what was going to become of us as a result of witnessing her despair. I'm speaking particularly of the boys, her sons. But even if she had foreseen it, how could she have kept quiet about what had become her own essential fate? How could she have made them all lie — her face, her eyes, her voice? Her love? She could have died. Done away with herself. Broken up our intolerable community. Seen that the eldest was completely separated from the younger two. But she didn't. She was careless, muddle-headed, irresponsible. All that. She went on living. And all three of us loved her beyond love. Just because she couldn't, because she wasn't able to keep quiet, hide things, lie, we, different as we all three were from one another, all three loved her in the same way.

It went on for a long time. Seven years. When it began we were ten. And then we were twelve. Then thirteen. Then fourteen, fifteen. Then sixteen, seventeen.

It lasted all that age, seven years. And then finally hope was given up. Abandoned. Like the struggles against the sea. From the shade of the verandah we look at the mountains of Siam, dark in broad daylight, almost black. My mother's quiet at last, mute. We, her children, are heroic, desperate.

My younger brother died in December 1942, during the Japanese occupation. I'd left Saigon after graduating from high school in 1931. He wrote to me just once in ten years. I never knew why. The letter was conventional, made out in a fair copy in careful handwriting without any mistakes. He told me everyone was well, the school was a success. It was a long letter, two whole pages. I recognized his writing, the same as when he was a child. He also said he had an apartment, a car, he told me the make. That he'd taken up tennis again. That he was fine, everything was fine. That he sent his fondest love. He didn't mention the war, or our elder brother.

* * *

I often bracket my two brothers together as she used to do, our mother. I say, My brothers, and she too, outside the family, used to say, My sons. She always talked in an insulting way about her sons' strength. For the outside world she didn't distinguish between them, she didn't say the elder son was much stronger than the younger, she said he was as strong as her brothers, the farmers in the north of France. She was proud of her sons' strength in the same way as she'd been proud of her brothers'. Like her elder son, she looked down on the weak. Of my lover from Cholon she spoke in the same way as my elder brother. I shan't write the words down. They were words that had to do with the carrion you find in the desert. I say, My brothers, because that's what I used to say too. It's only since that I've referred to them differently, after my younger brother grew up and was martyred.

Not only do we never have any celebrations in our family, nor a Christmas tree, or so much as an embroidered handkerchief or a flower. We don't even take notice of any death, any funeral, any remembrance. There's just her. My elder brother will always be a murderer. My younger brother will die because of him. As for me, I left, tore myself away. Until she died my elder brother had her to himself.

At that time, the time of Cholon, of the image, of the lover, my mother has an access of madness. She knows nothing of what's happened in Cholon. But I can see she's watching me, she suspects something. She knows her daughter, her child, and hovering around that child, for some time, there's been an air of strangeness, a sort of reserve, quite recent, that catches the eye. The girl speaks even more slowly than usual, she's absent-minded, she who's usually so interested in everything, her expression has changed, she's become a spectator even of her mother, of her mother's unhappiness, it's as if she were witnessing its outcome. There's a sudden terror in my mother's life. Her daughter's in the direst danger, the danger of never getting married, never having a place in society, of being defenceless against it, lost, alone. My mother has attacks during which she falls on me, locks me up in my room, punches me, slaps me, undresses me, comes up to me and smells my body, my underwear, says she can smell the Chinese's scent, goes even further, looks for suspect stains on my underwear, and shouts, for the whole town to hear, that her daughter's a prostitute, she's going to throw her out, she wishes she'd die, no one will have anything to do with her, she's disgraced, worse than a bitch. And she weeps, asking what she can do, except drive her out of the house so she can't stink the place out any more.

Outside the walls of the locked room, my brother.

He answers my mother, tells her she's right to beat the girl, his voice is lowered, confidential, coaxing, he says they must find out the truth, at all costs, must find out in order to save the girl, save the mother from being driven to desperation. The mother hits her as hard as she can. The younger brother shouts at the mother to leave her alone. He goes out in the garden, hides, he's afraid I'll be killed, he's afraid, he's always afraid of that stranger, our elder brother. My younger brother's fear calms my mother down. She weeps for the disaster of her life, of her disgraced child. I weep with her. I lie. I swear by my own life that nothing has happened to me, nothing, not even a kiss. How could I, I say, with a Chinese, how could I do that with a Chinese, so ugly, such a weakling? I know my elder brother's glued to the door, listening, he knows what my mother's doing, he knows the girl's naked, being beaten, and he'd like it to go on and on to the brink of harm. My mother is not unaware of my elder brother's obscure and terrifying intent.

* * *

We're still very small. Battles break out regularly between my brothers, for no apparent reason except the classic one by which the elder brother says to the younger: Clear out, you're in the way. And straight away lashes out. They fight without a word, all you can hear is their breathing, their groans, the hollow thud of the blows. My mother accompanies this scene, like all others, with an opera of shrieks.

They both have the same talent for anger, those black, murderous fits of anger you only see in brothers, sisters, mothers. My elder brother can't bear not being able to do evil freely, to be boss over it not only here but everywhere. My younger brother can't bear having to look on helpless at this horror, at what his elder brother is like.

When they fought we were equally afraid for both of their lives. My mother used to say they'd always fought, they'd never played together, never talked to one another. That they had nothing in common but her, their mother, and especially their sister. Nothing but blood.

I believe it was only her eldest that my mother called 'my child'. She sometimes called him that. The other two she called 'the younger ones'.

We said nothing about all this outside, one of the first things we'd learned was to keep quiet about the ruling principle of our life, poverty. And then about everything else. Our first confidants, though the word seems excessive, are our lovers, the people we meet away from our various homes, first in the streets of Saigon and then on liners and trains, and then all over the place.

It takes my mother all of a sudden towards the end of the afternoon, especially in the dry season, and then she'll have the house scrubbed from top to bottom, to clean it through, scour it out, freshen it up, she says. The house is built on a raised strip of land, clear of the garden, the snakes, the scorpions, the red ants, the floodwaters of the Mekong, those that follow the great tornadoes of the monsoon. Because the house is raised like this it can be cleaned by having buckets of water thrown over it, sluiced right through like a garden. All the chairs are piled up on the tables, the whole house is streaming, water's lapping round the piano in the small sitting-room. The water pours down the steps, spreads through the yard towards the kitchen quarters. The little houseboys are delighted, we join in with them, splash one another, then wash the floor with yellow soap. Everyone's barefoot, including our mother. She laughs. She's got no objection to anything. The whole house smells nice, with the delicious smell of wet earth after a storm, enough to make you wild with delight, especially when it's mixed with the other, the smell of yellow soap, of purity, of respectability, of clean linen, of whiteness, of our mother, of the immense candour and innocence of our mother. The houseboys' families come along, and the houseboys' visitors, and the white children from neighbouring houses. My mother's very happy with this disorder, she can be very very happy sometimes, long enough to forget, the time it takes to clean out the house may be enough to make her happy. She goes into the sitting-room, sits down at the piano, plays the only tunes she knows by heart, the ones she learned at the teacher training school. She sings. Sometimes she laughs while she plays. Gets up, dances and sings. And everyone thinks, and so does she, that you can be happy here in this house suddenly transmogrified into a pond, a water-meadow, a ford, a beach.

The two smaller children, the girl and the younger brother, are the first to remember. They suddenly stop laughing and go into the darkening garden.

I remember, just as I'm writing this, that our elder brother wasn't in Vinh Long when we sluiced the house out. He was living with our guardian, a village priest, in the department of Lot-et-Garonne. He too used to laugh sometimes, but never as much as we did. I forget everything, and I forgot to say this, that we were children who laughed, my younger brother and I, laughed fit to burst, fit to die.

I see the war as I see my childhood. I see war-time and the reign of my elder brother as one. Partly, probably because it was during the war that my younger brother died: his heart, as I've said, had given out, given up. As for my elder brother, I don't think I ever saw him during the war. By that time it didn't matter to me whether he was alive or dead. I see the war as like him, spreading everywhere, breaking in everywhere, stealing, imprisoning, always there, merged and mingled with everything, present in the body, in the mind, awake and asleep, all the time, a prey to the intoxicating passion of occupying that delightful territory, a child's body, the body of those less strong, of conquered peoples. Because evil is there, at the gates, against the skin.

We go back to the apartment. We are lovers. We can't stop loving each other.

Sometimes I don't go back to the boarding school. I sleep with him. I don't want to sleep in his arms, his warmth, but I do sleep in the same room, the same bed. Sometimes I stay away from high school. At night we go and have dinner in town. He gives me my shower, washes me, rinses me, he adores that, he puts my make-up on and dresses me, he adores me. I'm the darling of his life. He lives in terror lest I meet another man. I'm never afraid of anything like that. He's also afraid, not because I'm white but because I'm so young, so young he could go to prison if we were found out. He tells me to go on lying to my mother, and above all to my elder brother, never to say anything to anyone. I go on lying. I laugh at his fear. I tell him we're much too poor for my mother to start another lawsuit, and anyway she's lost all those she ever did start, against the land registrar, against the officials, the government, the law, she doesn't know how to conduct them properly, how to keep calm, wait, go on waiting, she can't, she makes a row and spoils her chances. With this one it would be the same, so no need to be afraid.

Marie-Claude Carpenter. She was American, from Boston I seem to remember. Very pale eyes, grey-blue. 1943. Marie-Claude Carpenter was fair. Scarcely faded. Quite goodlooking, I think. With a brief smile that ended very quickly, disappeared in a flash. With a voice that suddenly comes back to me, low, slightly grating in the high notes. She was forty-five, old already, old age itself. She lived in the sixteenth arrondissement, near the place de l'Alma. Her apartment was the huge top floor of a block overlooking the Seine. People went to dinner there in the winter. Or to lunch in the summer. The meals were ordered from the best caterers in Paris. Always passable, almost. But only just enough, skimpy. She was never seen anywhere else but at home, never out. Sometimes there was an expert on Mallarmé there. And often one, two or three literary people, they'd come once and never be seen again. I never found out where she got them from, where she met them, or why she invited them. I never heard anyone else refer to any of them, and I never read or heard of their work. The meals didn't last very long. We talked a lot about the war, it was the time of Stalingrad, the end of the winter of '42. Marie-Claude Carpenter used to listen a lot, ask a lot of questions, but didn't say much, often used to express surprise at how little she knew of what went on, then she'd laugh. Straight away after the meal she'd apologize for having to leave so soon, but she had things to do, she said. She never said what. When there were enough of us we'd stay on for an hour or two after she left. She used to say, Stay as long as you like. No one spoke about her when she wasn't there. I don't think anyone could have done, because no one knew her. You always went home with the feeling of having experienced a sort of empty nightmare, of having spent a few hours as the guest of strangers, with other guests who were strangers too, of having lived through a space of time without any consequences and without any cause, human or other. It was like having crossed a third frontier, having been on a train, having waited in doctors' waiting-rooms, hotels, airports. In summer we had lunch on a big terrace looking over the river, and coffee was served in the garden covering the whole roof. There was a swimming pool. But no one went in. We just sat and looked at Paris. The empty avenues, the river, the streets. In the empty streets, catalpas in flower. Marie-Claude Carpenter. I looked at her a lot, practically all the time, it embarrassed her but I couldn't help it. I looked at her to try to find out, find out who she was, Marie-Claude Carpenter. Why she was there rather than somewhere else, why she was from so far away too, from Boston, why she was rich, why no one knew anything about her, not anything, no one, why these seemingly compulsory parties. And why, why, in her eyes, deep down in the depths of sight, that particle of death? Marie-Claude Carpenter. Why did all her dresses have something indefinable in common that made them look as if they didn't quite belong to her, as if they might just as well have been on some other body? Dresses that were neutral, plain, very light in colour, white, like summer in the middle of winter.

Betty Fernandez. My memory of men is never lit up and illuminated like my memory of women. Betty Fernandez. She was a foreigner too. As soon as I say the name there she is, walking along a Paris street, she's short-sighted, can't see much, screws up her eyes to recognize you, then greets you with a light handshake. Hallo, how are you? Dead a long time ago now. Thirty years, perhaps. I can remember her grace, it's too late now for me to forget, nothing mars its perfection still, nothing ever will, not the circumstances, nor the time, nor the cold or the hunger or the defeat of Germany, nor the coming to light of the crime. She goes along the street still, above the history of such things however terrible. Here too the eyes are pale. The pink dress is old, the black wide-brimmed hat dusty in the sunlight of the street.

She's slim, tall, drawn in Indian ink, an engraving. People stop and look in amazement at the elegance of this foreigner who walks along unseeing. Like a queen. People never know at first where she's from. And then they think she can only be from somewhere else, from there. Because of this she's beautiful. She's dressed in old European clothes, scraps of brocade, out-of-date old suits, old curtains, old oddments, old models, moth-eaten old fox furs, old otterskins, that's her kind of beauty, tattered, chilly, plaintive and in exile, nothing suits her, everything's too big, and yet it looks marvellous. Her clothes are loose, she's too thin, nothing fits, yet it looks marvellous. She's made in such a way, face and body, that anything that touches her shares immediately and infallibly in her beauty.

She entertained, Betty Fernandez, she had an 'at home'. We went sometimes. Once Drieu la Rochelle was there. Clearly suffering from pride, he scarcely deigned to speak, and when he did it was as if his voice was dubbed, his words translated, stiff. Maybe Brasillach was there too, but I don't remember, unfortunately. Sartre never came. There were poets from Montparnasse, but I don't remember any names, not one. There were no Germans. We didn't talk politics. We talked about literature. Ramon Fernandez used to talk about Balzac. We could have listened to him for ever and a day. He spoke with a knowledge that's almost completely forgotten, and of which almost nothing completely verifiable can survive. He offered opinions rather than information. He spoke about Balzac as he might have done about himself, as if he himself had once tried to be Balzac. He had a sublime courtesy even in knowledge, a way at once profound and clear of handling

knowledge without ever making it seem an obligation or a
burden. He was sincere. It was always a joy to meet him in the
street or in a café, and it was a pleasure to him to greet you.
Hallo how are you? he'd say, in the English style, without a
comma, laughing. And while he laughed his jest became the
war itself, together with all the unavoidable suffering it caused,
both resistance and collaboration, hunger and cold, martyrdom and infamy. She, Betty Fernandez, spoke only of people,
those she'd seen in the street or those she knew, about how
they were, the things still left for sale in the shops, extra rations
of milk or fish, good ways of dealing with shortages, with cold
and constant hunger, she was always concerned with the practical details of life, she didn't go beyond that, always a good
friend, very loyal and affectionate. Collaborators, the Fernan-
dezes were. And I, two years after the war, I was a member
of the French Communist Party. The parallel is complete and
absolute. The two things are the same, the same pity, the same
call for help, the same lack of judgement, the same superstition
if you like, that consists in believing in a political solution to
the personal problem. She too, Betty Fernandez, looked out
at the empty streets of the German occupation, looked at
Paris, at the squares of catalpas in flower, like the other
woman, Marie-Claude Carpenter. Was 'at home' certain days,
like her.

He drives her back to the boarding school in the black limousine. Stops just short of the entrance so that no one sees him.
It's at night. She gets out, runs off, doesn't turn to look at him.
As soon as she's inside the door she sees the lights are still on
in the big playground. As soon as she turns out of the corridor
she sees her, waiting for her, worried already, erect, unsmiling.
She asks, Where've you been? She says, I just didn't come back
here to sleep. She doesn't say why and Hélène Lagonelle
doesn't ask. She takes the pink hat off and undoes her braids
for the night. You didn't go to class either. No, she didn't.

Hélène says they've phoned, that's how she knows, she's to go and see the vice-principal. There are lots of girls in the shadowy playground. They're all in white. There are big lamps in the trees. The lights are still on in some of the classrooms. Some of the pupils are working late, others stay in the classrooms to chat, or play cards, or sing. There's no fixed time for them to go to bed, it's so hot during the day they're allowed to do more or less as they like in the evening, or rather as the young teachers on duty like. We're the only two white girls in this state boarding school. There are lots of half-castes, most of them abandoned by their fathers, soldiers or sailors or minor officials in the customs, post, or public works department. Most of them were brought up by the Assistance Board. There are a few quadroons too. Hélène Lagonelle believes the French government raises them to be nurses in hospitals or to work in orphanages, leper colonies and mental homes. She also thinks they're sent to isolation hospitals to look after people with cholera or the plague. That's what Hélène Lagonelle thinks, and she cries because she doesn't want any of those jobs, she's always talking about running away.

I go to see the mistress on duty, a young half-caste herself who spends a lot of time looking at Hélène and me. She says, You didn't go to class and you didn't sleep here last night, we're going to have to inform your mother. I say I couldn't help it, but from now on I'll try to come back and sleep here every night, there's no need to tell my mother. The young woman looks at me and smiles.

I'll do it again. My mother will be informed. She'll come and see the head of the boarding school and ask her to let me do as I like in the evenings, not to check the time I come in, not to force me to go out with the other girls on Sunday excursions. She says, She's a child who's always been free, otherwise she'd run away, even I, her own mother, can't do anything about it, if I want to keep her I have to let her be free. The head agrees because I'm white and the place needs a few whites among all the half-castes for the sake of its reputation. My mother also said I was working hard in high school even though I had my freedom, and that what had happened with her sons was so awful, such a disaster, that her daughter's education was the only hope left to her.

The head let me live in the boarding school as if it were a hotel.

Soon I'll have a diamond on my engagement finger. Then the teachers will stop making remarks. People will guess I'm not engaged, but the diamond's very valuable, no one will doubt that it's genuine, and no one will say anything any more, because of the value of the diamond that's been given to this very young girl.

I come back to Hélène Lagonelle. She's lying on a bench, crying because she thinks I'm going to leave. I sit on the bench. I'm worn out by the beauty of Hélène Lagonelle's body lying against mine. Her body's sublime, naked under the dress, within arm's reach. Her breasts are such as I've never seen. I've never touched them. She's immodest, Hélène Lagonelle, she doesn't realize, she walks around the dormitories without any clothes on. What's the most beautiful of all the things given by God is this body of Hélène Lagonelle's, peerless, the balance between her figure and the way the body bears the breasts, outside itself, as if they were separate. Nothing could be more extraordinary than the outer roundness of these breasts proffered to the hands, this outwardness held out towards them. Even the body of my younger brother, like that of a little coolie, is as nothing beside this splendour. The shapes of men's bodies are miserly, paternalized. Nor do they get spoiled like those of girls such as Hélène Lagonelle, which never last, a summer or so perhaps, that's all. She comes from the high plateaus of Da Lat. Her father works for the post office. She came quite recently, right in the middle of the school year. She's frightened, she comes up and sits beside you and stays there without speaking, crying sometimes. She has the pink and brown complexion of the mountains, you can always recognize it here where all the other children are pale green with anaemia and the torrid heat. Hélène Lagonelle doesn't go to high school. She's not capable of it, Hélène L. She can't learn, can't remember things. She goes to the primary classes at the boarding school, but it's no use. She weeps up against me, and I stroke her hair, her hands, tell her I'm going to stay here with her. She doesn't know she's very beautiful, Hélène Lagonelle. Her parents don't know what to do with her, they want to marry her off as soon as possible. She could have all the fiancés she likes, Hélène Lagonelle, but she doesn't like, she doesn't want to get married, she wants to go back to her mother. She, Hélène L. Hélène Lagonelle. In the end she'll do what her mother wants. She's much more beautiful than I am, the girl in the clown's hat and lamé shoes, infinitely more marriageable, she can be married off, set up in matrimony, you can frighten her, explain it to her, what frightens her and what she doesn't understand, tell her to stay where she is, wait.

Hélène Lagonelle is seventeen, seventeen, yet she still doesn't know what I know. It's as if I guessed she never will.

Hélène Lagonelle's body is heavy, innocent still, her skin's as soft as that of certain fruits, you almost can't grasp her, she's almost illusory, it's too much. She makes you want to kill her, she conjures up a marvellous dream of putting her to death with your own hands. Those flour-white shapes, she bears them unknowingly, and offers them for hands to knead, for lips to eat, without holding them back, without any knowledge of them and without any knowledge of their fabulous power. I'd like to eat Hélène Lagonelle's breasts as he eats mine in the room in the Chinese town where I go every night to increase my knowledge of God. I'd like to devour and be devoured by those flour-white breasts of hers.

I am worn out with desire for Hélène Lagonelle.

I am worn out with desire.

I want to take Hélène Lagonelle with me to where every evening, my eyes shut, I have imparted to me the pleasure that makes you cry out. I'd like to give Hélène Lagonelle to the man who does that to me, so he may do it in turn to her. I want it to happen in my presence, I want her to do it as I wish, I want her to give herself where I give myself. It's via Hélène Lagonelle's body, through it, that the ultimate pleasure would pass from him to me.

A pleasure unto death.

I see her as being of one flesh with the man from Cholon, but in a shining, solar, innocent present, in a continual self-flowering which springs out of each action, each tear, each of her faults, each of her ignorances. Hélène Lagonelle is the mate of the bondsman who gives me such abstract, such harsh pleasure, the obscure man from Cholon, from China. Hélène Lagonelle is from China.

I haven't forgotten Hélène Lagonelle. I haven't forgotten the bondsman. When I went away, when I left him, I didn't go near another man for two years. But that mysterious fidelity must have been to myself.

I'm still part of the family, it's there I live, to the exclusion of everywhere else. It's in its aridity, its terrible harshness, its malignance, that I'm most deeply sure of myself, at the heart of my essential certainty, the certainty that later on I'll be a writer.

That's the place where later on, once the present is left behind, I must stay, to the exclusion of everywhere else. The hours

I spend in the apartment show it in a new light. It's a place that's intolerable, bordering on death, a place of violence, pain, despair, dishonour. And so is Cholon. On the other bank of the river. As soon as you've crossed to the other side.

I don't know what became of Hélène Lagonelle, I don't even know if she's dead. It was she who left the boarding school first, a long while before I went to France. She went back to Da Lat. Her mother sent for her, I believe to arrange a match for her, I believe she was to meet someone just out from France. But I may be wrong, I may be projecting what I thought would happen to Hélène Lagonelle on to her prompt departure at her mother's request.

Let me tell you what he did, too, what it was like. Well – he stole from the houseboys in order to go and smoke opium. He stole from our mother. He rummaged in cupboards. He stole. He gambled. My father bought a house in Entre-deux-Mers before he died. It was the only thing we owned. He gambles. My mother sells the house to pay his debts. But it isn't enough, it's never enough. When he's young he tries to sell me to customers at the Coupole. It's for him my mother wants to go on living, so he can go on eating, so he can have a roof over his head, so he can still hear someone call him by his name. Then there's the place she bought for him near Amboise, ten years' savings. Mortgaged in one night. She pays the interest. And all the profit from the cutting down of the woods I told you about. In one night. He stole from my mother when she was dying. He was the sort of person who rummaged in cupboards, who had a gift for it, knew where to look, could find the right piles of sheets, the hiding places. He stole wedding-rings, that sort of thing, lots of them, jewellery, food. He stole from Dô, the houseboys, my younger brother. From me. Plenty. He'd have sold her, his own mother. When she dies he sends for the lawyer right away, in the midst of all the emotion. He takes advantage of it. The lawyer says the will's not valid. It favours the elder son too much at my expense. The difference is enormous, laughable. I have to refuse or accept, in full knowledge of the facts. I say I'll accept: I'll sign. I've accepted. My brother lowers his eyes. Thanks. He weeps. In the midst of all the emotion of our mother's death. He's quite sincere. At the liberation of Paris, probably on the run for having been a collaborator in the South, he has nowhere to go. He comes to me. He's running away from some danger, I never quite knew what. Perhaps he informed on people, Jews perhaps, anything's possible. He's very mild and affectionate, as always after he's committed murders or when he needs your help. My husband's been deported. He sympathizes. He stays three days. I've forgotten, and when I go out I don't lock anything up. He rummages around. I've been keeping my rice and sugar rations for when my husband comes back. He rummages around and takes them. He also rummages around in a little cupboard in my bedroom. He finds what he's looking for and takes all my savings, fifty thousand francs. He doesn't leave a single note. He quits the apartment with the spoils. When I see him again I shan't mention it, it's too shaming for him, I couldn't. After the fake will, the fake Louis XIV chateau is sold for a song. The sale was a put-up job, like the will.

After my mother's death he's left alone. He has no friends, never has had, sometimes he's had women who 'worked' for him in Montparnasse, sometimes women who didn't work for him, at least to begin with, sometimes men, but then they did the paying. He lived a very lonely life. And more so as he grew older. He was only a layabout, he operated on a very small scale. He inspired fear in his immediate circle, but no further. When he lost us he lost his real empire. He wasn't a gangster, just a family layabout, a rummager in cupboards, a murderer without a gun. He didn't take any risks. Layabouts all live as he did, without any loyalty, without any grandeur, in fear. He was afraid. After my mother's death he leads a strange existence. In Tours. The only people he knows are waiters in cafés, for the racing tips, and the bibulous patrons of backroom poker games. He starts to look like them, drinks a lot, gets bloodshot eyes and slurred speech. In Tours he had nothing. Both houses had been sold off. Nothing. For a year he lived in a furniture warehouse leased by my mother. For a year he slept in an armchair. They let him go there. Stay for a year. Then they threw him out.

For a year he must have hoped to buy his mortgaged property back. He gambled away my mother's furniture from the warehouse, bit by bit. The bronze Buddha, the brass, then the beds, then the wardrobes, then the sheets. And then one day he has nothing left, that does happen to people like him, one day he has the suit on his back and nothing else, not a sheet, not a shelter. He's alone. For a year no one will open their door to him. He writes to a cousin in Paris. He can have a servant's room in the boulevard Malesherbes. And when he's over fifty he'll have his first job, his first wages ever, as commissionaire for a marine insurance company. That lasted, I think, fifteen years. He had to go into hospital. He didn't die there. He died in his room.

My mother never talked about that one of her children. She never complained. She never mentioned the rummager in cupboards to anyone. She treated the fact that she was his mother as if it were a crime. She kept it hidden. She must have thought it was unintelligible, impossible to convey to anyone who didn't know her son as she did, before God and only before Him. She repeated little platitudes about him, always the same ones. That if he'd wanted to he could have been the cleverest of the three. The most 'artistic'. The most astute. And he was the one who'd loved his mother most. The one, in short, who'd understood her best. I didn't know, she'd say, that you could expect that of a boy, such intuition, such deep affection.

* * *

We met again once, he spoke about our dead brother. He said of his death: What an awful thing, how dreadful, our little brother, our little Paulo.

There remains this image of our kinship: a meal in Sadec. All three of us are eating at the dining-room table. They're seventeen, eighteen. My mother's not with us. He watches us eat, my younger brother and me, then he puts down his fork and looks at my younger brother. For a very long time he looks at him, then suddenly, very calmly, says something terrible. About food. He says he must be careful, he shouldn't eat so much. My younger brother doesn't answer. The other goes on. Reminds him the big pieces of meat are for him, and he mustn't forget it. Or else, he says. I ask, Why are they for you? He says, Because that's how it is. I say, I wish you'd die. I can't eat any more. Nor can my younger brother. He waits for my younger brother to dare to speak, just one word, his clenched fists are poised ready over the table to bash his face in. My younger brother says nothing. He's very pale. Between his lashes, the beginning of tears.

It was a dreary day, the day he died. In Spring, I think it was, April. Someone telephones. They don't say anything else, nothing, just he's been found dead, on the floor, in his room. But death came before the end of his story. When he was still alive it had already happened, it was too late now for him to die, it had been all over since the death of my younger brother. The conquering words: It is finished.

She asked for him to be buried with her. I don't know where, in which cemetery. I just know it's in the Loire. Both in the same grave. Just the two of them. It's as it should be. An image of intolerable splendour.

Dusk fell at the same time all the year round. It was very brief, almost like a blow. In the rainy season, for weeks on end, you couldn't see the sky, it was full of an unvarying mist which even the light of the moon couldn't pierce. In the dry season, though, the sky was bare, completely free of cloud, naked. Even moonless nights were light. And the shadows were as clearcut as ever on the ground, and on the water, roads and walls.

I can't really remember the days. The light of the sun blurred and annihilated all colour. But the nights, I remember them. The blue was more distant than the sky, beyond all depths, covering the bounds of the world. The sky, for me, was the stretch of pure brilliance crossing the blue, that cold coalescence beyond all colour. Sometimes, it was in Vinh Long, when my mother was sad she'd order the gig and we'd drive out into the country to see the night as it was in the dry season. I had that good fortune – those nights, that mother. The light fell from the sky in cataracts of pure transparency, in torrents of silence and immobility. The air was blue, you could hold it in your hand. Blue. The sky was the continual throbbing of the brilliance of the light. The night lit up everything, all the country on either bank of the river as far as the eye could reach. Every night was different, each one had a name as long as it lasted. Their sound was that of the dogs, the country dogs baying at mystery. They answered one another from village to village, until the time and space of the night were utterly consumed.

On the paths of the yard the shadows of the cinnamon-apple trees are inky black. The whole garden is still as marble. The house too – monumental, funereal. And my younger brother, who was walking beside me, now looks intently at the gate open on the empty road.

One day he's not there outside the high school. The driver's alone in the black car. He says the father's ill and the young master's gone back to Sadec. He, the driver, has been told to stay in Saigon to take me to school and back again to the boarding house. The young master came back after a few days. Again he was there in the back of the black car, his face averted so as not to see people looking at him, still afraid. We kissed, without a word, kissed there outside the school, we'd forgotten. While we kissed, he wept. His father was going to live. His last hope was vanishing.

He'd asked him, implored him to let him keep me with him, close to him, he'd told him he must understand, must have known a passion like this himself at least once in his long life, it couldn't be otherwise, he'd begged him to let him have his turn at living, just once, this passion, this madness, this infatuation with the little white girl, he'd asked him to give him time to love her a while longer before sending her away to France, let him have her a little longer, another year perhaps, because it wasn't possible for him to give up this love yet, it was too new, too strong still, too much in its first violence, it was too terrible for him to part yet from her body, especially since, as he the father knew, it could never happen again.

The father said he'd sooner see him dead.

We bathed together in the cool water from the jars, we kissed, we wept, and again it was unto death, but this time, already, the pleasure it gave was inconsolable. And then I told him. I told him not to have any regrets, I reminded him of what he'd said, that I'd go away from everywhere, that I wasn't responsible for what I did. He said he didn't mind even that now, nothing counted any more. Then I said I agreed with his father. That I refused to stay with him. I didn't give any reasons.

It's one of the long avenues in Vinh Long that lead down to the Mekong. It's always deserted in the evening. That evening, like most evenings, the electricity breaks down. That's what starts it all off. As soon as I reach the street and the gate shuts behind me, the lights go off. I run. I run because I'm afraid of the dark. I run faster and faster. And suddenly I think I hear running behind me, and suddenly I'm sure that someone's after me. Still running, I look round, and I see. It's a very tall woman, very thin, thin as death, laughing and running. She's barefoot, and she's running after me to catch me. I recognize her, she's the local lunatic, the mad-woman of Vinh Long. I hear her for the first time, she talks at night, during the day she sleeps, often here in the avenue, outside the garden. She runs, shouting in a language I don't understand. My fear's so great I can't call out. I must be eight years old. I can hear her shrieks of laughter and cries of delight, she's certainly playing with me. My memory is of a central fear. To say it's beyond my understanding, beyond my strength, is inadequate. What's sure is the memory of my whole being's certainty that if the woman touches me, even lightly, with her hand, I too will enter into a state much worse than death, the state of madness. I manage to get into the neighbours' garden, as far as the house, I run up the steps and fall in the doorway. For several days I can't say anything at all about what happened.

Quite late in life I'm still afraid of seeing a certain state of my mother's – I still don't name it – get so much worse that she'll have to be parted from her children. I believe it will be up to me to recognize the time when it comes, not my brothers, because my brothers wouldn't be able to judge.

It was a few months before our final parting, in Saigon, late one evening, we were on the big terrace of the house in the rue Testard. Dô was there. I looked at my mother, I could hardly recognize her. And then, in a kind of sudden vanishing, a sudden fall, I all at once couldn't recognize her at all. There, suddenly, close to me, was someone sitting in my mother's place who wasn't my mother, who looked like her but who'd never been her. She looked rather blank, she was gazing at the garden, a certain point in the garden, it looked as if she was watching for something just about to happen, of which I could see nothing. There was a youthfulness about her features, her expression, a happiness which she was repressing out of what must have been habitual reticence. She was beautiful. Dô was beside her. Dô seemed not to have noticed anything. My terror didn't come from what I've just said about her, her face, her look of happiness, her beauty, it came from the fact that she was sitting just where my mother had been sitting when the substitution took place, from the fact that I knew no one else was there in her place, but that that identity irreplaceable by any other had disappeared and I was powerless to make it come back, make it start to come back. There was no longer anything there to inhabit her image. I went mad in full possession of my senses. Just long enough to cry out. I did cry out. A faint cry, a call for help, to crack the ice in which the whole scene was fatally freezing. My mother turned her head.

For me the whole town is inhabited by the beggar woman in the road. And all the beggar women of the towns, the rice-fields, the tracks bordering Siam, the banks of the Mekong – for me the beggar woman who frightened me is inhabited by them. She comes from everywhere. She always ends up in Calcutta wherever she started out from. She's always slept in the shade of the cinnamon-apple trees in the playground. And always my mother has been there beside her, tending her foot eaten up with maggots and covered with flies.

Beside her, the little girl in the story. She's carried her two thousand kilometres. She's had enough of her, wants to give her away. Go on, take her. No more children. No more child. All dead or thrown away, it amounts to a lot after a whole life. The one asleep under the cinnamon-apple trees isn't yet dead. She's the one who'll live longest. She'll die inside the house, in a lace dress. She'll be mourned.

She's on the banks of the rice-fields on either side of the track, shouting and laughing at the top of her voice. She has a golden laugh, fit to wake the dead, to wake anyone who listens to children's laughter. She stays outside the bungalow for days and days, there are white people in the bungalow, she remembers they give food to beggars. And then, one day, lo and behold, she wakes at daybreak and starts to walk, one day she goes, who can tell why, she turns off towards the mountains, goes up through the forest, follows the paths running along the tops of the mountains of Siam. Having seen, perhaps, seen a yellow and green sky on the other side of the plain, she crosses over. At last begins to descend to the sea. With her great gaunt step she descends the slopes of the forest. On, on. They're forests full of pestilence. Regions of great heat. There's no healthy wind from the sea. There's the stagnant din of mosquitoes, dead children, rain every day. And then here are the deltas. The biggest deltas in the world. Made of black slime. Stretching towards Chittagong. She's left the tracks, the forests, the tea roads, the red suns, behind, and she goes forward over the estuary of the deltas. She goes in the same direction as the world, towards the engulfing, always distant east. One day she comes face to face with the sea. She lets out a cry, laughs her miraculous bird-like coo. Because of her laugh she finds a junk in Chittagong, the fishermen are willing to take her, she crosses with them the Bay of Bengal.

Then, then she starts to be seen near the rubbish dumps on the outskirts of Calcutta.

And then she's lost sight of. And then later found again behind the French embassy in the same city. She sleeps in a garden, replete with endless food.

She's there during the night. Then in the Ganges at sunrise. Always laughing, mocking. She doesn't go on this time. Here she can eat, sleep, it's quiet at night, she stays there in the garden with the oleanders.

One day I come, pass by. I'm seventeen. It's the English

quarter, the embassy gardens, the monsoon season, the tennis courts are deserted. Along the Ganges the lepers laugh.

We're stopping over in Calcutta. The boat broke down. We're visiting the town to pass the time. We leave the following evening.

Fifteen and a half. The news spreads fast in Sadec. The clothes she wears are enough to show. The mother has no idea, and none about how to bring up a daughter. Poor child. Don't tell me that hat's innocent, or the lipstick, it all means something, it's not innocent, it means something, it's to attract attention, money. The brothers are layabouts. They say it's a Chinese, the son of the millionaire, the villa in Mekong with the blue tiles. And even he, instead of thinking himself honoured, doesn't want her for his son. A family of white layabouts.

The Lady, they called her. She came from Savanna Khet. Her husband was posted to Vinh Long. For a year she wasn't seen there. Because of the young man, the assistant administrator in Savanna Khet. They couldn't be lovers any more. So he shot himself. The story reached the new posting in Vinh Long. The day she left Savanna Khet for Vinh Long, a bullet through the heart. In the main square in broad sunlight. Because of her young daughters and her husband's being posted to Vinh Long she'd told him it had to stop.

It goes on in the disreputable quarter of Cholon, every evening. Every morning the little slut goes to have her body caressed by a filthy Chinese millionaire. And she goes to the French high school, too, with the little white girls, the athletic little white girls who learn the crawl in the pool at the Sporting Club. One day they'll be told not to speak to the daughter of the teacher in Sadec any more.

* * *

During break she looks towards the street, all on her own, leaning against a post in the school yard. She doesn't say anything about it to her mother. She goes on coming to school in the black limousine belonging to the Chinese in Cholon. She watches it go. No one will break the rule. None of the girls will speak to her. The isolation brings back a clear memory of the lady in Vinh Long. At that time she'd just turned thirty-eight. And the child was ten. And now, when she remembers, she's sixteen.

The lady's on the terrace outside her room, looking at the avenues bordering the Mekong, I see her when I come home from catechism class with my younger brother. The room's in the middle of a great palace with covered terraces, the palace itself in the middle of the garden of oleanders and palms. The same distance separates the lady and the girl in the low-crowned hat from the other people in the town. Just as they both look at the long avenues beside the river, so they are alike in themselves. Both isolated. Alone, queen-like. Their disgrace is a matter of course. Both are doomed to discredit because of the kind of body they have, caressed by lovers, kissed by their lips, consigned to the infamy of a pleasure unto death, as they both call it, unto the mysterious death of lovers without love. That's what it's all about: this hankering for death. It emanates from them, from their rooms, a death so strong its existence is known all over the town, in outposts up-country, in provincial centres, at official receptions and slow-motion government balls.

The lady's just started giving official receptions again, she thinks it's over, that the young man in Savanna Khet is a thing of the past. So she's started giving evening parties again, the ones expected of her so that people can just meet occasionally and occasionally escape from the frightful loneliness of serving in outposts up-country, stranded amid chequered stretches of rice, fear, madness, fever and oblivion.

* * *

In the evening, after school, the same black limousine, the same hat at once impudent and childlike, the same lamé shoes, and away she goes, goes to have her body laid bare by the Chinese millionaire, he'll wash her under the shower, slowly, as she used to wash herself at home at her mother's, with cool water from a jar he keeps specially for her, and then he'll carry her, still wet, to the bed, he'll switch on the fan and kiss her more and more all over, and she'll keep asking again and again and afterwards she'll go back to the boarding school, and no one to punish her, beat her, disfigure or insult her.

It was as night ended that he killed himself, in the main square, glittering with light. She was dancing. Then daylight came, skirted the body. Then, with time, the sunlight blurred its shape. No one dared go near. But the police will. At noon, by the time the tourist boats arrive, there'll be nothing left, the square will be empty.

My mother said to the head of the boarding school, It doesn't matter, all that's of no importance. Haven't you noticed how they suit her, those little old frocks, that pink hat and the gold shoes? My mother's drunk with delight when she speaks of her children, and that makes her more charming than ever. The young teachers at the boarding school listen to her with passionate attention. All of them, says my mother, they all hang around her, all the men in the place, married or single, they hang around, hanker after the girl, after something not really definite yet, look, she's still a child. Do people talk of disgrace? I say, how can innocence be disgraced?

My mother rattles on. She speaks of blatant prostitution and laughs, at the scandal, the buffoonery, the funny hat, the sublime elegance of the child who crossed the river. And she laughs at what's irresistible here in the French colonies: I mean, she says, this little white tart, this child hidden till then in outposts up-country and suddenly emerging into the day-light and shacking up in front of everyone with this millionaire Chinese scum, with a diamond on her finger just as if she were a banker's wife. And she weeps.

When she saw the diamond she said in a small voice: It reminds me of the little solitaire I had when I got engaged to my first husband. I say: Mr Dark. We laugh. That was his name, she says, it really was.

We looked at each other for some time, then she gave a sweet, slightly mocking smile, full of so deep a knowledge of her children and what awaited them later on that I almost told her about Cholon.

But I didn't. I never did.

She waited a long while before she spoke again, then she said, very lovingly: You do know it's all over, don't you? That you'll never be able, now, to get married here in the colony? I shrug my shoulders, smile. I say, I can get married anywhere, when I want to. My mother shakes her head. No. She says: Here everything gets known, here you can't, now. She looks at me and says some unforgettable things: They find you attractive? I answer: Yes; they find me attractive in spite of everything. It's then she says: And also because of what you are yourself.

She goes on: Is it only for the money you see him? I hesitate, then say it is only for the money. Again she looks at me for a long while, she doesn't believe me. She says: I wasn't like you, I found school much harder and I was very serious, I stayed like that too long, too late, I lost the taste for my own pleasure.

It was one day during the vacation in Sadec. She was resting in a rocking-chair with her feet up on another chair, she'd made a draught between the door of the sitting-room and the door of the dining-room. She was peaceful, not aggressive. She'd suddenly noticed her daughter, wanted to talk to her.

It happened not long before the end, before she abandoned

the land by the dyke. Not long before we went back to France.

I watched her fall asleep.

Every so often my mother declares: Tomorrow we'll go to the photographer's. She complains about the price but still goes to the expense of family photos. We look at them, we don't look at each other but we do look at the photographs, each of us separately, without a word of comment, but we look at them, we see ourselves. See the other members of the family one by one or all together. Look back at ourselves when we were very young in the old photos, then look at ourselves again in the recent ones. The gulf between us has grown bigger still. Once they've been looked at the photos are put away with the linen in the cupboards. My mother has us photographed so that she can see if we're growing normally. She studies us at length, as other mothers do other children. She compares the photos, discusses how each one of us has grown. No one ever answers.

My mother only has photos taken of her children. Never anything else. I haven't got any photographs of Vinh Long, not one, of the garden, the river, the straight tamarind-lined avenues of the French conquest, not of the house, nor of our institutional whitewashed bedrooms with the big black and gilt iron beds, lit up like classrooms by the red street lights, the green metal lamp-shades, not a single image of those incredible places, always temporary, ugly beyond expression, places to flee from, in which my mother would camp until, as she said, she really settled down, but in France, in the regions she's spoken of all her life and that vary, according to her mood, her age, her sadness, between Pas-de-Calais and Entre-Deux-Mers. But when she does halt for good, when she settles down in the Loire, her room will be a terrible replica of the one in Sadec. She'll have forgotten.

*   *   *

She never had photos taken of places, landscapes, only of us, her children, and mostly she had us taken in a group so it wouldn't cost so much. The few amateur photos of us were taken by friends of my mother's, new colleagues just arrived in the colony who took views of the equatorial landscape, the coconut palms and the coolies to send to their families.

For some mysterious reason my mother used to show her children's photographs to her family when she went home on leave. We didn't want to go and see them. My brothers never met them. At first she used to take me, the youngest, with her. Then later on I stopped going, because my aunts didn't want their daughters to see me any more on account of my shocking behaviour. So my mother has only the photographs left to show, so she shows them, naturally, reasonably, shows her cousins her children. She owes it to herself to do so, so she does, her cousins are all that's left of the family, so she shows them the family photos. Can we glimpse something of this woman through this way of going on? The way she sees everything through to the bitter end without ever dreaming she might give up, abandon – the cousins, the effort, the burden. I think we can. It's in this valour, human, absurd, that I see true grace.

When she was old, too, grey-haired, she went to the photographer's, alone, and had her photograph taken in her best dark red dress and her two bits of jewellery, the locket and the gold and jade brooch, a little round of jade sheathed in gold. In the photo her hair's done nicely, her clothes just so, butter wouldn't melt in her mouth. The better-off natives used to go to the photographer's too, just once in their lives, when they saw death was near. Their photos were large, all the same size, hung in handsome gilt frames near the altars to their ancestors. All these photographs of different people, and I've seen many of them, give practically identical results, the resemblance was stunning. It wasn't just because all old people look alike, but

because the portraits themselves were invariably touched up
in such a way that any facial peculiarities, if there were any left,
were minimized. All the faces were prepared in the same
way to confront eternity, all toned down, all uniformly
rejuvenated. This was what people wanted. This general
resemblance, this tact, would characterize the memory of their
passage through the family, bear witness at once to the singu-
larity and to the reality of that transit. The more they
resembled each other the more evidently they belonged in the
ranks of the family. Moreover, all the men wore the same sort
of turban, all the women had their hair scraped back into the
same kind of bun, and both men and women wore tunics with
stand-up collars. And they all wore an expression I'd still
recognize anywhere. My mother's expression in the photograph with the red dress was the same. Noble, some would say.
Others would call it withdrawn.

They never speak of it any more. It's an understood thing that
he won't approach his father any more to let him marry her.
That the father will have no pity on his son. He has no pity on
anyone. Of all the Chinese immigrants who hold the trade of
the place in their hands, the man with the blue terraces is the
most terrible, the richest, the one whose property extends the
furthest beyond Sadec, to Cholon, the Chinese capital of
French Indo-China. The man from Cholon knows his father's
decision and the girl's are the same, and both are irrevocable.
To a lesser degree he begins to understand that the journey
which will separate him from her is a piece of good luck for
their affair. That she's not the marrying kind, she'll run away
from any marriage, he must give her up, forget her, give her
back to the whites, to her brothers.

Ever since he'd been infatuated with her body the girl had
stopped being incommoded by it, by its thinness. And similarly, strangely, her mother no longer worried about it as she

had before, just as if she too had discovered it was plausible after all, as acceptable as any other body. The lover from Cholon thinks the growth of the little white girl has been stunted by the excessive heat. He too was born and grew up in this heat. He discovers this kinship between them. He says all the years she's spent here, in this intolerable latitude, have turned her into a girl of Indo-China. That she has the same slender wrists as they, the same thick hair that looks as if it's absorbed all its owner's strength, and it's long like theirs too, and above all there's her skin, all over her body, that comes from the rainwater stored here for women and children to bathe in. He says compared to the women here the women in France have hard skins on their bodies, almost rough. He says the low diet of the tropics, mostly fish and fruit, has something to do with it too. Also the cottons and silks the clothes here are made of, and the loose clothes themselves, leaving a space between themselves and the body, leaving it naked, free.

The lover from Cholon's so accustomed to the adolescence of the white girl, he's lost. The pleasure he takes in her every evening has absorbed all his time, all his life. He scarcely speaks to her any more. Perhaps he thinks she won't understand any longer what he'd say about her, about the love he never knew before and of which he can't speak. Perhaps he realizes they never have spoken to each other, except when they cry out to each other in the bedroom in the evening. Yes, I think he didn't know, he realizes he didn't know.

He looks at her. Goes on looking at her, his eyes shut. He inhales her face, breathes it in. He breathes her in, the child, his eyes shut he breathes in her breath, the warm air coming out of her. Less and less clearly can he make out the limits of this body, it's not like other bodies, it's not finished, in the room it keeps growing, it's still without set form, continually coming into being, not only there where it's visible but elsewhere too, stretching beyond sight, towards risk, towards death, it's nimble, it launches itself wholly into pleasure as if it were grown up, adult, it's without guile, and it's frighteningly intelligent.

I used to watch what he did with me, how he used me, and I'd never thought anyone could act like that, he acted beyond my hope and in accordance with my body's destiny. So I became his child. And he became something else for me too. I began to recognize the inexpressible softness of his skin, of his member, apart from himself. The shadow of another man must have passed through the room, the shadow of a young murderer, but I didn't know that then, had no inkling of it yet. The shadow of a young hunter must have passed through the room too, but that one, yes, I knew about, sometimes he was present in the pleasure and I'd tell the lover from Cholon, talk to him of the other's body and member, of his indescribable sweetness, of his courage in the forest and on the rivers whose estuaries hold the black panthers. Everything chimed with his desire and made him possess me. I'd become his child. It was with his own child he made love every evening. And sometimes he takes fright, suddenly he's worried about her health, as if he suddenly realized she was mortal and it suddenly struck him he might lose her. Her being so thin strikes him, and sometimes this makes him suddenly afraid. And there's the headache, too, which often makes her lie limp, motionless, ghastly pale, with a wet bandage over her eyes. And the loathing of life that sometimes seizes her, when she thinks of her mother and suddenly cries out and weeps with rage at the thought of not being able to change things, not being able to make her mother happy before she dies, not being able to kill those responsible. His face against hers he receives her tears, crushes her to him, mad with desire for her tears, for her anger.

*　　*　　*

He takes her as he would his own child. He'd take his own child the same way. He plays with his child's body, turns it over, covers his face with it, his lips, his eyes. And she, she goes on abandoning herself in exactly the same way as he set when he started. Then suddenly it's she who's imploring, she doesn't say what for, and he, he shouts to her to be quiet, that he doesn't want to have anything more to do with her, doesn't want to have his pleasure of her any more. And now once more they are caught together again, locked together in terror, and now the terror abates again, and now they succumb to it again, amid tears, despair and happiness.

They are silent all evening long. In the black car that takes her back to the boarding school she leans her head on his shoulder. He puts his arm round her. He says it's a good thing the boat from France is coming soon to take her away and separate them. They are silent during the drive. Sometimes he tells the driver to go round by the river. She sleeps, exhausted, on his shoulder. He wakes her with kisses.

In the dormitory the light is blue. There's a smell of incense, they always burn incense at dusk. The heat's oppressive, all the windows are wide open and there's not a breath of air. I take my shoes off so as not to make any noise, but I'm not worried, I know the mistress in charge won't get up, I know it's accepted now that I come back at night at whatever time I like. I go straight to where H.L. is, always slightly anxious, always afraid she may have run away during the day. But she's there. She sleeps deeply, H.L. An obstinate, almost hostile sleep, I remember. Expressing rejection. Her bare arms are flung up in abandon around her head. Her body's not lying down decorously like those of the other girls, her legs are bent, her face is invisible, her pillow awry. I expect she was waiting for me but fell asleep as she waited, impatient and angry. She must have been crying too, and then lapsed into oblivion. I'd like to wake her up, have a whispered conversation. I don't talk to the man from Cholon any more, he doesn't talk to me, I need to hear H.L.'s questions. She has the matchless attentiveness of those who don't understand what's said to them. But I can't wake her up. Once she's woken up like that, in the middle of the night, H.L. can't go back to sleep again. She gets up, wants to go outside, does so, goes down the stairs, along the corridors, out all alone into the big empty playgrounds, she runs, she calls out to me, she's so happy, it's irresistible, and when she's not allowed to go out with the other girls you know that's just what she wants. I hesitate, but then no, I don't wake her up. Under the mosquito net the heat's stifling, when you close the net after you it seems unendurable. But I know it's because I've come in from outside, from the banks of the river where it's always cool at night. I'm used to it, I keep still, wait for it to pass. It passes. I never fall asleep right away despite the new fatigues in my life. I think about the man from Cholon. He's probably in a night-club somewhere near the Fountain with his driver, they'll be drinking in silence, they drink arrack when they're on their own. Or else he's gone home, he's fallen asleep with the light on, still without speaking to anyone. That night I can't bear the thought of the man from Cholon any more. Nor the thought of H.L. It's as if they were happy, and as if it came from outside themselves. And I have nothing like that. My mother says: This one will never be satisfied with anything. I think I'm beginning to see my life. I think I can already say, I have a vague desire to die. From now on I treat that word and my life as inseparable. I think I have a vague desire to be alone, just as I realize I've never been alone any more since I left childhood behind, and the family of the hunter. I'm going to write. That's what I see beyond the present moment, in the great desert in whose form my life stretches out before me.

*   *   *

I forget the words of the telegram from Saigon. Forget whether it said my younger brother was dead or whether it said, Recalled to God. I seem to remember it was Recalled to God. I realized at once, she couldn't have sent the telegram. My younger brother. Dead. At first it's incomprehensible, and then, suddenly, from all directions, from the ends of the earth, comes pain. It buried me, swept me away, I didn't know anything, I ceased to exist except for pain, what pain, I didn't know what pain, whether it was the pain returning of having lost a child a few months before, or a new pain. Now I think it was a new pain, I'd never known my still-born child and hadn't wanted to kill myself then as I wanted to now.

It was a mistake, and that momentary error filled the universe. The outrage was on the scale of God. My younger brother was immortal and they hadn't noticed. Immortality had been concealed in my brother's body while he was alive, and we hadn't noticed that it dwelt there. Now my brother's body was dead, and immortality with it. And the world went on without that visited body, and without its visitation. It was a complete mistake. And the error, the outrage, filled the whole universe.

Since my younger brother was dead, everything had to die after him. And through him. Death, a chain reaction of death, started with him, the child.

The corpse of the child was unaffected, itself, by the events of which it was the cause. Of the immortality it had harboured for the twenty-seven years of its life, it didn't know the name.

No one saw clearly but I. And since I'd acquired that knowledge, the simple knowledge that my younger brother's body was mine as well, I had to die. And I am dead. My younger brother gathered me to him, drew me to him, and I am dead.

*   *   *

People ought to be told of such things. Ought to be taught
that immortality is mortal, that it can die, it's happened before
and it happens still. It doesn't ever announce itself as such –
it's duplicity itself. It doesn't exist in detail, only in principle.
Certain people may harbour it, on condition they don't know
that's what they're doing. Just as certain other people may
detect its presence in them, on the same condition, that they
don't know they can. It's while it's being lived that life is
immortal, while it's still alive. Immortality's not a matter of
more or less time, it's not really a question of immortality but
of something else that remains unknown. It's as untrue to say
it's without beginning or end as to say it begins and ends with
the life of the spirit, since it partakes both of the spirit and of
the pursuit of the void. Look at the dead sands of the desert,
the dead bodies of children: there's no path for immortality
there, it must halt and seek another way.

In the case of my younger brother it was an immortality without flaw, without commentary, smooth, pure, unique. My
younger brother had nothing to cry in the wilderness, he had
nothing to say, here or anywhere, nothing. He was un-
educated, he never managed to learn anything. He couldn't
speak, could scarcely read, scarcely write, sometimes you'd
think he couldn't even suffer. He was someone who didn't
understand and was afraid.

The wild love I feel for him remains an unfathomable mystery
to me. I don't know why I loved him so much as to want to
die of his death. I'd been parted from him for ten years when
it happened, and hardly ever thought about him. I loved him,
it seemed, for ever, and nothing new could happen to that
love. I'd forgotten about death.

*   *   *

We didn't talk to each other much, we hardly talked at all about our elder brother, or our unhappiness, our mother's unhappiness, the misfortune of the concession, the plain. We talked instead about hunting, rifles, mechanics, cars. He'd get furious about our worn-down old car, and tell me about, describe, the cars he'd have in the future. I knew all the makes of hunting rifles and all the brands of car. We also talked, of course, about being eaten by tigers if we weren't careful, or getting drowned in the river if we went on swimming in the currents. He was two years older than I.

The wind has ceased, and under the trees there's the supernatural light that follows rain. Some birds are shrieking at the tops of their voices, crazy birds. As they sharpen their beaks on it, the cold air rings with an almost deafening clamour.

The liners used to go up the Saigon River, engines off, drawn by tugs to the port installations in the bend of the Mekong that's on the same latitude as the town of Saigon. This bend or branch of the Mekong is called the River, the Saigon River. The boats stopped there for a week. As soon as they berthed, you were in France. You could dine in France and dance there, but it was too expensive for my mother, and anyway for her there was no point. But with him, the lover from Cholon, you could have gone. But he didn't go because he'd have been afraid to be seen with the little white girl, so young. He didn't say, but she knew. In those days, and it's not so long ago, scarcely fifty years, it was only ships that went all over the world. Large parts of all the continents were still without roads or railways. Hundreds, thousands of square kilometres still had nothing but pre-historic tracks. It was the handsome ships of the Messageries Maritimes, the musketeers of the shipping lines, the Porthos, D'Artagnan and Aramis, that linked Indo-China to France.

*   *   *

The voyage lasted twenty-four days. The liners were like towns, with streets, bars, cafés, libraries, drawing-rooms, meetings, lovers, weddings, deaths. Chance societies formed, fortuitous as everyone knew and did not forget, but for that very reason tolerable, and sometimes unforgettably pleasant. These were the only voyages the women ever made. And for many of them, and for some men too, the voyage out to the colony was the real adventure of the whole thing. For our mother those trips, together with our infancy, were always what she called 'the happiest days of her life'.

Departures. They were always the same. Always the first departures over the sea. People have always left the land in the same sorrow and despair, but that never stopped men from going, Jews, philosophers, and pure travellers for the journey's own sake. Nor did it ever stop women letting them go, the women who never went themselves, who stayed behind to look after the birthplace, the race, the property, the reason for the return. For centuries, because of the ships, journeys were longer and more tragic than they are today. A voyage covered its distance in a natural span of time. People were used to those slow human speeds on both land and sea, to those delays, those waitings on the wind or fair weather, to those expectations of shipwreck, sun and death. The liners the little white girl knew were among the last mail-boats in the world. It was while she was young that the first air-lines were started, which were gradually to deprive mankind of journeys across the sea.

We still went every day to the flat at Cholon. He behaved as usual, for a while he behaved as usual, giving me a shower with the water from the jars, carrying me over to the bed. He'd come over to me, lie down too, but now he had no strength, no potency. Once the date of my departure was fixed, distant though it still was, he could do nothing with my body any more. It had happened suddenly, without his realizing it. His body wanted nothing more to do with the body that was about to go away, to betray. He'd say: I can't make love to you any more, I thought I still could, but I can't. He'd say he was dead. He'd give a sweet, apologetic smile, say that perhaps it would never come back. I'd ask him if that's what he wanted. He, almost laughing, would say, I don't know, at this moment perhaps yes. His gentleness was unaffected by his pain. He didn't speak of the pain, never said a word about it. Sometimes his face would quiver, he'd close his eyes and clench his teeth. But he never said anything about the images he saw behind his closed eyes. It was as if he loved the pain, loved it as he'd loved me, intensely, unto death perhaps, and as if he preferred it now to me. Sometimes he'd say he'd like to caress me because he knew I longed for it, and he'd like to watch me as the pleasure came. So he did, and watched me at the same time, and called me his child. We decided not to see each other any more, but it wasn't possible, it turned out to be impossible. Every evening he was there outside the high school in his black car, his head averted from humiliation.

When it was due to sail the boat gave three blasts on its siren, very long and terribly loud, they were heard all over the town, and over the harbour the sky grew dark. Then the tugs came up and towed the boat to the middle of the river. After which they cast off their cables and returned to harbour. Then the boat bade farewell again, uttering once more its terrible, mysteriously sad wails that made everyone weep, not only those who were parting from one another but the onlookers too, and those who were there for no special reason, who had no one particular in mind. Then, very slowly, under its own steam, the boat launched itself on the river. For a long while its tall shape could be seen advancing towards the sea. Many people stayed to watch, waving more and more slowly, more and more sadly, with scarves and handkerchiefs. Then finally the outline of the ship was swallowed up in the curve of the earth. On a clear day you could see it slowly sink.

For her too it was when the boat uttered its first farewell, when the gangway was hauled up and the tugs had started to tow and draw the boat away from land, that she had wept. She'd wept without letting anyone see her tears, because he was Chinese and one oughtn't to weep for that kind of lover. Wept without letting her mother or her younger brother see she was sad, without letting them see anything, as was the custom between them. His big car was there, long and black with the white-liveried driver in front. It was a little way away from the Messageries Maritimes car park, on its own. That was how she'd recognized it. That was him in the back, that scarcely visible shape, motionless, overcome. She was leaning on the rails, like the first time, on the ferry. She knew he was watching her. She was watching him too, she couldn't see him any more but she still looked towards the shape of the black car. And then at last she couldn't see it any more. The harbour faded away, and then the land.

There was the China Sea, the Red Sea, the Indian Ocean, the Suez Canal, the morning when you woke up and knew from the absence of vibration that you were advancing through the sand. But above all there was the ocean. The furthest, the most vast, it reached to the South Pole. It had the longest distance between landfalls, between Ceylon and Somalia. Sometimes it was so calm, and the weather so fair and mild, that crossing it was like a journey over something other than the sea. Then the whole boat opened up, the lounges, the gangways, the portholes, and the passengers fled their sweltering cabins and slept on deck.

Once, during the crossing of the ocean, late at night, someone died. She can't quite remember if it was on that voyage or another that it happened. Some people were playing cards in the first-class bar, and among the players was a young man, who at one point, without saying anything, laid down his cards, left the bar, ran across the deck and threw himself into the sea. By the time the boat was stopped – it was going at full speed – the body couldn't be found.

No, now she comes to write it down she doesn't see the boat, but somewhere else, the place where she was told about it. It was in Sadec. It was the son of the district officer in Sadec. She knew him, he'd been at the high school in Saigon too. She remembers him, dark, tall, with a very gentle face and horn-rimmed glasses. Nothing was found in his cabin, no farewell letter. His age has remained in her memory, terrifying, the same, seventeen. The boat went on again at dawn. That was the worst. The sunrise, the empty sea, and the decision to abandon the search. The parting.

And another time, on the same route, during the crossing of the same ocean, night had begun as before and in the lounge on the main deck there was a sudden burst of music, a Chopin waltz which she knew secretly, personally, because for months she tried to learn it, though she never managed to play it properly, never, and that was why her mother agreed to let her give up the piano. Among all the other nights upon nights, the girl had spent that one on the boat, of that she was sure, and she'd been there when it happened, the burst of Chopin under a sky lit up with brilliancies. There wasn't a breath of wind and the music spread all over the dark boat, like a heavenly injunction whose import was unknown, like an order from God whose meaning was inscrutable. And the girl started up as if to go and kill herself in her turn, throw herself in her turn into the sea, and afterwards she wept because she thought of the man from Cholon and suddenly she wasn't sure she hadn't loved him with a love she hadn't seen because it had lost itself in the affair like water in sand and she rediscovered it only now, through this moment of music flung across the sea.

As later she had seen the eternity of her younger brother, through death.

Around her, people slept, enveloped but not awakened by the music, peaceful. The girl thought she'd just seen the calmest night there had ever been in the Indian Ocean. She thinks it's during that night too that she saw her younger brother come on deck with a woman. He leaned on the rails, she put her arms around him and they kissed. The girl hid to get a better view. She recognized the woman. Already, with her younger brother, the two were always together. She was a married woman, but it was a dead couple, the husband appeared not to notice anything. During the last few days of the voyage the younger brother and the woman spent all day in their cabin, they came out only at night. During these same days the younger brother looked at his mother and sister as if he didn't know them. The mother grew grim, silent, jealous. She, the girl, was afraid. She was happy, she thought, and at the same time she was afraid at what would happen later to her younger brother. She thought he'd leave them, go off with the woman, but no, he came back to them when they got to France.

She doesn't know how long it was after the white girl left that he obeyed his father's orders, married as he was told to do the girl the families had chosen ten years ago, a girl dripping, like the rest, with gold, diamonds, jade. She too was a Chinese from the north, from the city of Fushun, and had come there with relations.

It must have been a long time before he was able to be with her, to give her the heir to their fortunes. The memory of the little white girl must have been there, lying there, the body, across the bed. For a long time she must have remained the queen of his desire, his personal link with emotion, with the immensity of tenderness, the dark and terrible depths of the flesh. Then the day must have come when it was possible. The day when desire for the little white girl was so strong, so unbearable that he could find her whole image again as in a great and raging fever, and penetrate the other woman with his desire for her, the white child. Through a lie he must have found himself inside the other woman, through a lie providing what their families, Heaven and the northern ancestors expected of him, to wit an heir to their name.

Perhaps she knew about the white girl. She had native servants in Sadec who knew about the affair and must have talked. She couldn't not have known of his sorrow. They must both have been the same age, sixteen. That night, had she seen her husband weep? And, seeing it, had she offered consolation? A girl of sixteen, a Chinese fiancée of the thirties, could she without impropriety offer consolation for such an adulterous sorrow at her expense? Who knows? Perhaps she was mistaken, perhaps the other girl wept with him, not speaking for the rest of the night. And then love might have come after, after the tears.

But she, the white girl, never knew anything of all this.

Years after the war, after marriages, children, divorces, books, he came to Paris with his wife. He phoned her. It's me. She recognized him at once from the voice. He said: I just wanted to hear your voice. She said: It's me. Hallo. He was nervous, afraid, as before. His voice suddenly trembled. And with the trembling, suddenly, she heard again the voice of China. He knew she'd begun writing books, he'd heard about it through her mother whom he'd met again in Saigon. And about her younger brother, and he'd been grieved for her. Then he didn't know what to say. And then he told her. Told her that it was as before, that he still loved her, he could never stop loving her, that he'd love her until death.

Neauphle-le-Château – Paris
February–May 1984

WARTIME NOTEBOOKS

EDITED BY SOPHIE BOGAERT
AND OLIVIER CORPET

TRANSLATED BY LINDA COVERDALE

CONTENTS

BEIGE NOTEBOOK

NOTE ON THE TRANSCRIPTION

SINCE FIDELITY TO the text was the paramount concern, the transcription of the *Wartime Notebooks* required making choices and adopting certain conventions.

The texts have been transcribed in the order in which they appear in their notebooks, with the exception of those in the fourth notebook, the scattered pages of which have been grouped thematically. The texts are also presented in their totality, aside from the very rare exception of a few fragments that were too brief or illegible and were therefore dropped. Incomplete sentences (which usually followed or preceded a missing page) were also removed.

Square brackets – [ ] – identify all significant interventions on our part, meaning when a word was either illegible, or uncertain, or syntactically necessary and obviously over-looked by the author.

Through a concern for legibility, we finally decided to remove all crossed-out words and, where necessary, to choose what appeared to be the author's last correction. (The only crossed-out words we retained are those that Marguerite Duras did not replace and which remained indispensable to the meaning of the text.) The punctuation was occasionally very lightly modified: principally, commas were added to the longest sentences, and quotation marks were inserted where obviously required. Certain particularly dense passages were opened up with new paragraphs. Numbers were written out; lastly, spelling mistakes were corrected, along with errors in agreement and the sequence of tenses.

NOTE ON THE TRANSLATION

THE *Wartime Notebooks* are precisely that: notebooks, not novels. Although Marguerite Duras certainly knew that anything she wrote might someday be published (what writer does not?), not one piece was published by her as it appears in the *Cahiers de la guerre*. In that sense, these are *private* papers, and they present a translator with a particularly prickly problem.

The writing in these exercise books is by its very nature 'imperfect': exploratory, impassioned, sometimes rushed or overworked, often brutally frank, incomplete, even incomprehensible at moments, because the author has not licked these bear cubs into their final shape and sent them out into the world with her blessing. A translator always micro-edits while melting a work down in one language and recasting it in another, doing small things here and there to smooth out the rough spots and irregularities that inevitably appear. The author, after all, has taken care to present the original language *just so*: this way, and no other. Mixing and matching, the translator works to present the original text in a new language, but with the same degree of linguistic craft and finesse that distinguished the author's creation.

What happens, however, when the work is, as all these texts are, works-in-progress? There is a great temptation to help out, to make things more coherent, less abrupt, more musical, to tweak the writing subtly into a form perhaps more friendly to the reader – and less likely ever to set that reader wondering whether something strange might be going on in the translation.

Yet the whole point of this book is, in a way, its 'imperfections': the sudden shifts in tone, in point of view, the verbs veering between past and present, the same subject showing up in yet another guise, the chop-logic when the author wheels the narrative off in a different direction, just to see. . . . Different styles are tested, like lenses in an ophthalmologist's office: Is it better this way, or that way? With, or without? The writing here is protean, fluid, like water seeking its own level any way it can, as Duras exercises her voice, learning as she goes, and there's something for everyone here. Fairly conventional prose sits next to work that flows like what she later called *écriture courante*; we see her fiddling with compressive phrasing, techniques of repetition, the gaze as the primum mobile of writing; there are texts as brusque as a no-nonsense film or theater script, others where she's figuring out how to hide things in plain sight, and always, always, those moments of mathematical elegance when the writing hits its full stride and captivates us with the ruthless power of a voice like no other. Readers familiar with her published works will find their earliest expression here, and those who read her for the first time will see the startling and dramatic events of her tumultuous life just coming into focus as she begins creating and recreating her identity as a writer. The very rawness of this writing matches the raw material of a life whose themes appear here in their first and, perhaps, most honest avatars.

And so, these texts must be translated with even *less* linguistic leeway than usual, because their irregularities and idiosyncrasies are so revealing. I have tried to pay attention to the rhythm of the language on the page rather than follow by-the-book punctuation and phrasing. If Duras indulges in an orgy of comma splices, so be it. If her pages thicken with staccato exchanges of he said/she said, become overripe, or strangely mannered, or turn maddeningly telegraphic, well, that's her choice. Here Duras is already, clearly, some kind of a writer, and this book is her workshop, gymnasium, kitchen, treasure chest, the magic mirror in which she longs to see herself and which shows her to us, in a seductively elusive mise en abîme, as she would come to be.

A few practical considerations.

The French editors' additions are in square brackets: [ ]. (The brackets around small inserts like 'on' or 'to' have been dropped.) My additions are in fancy brackets: { }. They represent useful clarifications too slight for endnotes. Some of these clarifications come from the published works for which these texts were rough drafts.

The French editors supplied endnotes only for the introductions to the *20th Century Press Notebook*. All endnotes to the material in the notebooks themselves are the translator's, and when notes have been added, they appear at the end of the individual sections in each notebook: 'Ter of the Militia,' 'Rue Saint-Benoît,' and so on.

LINDA COVERDALE

PINK MARBLED
NOTEBOOK

INTRODUCTION

THE FIRST OF the *Wartime Notebooks*, called the *Pink Marbled Notebook*, is the longest of the four. This exercise book with a thick cardboard cover contains 123 pages, some fifteen of which are filled with a child's drawings (probably added later by Marguerite Duras's son, Jean Mascolo, born June 30, 1947).

The chronological references in the text indicate that Marguerite Duras began writing this notebook sometime in 1943. The first seventy pages contain a long autobiographical narrative focused on events from the author's childhood and adolescence in Indochina, including in particular the first known version of her relationship with the man who will become 'the Lover.' Written in an even hand with few deletions, this entire section appears to have been composed in a rather continuous fashion. Although the text occasionally alludes to the reactions of a potential reader, implicit in the impersonal pronoun 'one,' the only explicit motivations for the writing are personal: 'No other reason impels me to write of these memories, except that instinct to unearth. It's very simple. If I do not write them down, I will gradually forget them' (p. 129). Certain episodes will reappear, however, sometimes in an almost identical form, in published works (the novella *The Boa*, and especially *The Sea Wall*).

The rest of the notebook is more disconnected, with more crossings-out. It contains various fragments of *The Sea Wall* (in which the first person gradually gives way to fictitious characters, Suzanne and Joseph), followed by texts later rewritten and published in the collection *The War*, there entitled 'Ter of the Militia' and 'Albert of the Capitals.' In *The War*, the names of the characters in particular are different: {in both stories} the main character, Théodora (or Nano), becomes Thérèse,

{and Albert, one of the leaders of the interrogation center, becomes D.; the other leader, Jean, becomes Beaupain in 'Ter of the Militia' and Roger in 'Albert of the Capitals.'}

CHILDHOOD AND ADOLESCENCE
IN INDOCHINA[1]

IT WAS ON the ferry that plies between Sadec and Saï that I first met Léo. I was returning to boarding school in Saigon and someone, I no longer remember who, had given me a lift in his car along with Léo. Léo was a native but he dressed like a Frenchman, he spoke perfect French, and he was just back from Paris. Me, I wasn't even fifteen yet and had been to France only when I was very young. I thought Léo was quite elegant. He was wearing a big diamond ring and a suit of tussore, a lightweight raw silk. I'd never seen a diamond like that except on people who until that moment had never noticed me, and as for my brothers, they wore white cotton.[2] Given our resources, I found it almost inconceivable that they could ever afford to wear tussore suits.

Léo told me that I was pretty.

'You know Paris?'

Blushing, I said no. He knew Paris. He lived in Sadec. Someone living in Sadec knew Paris and this was the first I'd heard about it. Léo flirted with me, to my profound amazement. The doctor dropped me off at the boarding school in Saï, and Léo managed to tell me that we'd 'see each other again.' I'd realized that he was extraordinarily rich and I was dazzled. I was so impressed and unsure of myself that I couldn't answer Léo. I returned to the home of Mademoiselle C., where I boarded with three other people: two teachers and a girl two years younger than I named Colette. Mademoiselle C. relieved my mother of about a quarter of her schoolteacher's salary, in return for which she guaranteed a thorough education. Only Mademoiselle C. knew my mother was a teacher, which we tried hard to hide from the other boarders, who would have taken offense. Teaching positions in native schools were considered demeaning because they were so poorly paid. I took great pains to conceal this secret as best I could. Returning that evening to Mademoiselle C.'s house, I sank into despair – I told myself that Léo, who lived in Sadec, would surely discover my mother's occupation and inevitably turn away from me. I couldn't tell this to anyone, certainly not Colette, who was the daughter of an important government administrator, or Mademoiselle C., who would have sent me packing – which, I had no doubt, would have promptly killed my mother. But I consoled myself. Even though Léo knew Paris and was quite wealthy, he was a native and I was white; perhaps he would be satisfied with a teacher's daughter.

Being a teacher's daughter had cost me some setbacks in school, where I frequented only the daughters of customs officers and post-office employees, the sole positions on a par with teaching in a native school. Because she was broadminded and because my mother still had a great reputation for integrity, Mademoiselle C. had been willing to accept me, but she was both more strict and more intimate with me than she was with Colette. For instance, Mademoiselle C. had a cancer below her left breast and showed it to no one else in the house except me. She usually showed it to me on Sunday afternoon, when everyone had gone out, after we'd had our snack. The first time she showed it to me, I understood why Mademoiselle C. gave off such a stench – but showing it to no other boarder except me conferred on us a kind of complicity, which I attributed to my status as a teacher's daughter. I was not offended and told my mother, who took some pride in this mark of confidence. It would all take place in Mademoiselle C.'s bedroom. She would uncover her breast, go over to the window, and show me the cancer. Tactfully, I even contemplated the cancer for a good two or three minutes. 'You see?' Mademoiselle C. would say. 'Ah! Yes, I do see, that's what it is.' Mademoiselle C. would tuck her breast away, I'd begin to breathe again, she would do up her black lace dress and sigh;

I would then tell her she was old and it wasn't important any-more. She would agree with me, be comforted, and we'd go for a walk in the botanic garden.

My mother had been teaching in Indochina since 1903, and as a civil servant and the widow of a civil servant, she had obtained from the colonial administration a concession of rice fields in Upper Cambodia. At the time these grants were paid for in very modest annual installments and passed to the bene-ficiary only if the land had been put under cultivation by the end of x years. After endless efforts, my mother obtained a vast grant of 2,100 acres of lowlands and forests at the back of beyond in Cambodia, between the Elephant Mountains and the sea. This plantation was thirty-seven miles along a dirt track from the nearest French outpost, but that should not have posed any real problem. My mother hired fifty or so ser-vants who had to be transplanted from Cochin China and installed in a 'village' we had to build entirely on marshland, a little over a mile from the sea. That time was one of intense joy for us all. My mother had waited her whole life for that moment. In addition to the village, we built a bungalow on piling beside the track that ran along the edge of our planta-tion. That house cost us 5,000 piasters, a vast sum in 1925. Set on piling because of the floods, it was built entirely of wood that had to be felled, squared, and cut into boards on-site. None of these enormous potential disadvantages stopped my mother. We lived for six months straight at Banteaï-Prey (the name of the plantation), my mother having obtained a leave of absence from the Department of Education in Saigon. Dur-ing the construction of our house, we lived – my mother, young brother, and I – in a straw hut next to the one for the household staff (the servants' village lay four hours by boat from the track, and thus from our house). We lived completely as our servants did, except that my mother and I slept on a mattress. I was eleven at the time, and my brother thirteen. We would have been perfectly happy, if our mother's health had not broken down. Nervous irritation and the joy of seeing us so close to leaving all our troubles behind coincided with her change of life, which was particularly difficult. Then my mother had two or three epileptic fits that left her in a kind of lethargic coma that could last all day. Not only was it impossible to find a doctor, since telephones simply did not exist in that part of Cambodia in those days, but my mother's illness dismayed and frightened the native servants, who would threaten to leave each time she had an attack. They were afraid of not being paid. For as long as those fits lasted, the servants sat silently on the adjacent embankments all around the hut in which my mother lay unconscious and groaning softly. My brother or I would come out occasionally to reassure the servants and tell them that my mother wasn't dead. They had a hard time believing us. My brother would promise them that even if our mother died, he would pay them and send them back to Cochin China no matter what the cost. My brother, as I said, was thirteen at the time; he was already the bravest person I've ever known. He found the strength to both comfort me and persuade me not to cry in front of the servants, since there was no need for that: our mother was going to live. And indeed, when the sun would leave the valley to set behind the Elephant Mountains, our mother would regain consciousness. Those attacks were unusual in that they had no lasting effects, and my mother was able to resume her customary activities the very next day.

The cultivation of five hundred acres of the plantation that first year, added to the construction of both our house and the village, plus the transportation and installment of the servants, completely consumed the savings my mother had accumulated over twenty-four years of civil service. But that was of minor importance to us, confident as we were that the first harvest would recoup more or less all our setting-up expenses.

This calculation worked out by my mother, and carefully checked by her night after sleepless night, would of course prove infallible. We believed in it all the more because my mother 'knew' that we ought to be millionaires in four years. In those days, she was still communicating with my father, dead for many long years; she did nothing without seeking his advice, and it was he who 'dictated' to her all the plans for our future. These 'pronouncements,' according to her, only occurred at around one o'clock in the morning, which justified my mother's wakeful nights and endowed her in our eyes with fabulous prestige. The first harvest came to a few bags of paddy rice. The 2,100 acres granted by the colonial administration were salt land, flooded by the sea for part of the year. The entire standing crop 'burned' in one night of high water, except for the few acres around the house that were far enough away from the sea. As soon as the water dropped and the river running along the edge of our plantation was navigable again, we went to see our five hundred acres of salt-burned rice – thus making an eight-hour round-trip by boat to confirm our complete ruin. But that very evening, my mother decided to borrow 300,000 francs to build dikes that would place our rice fields definitively beyond the reach of tidal flooding. We could not mortgage our plantation, given that it did not yet belong to us and that even if it had, considering that it lay on alluvial salt lands regularly invaded by the sea, it was worthless. All the credit banks to which my mother turned formally refused to lend her that considerable sum, which we could guarantee with nothing. In the end, my mother went to a *chetti*, a Hindu moneylender, who agreed to advance her that amount in return for a bond on her teacher's salary. All three of us were deeply ashamed when the arrangement could not be made without the knowledge of the Department of Education. My mother was therefore obliged to return to work. On Friday evenings she used to leave Sadec, where she taught, covering five hundred miles by car and setting out on her return trip

Sunday night. The *chetti* demanded so much interest that he personally consumed about a third of my mother's salary. For as long as those dealings lasted, my mother never lost heart. The construction of the dikes, which were to be gigantic, plunged her into boundless excitement. My brother and I were quite close to her and shared her exaltation. My mother consulted no expert to determine if those barriers would be effective. She believed in them. She always acted by virtue of a superior and unverifiable logic. We brought in several hundred workers, and the barriers were constructed during the dry season under our supervision. Most of the money loaned by the *chetti* was spent on them. Unfortunately the dikes were chewed up by swarms of crabs that burrowed into the mud in high tides – and when the sea rose the next year, those barriers of loose earth, undermined by the crabs, melted almost completely away.

The whole crop was lost a second time. It was obvious that we could not build dikes without shoring them up with stones. My mother understood this; unable to find any stones, she considered crisscrossing the trunks of mangrove trees at the base of the embankments. Once again she'd found the answer. The evenings when she made such discoveries and told us of them are among the most beautiful of my life. Her own ingenuity filled her with an ecstasy so infectious that the few remaining household servants came to share it as well. The field workers, who lived isolated from us, stayed only because my mother treated them with extravagant generosity. They had come to settle in as farmers, but since the rice fields produced almost nothing, my mother found herself obliged to treat them as workers – which didn't help our finances. The last of the money loaned by the *chetti* went into the mangrove scheme. It wasn't that bad an idea: one section of the embankment held up, the other collapsed. The hundred acres of rice fields Mama christened 'the conclusive test' were her pride and joy. The crop flourished and we went to see it every

Saturday. Alas, we were disappointed again when harvest time arrived: working together, the village servants gathered the crop in secret and returned to Cochin China by sea – with the only paddy rice we'd ever managed to produce in three years. Once more, my mother made the best of it. The construction of the dikes had absorbed all her attention for three years. To her, the fact that one section had held fast represented a signal success. My mother's purity of soul was equaled only by her high-minded detachment. Tiring of the barriers, she tried to ignore the fact that the following year, those that had survived intact now crumbled in turn. Nevertheless, she continued afterward to sow a few acres every year on a trial basis. She claimed that the sea would soon withdraw from her rice fields and that she would reap the reward for her efforts. The acquisition of our millions was further off, she felt, but no less certain. Sometimes we doubted that alluvial land could silt up in just a few years, but my mother reassured us. She had emotional convictions like that, which we still shared.

We were utterly ruined. My mother more or less abandoned the plantation and tried to figure out how to reimburse the *chettis*. Turning her attention to me, she decided to see to my education and was as relentless in this project as she had been in constructing our house and the dikes. She didn't bother with my brother, whom she found unintelligent, and took me in hand. She considered me more promising educational material than he was, but her judgment was tinged with contempt. My brother didn't either {*sic*}. My brother used to say to me, 'I'm not very smart, myself – I'll stay on the plantation,' or, 'Me, I haven't got your intelligence, I don't deserve the sacrifices that Mama makes for you.' He was sincere. And he would tell me, 'Of course I have to stay in Sadec so you can study.' He stayed in Sadec. My brother's humility caused me constant sorrow. My mother had decided that he was obtuse, and he adjusted to that 'demotion' in all simplicity. In the same way, my mother had decided that I was naturally suited for

studies. My grades at the lycée were disastrous: I was at the
very bottom of the class in every subject until the eleventh
grade, but an acceptable mark would occasionally come my
way in French — and then my mother would weep with joy
and say her sacrifices had been worth it. At the beginning she
often came to see me at Mademoiselle C.'s home with my
brother, in our ancient Citroën, but since they were then making ends meet thanks only to my mother's incredible ingenuity, their visits quickly dropped off. That's when I began going
to Sadec on my own sometimes, taking the Saturday bus the
French never used because it required eight hours for a trip
that usually took four. That's how I came to accept the occasional ride home and how, during one of them, I met Léo.

The day after that encounter, back at Mademoiselle C.'s
house, I heard a car honk loudly. It was Léo. Colette was with
me, I was afraid to go out onto the balcony. Léo drove by
thirty-five times in a row. He would slow down in front of the
house without daring to stop. I did not appear on the balcony.
No one else thought to look outside; I must have been waiting
for Léo and particularly attentive to the sounds in the street.
I felt rather embarrassed, I might add, when I thought of the
trouble Léo was taking to please me. Still, I dressed as nicely
as I could and at two o'clock went down to go to the lycée.
Wearing another tussore suit, Léo was waiting for me along
the way, leaning against his car door. He came toward me and
said, 'It's not easy to meet you.' He invited me into his car.
Léo's car truly fascinated me. The moment I got in I asked
what make it was and how much it cost. Léo told me it was a
Morris-Léon Bollée and cost 7,000 piasters. I thought of our
Citroën that had cost 400 piasters, which my mother had paid
in three installments. Léo also told me that it wasn't his only
car, that he had another as lovely as this one but a touring car,
also a Morris-Léon Bollée, which was his favorite make of

automobile. Léo seemed quite pleased that we were having such a relaxed conversation. He asked me where I would like him to drive me. 'To the lycée,' I said, 'I'm late.' In gracious and carefully considered terms, Léo asked me if I wouldn't like to go for a drive; I said no. He drove me to the main gate of the school and asked my permission to come pick me up that same evening. He came that evening and returned the next day and all the days that followed. I was so proud of his car that I really counted on people seeing it, and I lingered in it on purpose to be sure my classmates would notice me. I was certain at the time that my using such a car would create a definite stir, thus making me suitable company for the daughters of important Indochinese officials. None of those girls had a limousine like that at her disposal: a green and black limousine specially ordered from Paris, of impressive dimensions, of such royal elegance, with a liveried chauffeur. Unfortunately, in spite of his wonderful car, Léo was Annamese. I was so dazzled by the car that I forgot this drawback. My lycée classmates dropped me permanently from their society. My only previous companions no longer dared compromise themselves in my company. I had no girl friends and wasn't unduly upset by that. For several weeks I continued to see Léo. I always contrived to get him talking about his fortune. An only son, he owned a huge number of buildings scattered throughout Cochin China and had access to considerable wealth. The figures comprising Léo's estimated fortune staggered me: I dreamed of them at night and thought about them all day long. They had nothing in common with any I'd ever heard at home. For as far back as I could remember, I'd known that my mother didn't have enough money. Her one preoccupation was to earn some, although her adventurous streak often led her quite a long way round toward her goal. It didn't matter – our mother had inculcated in us an almost sacred reverence for money. Without it, one was unhappy. Without it, virtue would not 'pass' and innocence was open to reproach. My mother was

convinced that if she succeeded in earning money, a series of
happy consequences would follow.

'There are teachers in native schools who married their
daughters to bankers. They exist, believe me, I know some.
But they're the ones who found ways to give their girls
dowries.'

When I met Léo, we were managing to live and to pay off
the *chettis* each month only by selling what remained of our
furniture and jewelry. We did this in secret, selling our jewelry
to native jewelers as quietly as possible. 'If anyone finds out,
we'll be disgraced,' my mother said. She had kept on our old
housekeeper and the cook, however, because if people in
Sadec had learned that my mother did her own cooking, they
would have dropped us flat. And Mama did have to make and
receive a few official visits. My mother did not sit in judgment,
by the way; she had neither the time nor the inclination for
that. I never heard her complain that money trumped all the
other values of the Indochinese colonial world. At that time,
fortunes were springing up like mushrooms in Indochina.
Rubber planters were swarming through the colony, earning
millions. Saigon was one of the richest and most corrupt cities
in the Far East. There reigned the strictest of hierarchies, based
on wealth and all its outward signs. The planters came first,
and then the body of high-ranking Indochinese civil servants.
Bribery was accepted, organized, and facilitated our access to
high society: a customs officer who had managed to smuggle
in three million in contraband opium would thus soon find
himself hobnobbing with the local administrator. The corps
of top Annamese public officials paid exorbitant (fixed) prices
for honors and decorations. It was common knowledge that
the Legion of Honor cost 18,000 piasters.

Although such considerations exceed the scope of my
narrative, they have a bearing here precisely because we never
gained any foothold in that society, and because my mother's
natural humility fueled her constant desire to achieve entry

there at all costs and by any means. I've forgotten to mention that among the French in the colony, 'Annamitophobia' was the rule. A very few Annamese moved among French circles. In principle, any 'native-lover' in the civil service was doomed never to rise in the ranks, and we were, given our mother's position, at the bottom of the civil service ladder. People said my mother had some merit, but no one received her. Our only friends were either post-office employees, or customs officers, or worked as she did in primary-school education. The very fact that my mother had never left the colony and that she had many Annamese friends there discredited her for good among the French. On that point, my mother was particularly uneasy and uncertain.

I don't wish to paint a portrait of Indochina in 1930; I want to speak above all about what my youth was like. My mother was often of two minds not so much because of external conditions and conventions, but by nature. And so, when the question later arose of my marrying Léo, my mother hesitated because he was native – which would have reinforced the disrepute from which she suffered so unaffectedly. The important thing is that she hesitated, although she knew, deep down, that anybody would have considered the whole thing absolutely unacceptable.

We suffered a lot from our poverty, and hiding it added insult to injury. It wasn't so obvious on the plantation, where we lived in perfect isolation. In Sadec, we stuck at nothing to prevent the sixty French people on the post from learning anything about our plight. So on the last evening of every month, when my mother would take the *chetti* a third of her salary to pay off the interest, she went in secret and after nightfall. Several times she wasn't able to do so, I no longer remember why. Then the *chettis* would come to our house. They'd settle into the sitting room and wait. Several times Mama wept in front of them, begging them to go because the servants could see them. The *chettis* did not leave. Silently, they stayed.

They knew they had only to appear, that for a white woman, borrowing from *chettis* was the very depth of shame. Finally Mama would throw the money in their faces. They would gather it up and go off smiling.

In such situations I'd shut myself into a room in the house, forcing Mama to come looking for me, which generally resulted in a proper thrashing. Mama often beat me, usually when 'her nerves gave way' and she couldn't help herself. Since I was the smallest of her children and the easiest to control, I was the one Mama beat the most. She used to hit me with a stick, and easily sent me spinning. Anger would send such a rush of blood to her head she'd speak of dying of a stroke. The fear of losing her would thus defeat my rebellion every time. I always agreed with Mama's reasons for beating me, but not with her methods. The use of the stick I found radically shocking and unaesthetic; the blows on the head, dangerous. But the slaps that marked my cheeks were my despair – especially while I knew Léo, to whom I couldn't possibly admit 'what was going on at home.' I knew he would not understand, that he would never approve of Mama's attitude toward me, while I agreed with her completely and could not have tolerated anyone criticizing her, not even Léo.

I'll have occasion to return to these blows. I really did get a lot of them. Shortly before I met Léo, when I was fourteen, my eldest brother, who was studying in France, returned to Indochina. Through some strange rivalry, he picked up the habit of beating me as well. The only question became who would hit me first. When he didn't like the way Mama was beating me, he'd tell her, 'Wait,' and take over. But soon she'd be sorry, because each time she thought I'd be killed on the spot. She'd let out ghastly shrieks but my brother had trouble stopping himself. One day he changed tactics and sent me tumbling; my temple struck a corner of the piano, and I could barely get up again. My mother was so frightened that from then on she lived in obsessive fear of those battles. My brother's massive biceps compounded my misfortune, and his Herculean strength overawed my mother, which probably spurred him on. I was quite small and thin, without any of my two brothers' superbly athletic appearance. In her good moments, my mother would tell me, 'You, you're my little waif.' Such marks of affection, which revealed that my mother loved me for the very reasons that so often turned her against me, were beyond price, especially since they were so rare. My brother's return home introduced insults and vulgarity to our household. Until then we had been polite through ignorance. My eldest brother came back from France with an education (the only one, since four years of tutoring with a priest had failed to earn him his baccalaureate diploma at the age of eighteen) in new insults, which arrived in the nick of time at a house where jangled nerves were reaching a flash point. My naïveté may seem exaggerated, but it was nonetheless real. When my brother beat me and called me a little crab louse, I had no idea what that meant and no chance to find out until years later, actually. Which doesn't mean that I didn't resent the insult 'crab louse' – on the contrary, I resented it all the more violently in that I was more or less confusing 'crab louse' and 'crap house' to get 'stinking little thing,' so I became even angrier at being thrashed for my tininess, which was hardly my fault. My brother insulted as he thrashed. His usual terms of abuse, aside from 'crab louse,' were 'piece of shit,' 'you're not even worth spitting on,' 'you pile of garbage,' and 'dirty slut,' which last also remained a mystery to me, but stabbed me any-way – I don't know why, perhaps because of the obscene sound of that word 'slut' – right in the heart. 'Bitch' seemed to me particularly unacceptable, much more so than 'sonofa-bitch,' which I thought was the diminutive version. The word 'degenerate' troubled my conscience and upset me, especially while I knew Léo, because my brother used it a lot during that relationship, along with 'snake in the grass' and 'venomous serpent' which, although more intellectual, seemed to me more treacherous. 'Stinker,' 'shit-ass,' 'ass-wipe' or 'whore' did not require backing up by blows, they were already every-day expressions. There were others and I'm greatly saddened not to remember them. I cannot hear them without feeling in my very soul the true taste of my youth; they have the aura of summers gone forever, of the raw, vivid angers of my fifteenth year. I received them with a seriousness that may be laughable, but that I will never feel again no matter what anyone says to me. I believed in them. I no longer do. They put me through the pangs of hell. Even Léo, in whom I confided regarding my brother, could not manage to grasp how they could make me suffer so.

The difference between my mother's and my brother's blows is that his hurt much more and that I refused to accept them in any way. Every time, a moment would come when I believed my brother was going to kill me, and my anger would give way to fear that my head would come off my body and roll along the ground, or that I would be beaten silly. When my brother took up opium, his violence even increased, so that I could not speak to him without provoking an attack. When he had smoked too much, he beat with skill and cunning, slowly, pausing after each blow to enjoy fully its effect. He also beat my brother {sic} at first, but as the opium took its toll, he no longer came out on top as often, and backed off.

One may wonder why my brother treated me like that. I wonder as well. I no sooner glimpse reasons than they slip away from me. He beat me because he couldn't bear me. My mother couldn't bear me either, even though she loved me deeply. I note that I did not have any friends in my lycée either, and that the girls and even most of the boys in my class found me unlikable. When my mother withdrew me from Made-moiselle C.'s care later on and placed me in a state boarding school, I was the bête noire of the monitors and most of the students. (True, I did have one friend there, Hélène, as well as three other girls who worshiped me with a kind of adoration that was rather ambiguous, but quite far from true friendship.) In those days I didn't try to understand; I endured the situation with fatalism. I didn't feel sad about it. I was detestable the way the others were amiable; I was as uninteresting to most of the girls my age as they were fascinating to me, because before I came to the lycée, before I was fifteen, I'd had precisely no contact whatsoever with French girls. There were specific reasons for their antipathy and indifference. First of all a kind of perfectly understandable unsociability that I tried to conceal with arrogance, if not downright meanness. I was never pleasant with anyone. Amiability, *terra incognita*. When I encountered white society in Saigon, I discovered amiability. I thought it was the prerogative of wealth and happiness. It never occurred to me to smile. I'd never felt pleasure except with my mother and brothers, and at home we knew only wild, uncontrollable laughter, since smiles had been banished from our relations. We were modest and hard with one another, using speech to hurl insults or inform ourselves about various strictly material things. Chatting was unknown at home, except on certain evenings of general gaiety that occur in any family, but which in mine took on a frenzied note, probably because they appeared after months of silence. And that chatter, in fact, was not the real thing. The main idea was to have some fun, because we could no longer stand going without it. Then we could laugh at anything – we even went so far as to turn the story of our plantation into an irresistible farce. And all in the interest of the cause. 'It's falling-down funny, the story of our dikes,' my eldest brother would say. 'I don't know anything more hysterical. Everything turned against us, even the crabs that chomped them right out from under us – trust Mama to come up with an idea like that.' On those evenings I'm sure we all attained the highest state of bliss.

We'd lost everything but would laugh ourselves into fits (there's no other word) over losing everything.

Well, when I arrived in Saigon, I had no intention of changing. I remember what a painful chore it was to shake hands with my classmates. During the three years I remained at the lycée, I never got used to that, it provoked an involuntary coldness in my manner, just as I could never answer my teachers' questions without arrogance. I had one English teacher who took such a dislike to me that he actually felt ill at the sight of me, he *could not stand* to look at me anymore, and flouting the custom observed in co-educational schools, he seated me at the very back of the classroom, claiming that I was hopeless in English. At the boarding school, I made a monitor 'sick' through my mere presence in the study hall and dormitory. She could not speak to me without choking. And yet I wasn't unruly, and given how indifferent or hostile most of the other students were to me, I could hardly have induced them to misbehave.

If I stress this aspect of my relations with others (with both my family and my classmates), it's because this is important – and left its mark on me for years. I lived in a more or less constant state of guilt, which only increased my arrogance and spitefulness, because I took pride in never feeling sad about this. A single person, before Léo, took an interest in me. He was one of the class dunces, a half-caste. I wouldn't let him touch me because he had rotten teeth. Everyone looked down on him. His father ran a store in the Chinese quarter. He was over twenty and still in the ninth grade, he'd been left back so many times. We both sat in the last row in English class and he regularly asked me for a ring I wore. I would pass it to him. Saying that it was still warm from my heat, he'd hold it tightly in his hand, bring it to his mouth, kiss it and close his eyes, breathing deeply, and each time I'd be afraid he might swallow the ring. I'd look at him, curious; I didn't know what he was talking about when he'd tell me that the ring was making him excited. That creature was a calamity. I couldn't bear seeing him because he embodied the species to which I belonged – and from which I wanted to escape: the poor and despised. For more than a year he pursued me like an evil spell. At that time in the school in Saigon there were some planters' or governors' sons who had their own cars, and who crossed the girls' courtyard with tennis rackets tucked under their arms, arriving with 'their' girls. And some of them were handsome. I used to hide and watch them go by. Seeing them hurt me, because I already knew that they would never take me away in their cars. I gazed at them as if they were displays in a shop window; sometimes I would dream that one of them noticed me, and I'd wake up in tears.

I think that I lacked the slightest bit of charm to an unbelievable degree – especially since my mother rigged me out after her own taste, which must have lagged ten years behind the current fashion. Unlike the other girls, who wore straw hats, I was outfitted with a colonial helmet with a large round brim that probably protected my shoulders as well as the back of my neck. It was a model of an impressive size that my mother had ordered specially for plantation life, and which I dragged around for years. When I managed to lose it at last (it fell into the river during a ferry crossing), my mother bought me a man's fedora that was originally the {brownish-pink} color of rosewood and later turned a yellow mottled with green. Everyone wore white sandals in those days. My mother, well, she saddled me with black patent-leather pumps I wore on bare feet. My dresses were consistently made to my mother's specifications by our Annamese housekeeper. They were the very same ones I wore at eleven or twelve years old; the hems were let down as I grew up, and that was that. Those dresses were so huge ('Above all, let's be practical,' Mama used to say) that at fifteen I was still wearing them. They were usually of Japanese or native fabric and my mother, for hygienic reasons, had them laundered, which meant that their colors soon washed out of them. I remember a vivid blue cotton dress (seams on the shoulders and at the sides: the pattern followed for sixteen years of my life) with a design showing a flowering cherry branch reaching from my right shoulder to my left knee; on this branch, at my waist, an enormous bright pink bird was poised to take flight – a design repeated in reverse on the back. If I remember that dress, it's because I suspected that it wasn't in good taste and felt that the fabric was better suited to a folding screen. My mother assured me peremptorily that the dress was wonderful and I believed her. It's true that she herself dressed in a more or less similar fashion and was famous throughout Cochin China (I only learned this much later) for her almost unique way of dressing. I believed in my mother as much as in God. If she liked a dress, I do believe I would have worn it proudly before the jeers of the whole world. I forgot to mention that when I met Léo, I was wearing the brownish-pink fedora that Mama particularly liked and that she placed on my head herself in a rather unusual way, tilted to the side, like those cowboy hats in American silent films. Léo spent a whole month trying to make me understand through increasingly direct allusions (and with good reason) that this hat was unsuitable for a girl. But I had such faith in my mother's taste that, even though I had never seen anyone wear a hat like it, and even though Léo finally told me flat out that it upset him, I wore it anyway, behind Léo's back and before the eyes and under the nose of the entire lycée.

Besides lacking charm and dressing in a manner so absurd it almost defied description, I was not conspicuous for my beauty. I was small and ungainly, thin, covered with freckles, burdened with two carrot-red braids that hung to the middle of my thighs – I say braids but *cables* would be the better word, my mother pulled and twisted my hair so tight. I was sunburned from being almost always outdoors on the plantation and at the time, white skin was the fashion in Saigon. My features were reasonably even and might have passed for beautiful but were so distorted by my stubborn, disagreeable, tight-lipped expression that no one could notice them. I had an evil look my mother described as 'venomous.' I'll simply say that when I come across any photos from those days, I look in vain for a hint of softness, of sweetness in my face. My mother's few friends used to tell her that I would turn out pretty, that I had beautiful eyes but needed to wear glasses because there was certainly something wrong there, my gaze didn't look right. In the outpost of Vinh Long, where my mother taught when I was just a little thing, that look had already provoked comment, from the administrator's wife. I had turned around toward her at Mass and the look in my eyes, it seems, had 'frightened' her. A kind soul, she told my mother to have my eyes checked. My mother never did – she knew there was nothing wrong with my eyes, and she claimed that if I had a venomous gaze it was also intelligent. She used to tell me as well that I was very pretty, she told me so in private: 'Don't worry, you're awfully pretty.' I didn't worry. I think my mother was trying to convince herself that she had a pretty daughter. My eldest brother, on the contrary, positively insisted that 'Aside from me, your kids are all duds.' It's true that he was astonishingly beautiful. I'm not saying that lightly: within a month of his arrival in Cochin China, he was known as the handsomest man in the colony. My brother had this quirk: he could not mention any woman he found pretty without adding a remark aimed at me ('So much for you!') or my mother ('So much for your daughter!'). Sometimes he looked at himself in the mirror and called me over. 'You ever seen a mouth like this?' he'd ask me, pointing to his. I'd reply prudently that with a thorough search, one might perhaps be found. 'Stinker,' my brother would answer, 'so much for you. . . .'

Nothing distressed my mother more than to have my brother question my beauty. True, I had no dowry, and my mother agonized over the thought that one day she'd have to marry me off. When I turned fifteen, this became a topic of discussion at home. 'To get her fixed up,' my eldest brother would say, 'you can just go whistle: you'll still have that one on your hands when she's thirty.' This was a sore point with my mother and she'd get angry: 'I'll marry her off tomorrow if I feel like it, and to whomever I please besides.' I found the idea of winding up an old maid chilling – even death paled in comparison. I kept my ears open. I knew my mother was lying when she said she could marry me to anyone at all, but I still hoped that I might find 'a match.' My mother preferred to confide in my younger brother, and would sigh, 'How will we marry her off?' My younger brother was an idealist, and he was fond of me. 'You never know,' he'd say, 'but we should get her out and about.' He was the one who insisted that I go to boarding school. 'If she's well brought up and has a profession in hand, even without a dowry, she just might find a husband.' I think all mothers with children worry about these things. In my house, though, they thought it wise to let me know how matters stood. 'She has to understand what life is like,' my mother said. The professions they wanted to 'place in my hands' varied from year to year. They considered in turn that I would be nothing less than a teacher, lawyer, doctor, newspaper editor, and explorer. I had my own ideas; until I was fifteen I wanted to be a trapeze artist or a movie star. 'You'll do what you're told,' my mother would say. The most surprising thing was that my brothers never gave a thought to their future. 'They'll have the plantation,' my mother said, which wasn't a solution; long after experience had shown that we couldn't count on that, she continued to say that my brothers 'would have the plantation,' which reassured her all the same. My brothers never went to the lycée or any kind of school. There wasn't ever any question of that. They lived in Sadec, and the complete idleness of those young men of seventeen and eighteen seemed scandalous to everyone, except of course to us. We made no effort to excuse it. When people told my mother that the situation was 'a great misfortune,' she would regularly reply, 'You're telling me!' – but without any real conviction. My younger brother had decided to become a hunter, the greatest hunter in Indochina, and pass up the plantation. By the age of fourteen he was hunting in the Elephant Mountains, and at twenty-one he had bagged twelve tigers and a black panther. 'It's a goddamn lousy profession,' my older brother kept telling him, only to be told that it was the sole career suitable for a man who had 'courage but no talent for studying.'

Léo's intrusion into the family changed all our plans. As soon as we learned the extent of his fortune, it was unanimously decided that besides providing everyone in the family with his or her own car, Léo would pay off the *chettis* and finance various undertakings: a sawmill for my younger brother and a studio-workshop for my elder one, the blueprints for which my mother studied carefully. I was delegated to inform Léo of these projects and 'sound him out' on them, without promising anything in return. 'If you could manage not to marry him,' my mother said, 'that would be better: he's native, after all, no matter what you say to me.' I rebelled and said I would marry Léo, to which my mother's answer was always, 'If you're clever and know how to manage it, you can definitely avoid that.' If I persisted, I got a beating. My mother would make me swear 'on her head' that I would never give myself to Léo. 'You can do absolutely whatever you like, but don't sleep with him: get everything you can out of him, you have the right – think of your poor mother – but don't sleep with him, or no one else will want you.' My mother had complete faith in the virginity of girls: 'A girl's greatest treasure is her purity.' If I slept with Léo, nobody would ever want me, not even Léo. Later, a year after I'd met Léo, he announced that to his great sorrow he could only marry me completely disinherited by his father, who would not accept such a marriage at any price. My mother then spoke of 'taking him to court' for having compromised me. My mother had so counted on Léo that she considered this refusal a disaster not only for me but for my brothers, who had been naïve enough to bank on him. But my mother was kind and allowed Léo to keep seeing me anyway. She saw him rather often herself; perhaps she hadn't given up all hope that he would marry me, and meanwhile she and my brothers took considerable advantage of the situation, and I'll come back to that.

Why did Léo notice me? He found me to his liking. The only explanation I can think of is that Léo himself was ugly. Left badly scarred by smallpox, he was distinctly uglier than the average native but was always dressed with perfect taste, meticulously groomed, and unfailingly polite, even at my house where rudeness was the rule, even toward him. Léo was, moreover, truly generous, but sharp enough so that one couldn't ask 'just anything' of him. So when he met my family he was shrewd enough to realize how dangerous they would be if he didn't watch out for himself. Despite this natural caution Léo was more or less unintelligent. He was the worst kind of 'European' snob, yet he seriously impressed me because he knew how to dance the Charleston, he ordered his ties from Paris, and he'd seen Joséphine Baker in the flesh at the Folies-Bergère. He missed Paris, trailing an aura of nostalgia that was not without charm. For almost two years he dragged my family and me through every nightclub in Saigon. He would come fetch me in his Léon Bollée, in which he carted around my mother and two brothers. My mother would request 'special permission' from the directress of the Pension Barbet, my boarding school, and I would go out with them. That's what Léo called 'hitting the town' or 'going off on a spree.' My family annoyed him and he would have gladly dispensed with them, but I'd told him once and for all that if he didn't 'hit the high spots' with them, I wouldn't go out with him. My mother was unshakable on this point: a girl must not go out alone with a young man, or she'll be compromised forever and won't find a husband. But my refusal to go out alone with Léo reflected above all – aside from the trust I placed in my mother's words – the most sincere and steadfast desire to see my mother and brothers profit as well from my good fortune. I felt as if I were 'taking them out' in turn, because without Léo that would never have happened, since at the time my mother could not buy even a few gallons of gas to come get me in Saigon.

How often did Léo haul us around like that? No doubt many, many times. They all blend into one. We were known in every bar, tearoom, and nightclub in the city. We used to go above all to La Cascade, which was about twelve miles outside the city and featured a 'night' swimming pool cut right into the bed of a mountain stream. This pool was lighted from the inside by electricity, and the swimmers' bodies, fluid and supple, were silhouetted in the diverted waters of the torrent. My brothers and I used to swim there before the ritual cold supper and dancing. Those were strange evenings; they were not cheerful occasions. My brothers, who despised Léo, wore set expressions of silent dignity; my mother displayed a fixed sad and gentle smile as she proudly watched her children dancing. As usual, her dresses looked like peignoirs, with side and shoulder seams, no belt, and she wore cotton stockings with her down-at-the-heel shoes. She sat a little aside from the table, holding on her knees the large handbag she 'never let out of her sight,' in which she always carried the land-office map of the plantation and her receipts from the *chettis*. At that time people were calling her a martyr to her sons, especially the eldest, for whom she went daily deeper into debt without any idea of how she could ever get out. She used to say herself that she was a martyr and we believed her; she said it every day, each time she beat me, and whenever she was resting,

taking time to think. To us she had by slow degrees reached
the condition of martyrdom the way one advances toward a
diploma in disaster. She was a 'martyr' the way one would be
anything else. She used to say, 'I'm chained to my troubles';
'I'm worn out, it would be best if I died'; 'I'll have to shoulder
my burden until the end'; 'Sometimes I wonder what I did to
Heaven to deserve such tribulation.' She talked like that too
often, we never listened anymore. People criticized her in
those days for being too indulgent, especially because of that
business with Léo, which did her serious harm. They used to
say, 'Madame D. lets her daughter go out with Annamese –
that girl is completely ruined, it's a shame.' They always saw
us with Léo and his friends, and said that I 'slept with natives.'
I was fifteen. Léo hadn't yet touched me when all Saigon considered me 'the dregs of the city.' We suspected as much, but
we used to interpret that gossip in a reassuring way. Finally,
when no one would have anything to do with us anymore,
Mama said, 'They're jealous, who cares?' I think my mother
found real relaxation in those nights spent in the clubs. She
did not touch the champagne. Her big hands resting on her
purse, she was entirely at our service, never saying a word
about going home. From time to time she would say something nice to Léo, as a token of gratitude and because she felt
my brothers were too frosty with him. (I can see my mother's
hands now, clutching her purse as if clinging to her fate.
God's hands do not seem more beautiful to me. When I was
very little and noticed something disturbing or had a frightening thought, for example the possibility of my mother's death,
when I learned at the age of five that she was mortal, I would
go to her and tell her. Then she would pass her hand over my
face, gently, and tell me, 'Forget.' I would forget and go away
comforted. With those same hands, later on, she beat me. And
she earned my daily bread by correcting exercise books or doing accounts all night long. She devoted that same full effort
to it. She beat hard, she slaved hard, she was profoundly good,

she was made for tempestuous destinies, for hacking her way in exploration through the world of emotions. She was deeply unhappy, but she found her share of happiness in that very misfortune because she loved work and sacrifice, and what she preferred above all else was to forget herself, to lose herself in endless illusions. My mother dreamed the way I have never seen anyone dream. She dreamed her very unhappiness, she spoke of it with pride; she never knew real sadness but only pain, because she possessed a soul of royal fierceness that would have disdained to wallow in the acceptance all sadness entails.)

If she seemed sad while we were dancing, it was without realizing it; she wasn't sad in fact, she was simply pleased. Her manner could be misleading. Léo would not have allowed me to dance with anyone but him, aside from my brothers. In the cabarets my brothers spent their time watching girls they found attractive. When there was one they both fancied too much, things almost always ended badly, so Mama, who kept an eye out, would announce she was tired and suggest that we leave. I didn't like dancing, except with my younger brother, with whom I waltzed. Léo, who danced consistently off the beat, considered himself a fine dancer. At first the other customers laughed at us, but in the end everyone knew us and no one paid any attention. Léo was short and wore suits with sloping shoulders, which did not look good on him. There was a tango he considered irresistible because he had danced it in Paris: 'Not That I'm Curious, But I'd Like to Know Why Blondes Always Have Black Muffs.'

Léo was perfectly laughable and that pained me deeply. He looked ridiculous because he was so short and thin and had droopy shoulders. Plus he thought so much of himself. In a car he was presentable because one couldn't see his height, only his head, which, albeit ugly, did possess a certain distinction. Not once did I agree to walk a hundred yards with him in a street. If a person's capacity for shame could be exhausted, I would have exhausted mine with Léo. It was just simply awful. I would dance only tangos with him because the bright lights were then replaced by a very subdued, reddish glow, which allowed the two of us to escape much notice. I'd come to an agreement with him about dancing only the tango; since that dance was quite popular at the time, I danced enough with Léo for him to feel it was still worthwhile to take us out. I claimed that I loved no other dance but the tango (which, by the way, I haven't much cared for ever since). I'd already had an instinctive dislike for that dance, which I soon hated. Since it was for months Léo's only chance to get close to me, he danced it in a rather lewd fashion, glued to me, his belly thrust forward, with an expression of painful concentration. As for the Charleston, it was all the rage in Paris, but in Saigon it was only beginning to catch on. Léo knew the Charleston and loved it madly. For months he begged me to learn it so that we could dance it together. The prospect of dancing with him on a half-empty floor always repelled me. I never learned the Charleston. Given the way I felt, the very idea drove me to despair whenever Léo unfortunately insisted that we try. A few rare times, crazed by his exasperated longing for the Charleston, he danced it with some other girls in the room; since he was native, and to avoid being rebuffed, he could only try inviting the girls who seemed decidedly middle-class and displayed a certain coarseness. He believed that these desperate decisions (because one never knew, he might be rejected anyway) would impress me. They did not leave me indifferent, true, but what tormented me the most was seeing the man who passed for my lover and with whom I was supposed to spend my life making such a fool of himself.

When Léo talked to me it was exclusively about love. In general he complained about me, and claimed I was making him suffer terribly. His jealousy poisoned our relationship. But looking back after fifteen years, I do realize that without that jealousy I could never have continued seeing him. He squabbled with me and imposed conditions on our 'outings,' which he had realized I enjoyed. He'd tell me, 'Now that I've pulled you out of the soup, you're going to betray me.' He was obsessed with that and must have been innately pre-disposed toward jealousy, because from the beginning I took our relationship quite seriously and never gave him any reason to be jealous. After the Charleston, it was movies Léo loved, American movies. So he would tell me, 'It's real simple: if you betray me I'll bump you off.' How could I have betrayed him, and with whom? I only slept with him once and after two years of pleading. What he called 'betrayal' would have been kissing someone else, for example, or dancing with a European. I gave him a detailed schedule of my activities, I yielded to all his arbitrary demands. I obeyed them rigorously. I thus spent a certain part of my life creating imaginary obligations for myself and observing them with uncommon strictness. I truly believed I was at fault where Léo was concerned, and I felt wretched for not being able to 'do more.' I spent a good part of my time with him swearing on the heads of my mother and brothers that I was faithful to him. But Léo never entirely believed me. My elder brother would tell him, 'My sister's a tart,' and Léo would [press] me to give him explanations I could not provide. To the best of my recollection, the rare moments I spent alone with Léo were formal interrogations. Or else, when the surroundings were convenient, serious struggles during which Léo tried to kiss me on the mouth. Yet I was in love with him in my fashion, and when he would go a week without seeing me, to punish me, I was very unhappy. I was in love with Léo-in-his-Léon-Bollée. Sitting in his magnificent limousine, he made a considerable impression on me, and I never got used to it. I was also in love with Léo when he paid for the cold suppers and champagne in the nightclubs. He did it casually, with an offhandedness that went straight to my heart. Never, precisely never, would my mother or my brothers have offered to pay for anything at all; never (although yes, perhaps once in two years, and I'm not even sure about that) was he invited to lunch in our home. Often, before going to the nightclubs, he took us to dinner in a Chinese restaurant in Cholen. That would happen when I had been 'nice'; then he'd cough up a hundred piasters (a thousand francs in 1931) and that was just for a start. My mother and brothers felt he never shelled out enough and often groused about it, but they didn't dare say so to his face.

It was to me they said or argued that. 'He should already be quite happy to go out with a white girl,' my mother used to say. My elder brother, when he did mention him, never referred to him as anything but 'the fetus' or 'your lousy fetus' or 'your syphilitic jerk.' I was willing to go along, indeed that's all I was, not being very enterprising. Timidly, I began to complain to Léo about needing money. I still wonder how I wound up taking such a drastic step. Search as I may, I can't find a clear motive for that decision anymore. Obviously, above all, I was trying to make sense of myself. I had brought Léo to the house and with him the considerable comfort of his cars, as well as the distraction and luxury of our nights on the town. But that was not enough. Léo would get his back up: he did a lot but not *everything* that was asked of him. For example, he had indeed placed one of his cars at our disposal – to be driven only by his chauffeur: my brothers were not allowed to touch it. This condition struck them as a grave affront, and my elder brother considered it a provocation. He could not climb into the car without remembering it. 'If this isn't pathetic, to have to put up with stuff like this. ... If I weren't keeping a grip on myself, I'd bash in the ribs of that lousy fetus of yours.' And my mother would add, 'Let it go, things won't always be this way.' To understand such naïveté, which might seem far-fetched, one must realize that we were sunk in a boundless childhood from which, all in all, we were trying in vain to escape. We were even spending our whole lives trying to get out of it any way we could.

When I say that I was trying to make sense of myself, I mean something quite specific. I was seeking this meaning within my family, where my insignificance was such that every time I tried to assert myself, if only by giving my opinion, I was energetically put back in my place. When I first brought Léo to the house, I hoped to become an interesting and perhaps even an indispensable person. My family soon became accustomed to the comforts and opportunities Léo provided. They got used to everything with disconcerting ease. When an advantage went missing, they became indignant with the utmost sincerity. Whenever Léo happened to 'go down' to Saigon without taking them along, they felt this was a dirty trick that spoke volumes about what Léo really was. 'I saw through him long ago, that little runt,' my elder brother would say, adding, 'One day I'll get him back for all this.' I must note that we also became accustomed to the worst inconveniences as well as the pleasant changes. In the same way that we had grown used to running out of money, to selling our remaining jewelry and later the furniture, so that we could eat until the end of the month, we got used to nasty gossip (slander, my mother called it, saying, 'Let them foam at the mouth, my conscience is cleaner than theirs'). Likewise, we grew accustomed to Léo, but with this difference: the acquired advantages immediately joined our most basic needs. All acquisitions were permanent, and our eyes then turned toward possible future gains. And so, I had no right at all to rest on the laurels of any advantages Léo offered through me, which meant I was always on the alert, constantly looking for what Léo might do next for my family. Léo needed a lot of coaxing, he was stingy, and he told me that my family disgusted him deeply, which neither bothered nor angered me in the least.

When he was willing to give me some money, I led him to believe that it was for me to buy certain things I needed. These sums were not large, but still, they were something. I would waltz home in triumph, planning my performance, and announce: 'Léo gave me fifty piasters.' My mother would come over to me and say, 'Give.' Basically, I wasn't very nice: 'Why should I?' I'd say, wanting to be begged. My elder brother would show up in turn; when there was talk of money, when he heard it mentioned in conversation, he arrived all aquiver, like the hunter who hears the tiger roar. 'How much?' he'd ask. My younger brother would declare, 'I think this is revolting.' Me, I still had the money and while I had it, I knew what happiness was. It didn't last long. 'Give me that money,' my mother would insist, adding remarks such as, 'You cannot keep that on you, it's not proper, hand it over, I'll give it back to you.' She never did give me back anything whatsoever, poor woman, it would have been completely impossible for her – the little bit of money I gave her was immediately swallowed up by the family's needs. I made them plead with me, it was a kind of revenge. For a moment I experienced the illusion of power. I'm not saying that my mother didn't feel a twinge of shame at such moments, but money had an extraordinary power over her. When she knew that I had some, she entered a kind of trance. She would dog my footsteps all through the house: 'Give.' My brother prowled around us, bare-chested in his silk trousers. I'd announce my news in a loud voice, on purpose, because my mother had told me one day, 'Don't tell your brothers anything, it's not worth it.' I wanted to know how far, to what extremes, my mother would go; I felt a terrible joy in watching the limits to her injustice expand with each passing day. My mother knew this, but she never had the strength to do otherwise. Afterward I was punished but I deserved it, I knew that too. Things weren't to be pushed too far; even in that case, there were boundaries to be observed. The moment when I had to hand over the money always arrived: 'You're going to give it to me this instant.' The hand was suspended above my face, ready to fall. I gave. The money vanished into the purse and we thought no more about it – that's a manner of speaking, by the way, because once Léo began giving me some money, my brother's insults acquired a fresh nuance. From 'crab louse' I passed to the status of 'tart,' 'bit on the side,' and 'bitch who sleeps with natives.' My mother, speaking of that aspect of my relations with Léo, used to say, 'It's a dreadful misfortune.' Still, fifty piasters – why let them go to waste?

Such reflections do prove that they more or less realized that the situation was somewhat scandalous, but they always managed to make that all my fault. Especially since my mother was not unaware that such behavior (I was sixteen) might present a few drawbacks for the future. The particular nature of her attitude sprang precisely from the contradiction between her conduct and her observations. Regarding the conduct of young women my mother's opinion never changed, and although her ideal was doubtless a touch naïve, she believed in it passionately, an ideal that never, ever, became more flexible or nuanced, even when she accepted my behavior with Léo and his money. 'There is nothing more beautiful than a pure young woman,' my mother would tell me, and she described her so well and with such grace that she tortured me, because I recognized none of my traits in those portraits. Even when my reputation was such that it was now just about useless to try passing me off as 'marriageable,' I could not arrive anywhere without my mother whispering to me, 'Smile, a girl should smile,' and she herself would present a kind of pathetic grimace she probably considered the happy-smile-of-the-happy-mother-of-the-smiling-young-woman.

I add that her chief character trait was a complete incapacity for despair. Until the last day of my time in Indochina, she hoped to marry me off. This idealistic aspect of her character was balanced by a kind of unshakable good sense: 'Demand whatever you like from him,' she'd tell me when speaking of Léo, 'you can accept everything, but don't sleep with him.' And when I managed to extract some money from Léo, she felt a certain pride in that. She used to say of me, 'I'm not worried about her, she'll manage.' I began to hand over the

money Léo gave me to my mother, but my elder brother
quickly asked me to help him out. On such occasions he was
charming and irresistible – and I could not resist him. 'Dear
little N., couldn't you let me have ten piasters?' I'd give it to
him in secret; there wasn't a single time when I didn't believe
we would be friends again forever. My gullibility was equaled
only by my stupidity. When my brother and I later lived in
France and I began playing my little game with the boys at the
lycée, he got into the habit of turning out my pockets every
evening. Then he'd beat me, claiming that I was being 'kept'
and that he'd 'teach me how to live,' that he was 'doing this
for my own good.' I refrain from passing judgment just as
I refrained from doing so at the time. I would like to keep
intact the radiance of the unique Event that my elder brother
was for me. He was unfair and cowardly, like fate itself and
every destiny. There was something thorough and fundamentally pure in his ferocity toward me. His life unfolded with the
implacability of the inevitable, and he filled us with respect.
The weave of blows and insults he gave me is the very fabric
of which his soul was made, there was no extra margin. He
was always of the *greatest* injustice, what no one could surpass,
which best evokes the unjustness of Destiny and falls upon you
with the unpredictability of fate. Not for anything would
I want that in the name of some morality, no matter how all-
inclusive, he be found reprehensible, and judgment be passed
on him. My brother was cruel, of course, but with a cruelty
such that I never found any human measure for it, and that is
the important thing, that is why I ask not for indulgence, but
for a reprieve from all morality. If he is found blameworthy,
along with my mother, I consider that these recollections are
not those I would have liked them to be. No one is entitled to
offer explanations for the conduct of others, or even to try,
everyone certainly agrees on that. Even when I was tiny,
I believed that my mother and elder brother were answerable
directly to God: they beat and passed judgment by virtue of

superior reasons, imbued with infinite mystery. When, older, I rebelled, it was always a bit reluctantly, and the joy I felt thereby was not unrelated to a blasphemous delight. I always felt a twinge of guilty conscience when accusing them in turn, and forcing them to a lucidity that diverged, however slightly, from the quasi-divine irresponsibility in which they moved with incomparable ease.

One may well wonder why I write down these recollections, why I present behavior I announce it would displease me to see judged. Doubtless, simply, to bring such behavior to light. I feel, since I began recording these memories, that I am unearthing them from a thousand years of drifting sands. It was barely thirteen years ago that these things happened and that our family broke up, except for my younger brother who never left my mother and who died last year in Indochina. Barely thirteen years. No other reason impels me to write of these memories, except that instinct to unearth. It's very simple. If I do not write them down, I will gradually forget them. That thought terrifies me. If I am not faithful to myself, to whom will I be? I no longer really know what I used to say to Léo. It's so frightening, and at the same time it isn't very important. Believing in the insignificance of one's childhood is, I think, the sign of a deep-seated unbelief: definitive, complete. What can I do about it? Everybody agrees about childhood. All the women in the world would weep over the story of any old childhood, be it even that of murderers, tyrants. Not long ago I saw a photo of Hitler as a child in embroidered petticoats, standing on a chair. From childhood on, every destiny is infinitely piteous. I am doubtless led to believe only in the childhood of others, for in mine I see nothing but a precocity more likely to horrify me on the whole. My childhood photographs nauseate me. Whenever I happen to read accounts of someone's childhood or youth, I am astonished at the world of unreality they contain. Even in the stories of children referred to as 'unhappy' (as if there were happy children), one finds artificial hells, desperate recourse to dreams, escape into enchantment, the supernatural. That always staggers me, and I tend to believe that it's a question more of involuntary betrayal – or more simply, a poetic transposition with which people feel childhood must be endowed, else it would be dishonored. For as far back as I remember, my childhood unfolded in a stark and barren light, nothing like the world of dreams, which was barred from my earliest years. It's always awkward to assert such things. I can therefore say that I do not recall having dreamed about anything whatsoever, be it even a better life. If I was dreaming about marrying Léo, my 'hell' was following me into the dream, and the dream – that was the confrontation between this reality and what one might call happiness.

I state immediately that this lack of dreaming does not imply that I was lucid. No. I remember (and perfectly) that in class, I was worse at studying than most of the pupils. Not that I was particularly unintelligent, but I didn't know how to work, I didn't find it at all interesting or useful. I think that despite my apparent attention, I was almost completely distracted. For example, I would listen to the teacher talk about some subject. What used to intrigue me was how he went about it, his way of explaining, more than what he was explaining. I make an exception nevertheless for mathematics, which fascinated me, even though I was basically hopeless in that subject as well as everything else until the eleventh grade. Sometimes I would receive an 'outstanding' grade in French, it depended on the teachers. For six months I had a French teacher who considered me far and away his best student, and he never gave me less than ninety percent. He left; his successor banished me to the bottom of the class, and never gave me even an average grade. I felt truly repelled by certain subjects or classic authors. Madame de Sévigné filled me with a discouraging disgust against which I struggled in vain. An assignment on her {close} relationship with her daughter earned me a failing mark and I was singled out for criticism. I no longer remember very clearly what I did to deserve that grade. On the other hand, Molière and Shakespeare enraptured me, whereas Corneille and even Racine bored me to pieces. There were some classes I decided to 'cut' because I felt they were useless. For a few weeks, I dropped out of English; they were reading *A Christmas Carol* at the rate of ten lines per class hour, and every class almost gave me a nervous breakdown. I did the same thing later with biology when it went too slowly for my taste, and then with history, and geography. This meant saving many hours, which I devoted to Léo. The principal of the lycée noticed, of course; I was threatened with expulsion and summoned to the vice-principal's office. I went to see him in an indescribable panic, but he invited me in and let me know right away that if I was nice, he would not expel me. Then he tried to kiss me on the mouth, and the session wound up in a boxing match [since] I didn't want to kiss him because of his huge black beard, and because I'd promised to remain faithful to Léo, whom I told about all this. Léo didn't believe me, he took it very badly, and would have liked me to leave the lycée immediately, which I found a bit excessive. As for my mother, she was delighted, even though she affected a sincere indignation: 'That's what it's like – when you have pretty daughters you must keep a sharp eye out.'

I stayed in school where I did exactly nothing at all. My report cards were catastrophic. At the end of the year, the over-all evaluation was: 'Does not use her great gifts.' My mother, who remained more or less indifferent to my grades, took only the general evaluation seriously, and she was jubilant: 'When I say she's intelligent, I know what I'm talking about.' At such moments she took greater care of me, had new dresses made for me, and she'd say, 'Eat, sleep, start building up your strength to be at your best when you go to college.' She thought the grades I received were unfair and managed to make me believe that the teachers had it in for me personally in the same way everyone had a grudge against us. 'Don't let it bother you,' she'd say; 'they'd never give such grades to the daughter of some administrator.' End of discussion. Besides, there was some truth to that. The sons and daughters of planters and important officials were seated in the front rows of the classroom; behind them came the minor civil servants, then the natives. And among the natives, those with well-to-do fathers were placed immediately behind the French students.

It is not for me to criticize that state of affairs, but it deeply amazed me. I'm not saying that some students' grades were related to their higher social standing, but it is true that those students received more attention. When they entered tenth grade, any native students considered anti-French were singled out for stricter supervision. I knew one, the son of a native doctor, who became a close friend; he was exceptionally intelligent and in ninth grade began winning all the first prizes. I admired him greatly, because he regularly refused to have anything to do with the French, and he never abandoned his pride. He refused to sit near the front of the class, for example, and stayed resolutely with his compatriots. He was said to be 'dangerous.' And so, even though he was by far the best student, he was never congratulated by the teachers' committee, which 'passed over' his grades. How many times did I hear French people say, 'With that race, you have to be careful, you mustn't flatter them, they'd immediately start thinking they're our equals.' We saw one another in secret, since he didn't want to be seen with a French girl. He was a boarder at the lycée because his father couldn't afford to pay for a room in town. I believe we came very close to being in love. The day before school let out for the summer, just before my departure for France, we met in an empty room after our last class. Saying good-bye to one another affected us deeply. 'You're French,' he told me, 'I'm Annamese, I can't allow myself to love you. I'll be going to Hanoi to study law because I don't have enough money to go to France, and besides I don't want to, I don't like the French.' Having no faith in the possibility of a Franco-Annamese rapprochement, he was in despair. I haven't seen him since, and don't really know what happened to him. He was afraid he had tuberculosis; I have no idea if his fears were justified. If he is alive, I suppose he's a leader in the Indo-chinese Nationalist Movement and I think of him and all his brothers with emotion, and I wish to tell him here of my admiration and complete sympathy.

(A remark, which is perhaps out of place here, but which I do wish to make: the school in Saigon admitted only the Annamese sons of French citizens, exclusively. Moreover, European dress was strictly required. In 1931, when I left Indochina for good, a few Annamese girls were attending the lycée. They were forced to disguise themselves as Europeans, which did not suit them at all, for the most part, and that bothered them. European dress was likewise obligatory in the state boarding school where I lived. On Sundays the Anna-mese boarding students could be seen out walking in the streets of Saigon, all dressed in the French style and making fools of themselves in public. What is the point of unforgivably stupid measures like that? I think such requirements, which may at first seem insignificant, come close to being criminal. In addition, the children of non-citizen natives were not allowed to go beyond primary school. Granted, tuberculosis and leprosy have been considerably contained in Indochina, thanks to us, but the physical world provides no possible moral compensation. To save children from death only to restrict them later to a sanctioned, limited development, the very limits of which are codified, seems to me much more repre-hensible than it was commendable to save them from death.)

Léo had no interest in politics. The management of his wealth and its astounding dimensions were a constant shelter from such preoccupations. Let's remove him from the Annamese setting and consider him as what he was. I mean that I'm returning to my adolescence. The more I think about it, the more I believe that Léo displayed a very characteristic stupidity that was not, however, without charm, at least for me. He had spent two years in Paris on one long spree during which, as he said, he had 'learned how to live.' He claimed to have known many women there, and as proof he showed me some photographs: in one of them he was sitting on the floor, his head on the lap of a laughing, heavily made-up brunette of about forty. Other women, each one supplied with an Annamese, lounged about either on divans or on the floor, in equally erotic poses. The setting must have been a hotel room, at night. The women were all stamped with a sinister vulgarity. It's not for nothing that I remember so well that photo in which Léo, his head clamped between the woman's knees, had his eyes half-closed and resembled a corpse. It was a revelation for me: I told myself that I was following these other women in Léo's life and, I don't know why, the anguish this thought gave me was like that I later felt at the idea of death. It then dawned on me that Léo was a truly pathetic fellow, and that I would spend my life in his company, that it was my lot to have Léo after having had my family and that I would never escape. I didn't leave Léo because of that, however; I never even mentioned anything to him. But after seeing that photo, I spent an entire month trying to familiarize myself with the idea of an absolute abandonment. I said nothing about this to my mother. I could not have done that. It was through the photo that I thought I understood that she had abandoned me, as had my brothers: she was letting me sink imperceptibly into that liaison with Léo, when she should have realized that he would not bring me happiness. I [thought] she was abandoning me not willingly, but because of a weakness I sensed was without limit or remedy, and which meant that from that moment on I loved her differently.

Léo showed me that evidence of a past life to try to make me fall in love. The things he said to me were not so different from those scattered through American movies and cheap romance novels. He told me he would love me 'till death,' that I had 'a heart of stone' and that I was 'breaking' his own heart; I loved him 'for my money,' he said, and 'not for myself.' He said that he was 'born to be unhappy,' that 'money can't buy happiness,' that he was too sentimental and that the world was cruel. He would also say, 'What I want is quite simple – a humble home, a loving heart, and I ask for nothing else on this earth.' He said that I was 'made to make men suffer' and to back this up, in his moments of despair, he would sing, 'Women love to drive men mad, live to make their poor hearts sad . . .' in such a mournful voice that I begged him every time never to sing that song, which I told him was passé. That's the language my first lover used with me for two whole years – a singular contrast with the way my family talked. I was aware of how shabby and outdated Léo's words could be, but that nonsense touched me, I usually found it flattering. I gave up trying to change Léo. He said things that ought to have proved to me a thousand times over his profound stupidity. An example of Léo's finesse: 'Parisiennes are adorable. Whenever I arrived at my mistress's place later than the appointed time, I'd find my photograph upside down. It was a charming way to let me know that she was hurt because I was late. When we're married, will you often turn my photograph upside down?'

I gave up trying to change him because it was too much work. I accepted Léo's trite remarks. I accepted everything. My mother, my elder brother, the showers of blows. Every-thing. I thought the only way to extricate myself was still to marry Léo, because he had money, because with that money we'd go to France with my entire family and there life would be good. I did not plan to leave my family in Indochina, because I thought life alone with Léo would be beyond my

strength. Therefore I accepted everything with a certain simplicity: I was not without hope, but I did not separate that
hope from a present that was rather fearsome. I thought that
one day I would no longer be beaten or insulted, that people
would listen to me, that I would be beautiful and brilliant,
rich, that I would ride around only in limousines, that perhaps
someone other than Léo would love me. Someone other than
Léo . . . But for that Léo's millions were needed so I could have
my nose straightened (advice from my elder brother, who was
aware of the new profession of plastic surgery), and patronize
the great fashion designers (more advice from my elder
brother), and know 'how to talk to men' (advice from my
mother). It was as clear as day. I believed it all. Without that,
no chance of a future. When I claim that I come from the most
colossal stupidity, that in losing my youth I lost an empire of
stupidity, I certainly know what I'm talking about. Whenever
I'd managed to make Léo angry and he was sulky with me,
I was despondent because in losing Léo I would lose everything, I'd fall back into my family, and grow old in their
shadow. It was horrible to contemplate. To escape all that,
I needed Léo.

How did I manage to overcome the kind of physical loathing I felt for Léo? The first time he kissed me on the mouth,
it was one evening in his Léon Bollée. He had come to get
me after class and was taking me back to Sadec for the week-
end. I rarely saw him alone and at that hour; perhaps it was
even the first time that had happened. Along the way, Léo put
his arms around me and I felt desire for him. I think it was
desire. It was a peacefulness that fully contented me. I was
comfortable, there, in Léo's arms. I believe it could have been
anybody, I would have felt the same. Léo was anybody: anybody could have told me what Léo told me, anybody could
have had Léo's arms and kindness in the darkness of the car,
in the black night that was my youth. When his cheek touched
my cheek, it was pleasant. I did not see his face. It was a cheek

that wanted my cheek – Léo's cheek, and nothing else. I sensed that he desired me because his hands were shaking and because they sometimes encountered my breasts; I preferred to have them around my waist, where I put them back, so that was fine. Quite moved, Léo said, 'You have lovely breasts.' I said nothing. Léo's desire slipped gently into me and induced mine. I did not desire Léo directly, I desired Léo because he desired me. His desire aroused mine without him having anything to do with it. I found that desire was good to experience, I felt it as a kind of solution to all sorts of things. While Léo held me in his arms, when I thought of my family, I suddenly pitied them for not being as happy as I was, and I thought it was good to think that. I was reconciling myself with the world: I hadn't felt that plenitude except when coming home from hunting with my younger brother, when there had been a storm, and we were returning barefoot in the soft mud of the rice paddies. 'Give me your breasts,' Léo was saying. I did not want to give him my breasts to touch, I didn't think that was worth it, that would not have added anything more. What I wanted was to feel his desire, that was all. 'I love you,' Léo said quietly. He did not rush me, he knew I was a virgin, he had principles concerning 'the first time'; he left my breasts alone and settled for my waist and my hair, my cheek. When he told me he loved me, I felt penetrated by a kind of fierce generosity and was forced to close my eyes. Anyone else could have said it to me. Under the same conditions, it would have had the same effect.

I had read a {popular sentimental} novel, *Magali* by Delly; this book played a major role in my youth. It was the most beautiful/the only one {*sic*} I'd read, and in it the words 'I love you' were pronounced a single time, during a conversation between the two lovers that lasted barely a few minutes but justified months of waiting, of pain, of devastating separation. I'd heard that declaration at the movies, and each time it overwhelmed me. I thought one said that only once in a lifetime, the way it was in *Magali* and {romantic} films about Casanova: only once to only one person, and never afterward to anyone else, like the way it was with death. I was convinced of that. And that evening, when Léo told me he loved me, I felt giddy. Not only was he saying it, but he would never say it again — and he was saying it to me. I was so young and so naïve that I imagined that once those words had been spoken, you couldn't say them again without being ashamed and dishonored to such an extent that suicide was the sole remedy for such despair. Later, Léo said them to me many times, and although I was not as deeply stirred as I had been the first time, I was moved all the same. Those words had a magical effect on me. Later on, I often asked Léo to say those words: 'Say them to me' — and I received them the way one receives the wind, eyes closed, paying attention with all one's being. Later on, long after Léo, other men happened to say them to me, when their meaning seemed more than doubtful to me. Nevertheless, the words have always obliged me to listen to them seriously, even when they were said only in the distraction of desire. I used to say to Léo, 'Even if it isn't true, say it.' They were key words: even in moments when I felt the most foreign, the most closed to Léo, those words opened me up and I became kind to him.

It was on that evening that Léo kissed me on the mouth. He did it by surprise. All of a sudden, I felt a cool and moist contact with my lips. The revulsion I felt truly cannot be described. I shoved Léo, I spat, I wanted to jump out of the car. Léo was at a complete loss. In a single second, I felt myself stretched tight like a bow, ruined forever. I kept saying, 'It's over, it's over.' Léo was saying, 'What do you mean?' He did not understand. At one point, he laughed, and explained to me that it wasn't letting herself be kissed on the mouth that cost a girl her virginity. 'I know that,' I cried, 'but it's still over.' He tried to calm me and put his arms around me again but I shouted, I begged him to stop the car and let me out. It was mid-evening in the middle of nowhere, but I wasn't thinking of that anymore. I'm retracing the scene the way it happened; I cannot explain it. I was disgust itself. But as for explaining what I meant by 'over,' I cannot do it, I don't know anymore. I did calm down, however, and slid over to the end of the seat, as far from Léo as possible. And there I spat into my handkerchief, I kept spitting, I spat all night long and the next day; whenever I thought about it again, I spat some more. Obviously quite miserable, Léo no longer tried to touch me; he could see that I was spitting and asked, 'Do I disgust you?' I could not reply. I was remembering his face, which was at that moment in darkness: his pockmarked face, his large, soft mouth; I recalled the photograph in which he was so pathetic and I was thinking that the mouth, the saliva, the tongue of that contemptible creature had touched my lips. Truly, I felt a kind of aftermath of rape. Nothing could make it so that he had not touched my mouth with his mouth that had touched so many others, that opened only to tell me despicable or ridiculous things, that seemed to me degraded, vain, and stupid, lost, as Léo was lost. 'I see that I disgust you, you don't need to hide.' I did not reply. I thought about the words my brothers used to describe Léo. 'Fetus': I had been kissed by a fetus. Ugliness had entered my mouth, I had communed with horror. I was violated to my very soul.

If I wanted to jump out of the car, it was to put an end to the horror: I was discovering my existence in a horrifying light, naked and bleak. For once, I was not deluding myself, and I *knew* what I would find in Sadec. My elder brother befuddled with opium, my mother in a frenzy of exasperation, and the blows, the blows, endless, the inadmissible blows, the shameful blows. It was as if a machine to manufacture lucidity had suddenly started up inside me. I saw things clearly. I was setting out in life with the misshapen creature that was Léo and there was no escape for me. I couldn't escape from anything – perhaps that was what it was to be 'over': I had nothing left.

Whereas I hadn't known a moment before that I still had my mouth, now it no longer belonged to me, I didn't recognize it anymore. I was suffering its violation, its pollution, just as I was suffering what I thought was life: my life. I rinsed my mouth with my own saliva that I spat out into my handkerchief, and with my handkerchief I rubbed my lips. But that wasn't enough – never enough: I still believed that some portion of Léo's saliva yet remained in my mouth and I spat again and again without stopping. Of course I knew that Léo must have been terribly hurt by all this but I put that off until later, there was nothing else I could do. I was busy cleansing my mouth. I opened it and dried it in the onrushing air. But when I closed it and my saliva began flowing, the tragedy would begin again, I would imagine that my saliva was forever mixed with Léo's. At some point I cried, and then I drew closer to Léo and said, 'I'm being silly, it's because it's the first time.' He put his arms around my waist and said, 'You're making me suffer dreadfully.' I clung to him, my head against his chest, hidden, and I tried to start swallowing my saliva again in tiny amounts, to get used to it. When I couldn't manage it, I would spit discreetly into my handkerchief. 'Above all, you mustn't be angry with me,' I told Léo. I wanted him to console me; he could not. But his enveloping arm consoled me. I could count only on Léo's arm and I used it that evening as much as I could. I found that arm inoffensive and kind, it wished me no harm, it was willing to have me, and I managed to make do with that for consolation.

My elder brother had a monkey, a marmoset, which he loved to distraction. He could shed tears over this monkey. When he was forced to leave it at the plantation – after the adventures I am about to relate – he sometimes worried seriously about it: 'I wonder what those bastards are doing with my monkey.' At the time I'm speaking of, my brother had gradually reached the point of smoking {opium} for much of the night and was coming home at around six in the morning. He would go to bed right away and get up for lunch, then go back to sleep, after which he would play with his monkey until our five o'clock snack, then play with his monkey again, have dinner, and go off to smoke. We kept this monkey in a cage, in a small courtyard. It was an exceptionally intelligent and amusing animal. He wound up playing a major role in my brother's life. When my brother wasn't sleeping, he would let the monkey out and put him on his shoulder; he used to play the piano to him and would give him so many sapeks (a bronze coin of the native currency) to put in his mouth that his jowls were stuffed full and so heavy that he could only move about with his head hanging. The monkey would then take the coins out and give them back to my brother one by one. My brother found this howlingly funny – I've never seen anyone laugh like he did. He would call my younger brother and me to come see the performance. We had to be there or risk making him dangerously angry. We had to watch. Sometimes it took an hour. Whenever I didn't laugh, my brother was furious. Sometimes my mother would appear and tell him, 'I beg you, do something, anything at all but do something, don't waste all your days. . . .' My brother would put her in her place more or less roughly, it depended, but he'd keep playing with the monkey. We were also raising a rooster, which my brother sometimes put into the monkey's cage, where the monkey would pluck out its feathers with shrieks of joy. The rooster would squawk and the scene would amuse everyone, even my mother, so there were some things that brought us together. Perhaps it was cruel, but we didn't think about that. One day the monkey escaped and spread panic through the native girls' school where my mother was the principal. Within a minute the entire school fled outdoors, the girls all screaming. My brothers and I were in heaven although my mother took it quite badly, spoke of being dismissed, and persuaded my brother to send the monkey back to the plantation. That was when he began taking an interest in the place, going out there to see his monkey, which was pining away from boredom. One day the animal began to lose his teeth because he wasn't being given enough to drink; my brother couldn't resist bringing him back to Sadec where the monkey, having picked up a few vices, would spend his entire day masturbating, to the huge disgust of everyone but my elder brother. My brother would show the same infatuation with certain people for a while, then drop them as completely as if they'd never existed.

Why remember the movie theater all of a sudden? Urgent to write it down. It happened when she was fourteen, that girl I once was. I did not want to go walking with the young ladies of the Pension Barbet every Sunday, in a line, through the streets of the city. I was ashamed of going out all lined up. It was just impossible to consider – impossible. I had said so to my mother. My mother understood that this was impossible. She knew that certain things I felt were impossible should simply be abandoned. Or was it that I managed to win her over? I don't think so. Just as my mother had given up hope of making me tell her I was sorry, she gave up hope of seeing me go out walking in a line with the Pension Barbet. I had told her, 'That's impossible,' without explaining myself. I had added, 'It's ridiculous.'

I would have been unable to explain myself, I was not in the habit of doing that. I had never explained what I meant about anything whatsoever. Everyone in my family was like that. Never, anywhere, in any milieu, have I encountered such an acute sense of the immodesty of language. Never was it used for anything except describing actions to be taken or situations requiring definition. Insults could not have been more gratuitous: we could have refrained from insulting one another, so if we insulted one another, it was thanks to a spirit of poetry.

Never in my home did words serve to describe a mood, to express a complaint. My elder brother's 'You make me fucking sick' meant, to us, that *everything* made him fucking sick, and that he found himself in a state of what in another milieu is conventionally known as despair. And so it was not without solemnity and respect that we avoided speaking to him at such moments. Insults – they were our poetry, sharing its truest, most undeniable characteristics. First, gratuity, which was not rash, but said exactly the right thing, lit us up with anger, and flooded us with revelations of all kinds. 'Your house is a shit-hole,' my brother would tell my mother, 'a real shithole and boring as shit.' Those words found in us that 'always hollow' space evoked by Saint John of the Cross, and they filled us with something evident, with a revelation. In such cases, I could tell that the house really was a shithole, that I was up to my neck in shit, and I suspected that everything was a shithole and that no one ever got out of it. There were the words, and the look that went with them, and the tone – clipped, unaffected, utterly suitable and sincere – that drove all doubt from those golden words.

I have not experienced revelations that powerful in my life, as powerful and as supremely convincing as certain of my elder brother's insults, save in my reading of Rimbaud, of Dostoyev-sky. My brother was perhaps the first to inculcate in me that tendency I still possess to prefer the work of inspiration to absolutely any other, and to hold human intelligence in dis-favor. In the matter of intelligence, I am tolerably responsive only to that of certain animals, precisely those that possess so little of it that the rare traces they do display seem to spring from sudden inspiration. For example I prefer stupid cats to intelligent ones. I can't help it. I prefer cats that don't recog-nize me to those that do. When my brother caught syphilis, he said, 'Rotten fucking life, I'm fucked rotten.' From then on, I felt infinitely compassionate and fraternal. I felt inconsol-able, just inconsolable to learn that such things happen in life, but I did indeed learn this, and no one, afterward, had to teach me that lesson better than he had.

When I insisted to my mother that it was impossible for me to go walking with the girls of the Pension Barbet, my mother must have felt that I couldn't help it. She was so used to 'things one can't help' that she gave in. She went to see the principal of the Pension Barbet. I waited for her outside the office door. It was an awkward request. The discussion lasted a long time. My mother emerged flushed and still unsettled, and she told me I'd been excused. I don't know what argument my mother used, but she was not a little proud of having carried the day. The principal felt strongly about those Sunday walks, she wanted to put the perfect behavior of her students on public display. I still wonder what made her give in, especially since my mother had asked her to allow me to go out alone, which should have seemed inadmissible to her. At that time, I did not know Léo, and my mother surely never thought I might misbehave on my walks; to tell the truth she wasn't thinking of anything, and she didn't wonder what I could do on my own in the city, at fourteen years old, every Sunday afternoon.

Indeed, the following Sunday, when I faced this prospect, I had no idea what to do with myself. I got dressed up at four o'clock, however, and I went out. I had a bright green straw hat my mother had bought me on sale (of course) to be worn on outings. I was wearing a dress of raw silk with blue flowers. It was only when I got outside that I found myself helpless to deal with the utter absurdity of my outfit, which seemed somehow inevitable. It never even occurred to me to change any part of it. Just as I had the mug of a 'crab louse,' of someone to whom one would say, 'So much for you,' so also that outfit prescribed by my mother was part of my public image, and I dragged it around as sadly as I did my face. Through the city, off I went. Believing the human race spent Sunday afternoon the same way in every city in the world, I did so too. I had always been taught the significance of social conventions, whose meaning had been deeply instilled into me. And I can affirm absolutely that throughout a great part of my youth, I strove to be 'like others,' to 'pass,' which brought me a considerable amount of pain and a latent despair that stayed with me for a strangely long time. After leaving the Pension Barbet, I set out to walk along the street with the air of a girl who knows where she's going, someone behaving normally. Well, once outside, I stiffened up and walked so bizarrely that people were looking at me. I think I must have been walking with an expression of extraordinary concentration – especially since I didn't know where I was going. I was mulling over what had led up to this outing: my refusal to walk in the Pension Barbet line; my wish to go off on my own. At that time, colonials all had their own cars. One hardly ever saw a French pedestrian. Because of the throngs of natives in the streets, girls went out with their parents – one certainly did not encounter a girl on her own, it just wasn't done. One kept girls 'on a tight rein.' As for me, in the shade of the tall tamarind trees, I walked along and as I walked, it became ever clearer that where I belonged was not where I was. People noticed me, looked back at me, smiled, surprised, sorry for me. No, it's difficult to imagine. I was fourteen, with breasts, an apple-green hat, a blue-flowered dress with a hem below my knees, patent-leather shoes, a small handbag, and I was walking with downcast eyes, looking at no one, just my feet, in a state of horrible embarrassment I've never experienced since. I felt disguised; I was. I encountered bands of girls going to play tennis, bareheaded, all in white, athletic, tripping lightly along. Me, I could have been taken for either a little girl or a little whore. I was a walking ambiguity. I didn't know, others didn't either, looking at me and wondering what this was that no one had ever seen before: she might have been young, except for that drawn expression, that age-old look of shame and misery shriveling her made-up face. I did not dream of going back. It was not possible. Not possible to retreat; furthermore, that never occurred to me. It was Sunday afternoon, and I was out for a walk. No one to go visit; I knew no one in the city. I walked, I walked, I left the wide avenues, I took the little streets. I couldn't go back until seven o'clock. I was waiting for evening, for darkness, to hide, and meanwhile I tried to conceal myself as best I could in narrow suburban streets edged with houses, where I knew there would be no French people, where only natives would be astonished, which seemed less serious to me, more bearable, because there were many more of them than there were French people, it was less important, less painful, everything was relative: a native would be less astounded, unprepared to take the full measure of my absurdity. I was bathed in perspiration: sweat poured from my hair down my face. Even so, I did not return to the Pension Barbet. I became stubborn. I decided to go to a movie matinee. That abrupt resolution came to me at the moment when my strength deserted me. I turned back and headed for the center of town. I kept running into French people. On my apple-green hat there was a red rose. 'Moss rose,' my mother called it. And my little handbag for that older look, 'all dressed up,' the finishing touch that gave me a serious air. I was suffering like a soul in hell. I walked very fast to go to ground in [the Éden Cinema].

I arrived there and went to the ticket window. I hadn't thought about this. I had barely enough money for a seat 'down in front.' The front seats were taken only by the 'scum' of the city. Half-castes, Annamese, all piled into rattan chairs, three rows separated from the orchestra seats by a great gap: difference.

I found enough money for my ticket by counting out some small change, without fainting. When I went inside to the theater, the lights were still on. I was too early, the show hadn't started yet. At the back of the orchestra, there were already three rows of French patrons. Down in front, a gang of rowdies laughed and whistled. I had to walk the length of the theater watched by everyone in the orchestra. Alone. Because no one escorted the patrons down front to their seats. Not one White in the front rows. I did not flinch. I walked down the aisle. The crossing of that theater by my public persona took place in the profound silence my public entrance had provoked. I remember that I no longer remembered how to walk. The whole of humanity was watching me. I was white, no doubt about that. Nobody had ever seen a white girl in the front seats before. Everything, I knew everything people were thinking, and I was thinking the same thing at the same moment. Everything danced before my eyes, and I found myself in a truly advanced state of unreality. I had bonded deeply with shame. I was a walking shame. I was simply ridiculous. I had no business being in that movie theater and my outfit was not normal but laughable to say the least, if not pitiable. Everything was giving way. I found myself giving way, on a rattan chair, my handbag on my lap, streaming with sweat. I could not say anymore whether ten minutes or an hour went by before the lights went out. But suddenly it was dark, and someone began playing the piano. I roused myself from my torpor. They were showing *Casanova*. I found this film to be decisively beautiful. I left consoled. I had seen Casanova confess his love to a woman and kiss her on the mouth.

IN THE EVENING, there was a faint dry clatter on the Ramé road. 'It's Paul coming home,' my mother said, and soon afterward he appeared in his small open carriage on the flat road to Ramé. We were in such need of money that he had come up with the idea of providing public transportation. So he'd bought an old horse and a cariole and all afternoon long he shuttled between Bantai and Ramé, which brought him at most enough to buy himself some cigarettes. My mother had gone along with the project.

From a distance we watched three natives alight from the carriage, pay Paul their fare, and Paul then turn onto our road and arrive at the house.

'Filthy job,' said Paul.

My mother was having palm trees and flowers planted along the side of the house. She had been supervising a servant hard at work all afternoon. For a long time now we had known there was no hope of earning any income from the plantation. The mother {*sic*} could not bear idleness; she had flowers planted and kept her servants busy that way. The scorching dryness, moreover, had defeated her efforts several times. But the mother still kept trying.

That day I had spent part of the afternoon in the shed under the eaves where we kept the game my brother bagged. Four does and a stag were hanging there from iron hooks. I often shut myself up inside, without my mother knowing. It was cool in that shed, and no one disturbed me there. The does were losing their blood drop by drop, and the soft sound – ploc – of the blood dripping on the floor must have lulled I don't know what far-away melancholy in me. My brother's hunts poisoned my existence; they were my mother's pride.

As soon as evening came, my brother would go out onto the veranda and sniff the air: 'Tonight, I'm off,' he'd say. I had made it a sort of personal duty to visit the dead does in the shed. I too was proud of my brother's exploits, but above all I found them wrenching. The animals decomposed quickly in the heat and were then unhooked and thrown into the river, where they drifted downstream to the sea. We ate so many that we grew sick of them, and in the end preferred something else, for example the black-fleshed wading birds my brother killed in the mangrove forests along the seashore and which we ate almost raw, barely roasted over a wood fire. At one time, we used to feast on the pickled flesh of young crocodiles, but in the end we tired of everything. The region offered little in the way of meat; the only pigs there were [*illegible*] and fed on sewage from the village. We were reluctant to eat them. The region was very poor. The natives made up for that with dogs; one of our servants would chase them with axes and decapitate them in mid-gallop: they would keep on running, covering ten yards or so without their heads, which literally threw me into a panic. We could not bring ourselves to eat dog, which my mother had always opposed because she loved dogs. We could not keep a single one, unfortunately, without seeing it end up in that pitiable fashion.

When I'd heard the rumbling of the carriage, I had come out of the shed. I went over to my brother. He was pouring with sweat, rapidly unharnessing the horse, which had grown even thinner.

'I don't know what's wrong with him,' my brother was saying. 'He's going to croak. He must be tubercular.'

He released him into the meadow. The animal was no longer eating. We looked at him for a moment.

'He won't last much longer,' my brother said. 'Come swimming.'

I went quickly back up to the bungalow and put on my suit.

In his room, my brother did the same. Going back down we passed my mother.

'You're going there again,' my mother said.

Without answering we made our way through the rice field toward the little wooden bridge where the river ran deep. My brother, a wonderful swimmer, jumped in first. The cove itself was wide and rather shallow; he went round in there like a goldfish in a bowl. I always hesitated, because of the things one encountered in that water. The river flowed out of the forest a few hundred yards from there, and often dead birds, squirrels, even tigers – in the rainy season – would go down that river. We almost always emerged from it with leeches. My brother would insist, and I always gave in at last. He was teaching me to swim. We'd stay in the water until nightfall, when we heard my mother yelling, threatening us with punishment. We'd go back up and rinse away the muddy river with jars of rainwater.

We used to tear leeches out from between our toes. My mother always spotted that.

'You'll wind up bled completely dry,' she'd say.

NOTES

1. The Union of Indochina was created in 1887, comprising Laos, Cambodia, Cochin China (the southern part of present-day Vietnam), Annam (central Vietnam), and Tonkin (northern Vietnam).

2. Born in 1914, Marguerite Donnadieu was the youngest of three children. Her brother Paul was born in 1911, and the oldest child, Pierre, in 1910.

TER OF THE MILITIA
(ROUGH DRAFT)

IT ALL STARTED three days ago. Maxime had come back reporting that he'd put {the prisoners} in a barn in Levallois with some clean straw and they'd been joking around, saying 'Kaput.' Maxime was laughing. This was in the canteen. The others laughed, listening to Maxime. Théodora had insulted them, then burst into tears. She'd been unapproachable ever since. 'She's awful, she's a savage,' the other women at the center were saying about her. Maxime and Théodora had shouted at each other. Almost everyone was on Maxime's side. For three days now, he'd avoided speaking to Théodora. Obviously disgusted with her, the women were keeping their distance. Albert was the only holdout. 'Just leave her the fuck alone, all right?' he told the other women. He agreed with Maxime about how to handle {the prisoners}, but made sure everyone knew not to give Théodora any shit about it.

'I'm off,' said the girl. 'Tell Albert I came by.'

'Everything's a goddamned mess,' said Théodora.

It was quite hot. Still machine-gun fire. The women took care of the canteen or the mutual aid center. Théodora wasn't doing anything. As a rule, she stayed in the bar[1] because of the phone numbers. Still machine-gun fire in the distance. It seems to be getting closer. It's hot. The militiamen[2] – eleven in a room on the fourth floor – must really be hot; maybe they need some water. It has already been over now for three days. In a small room across from the bar, six collaborators are playing cards; they've banded together because they found those out in the hall too lower-class. 'I've had it with prisoners,' thinks Théodora. She knows one prisoner who is perhaps being shot at that very moment. Shot by the Germans. He was at Fresnes[3] three weeks ago; now she hasn't any idea anymore.

Yesterday, in another center linked to the Richelieu center, there was also some shooting: a Gestapo agent. That was on the rue de la Chaussée-d'Antin, in a courtyard. She, Nano, had gone there with Albert and Ter, the militiaman. Ter had to be interrogated.

Entering the big empty room that was headquarters at the rue d'Antin center, they'd passed a stretcher going out: flabby, still soft. 'Two minutes ago,' Jean had said, 'you just missed it.' The Hernandez group had done it, he explained. Three revolver shots in the back of the neck, out in the courtyard. Albert and Théodora had gone to see the courtyard. On one stone, a puddle of blood was already congealing. In the hall, it was hard to talk over the loud voices of the Spaniards; in the courtyard, there was only some blood. The fellow had wept and pleaded while the Spaniards argued about who would get to kill him. Jean and Albert were talking about it; Jean was pale, like someone who's seasick. 'I don't like it,' he told Albert.

The militiaman, leaning back against the fireplace, had seen the Gestapo agent's corpse go by, and looking through the doorway, he'd seen the blood. He was quite pale. Of all the prisoners in the center, he was by far the one Albert and Théodora liked the best. 'If you've brought me here to shoot me,' he'd said very quietly to Albert, 'I'd like to know it: I'd like to write a note to my parents.' Suddenly, while they were talking to Jean, they'd realized that the militiaman had seen the corpse of the Gestapo agent. Ter's pallor was the kind that should happen only once in this life. 'No, we didn't bring you here to shoot you,' Albert had replied with a smile. 'Oh, good,' the militiaman said, 'because I would have liked to know.' Then he'd said nothing more. For a moment, Albert had remained thoughtful.

In the two neighboring rooms, men were carefully oiling their guns. Sweating heavily, Jean was giving orders about where various groups would be staying that evening. The Spaniards were yelling in the empty rooms. Smiling, Albert had offered a cigarette to the militiaman. Albert was friendly with the militiaman and Théodora. He'd also offered Théodora a cigarette. He liked Théodora, he took her around just about everywhere; he found women a bother but not Théodora. The militiaman had smiled back at Albert when he'd offered him the cigarette. Théodora had smiled too, of course. It was a nice moment. The militiaman was smoking his cigarette as hard as he could, taking deep drags. He was twenty-three. You could see his trim waist, and the muscles in his long young forearms. He would have blended right in with the other men moving around and oiling their guns if he hadn't been so pale, and smoking like that. But he had a dirty past; if men's pasts could be forgotten, there would never be any war. Smoking his cigarette, he might have managed to believe he was starting to live again and that this past had vanished, but no. Off in every corner men were oiling their guns and preparing to go out again. Albert might have offered that smile and that cigarette to just anyone, once this man had passed, alive, from the utter certitude of death to life. But just anyone would not have smiled at just anyone like that. Albert was intelligent. He was even the triumph of intelligence, that Albert, thought Théodora, in the sense that this smile was one of understanding with the militiaman. He was not kind, but was so understanding that you could say nothing escaped him, while he understood everything. Standing by the fireplace, Albert waited for Jean. 'When you have a second, can I? . . .' 'Now is good,' said Jean. The militiaman didn't wonder what he was doing there. He smoked his cigarette. Since he hadn't been shot, he was now at loose ends. He must have suspected he'd be a topic of interest, but only vaguely. That was no ordinary smile they'd exchanged, he and Albert: a smile of complicity. A priest wouldn't have done that, because religion has disfigured death, and that's the least of its crimes. Neither Albert nor the militiaman believed in God. No other way.

Jean has a second. He and Albert talk. Théodora stays by

the fireplace with the militiaman. It was yesterday they'd interrogated him. She knows him as well as she knows her own
brother. He was a friend of Bony and Lafont. He went off on
sprees with them. He rode around in Lafont's armored car.
'Why did you join the militia?' 'Because I wanted to have a
gun.' 'Why a gun?' 'Because guns are swell.' For an hour
they'd been after him relentlessly to find out what he'd done
with it, if he'd killed anyone in the Resistance with that gun.
'I was the lowest of the low,' he'd said. 'They wouldn't have
let me kill any Resistance fighters.' He hadn't said that he
wouldn't have tried if they had let him. Albert's group had
arrested him in another FFI group,[4] one that didn't take
prisoners, so they'd unloaded him back on Albert's men.
'What the fuck were you doing in the FFI?' 'I wanted to fight.'
'With what weapon?' 'With my gun.' 'Was it to hide out?'
'No, because I knew that sooner or later ... It was to fight.'
'Why weren't you wearing an armband?' Then Ter had
smiled. 'Come on, you must be kidding. ...' That answer was
what had made Albert and Théodora take a liking to the militiaman. In one year he had made six million in a German
purchasing office, and he'd spent it all. 'How much did it bring
you?' 'Six million in 1943.' He'd come right out with it.
Théodora thought he looked like a guy who liked sex and
good times. He was convinced he was going to be shot. During his interrogation, he'd looked at Théodora in a certain
way. Now she knew he must have been a skirt chaser. A fucking idiot, too, but that wasn't the moment to think about it.

    Albert had rejoined Ter and Théodora. 'We're leaving.'
They'd headed straight for the door. On the way out, Albert
had given a friendly wave to Hernandez, and so had
Théodora.

    Hernandez was a Spanish giant in the FAI[5] who said he was
in training to return to Spain. It was his group that had
executed the {Gestapo} agent, and all the French considered
those seventeen men their battle-hardened superiors. The

agent's execution made Albert feel his friendship was well founded; the friendly wave he'd given him confirmed this. Hernandez would have died in an instant for the Spanish republic: he had the right to kill. The honor of executing the agent had fallen to his group, and rightly so. Even though the agent was French, the French hadn't protested. They'd been less than certain that the man deserved to be executed; Hernandez, no. Now Hernandez was laughing, as usual. He was a barber by trade, and a Spanish Republican by conviction: he would just as willingly have blown his own brains out to advance the civil war. When they weren't fighting, the Spaniards oiled the guns they'd gotten their hands on. The insurrection in Paris made them homesick, and they thought of Spain. They felt they'd be able to leave in the following month. 'It's Franco's turn,' Hernandez kept saying. They were sure about that, and anxious to regroup, but the Socialists were setting conditions unacceptable to those in the FAI. The FAI and the Communists wanted to leave for the border immediately; the Socialists wanted to wait, and talked about an organized expeditionary force. They had all left their jobs to go back.

Going past Hernandez, Théodora thought he might be the one who would execute the militiaman in a few days. She preferred Hernandez. She smiled at him. Only Hernandez knew how necessary it was to kill him. No question of meddling in that: preventing Hernandez from killing would have been a crime against the people. The Gestapo agent's death had been a true execution, Hernandez didn't doubt that. Théodora had even less doubt on that score – a few days earlier she'd wanted to kill the German prisoners. Théodora didn't know what Jean and Albert had said to each other. Why had the militiaman been brought from Richelieu to the d'Antin center? Théodora couldn't figure out what Albert had in mind. But that wasn't important.

When they got into the car, Terrail had politely opened the door for Théodora. He was naturally pleased to be leaving the d'Antin center, but it was also because Théodora was driving, and women who drove must have impressed him. The militiaman had sat beside Théodora; Albert, in back, with a small – very small – revolver. It didn't work, this revolver; it was all he had left, since his comrades had stolen the rest of his guns. The militiaman didn't know this revolver didn't work; he sat quietly, sticking out his arm at every turn, paying attention to the driving. At one point, Albert and Théodora had exchanged gleeful looks over the revolver: if he only knew. . . . The militiaman, though, was serious, quite serious, signaling the turns with his arm. This militiaman was the kind of person who can enjoy a car ride even if he knows it's his last – after all, at least it's something – and for whom the handling of a car in Paris is fascinating in itself. He had hung on to his gun for the same reason.

In the streets, no policemen. Swarms of FFI vehicles went in all directions. In particular, cars went in the wrong direction along one-way thoroughfares, especially Haussmann, which Théodora had taken to return from the Chaussée-d'Antin center. Still no police. Lots of accidents. From almost every car {bristled} the barrels of rifles and machine guns held by guys with the mugs of proles. Now and then, the warbling of machine guns: the shooters on the roofs. Every evening, people come to the center to report seeing shadows passing across neighboring rooftops. That's how Théodora almost got some American soldiers killed when they were setting up an anti-aircraft defense post on a bank roof. There are women in all the jeeps, and little tarts as well, as in the FFI cars. The biggest bellyachers are the AS.[6] A whole bunch of them had turned up – in uniform – at the Richelieu center the day after Leclerc's entrance into Paris.[7] They had complained indignantly about the disrespectful treatment they'd received. They had come 'to take possession of the premises.' When she'd gotten back there yesterday, Théodora had run into them in the hall as the general was saying, 'I thought we'd be able to

keep them, but they're too much in the way, it's impossible.'
He was talking about the FFI.

Théodora was sorry that the insurrection was over and they
hadn't been allowed to wipe out the mothball brigade.[8] Many
things saddened her, and not the least of them was those mothballs. It was one of the most depressing things she'd ever seen.
They had come 'to put an end to irregularities.' Addressing
men who hadn't washed or slept properly in two weeks, they'd
said, 'Boys, these mattresses must go, enough of that.' The
mothball general never went anywhere without six other
mothballs, even to order the hall swept, whereas gasoline-
bottle 'missions' were carried out by two men.

Albert was ashamed for the mothballs. The men at Levallois
were bitching like crazy. Those at Porte Champerret, while
they were at it, wanted to burn the whole place down. Only
the prisoners were reassured, because they'd wind up in the
hands of the military police. The mothballs had spent the last
two weeks taking inventory of everything the FFI had stolen
from collaborators. In the end the list became so long they'd
given up trying to get it all back and had started minding their
own business. They impressed no one but the prisoners; the
Levallois men didn't even step aside when they passed them
in the building. The FFI men had been hard up for food for
several weeks, but the mothballs were eating like kings, on
tablecloths and at noon. The FFI ate the leftovers at one thirty.

The same day the Gestapo agent was executed, Théodora
had gone that evening to the Prisoners' Bureau to get some
bread requisition coupons. There she'd run into a number of
people conscripted for public service who'd come to get paid.
In the office of the minister's secretary, a man was saying, 'I've
got a stiff and no idea where to put it. It was dropped off at the
station three hours ago, the morgues don't want it, I'm fed up!'
The secretary had told him she had other things to do. 'It's
from the rue de la Chaussée-d'Antin – I've phoned all the
hospitals, he's downstairs in the vehicle, and what am I

supposed to do with him?' Théodora hadn't said a thing. It was the agent. The secretary was growing impatient and so was the guy, who finally went away, leaving on the secretary's table a small gold medal on a chain: 'They found that on him; it's got nothing to do with me.' And he'd left. Théodora, who knew the secretary, had ventured to look at the chain. A first communion medal. She'd wondered why the guy had taken it off him, that complicated things. 'And me, what do you want me to do with him?' the secretary had said with a shrug. The guy had slipped away. While Théodora was signing the requisition coupons, the chain had been lying on the table like any old thing. She had felt like touching the chain to see if it was still warm. That was silly. The guy had said that the stiff hadn't a single paper on him, he hadn't a clue who it could be. Théodora didn't know either, but she could have found out by phoning Jean. The thought had never even crossed her mind. She'd laughed. And then she had left. Although she'd laughed, the chain had also made her feel sick. That was enough of that.

NOTES

1. 'That's what we called a kind of checkroom with a counter where we'd distributed provisions during the insurrection.' *La douleur* (*The War*).

2. In January 1943, a collaborationist militia run by Joseph Darnand became the Milice Française (French Militia), a volunteer force with political and paramilitary powers charged with supporting German operations against the French Resistance. Pierre Laval was its first head, but the Milice was led by Darnand and underlings such as Paul Touvier. The Milice also worked with the likes of Klaus Barbie to round up the men, women, and children sent to French detention centers for shipment to German concentration camps.

3. Built at the end of the nineteenth century just outside Paris, Fresnes prison was used by the Germans to house political prisoners, some of whom were executed there, while others were sent on to Germany for execution or internment in concentration camps.

4. The Forces Françaises de l'Intérieur (French Forces of the Interior) refers to the resistance fighters of various organizations in France placed under the command of General Koenig by Charles de Gaulle in June 1944 to unify domestic armed opposition to the Germans. About two hundred thousand strong, the FFI wore civilian clothing with an FFI armband and mostly used their own weapons.

General Patton, among others, paid tribute to their invaluable support in the liberation of France.

5. The Federación Anarquista Ibérica (Federation of Spanish Anarchists) was a militant Spanish trade union organization that fought against Franco in the Spanish Civil War, and was one of several such Spanish groups that fought later as independent but integral forces within the French Resistance.

6. By the end of 1942, some independent Resistance organizations had combined into the Mouvements Unis de la Résistance; the armed wing of the MUR was the Armée Secrète. The armed wing of the Communist-led Front National, formed in May 1941, was the Francs-Tireurs et Partisans Français. The more right-wing MUR recognized de Gaulle as their leader and thus benefited from his – and Allied – support, whereas the Communists, more suspicious of the general's growing authority, retained their independence, but were often left to scrounge for their supplies and weapons.

7. As the Germans lost control of Paris during the last stages of the Allied advance, brutal fighting broke out in the capital among the German occupiers, collaborationists, and the French Resistance, whose strongest element in Paris was the Communist movement led by Colonel Henri Tanguy (Colonel Rol-Tanguy). General Philippe Leclerc entered the capital at the head of the first detachment of the second armored division on August 24, 1944. General Dietrich Von Choltitz surrendered the next day.

8. *Les naphtalinés* – members of the French armed forces who decided not to fight the German occupation – put their uniforms away in mothballs to be safely donned years later at the Liberation, when they smelled richly of naphthalene.

WIFE TO MARCEL

I'M THE LOWEST thing there is in society, I'm wife to Marcel. Marcel works nearby, at the factory. Before the war he made airplane engines, now he makes churns. He's a skilled worker, makes good money. Yes. He makes enough, I've no complaints. He's a working man. We had three children: two died, the third's a working man as well, married. He's got a four-year-old son. Me, I'm wife to Marcel. No special skills. I keep a good house. Marcel's pals, when they stop by of an evening, it's 'Where's Marcel?' 'He's at the union hall,' I say. So then they say, 'I'll come back tomorrow. ... How's it going?' 'Fine.' They leave. Why would they stay? I got nothing to say to them. I'm wife to Marcel – besides that I don't see what. Our son comes by on Sundays: 'Hello M'ma.' Then he talks with his father. I fix the food. My daughter-in-law, she talks with them, and sure she helps me but we haven't much to say to each other. I've never had much to say.

ALBERT OF THE CAPITALS
(ROUGH DRAFT)

AFTER A WHILE, they'd all had enough of interrogating the prisoners. At first everyone was interrogating, then only a few, then Albert and Jean. Then even Albert and Jean had gotten fed up. Théodora had questioned the first prisoner, brought in at five one afternoon. An owner of the bistro he frequented had come by: 'There's a traitor in my place, an informer – you should come get him.' Three men had gone to pick him up. He was the first one they'd had at the center, a guy of about fifty. Everyone had come to see him, so they'd put him in the bar. They'd left him in the center of the room for an hour. They just couldn't believe it: a squealer – they'd gotten their hands on one. The men surrounded him, went up to him, stared at him, sniffed him. Traitor. Bastard. Pig. A little fifty-year-old fellow. He had a squint, wore glasses, a wing collar, a tie. The men went right up to his face and yelled 'Traitor!' The informer warded off blows, he was scared, sweating, saying no monsieur, yes monsieur, no madame. He had a refined voice; you might have taken him for a retired municipal employee, for example. 'I assure you, monsieur, you are making a mistake.' Théodora was furious, eager to deal with him right away, but Albert had said they should wait for dinner, that they'd 'take care of him' afterward. Everyone agreed that Théodora would be the one to handle him. Théodora's husband had been arrested by the Gestapo; she didn't know whether he was still alive, she was heartsick over it – she was the one who should deal with the Gestapo agent. The men were disappointed, but it was only fair. They had gone off to eat. Théodora hadn't eaten much. Then, after dinner, she had asked for two men. They were all busy eating in the dining hall up on the seventh floor. 'Who's coming with me?' Twenty

had stood up, their mouths full, and gathered around Théodora. They all had good reasons, but Théodora had picked two
who'd been through Montluc, that was only fair, been
through Montluc {Prison, near Lyon,} and been savagely
beaten. No objections. The two young men had gone to fetch
a couple of hurricane lamps; Théodora, a pencil and some
paper to take notes on the interrogation. She'd heard that
records were kept during questioning. There wasn't any electricity. Théodora had gone down the main stairs of the newspaper building with the two men. Outside, you could hear
machine guns over by the Louvre. It was still going on. In the
distance, the rumbling of tanks. Now and then, artillery. Paris
was free – almost. Théodora wasn't particularly vicious, she
was heartsick.

One of the young men had gone to get the informer, then
the four of them had gone into a room, empty except for a
table and two chairs, and closed the door. 'Well?' 'Go ahead,
get his clothes off,' {she said.} 'Get undressed!' the young guys
had told him. 'And hurry it up.' They'd been through the same
thing in Montluc: first their clothes had come off and in the
end they'd lost three toenails, gritting their teeth. One of them
was a redhead, thirty, a garage mechanic; the other an unskilled worker, twenty-five – good guys, courageous. While
the fellow was undressing, Théodora wondered what she was
doing; she wouldn't have known how to put it, but it was
necessary. For four years, she'd been hearing, 'When we catch
hold of one, will he ever get it!' This was one of them. The
informer had first removed his jacket. He was taking off his
trousers. Suspecting what was coming, he was undressing
slowly. He'd placed his jacket on a chair. 'Speed it up,' said
one of the men. Maybe they were going to kill him. His tie;
he was taking it off. She reminded herself: 150,000 shot. His
collar; the shirt was dirty. In the rue des Saussaies there were
a hundred women waiting to give their husbands or sons pack-
ages, which had been stopped since the {Allied} landing.

Théodora had waited two days running, twenty-two hours in line so he could have a package weighing a little over two pounds. The man's shirt was dirty, beneath his white collar; he was a snitch. *He* didn't have to line up on the rue des Saussaies. 'You going to hurry it up or not?' said Théodora. She had stood up suddenly. The men looked at her; then, 'You were told to get a move on, you bastard!' They hustled him out of his underpants. He didn't wait anywhere, he didn't line up on the rue des Saussaies: he would show a card, then go inside, then knock, then say he had the description, the address, the hours. They'd give him an envelope. Now he was removing his shoes. All his clothes were on the chair; he was trembling. In the line, there was a young pregnant woman in mourning: he'd been executed, and she was standing in line because she had received a notice – she'd been in line for twenty-two hours to come get his bundle of things and the baby was due in two weeks. Now it's the socks. She wanted his things, she wanted to see them again, she'd read his last letter out loud, she read and reread that letter: 'Tell our child I was brave,' and she wept aloud – she must have been twenty years old and she kept saying, 'It's not possible, it's not possible.' All the women were crying. Someone had offered her a folding stool but she didn't want anything, she couldn't bear it except standing up. Now he's completely naked: he has taken off his glasses and placed them on top of his clothes. The young men await Théodora's orders. He's completely naked: he has an old penis, shrunken testicles, no waist, he's fat, he's dirty. He's fat.

'Hey, you sure haven't gone hungry for four years, have you?'

'How much a head did they pay you?' says Théodora.

He whimpers.

'I'm just a poor innocent guy, I keep telling you.'

'What we want is for you to tell us the truth. You're denying everything?'

'But I told you . . .'

Now the room is full. The women up front. The men in back. It bothers Théodora, it's as if she were doing something erotic.

And yet she can't ask them to go away, there'd be no reason. She simply stays behind the hurricane lamp, where you can see only her short, dark hair – but not her face.

'Go ahead,' says Théodora.

The first blow. It sounds strangely loud. The second blow. The old man tries to deflect it. 'Ow! Ow!' he wails. You can see him clearly in the lamplight. The young guys are hitting hard. The others, in back, say nothing. The men are punching him in the chest, slowly but hard. Then they stop: 'D'you get it now?' He rubs his chest; without his glasses, he can't see where the blows are coming from.

'How'd you get into Gestapo headquarters?'

'Uh . . . like everyone else. . . .'

He's rubbing his chest with both palms. He cries as he speaks. He has the voice of someone crying.

He said 'like everyone else.' Rue des Saussaies, handcuffed prisoners and Gestapo agents went inside. Other people never, ever, got inside. Théodora had applied for permission to send a package; three weeks later they'd told her she had to come get a number, which she'd been given at the concierge's lodge at the entrance to the Gestapo building. Then she'd waited twenty-two hours and had shown a special paper they'd torn up at the exit. He said 'like everyone else' because he's lying, plus he hopes that Théodora thinks people could easily get inside there. He's lying. Big purple bruises are coming out on his chest. He's lying.

'You said, "like everyone else"? Everyone went inside the Gestapo building?'

There's muttering from those in the back: 'Traitor, traitor, traitor, he's scared.'

'Uh, yes, you had to show your identity card.'

'You're sure that was enough?'

'Well, yes.'

A thin trickle of blood appears on his chest. He's still lying.

They had heard about informers. And the Germans. The tortures, too. Everything. Enemies. They'd shot her husband because he was a Communist, he was twenty-five years old. {This guy} turned in Communists, because he earned 500 francs a head for them. He's a liar. His tie, his shoes, he bought them with those 500 francs they paid him for each Communist head. 'Thank you, monsieur.' In the background: 'Traitor, pig, sonofabitch, bastard, scum.' Yes. Yes. Them, they didn't squeal: they weren't perfect, but they weren't snitches. The two young men – they never talked in Montluc.

'Go ahead, guys!'

Strange, thinks Théodora: they don't hit unless I tell them to, even though I have no more authority than they do. Maybe it's because they think I know how to interrogate while they don't, but they've got fists, they clenched them in Montluc but they didn't talk, and a few days ago – factory workers, in normal life – they were throwing bottles of gasoline into German tanks.

'Go to it!'

They take pleasure in it. It pleases me to give them pleasure. They're thinking of their comrades. Up against a wall: there's a man standing against a wall and in front of the man, Germans. Gunfire. The man clutches at his heart, shouts Long live France, Long live the Communist Party, falls facedown in the mud. That earned him 500 francs he spent on cigarettes and new shoes. To think that they might well not have found him, that he would have gone free. ... The young men stop and look at Théodora.

'So what color was your identity card?'

The two guys laugh. They know. Théodora's clever, and they like that. They've been hitting hard. His eye may have burst: blood's running down his face. He's weeping, there's bloody mucus coming from his nose and he's moaning 'Oh, oh, oh, oh, ow, ow, ow . . .' He runs his palms over his chest, the many places where the skin has split open, bleeding. His hands are white. To do what he did, he never had to lift a finger. Now, whether he lives or wriggles out of it doesn't matter. There's blood on the floor.

'We asked you the color of your identity card, you hear me – you old bastard!'

They're ruthless, and they stick their faces right up to his. Behind them a woman says, 'Maybe that's enough now . . .' The other women back her up. The two guys stop and try to see the women who spoke up from behind the hurricane lamp. Théodora has turned around. 'Enough?' says one of the young men. 'What?' says the other. 'For us, was it enough?' 'That's no reason,' says a woman.

'For the last time, what color was the identity card you used to show?'

'Answer!'

'Answer! You're going to answer!'

In the background, another woman, her voice indignant: 'It's starting up again. . . . Me, I'm leaving. . . .' Théodora turns around.

'Any women who can't stomach this don't have to stay, we don't need them – if they fuck off that suits us fine. Go ahead, guys!'

'Ow!'

But the women stay, and whisper things, all against Théodora. Only Théodora's hair is visible and – when she's asking questions – her white forehead and her eyes, half-closed, as if blind. The men say nothing, except for one: 'Shut up!' But the women stay.

'So, quick, what color?'

The two guys laugh. They know. They start punching again, on places they've hit before. The informer tries to fend them off. He's covered in blood. He moans.

'Well, like all the other identity cards. . . .'

'Go ahead, guys.'

They're hitting very hard. They're tireless. A man up against a wall falls clutching at his heart: he dies because he believes in something that is true for all men. The 500 francs went to buy little treats for himself. Those shooting at the man believe in their duty. Him, with his 500 francs, he bought himself petty solitary luxuries. He wasn't anti-Communist, he was earning himself some pin money. He's still lying. A man can lie like nobody's business. With the 500 francs he picked himself out a tie.

Théodora stretches her legs. There's no doubt, none at all: there's no choice.

'Go for it, guys, let him have it, and hard!'

And they let him have it, and how. In the background: 'Traitor, scum, pig.' The women leave. He groans loudly, he pleads: 'I'm begging you, please – I'm not a traitor!' But he's still afraid of dying, because he's not yet telling the truth.

Still not enough. Théodora stands up. There is a man, a man up against a wall, against a wall – a man she knows, who hasn't talked, forever, against that wall, God damn it all to hell, that man against that wall. God damn it. 'Don't make us laugh, you and your Resistance. . . .' Those who say that – if they were here, if they were to laugh, on top of everything else. . . . A man alone against a brick wall; beyond that wall, nothing. She can't see anymore, Théodora. She hears the 'Marseillaise' of those condemned to death, the 'Internationale' yelled out in police vans; the bourgeoisie peer from behind their closed shutters: 'They're terrorists. . . .'

'Get on with it, guys, get going!'

In the gleam of the hurricane lamp, he struggles. Every punch sounds clearly in the quiet room. With each blow he cries 'Ohhhhh!' in long wails. The women have left. Silent behind the hurricane lamp, the men say nothing when the blows land. It's when they hear his voice that the insults well up in the background, through clenched teeth, with clenched fists, single words, solemn words. It's when he speaks that the insults come because he's still lying, he still has the strength, he hasn't yet reached the point where the lies stop. Théodora watches the fists land, she hears the thudding blows and thinks that in a man's body there are protective layers that are hard to split open. When the insults rise behind her, it does her good, encourages her, she really appreciates those insults. In the silence, only once did she ask herself why the women left; impossible to understand. As for her, she can't feel her heart. When they punch his belly, he shrieks and grabs it with both hands and one of the guys takes advantage of the opening to kick him in the balls. He's bleeding a lot, especially his face. He's not like other men. You can kill him. For other men he was a lost man, informing on men. He betrayed men for 500 francs each, without bothering to find out why their enemies were paying him. A pig, now that's more valuable, you can eat it. And him, if they kill him, he'll just be something in their way.

'Enough!' says Théodora.

Her voice seems shrill after the muffled booming of the punches. She stands up and approaches the informer. The men in the back are letting her see it through, they trust her; no one's giving her any advice, but she's not making any 'mistakes,' and each time she feels warmed by the fraternal litany of insults. It's quiet in back; the two young men are watching Théodora closely. Everyone's waiting.

'One last time: we want to know what color your card was,' says Théodora. 'One last time . . .'

The man looks at her. She's quite close to him; he's not tall, she's about his size. She's slender, she's young and cruel. And she has said: 'One last time.'

'What is it you want me to say. . . .'

He's sniveling. Not so long ago, she sniveled too. But that's because she's a woman. The men standing against walls don't snivel. The informer is giving off a peculiar odor, nauseating and sweetish: the smell of blood.

'We want you to tell us what color identity card got you inside the Gestapo building.'

'I don't know. . . . Don't know . . . I keep telling you I'm innocent. . . .'

That does it: the insults flare up. Traitor. Scum. Bastard. Pig. Sonofabitch. Théodora sits down again. She says nothing more. A brief pause. The insults keep coming, one by one.

For the first time, a guy in the back says: 'Just finish him off. . . .' The informer has looked up. Silence. A pause. The informer is afraid. He speaks in a high, whimpering voice, one you feel he wishes could melt stones.

'If I knew what you wanted of me . . .'

The two young men are sweating; they wipe their brows with bloody fists, look at Théodora, and wait. Théodora seems tired and distracted.

'It's not enough yet,' she says suddenly.

The two guys turn toward the informer, fists cocked.

'No,' says Théodora.

She leaps up and shouts.

'Let's go, guys, together with me.'

An avalanche of fists. A final avalanche. Silence once more in the background.

'Was your card red you bastard?'

'Ohhh! Oh – you're hurting me!'

'Good,' [yell] the men. 'Just what we want: imagine that!'

Blood is dripping.

'Ohhh . . .'

'Red? Speak up! Red?'

He opens an eye. He's going to understand.

'Red?'

Théodora is screaming. The two guys *know in advance*. The informer tries to think about his answer.

'Red?'

Still no answer.

'Go at it harder, harder, don't hold back.'

'Red? Red? Red?'

'No . . .' moans the informer.

Laughter. The young men are laughing.

'Me – I waited twenty-two hours with a yellow identity card. Twenty-two hours, you bastard! Twenty-two hours. How do you explain that? It was yellow. And yet, you said you had the same one. Identity cards are normally yellow!'

Théodora is shouting. In the background voices swell, warm and full.

'Twenty-two hours! We waited twenty-two hours with a yellow card. Maybe yours was yellow?'

The informer is moaning constantly, constantly trying, now, to huddle in a corner. The two guys pull him out.

'Yellow?'

They pull him from the corner and then throw him back there. The chair with his clothes tips over, spilling them on the floor.

'Yellow?'

He opens and closes his mouth. He'd like to answer. He's terrified. He groans. He'd like to say something. For the first time, he's beside himself.

'Yellow?'

Théodora is still on her feet. They know she won't sit down again until he has confessed.

'Noooo . . . not yellow!' cries the informer.

The men keep at it. He's choking. Now he understands. They won't let up anymore. Théodora keeps at it.

'Well? What color?'

She's still shouting. Now the blows and the questions are coming with the same dizzying rhythm.

'What color?'

Maybe he has chosen to die, she thinks. But, no: he's

incapable of choosing to die – in the name of what? He'll say it.

'What color?'

He's silent. He pretends not to hear. He's acting like a guy overwhelmed by pain. Théodora knows this as surely as if she were inside him.

'Quick, what color?'

How will all this end up? wonders Théodora. If he doesn't say it, we won't even be able to kill him. We'll have failed completely.

'Still harder!' says Théodora.

They're hurling him back and forth like a ball, now punching, now kicking. They're streaming with sweat.

Théodora advances on the informer.

'Enough!'

She keeps coming, compact, unfathomable. The informer recoils. He has seen her. Again, silence.

'If you say it, we leave you the fuck alone. If you don't say it, we polish you off. Go ahead, guys. Go ahead.'

The informer doesn't know which way to turn. He's going to talk. He attempts to raise his head, like a drowning man tries to breathe. He's going to talk. This is it. He'd like to say something. The blows are what's keeping him from speaking. But if the blows stop, he won't talk. Everyone waits in suspense for this birth, this deliverance. But he still doesn't talk.

'I'm going to tell you,' says Théodora. '*I'm* going to tell you the color of the card you showed to get inside.'

The informer starts yelling. He's still completely conscious. The blows are leaving him completely conscious.

'Green!' yells the informer.

The guys stop. The informer looks at Théodora. He isn't moaning anymore. He's consumed by curiosity. He wonders how he talked.

'Yes,' says Théodora.

Silence. Théodora takes a cigarette and lights it. Then, in a tired voice: 'Get dressed.'

She stands up. Before leaving, she says simply, evenly, 'The cards carried by the SD agents, the German Secret Police, were green. There's no longer any doubt.'

While he gets dressed, both young men insult him some more.

'We'll pick it up again tomorrow?' says one.

'Have to know whom he betrayed,' says the other.

'We'll see,' says Théodora.

She leaves. All the men leave with her. They go to the bar.

All the women have taken refuge there. They're sitting in arm-chairs, some on {wooden} chairs.

'He confessed,' says Théodora.

No one replies. Théodora understands. They don't give a damn that he confessed. There's a man with them, and he doesn't give a damn about the confession either. They're simply against Théodora, that's all. Théodora sits down and looks at them with curiosity. She herself has no idea yet what she has just done. Perhaps she has done something evil. She suspects as much: she had a man tortured. That's what it's called. The Germans tortured. She did too. While she was in that room, what were they doing in here? What? Théodora smiles, with immense disdain: they were ripping her to shreds, they must have been saying vile things about her and enjoying every second, thinking more about her than about the informer. These women know better than Théodora what has just happened to her.

'You disgust me,' says Théodora.

A woman blanches with rage and shouts, 'Oh! And just what about you, you've no idea . . .'

She stops, choking with indignation. Albert goes over to the woman.

'Are you going to fucking leave her alone or what?'

Jean looks at her and shrugs. The woman says nothing. Albert comes over to Théodora and Jean. He seems quite upset by what has just happened.

'Let's have a drink,' says Albert. 'You'll have some wine with us, my dear Théodora.'

Théodora smiles. Jean and Albert put their arms around her. The three of them are at the counter. Jean and Albert, they're the head men at the center. Behind her back, the women keep quiet. The livid silence of hatred.

'Then you're going to go sleep like a good little girl,' says Jean.

'Yes,' says Théodora. It's late.

It's an effort for her to speak. She feels like crying. Albert hands her a glass of wine.

'What a bastard he was . . .' says Théodora uncertainly, looking up at Jean and Albert.

'Yes,' says Albert, 'a real bastard – here, drink up.'

'Drink, Théodora my dear,' says Jean.

Théodora drinks. She doesn't know what's happening to her. Why this sense of relief. . . . She has trouble swallowing. She feels like crying. The men, they drink. They talk about the informer and say he must be liquidated.

Once again, the women walk away, leaving the bar without saying good night.

'I disgust them,' says Théodora.

Albert looks at her and smiles.

'It's nothing, they're just a little jealous – come on, time for bed. . . .'

'Jealous?' says Théodora. 'Of what?'

'Yes,' says Jean. 'It doesn't matter if you don't understand.'

He laughs. Albert laughs. They leave, with their arms wrapped around Théodora. Then Théodora remembers that neither of them had shouted abuse at the informer, not even once.

*   *   *

There was a big blonde named Marie, who was loyal and good hearted. The other women were nice too, even the one named Colette, who'd never thought much about the war. And the young man who was twenty and who'd thought too much about the war – well, he was kind and courageous too. They all hated Théodora at this moment.

One time, Théodora asked herself how she could stand the sight and smell of that blood. I'm evil, I always suspected that. Finally, she was releasing all her cruelty. As a little girl she'd been hit many times without ever being able to hit back; she used to dream she was hitting her elder brother.

Triteness – the guys getting carried away at the last minute – one of them is vicious (Tessier); differentiate more between the two young men – light, hurricane lamp – interrogative point of departure: I used to buy things from the Germans – not objective enough [about] Théodora.

They'd been put in a room on the sixth floor, in what had been the cashier's office, overlooking a courtyard. The door was sheathed in metal. The window, barred. Only a small wicket communicated with the outside. Depending on the seriousness of each case, as people were brought in they were put in either the hall or the safe-room. In the end there were eleven, including four militiamen, an elderly Russian couple, and three other couples no one knew much about, except that they were collaborators.

THE RUE DE LA GAIETÉ

THE RUE DE LA GAIETÉ on Sunday afternoon. People are coming down the street with the sunshine at their backs. All shops open: direct communication between the crowd and what's in the shops. The girls' heavy legs. Boys' jackets nipped-in at the waist. And the crowd keeps coming. In the bus I took, there was a ticket collector who was inaugurating the new route: 'Get in messieurs, get in madame, seats for everyone. Colombier! Rennes! Montparnasse, everyone gets out.' He was very happy. Of course, he'd just finished four years in the métro and he doesn't work for the métro, this guy, he's with the TCRP. Because of that blasted war – no more gas, bus routes cancelled. They'd assigned him to the métro; it wasn't his profession. Fed up with the métro, he was – got to have a feel for it to last long there. Everyone on the bus was really happy for him. Except for two Americans who hadn't a clue.

THE SEA WALL
(ROUGH DRAFT)

'SHIT!' SAID PAUL. 'He won't go anymore.'

Paul and Marie looked at the horse. It was an old, gray, tubercular horse he'd bought for a hundred francs. The animal lowered its head; its flanks were so thin you'd have thought it had swallowed a wicker cage that made it look like a horse.

They'd been invited to this dance on account of her. Because the son of the flour mill owner was in love with her. Ordinarily, given their social standing, they would not have attended. It was a huge society ball. All the important figures in the city – public, administrative, and commercial – were present. The mayor was there. The man giving the ball, Monsieur Sales, owned all the flour mills in the area, and he had become impressively rich.

{The animal} lowered its head sadly and half closed its eyes. Its breathing was shallow and wheezy. This was really the end.

'Shit,' said the boy.

The mother came to see the horse and looked at it thoughtfully. She was barefoot in the sand, wearing a large hat that covered her ears and came down to her eyebrows. Her dress was of garnet red cotton, worn thin at the bust; she still had large breasts, she'd had lots of children. She began to scold her son.

'I told you not to buy him: a hundred francs for a half-dead horse – you always do the same stupid things, you're useless, you good-for-nothing.'

'Shit,' said the boy. 'Shit and shit, there's still the carriage, I don't give a damn, I'm through with the whole thing, it's just not worth it. First off I'm getting the hell out of here – you do what you want.'

The girl arrived next and contemplated the horse. She was seventeen. She had reddish-blond braids hanging down to her waist and was barefoot as well on the burning sand. She wore black pants reaching below her knees, and a blue blouse. She too had a large hat that completely framed her face. Her blue eyes made two very pale, bright spots among her freckles.

'You'd be right to get the hell out,' said the girl.

It was in the evening, after dinner. It had been a hot day. The man was resting on a chaise longue.

EXPECTING

IT'S BETWEEN THE hip and the ribs, in the place called the flank, that's where it turned up. In that hidden, quite tender place, that covers neither bones nor muscles, but delicate organs. A flower has sprung up there. Which is killing me.

THE SEA WALL
(ROUGH DRAFT)

ONE DAY, coming back from Ramé, the mother had said to Suzanne, 'I met a beggar woman who tried to give me her little daughter. If you want her, tell Joseph to go fetch her.'

1) The bath. 2) The plain. 3) Encounter with Monsieur Jo. 4) Scene with Monsieur Jo. 5) Joseph.

'The reason why you don't go swimming is because you're badly put together,' said Suzanne. 'Joseph is right when he says . . .'

Monsieur Jo stopped knocking. Now Suzanne was rinsing herself.

Suzanne continued: 'When Joseph says that . . .'

Suzanne fell silent. She knew that Monsieur Jo was behind the door. She was waiting for him to ask her what Joseph had said. When he didn't ask, Suzanne began softly to sing. A minute later, Monsieur Jo started knocking on the door again.

'One second, I beg you, Suzanne – one second.'

'What Joseph said about you doesn't interest you?'

'I don't give a damn,' said Monsieur Jo. 'I don't care a damn about Joseph, open up. . . .'

Suzanne stiffened. She went up close to the door.

'Joseph says you look like a fetus,' said Suzanne.

The knocking stopped. Suzanne went back to rinsing herself. She was sure that at that moment Monsieur Jo was feeling the insult and this brought her violent satisfaction, a kind of exultant revenge.

'I believe I have never known anyone as wicked as you,' says Monsieur Jo.

Suzanne laughs. Bright laughter mingling with the sound of water comes from the bathroom.

'I can't even hear you laughing,' says Monsieur Jo. 'You've put me in such a state. . . . Let me, for one second . . . It's not bad to show oneself naked, I won't touch you.'

'Go see if they're still over on the other side,' says Suzanne.

'Right away,' says Monsieur Jo.

Monsieur Jo crosses the dining room and lights a cigarette. Then he plants himself in the doorway with a relaxed air. The mother and Joseph are watching two workmen repair the bridge. The scorching white sun is going down; it's five in the afternoon. The shadows are lengthening. Many peasants in colorful *pagnes* are crossing the plain, heading for the *rac.*[1] Monsieur Jo returns.

'They're still out there – quick, Suzanne, quick.'

Suzanne cracks open the door to show Monsieur Jo her white body. Monsieur Jo looks at this body and moves toward it, staring. Suzanne closes the door. Monsieur Jo remains behind it. Suzanne towels herself off and gets dressed.

'Now go into the sitting room.'

'Yes,' says Monsieur Jo.

Suzanne opens the door and puts on makeup. Then she does her hair and pins her braids up around her head.

She goes to find Monsieur Jo, who is smoking and looking at the floor.

'How am I, naked?' asks Suzanne.

'You're beautiful,' says Monsieur Jo. His voice is low and sad.

Suzanne sits down, looks off into the distance. They're still working on the bridge. The sun is already slipping down and part of the mountain is in shadow. They hear children shouting in the *rac.*

'You're beautiful and desirable,' says Monsieur Jo.

'I'm only fifteen years old,' says Suzanne. 'I'm going to become even more beautiful.'

'Yes,' says Monsieur Jo.

Suzanne smiles. She has forgotten Monsieur Jo.

The mother and Joseph arrive, come up the stairs. Joseph wipes his forehead with a handkerchief. The mother takes off her straw hat. She has a red line across her forehead, left by the hat.

'This heat . . .' says Joseph. 'You're a sight,' he says to Suzanne. 'You don't know how to use makeup, you look like a tart.'

'She looks like what she is,' says the mother.

With a disgusted expression, Joseph goes into his room.

'Just what have you been up to, the both of you?' says the mother. 'If I ever see anything I shouldn't, I'll make you marry her within the week.'

'Madame, I respect your daughter too much,' says Monsieur Jo.

He stands up, adopting an offended air.

'Of course,' says the mother. 'The old story: dogs, that's what you are – wasn't always an old woman, you know.'

'We didn't do anything,' says Suzanne. 'Mama I swear we didn't do a thing, we didn't even touch each other,' she says.

'Shut up, good-for-nothing, dirty good-for-nothing.'

The mother collapses into an armchair.

'What a life!' says the mother, 'and there's never any rest. . . .'

'No one's forcing you,' says Suzanne.

The mother puts her feet up on an easy chair.

In the straw hut, the corporal's wife was grilling fish, and her daughter was singing.[2] And when night had fallen, in one of the villages bordering the plain the sound of the tam-tam was heard, rising from the plain. Indeed almost every evening, the tiger came down to the farmyards and the villages were wreathed in the smoke of great fires of green wood, and when a tiger was announced, the tam-tam called out and from all the neighboring villages men came toward the one under threat, armed with clubs.

Joseph, still lying on his couch, heard the call of the tam-tam. He tossed away his cigarette and sat up, listening to where it might be coming from. The mother, too, had stopped moving around, and looked out the open window at the black screen of the forest. Joseph would hold out when that tam-tam was silent, but when it called he could never resist.

'I'm going there tonight,' declared Joseph.

The mother went over to Joseph. It would start all over again.

'You're not going,' she said. 'I'm the one who's telling you: you're not going.'

'Shit,' said Joseph. 'We'll see about that. I'm going.'

'Take me along,' said Suzanne.

The mother let out her usual cries.

'If I have a seizure it will be your fault — three times this week ... If I die you can say you killed me.'

'Take me along,' said Suzanne.

'Shit,' said Joseph. 'I don't take women along. During the day – all right; at night – no, and you, if you holler, I'm leaving immediately.'

He stood up, went over to the corporal, and asked him to go get the trackers, then shut himself up in his room to get his Mauser ready. The mother was still grumbling, but she'd begun preparing her dinner. The battle was already lost; she was carrying on for the sake of appearances. Suzanne stayed out on the veranda. The evenings when Joseph went hunting were unlike all others, because everyone went to bed late.

The mother did not sleep on those nights. She would follow all the sounds of the forest and get up to track the gleam of the acetylene lamp in the darkness. Every evening Suzanne hoped that Joseph would go hunting, and at the same time she hoped he wouldn't kill anything.

'Dinner's ready!' shouted the mother.

They were having wading birds again. The corporal's wife brought up a few fish and some rice.

'You'll have to go down to the sea,' said the mother. 'They're nourishing, waders.'

She seemed flushed and tired in the lamplight. Her pills were starting to take effect. The mother yawned and groaned.

'Another sleepless night, with me so tired.'

'It's the change of life, come on Mama, don't worry, I'll be back early,' said Joseph kindly.

'It's not because of me,' said the mother. 'It's you I'm always afraid for.'

She rose to fetch a can of salted butter and one of Nestlé milk. Suzanne poured a great glassful of Nestlé milk over her rice. The mother made herself some bread and butter and dunked the slice in coffee. Joseph ate the fowl, its fine flesh dark and rare.

'It stinks of fish,' said Joseph, 'but it is nourishing.'

'That's what's important,' said the mother. 'You'll be careful, Joseph, you promise me?'

'Don't you worry, Mama, I'll be careful.'

'So once again we won't be going to Ramé this evening,' said Suzanne.

'We'll go tomorrow,' said Joseph, 'and well shit, you won't be finding any husband in Ramé, they're all married over there, except for young Agosti.'

'I'll never give her to the Agosti boy, that lout,' said the mother.

'In the meantime,' said Suzanne, 'there's no point in looking here.'

'It won't be easy,' said Joseph. 'We'd need money. Some do get married without money but they have to be awfully pretty, and even then it's a long shot.'

'Meanwhile,' said Suzanne, 'what I was saying about Ramé wasn't just for that – there are things going on in Ramé, there's electricity in the canteen and a fantastic phonograph.'

'You're a whore who's missed her calling,' said Joseph. 'Stop your goddamn nagging about Ramé.'

'Especially since it's not a place for young ladies,' said the mother.

The mother set food down before her children: the bread the bus brought every day and her inexhaustible reserves of Swiss and American canned goods.

The next day, as promised, Joseph announced that they were going to Ramé. The mother began by shouting, as usual, but she couldn't resist what her children wanted. On days when they went to Ramé, the mother put her hair up and wore shoes. Suzanne would wear a dress, she wound her braids around her head, and she put on lipstick. Joseph dressed up too. It was mail day. Going to Ramé meant going for a beer at the outpost canteen. Joseph asked the corporal to wash the car. It was an old {Citroën} B-12 and its battery was shot, so Joseph drove it with his acetylene lamp on his forehead; when there was a full moon, he drove without any light. The B-12's exhaust awakened all the village dogs along the way and set them barking. It took a good hour and a half to cover the thirty-seven miles from the bungalow to Ramé.

Joseph pulled up in front of the canteen. A magnificent limousine was parked there. 'Shit,' said Joseph. And they went inside the bungalow. It was mail day; the packet boat was lighting up the sea in front of the canteen. Inside the bungalow serving as a canteen were naval officers and a few passengers. Off in a corner, sitting next to the proprietor of the canteen, young Agosti was drinking a Pernod. He was a Corsican, short and thin, with an unhealthy air; he spent all his evenings in Ramé smoking opium and drinking Pernod. He nodded at them and kept talking. The proprietor saw them and came over. He had arrived in Ramé twenty years before and never left. He was a huge apoplectic man who had taken a native wife and adopted a child from the plain who served the aperitifs and the contraband Pernod, and who fanned him when he took his siesta. The man was always sweating. He came and shook hands with the mother.

'How's business?' he asked the mother. 'And the children?'

'Not bad,' said the mother, 'not bad. Thank God for good health.'

'You have some fancy customers,' said Joseph. 'Shit, that limousine.'

'He's a big landowner from the North,' said the proprietor. 'They're a hell of a lot richer than we are.'

'You've no reason to complain, with the Pernod,' said the mother.

'That's what people think,' said the proprietor. 'It's a risky business. Now they're coming down every week, so it's a free-for-all. That's not a life.'

'Point out this rubber planter to us,' said the mother.

'The guy in the corner, next to Agosti.'

He was a half-caste. He had set his fedora down on the table. He was wearing a tussore suit and on his finger, a magnificent diamond.

'Shit, that diamond,' said Joseph, 'but otherwise he's a monkey.'

They considered the diamond, the silk suit. The face had been marked by smallpox; the rest of him was stunted and sickly. He was on his own, and he was looking at Suzanne with a complacent eye. The mother had noticed that he was looking at Suzanne.

'Smile,' said the mother. 'You always look as if you were at a funeral.'

Suzanne smiled at the planter from the North. The mother looked at her daughter and found her pretty in spite of her freckles. When the record player started up, the planter from the North came over to Suzanne and asked her to dance.

Standing, he cut a distinctly poor figure. Everyone was looking at his diamond, especially the people from the plain – the
mother and Joseph, the proprietor and young Agosti. That
diamond was worth more, by itself, than all the salt lands of
the plain put together.

'With your permission, madame?' he said to the mother.

The mother gave her permission. A post office official was
already dancing with the young wife of the Ramé customs
officer.

'May I be introduced to your charming mother?' said the
planter. 'Are you from this area?'

'Of course,' said Suzanne. 'Yes, we're from around here,
we have some rice fields on the plain. Is that your car outside?'

'It's one of my cars. After our dance, you will introduce me
to her as "Monsieur Jo."'

'It's a really lovely car,' said Suzanne.

'You like cars?' said Monsieur Jo.

'Very much,' said Suzanne. 'It's a limousine. There aren't
any of those around here.'

'Doesn't a pretty girl like you get bored out on the plain?'
said Monsieur Jo.

Suzanne did not reply. She was thinking about the car. She
was thinking that she, Suzanne, was dancing with the owner
of a car like that. In her right hand, she was holding the hand
wearing the diamond.

'What make is it?' said Suzanne.

'It's a Morris-Léon Bollée,' said Monsieur Jo. 'That's my
favorite make. If you'd like, we could take a drive. Don't
forget to introduce me to your charming mother.'

'Fine,' said Suzanne. 'How much does it cost, a Morris-
Léon Bollée?'

'It's a special model,' said Monsieur Jo, 'custom-built in
Paris. I paid 50,000 francs for it.'

Suzanne thought about the B-12, which had cost 4,000
francs. The mother was still paying it off. Suzanne would never

have believed that a car could cost so much money.

'If we had a car like that, we'd come to Ramé every evening,' said Suzanne. 'That would make a nice change for us.'

'Money can't buy happiness,' said Monsieur Jo dreamily.

Suzanne told herself she'd heard that somewhere before. The mother said it sometimes. She also said the opposite, it depended on her mood. Suzanne definitely thought that money . . . was happiness. So did Joseph.

'I would have liked to keep on dancing,' said Monsieur Jo.

He followed Suzanne over to the table where the mother and Joseph were sitting.

'Allow me to introduce Monsieur Jo to you,' said Suzanne.

The mother rose to say hello to Monsieur Jo. She smiled at him. Joseph stood up too, but without the smile.

'Sit here at our table,' said the mother. 'Have a drink with us.'

'Let me invite you,' said Monsieur Jo. He turned toward the proprietor. 'Some champagne, well chilled,' he called out. 'I haven't managed to taste decent champagne since I got back from Paris.'

He grinned broadly. Joseph gave him a shifty look.

'You've just returned from Paris?' said the mother.

'Yes, fresh off the boat,' said Monsieur Jo. He was clearly enjoying the effect this had on them.

'It's a Morris-Léon Bollée,' said Suzanne to Joseph.

Joseph seemed to wake up.

'What horsepower?'

'Twenty-four,' said Monsieur Jo casually.

'Shit,' said Joseph, 'twenty-four horsepower. Four gears, of course?'

'Yes, four,' said Monsieur Jo, 'and you can start it up in second. What kind of car do you have?'

'Shit,' said Joseph. He laughed. 'Ours, it's not worth talking about.'

'It's a good car,' said the mother. 'A good old car that has served us well, you shouldn't disparage it. For these roads it's just fine.'

Joseph put on his mean look.

'Shit,' he said. 'It's easy to tell you're not the one driving. What mileage does yours get?'

'Fifteen, sixteen miles to the gallon on the highway,' said Monsieur Jo, who was beginning to lose interest in this conversation. 'I believe Citroëns use less.'

Suzanne's eyes were shining. She was thrilled by the effect Monsieur Jo's replies were having on Joseph and the mother. Especially since the champagne was beginning to have an effect on the mother, Joseph, and Suzanne. Joseph laughed heartily.

'Ours, ours gets almost ten miles to the gallon. But there's a hole in the gas tank, so that explains it.'

Joseph's merriment was contagious. The mother turned red and shouted with laughter.

'Ha-ha! It's not just the gas tank,' said the mother. 'If it were just the gas tank.'

Suzanne began laughing helplessly. Joseph and the mother were shaking with laughter.

'The carburetor too,' said Suzanne.

'If it were just the carburetor and the gas tank,' said Joseph.

Monsieur Jo tried to laugh. He felt as if they'd forgotten him. The mother had a full-throated laugh that jiggled her breasts.

'If it were just that,' said Joseph, 'but here's the thing: us, we've got tires we stuff with, with – we drive on tires with holes in them.'

Each time, a fresh burst of laughter would shake all three of them. Monsieur Jo seemed delighted and embarrassed.

'Guess what we drive on in the tires,' said Suzanne.

'Guess,' said the mother. 'Oh! It's so good to laugh.'

The proprietor had brought over another bottle of champagne. Young Agosti, who could hear the conversation, was laughing uncontrollably, along with the proprietor. The mother, Joseph, and Suzanne were choking. Everyone was looking at them. It was hard to understand what they were saying.

'On bicycle tires,' said Monsieur Jo, pouring some champagne.

'Ha-ha!' said the mother. 'That's not it, not at all. . . .'

'On banana leaves,' said Suzanne.

'We stuff the tires with banana leaves. . . .'

'And leave it to us. . . .' said the mother. 'Leave it to – leave it to Joseph to come up with that.'

Monsieur Jo really began to laugh. Joseph had reached such a paroxysm of laughter that he was strangling. The three of them hardly ever got going, but when that happened, they could hardly ever stop themselves. Monsieur Jo had obviously given up on inviting Suzanne to dance. He was waiting for things to calm down.

'That's original,' said Monsieur Jo. 'That's the very limit, as they say in Paris.'

But no one was listening to him.

'Us, when we go off on a trip,' said Joseph, 'we tie the corporal to the mudguard and hand him a watering can.'

'Shut up, shut up,' said the mother. 'Ha-ha-ha! Oh, it's so good . . .'

'Then we wire the doors shut,' said Suzanne, 'because, because . . .'

'Because the door handles are gone.'

'We don't even remember them,' said the mother.

'Us? Don't need any door handles,' said Joseph. 'Completely useless.'

'Shut up, Joseph,' said the mother. 'Stop it, I can't breathe. . . .'

'It's a pleasure to run into people as cheerful as you are,' said Monsieur Jo.

They burst out laughing again.

'As cheerful as we are,' said the mother, pretending to be dumbfounded.

'He said we were cheerful,' said Suzanne. 'It's clear he has no idea, no idea.'

'If only he did,' said Joseph.

Joseph was off and running now.

'If it were just the carburetor, the gas tank, the tires,' said Joseph. 'If it were just that . . .'

The mother and Suzanne looked at Joseph. They didn't know what he would come up with. Even before he said it, laughter began welling up inside him.

'If it were just that, it would be nothing.'

'What? Joseph, say it, quick!'

'We had some dikes,' said Joseph, 'and the crabs poked holes in them for us.'

Suzanne and the mother screamed with laughter again.

'It's true,' said the mother. 'Even the crabs . . .'

'Even the crabs are against us,' said Suzanne.

'The story of our dikes,' said Joseph, 'it's priceless, definitely priceless. We were confident, then when the sea rose – they leaked like sieves.'

'Oh, it's true,' said the mother, 'even the crabs. Oh yes, even the crabs.'

Joseph wriggled his hand like a crab. They were still convulsed with laughter. With two fingers, Joseph imitated a crab walking toward Monsieur Jo.

'The crabs gobbled up our entire fortune,' said Suzanne.

'Oh, you're funny,' said Monsieur Jo. 'You're incredible.'

He was laughing, but he would rather have been dancing with Suzanne.

'The story of our dikes is incredible,' said Joseph. 'We'd thought of everything, but not of those crabs. Our dikes were in their way.'

The laughter had subsided a little.

'They're tiny little crabs,' said Suzanne. 'They're black,

rice-paddy color, they were just made for us – leave it to us. . . .'

The laughter began again.

'On that score, it's true: leave it to us.'

'These dikes were to hold back . . .' said Monsieur Jo.

'To hold back the sea,' said Suzanne. 'You should know that us, we bought some sea – it's an idea no one would ever have, right? It was my mother's idea.'

The mother became serious again.

'Shut up or you'll get goddamn slapped,' said the mother.

Monsieur Jo started in surprise. But Joseph jumped right in.

'We wound up in the soup, all right,' said Joseph. 'The story of our rice fields is falling-down funny, and there we are waiting like goddamn jerks for the sea to pull back, and we're rotting away. It was sea-soup on salty mud. When we bought it . . .'

Joseph lit a cigarette without offering one to Monsieur Jo. Monsieur Jo took out a pack of American cigarettes and offered them to the mother and Suzanne. The mother and Suzanne were listening, enthralled, to Joseph.

'When we bought it, we believed we'd be millionaires within the year,' said Joseph. 'It was a sure thing. We built a house, then we waited for everything to grow, then the sea rose, then everything was goddamn ruined, and now there we are waiting for the Messiah in the house, which isn't even finished.'

'It rains inside, and there aren't any railings,' said Suzanne.

The mother laughed again; she had forgotten she'd lashed out at Suzanne.

'Don't listen to them, Monsieur Jo,' she said. 'Maybe it doesn't have any railings, but it's a good house, I'd get a good price for it if I sold it – I'm sure I would get 30,000 francs.'

'You can say that all you like,' said Joseph. 'Who would buy that tumbledown place? Crazy people like us,' said Joseph.

Suzanne began to smile fiercely and gazed into the distance. 'It's true that we're crazy,' said Suzanne ecstatically. 'Completely crazy,' said Joseph.

NOTES

1. A *pagne* is a piece of native cotton cloth worn wrapped around the body as a dress, skirt, or loincloth.

   A word of Vietnamese origin, *rac* means a stretch or stream of water such as a canal, backwater, or river. Here it refers to the river where 'Paul' and his sister go swimming in an earlier sketch.

2. The corporal is a Malay laborer in *The Sea Wall*, where Marguerite Duras describes his wretched life with cold outrage. To build their roads through swamps and forests, the French authorities used chain gangs of 'convicts' who were often political prisoners and poor peasants, whose wives were used as prostitutes by the native overseers. 'The corporal said he had been flogged almost to death, but at least he had not starved'; when 'his' road is finished, he and his family become homeless beggars living on garbage until he finds work on the mother's plantation. His one hopeless ambition had been to be a bus conductor on the highway he'd helped build; instead, he gleefully ties himself to the family Citroën's mudguard with water for the leaky radiator, blinking in amazement to see flashing by 'the road that had claimed six years of his life.'

   In *Marguerite Duras*, Laure Adler says that even today, *The Sea Wall* is admired in Vietnam for the honesty with which its author described the injustices of the French colonial period, and her compassion for 'the children of the plain,' who died year after year of sunstroke, cholera, and worms, simply returning to the earth like 'the drowned little monkeys at the mouth of the *rac*.'

20TH CENTURY PRESS NOTEBOOK

INTRODUCTION

THE SECOND of the four *Wartime Notebooks* is called the *20th Century Press Notebook* because of handwritten notations on its cover. It is one of the 'two notebooks in the blue armoires at Neauphle-le-Château' mentioned by Marguerite Duras in the preamble to *The War*, and it was probably written between 1946 and 1948.

Of the forty-four lined pages of this small notebook with a sturdy cover of blue-gray paper, the first twelve are devoted to 'Théodora,' the only unfinished novel by Marguerite Duras. A fifth notebook entitled 'Théodora, novel,' has deliberately been omitted from the *Wartime Notebooks* in spite of its chronological proximity to the texts presented here. The rough drafts of this narrative, written in 1947, form in fact a completely separate entity, which includes not only this fifth notebook, but also about a hundred typed pages marked with several layers of successive corrections. In addition – which was not the case with the *Wartime Notebooks* – Marguerite Duras clearly stated her refusal to publish the text in that form, which she considered irremediably flawed. She did, however, publish an excerpt from it in *Les Nouvelles littéraires* in 1979, which she also included in the collection *Outside*, with this introduction: 'I thought I had burned the novel *Théodora*. I found it in the blue armoires, unfinished, unfinishable. *Les Nouvelles littéraires* asked me for an article on hotels; I gave them an excerpt from *Théodora*.'[1]

Even so, the figure of Théodora, a young woman characterized by her subversive taste for freedom, threads her way through some of the author's published work. Alissa, a central character in *Destroy, She Said*, may be considered an avatar of Théodora; above all, the character now baptized Théodora Kats in *Yann Andréa Steiner* establishes an explicit filiation with the *Wartime Notebooks*, borrowing the principal characteristics of the daughter of Madame Cats described in the *Hundred-Page Notebook*. This same girl, named Jeanine in *The War* and called 'the friend' of the narrator, was supposedly 'deported to Ravensbrück with Marie-Louise, the sister of Robert {Antelme}.'[2] In *Yann Andréa Steiner*, the dialogues between the title character and the narrator diverge from that initial assertion and endow Théodora with contradictory life stories, in the service of both remembrance and invention.

The subsequent pages of the notebook, numbered by Marguerite Duras, contain the beginning of what would become *The War*. The essential content of these pages filled with small, compact handwriting was retained in the published work – with the exception, chiefly, of the most virulent passages attacking the Catholic Church and the government of General de Gaulle. Marguerite Duras made annotations in the margins with a red felt-tip pen, which indicate that she reread the manuscript several decades later. This text, which she referred to at that time as a 'diary,' was composed after the events it relates, and the manuscript reveals that the dates therein were quite probably added after the first version was written. Pages 219–21, greatly abridged and reworked, form part of the second fragment of 'Did Not Die Deported' published anonymously in the {feminist} magazine *Sorcières* in 1976.

NOTES

1. *Outside* (Paris: Éditions P.O.L, 1984), p. 293.
2. La Douleur (Paris: Gallimard, coll. 'Folio,' 1993), p. 57.

THÉODORA

IT WAS SHORTLY after entering the hotel dining room that we noticed that Bernard was being punished. We could hardly help noticing that in particular, since the table closest to ours happened to be the one occupied by the governess and the children in her care. Théodora, who had arrived at the hotel three weeks after I did, was not as familiar as I was with the governess and her handling of the children. Under the circumstances, and even though I'd spoken to her about this, Théodora could not be as sensitive as I was to the punishments inflicted on Bernard by his governess. Still, we had all formed opinions of one another, and although we pretended to ignore one another completely, the willpower thus expended would alone have proved that we were far from indifferent. This situation stemmed from the fact (at least in the beginning) that we had not found any excuse to approach one another. After three weeks, this missing excuse had become something like one more excuse not to approach one another. There was no reason anymore. We had become for one another the living proof of our lack of ingenuity. But this complete lack of interaction had not prevented me from noticing, for example, the children's perfect manners. At least at the table, where their behavior was exemplary. And Bernard's punishments, which occurred four times a week without fail, intrigued me all the more in that his attitude at the table was perfect. So perfect that it seemed suspect to me, and not unrelated to the reason for the punishments the boy endured.

However, I did have an opinion. And the governess must have known that I had one. She did not know what it was. Nor did I know the reasons for the punishments. Still, we did have our opinions and we could not simply ignore them.

The punishments landed on Bernard with remarkable regularity. He endured them as an obligation, and appeared not to suffer from them at all. When Germaine, the maid, brought him his plate, he himself pushed it away. These punishments, the nature of which never varied, seemed pointless, since for three weeks their schedule had remained strictly the same, as did their form, as did the indifference with which the governess dispensed them and Bernard endured them.

Despite everything, though, it gave me pleasure to see, to confirm once more that Bernard, once more, was being punished. A pleasure no doubt minute but certain, to see that it was all continuing, for the longer it continued, the more likely it was to continue to continue. This kind of confirmation is always certain to bring pleasure, to bring a certain well-being, perhaps because it all usually ends badly. I was just about certain that Bernard was always punished for a single invariable reason, and I told myself that it must be worth it. The reason might have been, simply – it wasn't impossible – to see when the governess would stop punishing him, when she would begin to flag. That particular reason was not my least favorite one. In the same way I have hoped that a myriad of things would continue in my life; among others, I experienced the war while hoping it would not end. Likewise, I had an old cat that had lasted two years beyond the average age for cats, which pleased me; perhaps they'd forgotten about that one, he's not going to have an ordinary death, I said to myself, not him. I took extremely – indecently – good care of that cat, knowing perfectly well he would die someday, of course, but I knew it the way one knows those things, at the same time hoping that perhaps . . .

Although Bernard's punishments were of a different *order* and in reality depended only on his governess, whereas the end of the war and my old cat's death definitely depended on something else, these punishments of quite a different nature did bring me a bit of the same pleasure: not knowing how it would all end up. I am aware that I will be disappointed. Because in the same way that the war ended, and my old cat died, these punishments will end. And no matter how they end, I'll be disappointed. Only, while I'm waiting, what fun! (I mean, while waiting for Théodora.) Whenever I notice that Bernard isn't touching his chocolate cake or apple tart, I smile at him in a certain way, the least obvious way possible, for even though the governess increasingly avoids looking at me, and especially when Bernard is being punished, I'm afraid she might see me smile. She knows I'm smiling because Bernard smiles back at me, almost imperceptibly, no doubt, but not to she who knows him well. If he is smiling at me – since he's well brought up and she has taught him that a boy must not take this kind of initiative with grown-ups – if he is smiling at me, she knows it's because I'm smiling at him. But not obviously enough for her to therefore point out to me the impropriety of my conduct. The best thing, for her, is to pretend to ignore my secret complicity with Bernard. For if she were to look at me, then it could only be sternly. Well, apparently, she is loath to do so, a point in her favor, which makes me believe she is playing her role reluctantly, and in short, that she is not altogether certain about the usefulness of her punishment of Bernard.

And so, I had my way of encouraging Bernard and supporting him, of urging him to carry on, of showing him my admiration and my faith in the success of his experiment.

Our complicity came to an end this evening, in a way that neither of us could have foreseen.

When we arrived this evening in the dining room, Théodora and I, I noticed that the governess was looking with singular persistence at Madame Mort's back. The latter did, in fact, happen to be in the former's immediate field of vision, and to make things even easier, Madame Mort {Madame Death} had her back to her. This openly curious stare might have made me believe, early in my stay at the hotel, that the governess was wondering for whom Madame Mort was in mourning. Very quickly, however, I realized that she must have known that Madame Mort was in mourning for her husband and that the Monsieur Théo who was accompanying her was his brother, and I thought that if she knew this, it was because she must have learned it from Germaine, who had enough generosity of soul to understand that curiosity about someone at a neighboring table can become excessive, and even distressing, if it is prolonged, and that a chambermaid's duty is to satisfy such curiosity with the requisite discretion. Therefore, if she knew, like everyone in the hotel, that Madame Mort was plunged in the deepest mourning, and that in spite of what one might have hoped, she was not sharing Monsieur Théo's room – if she knew this and was nevertheless staring so obstinately at Madame Mort's back, it was because Bernard was once again being punished, and because once again she had noticed me noticing the apple tart untouched on the boy's plate.

I had spoken of all this, casually, to Théodora. This evening, my pleasure at seeing Bernard punished was increased by that of learning what Théodora would think about this, for knowing Théodora as I did, I knew she could not be indifferent to the hint of grandeur in Bernard's endeavor. I anticipated the sort of pleasure she would take in it, which could not fail to affect the nature of mine. Théodora's arrival had brought a certain period to a close; one might call it that of my pure complicity with Bernard. I enjoyed in advance watching Théodora pass through the same stages as I had. And from now on it would be my pleasure to see what attitude someone like Théodora would take toward Bernard's mysterious punishments; it would have to be different from mine, but in any case, could bring me nothing but pleasure. Because already for quite some time now, Théodora has been my joy. Whatever she does, whatever she does to me, none of her words, none of her actions, even if they are (to use the common phrase) directed against me, can bring me anything but joy.

Marie was not eating any of her apple tart, either. This development is so new that Marie emerges from the kind of background in which I have kept her until now. While Marie is not eating, the governess eats with particular attention, as does Odile. Théodora has not noticed anything yet, which makes it easier for me to observe the scene. Marie is not eating. She does not seem to know that anything is on her plate, even though the governess served her as usual; Marie now appears, however, to have forgotten completely about eating. In front of her, Bernard isn't eating either. For the first time I have not smiled at him, and he has not once looked at me. He is clearly jealous and feels forsaken because he has ceased to interest me.

Marie, motionless, stares at the dining-room chandelier. She is beautiful, and is at least eighteen years old. She must be a good fuck. Her eyes are green and shining, her dress is red, that's the situation. Between her red dress and her green eyes, there is a still, set harmony, like a question asked, which it falls to me to try answering. She's so beautiful, Marie, that I wonder if she isn't more beautiful than the scene in progress, and might not carry off the prize. Now Théodora has noticed that Marie interests me. I do not forget Théodora, ever. But Marie is beautiful for me. 'I, too, am beautiful; Théodora isn't the only one.' That's true: not noticing Marie before this evening is my responsibility, Théodora has nothing to do with that, although her presence is not unrelated to Marie's new attitude. Théodora exists. As usual, she doesn't speak to me. It's been so long since we've had anything left to say to each other, except once in a while, and always on the same subject. I'm busy with Marie's eyes; Théodora can only acquiesce, she always does, nothing can change that. Marie does not acquiesce.

'You're not eating, Marie?' says the governess in a loud, firm voice.

Marie shifts her green gaze from the chandelier to the face of her governess.

She says: 'No.'

The governess is a trifle pale, but not enough yet in my opinion.

'This is the first time you haven't eaten, Marie. Are you ill?'

Marie smiles at her governess. I am more or less sure that she is joining in Bernard's punishment only to please me, because she has noticed something: that it pleased me to see punishments refused. Her smile is assured.

'No, Mademoiselle, I feel fine.'

Now Théodora is following the scene as I am, as oblivious of me as I am of her. The governess becomes visibly angry. Her hands tremble. She looks over – but we, we are so used to being looked at that it doesn't make us lower our eyes.

'Marie, you will go upstairs to bed after dinner.'

Marie's smile broadens. Her eyes travel back up to the chandelier and Marie says: 'No.'

I experience Marie's refusal, like her beauty, as being addressed to me. It isn't certain that everyone heard that 'No.' It was said quite softly, and at the moment when I've already become unable to take my eyes off Marie's mouth – which means that I saw that 'No' more than I heard it. If Marie had pronounced it distinctly, it would not have the same character; I would not have wondered if she'd been addressing only me, and would not have taken that refusal as a provocation meant for me. If that word had been spoken for everyone, Marie would not have emerged from it full blown as she just has with breasts, mouth, eyes, hair, multiple and varied shapes melded into a single one, ripe for me. Perhaps, as she said that 'No,' she doubted her right to do so, but once it was said, she must have been as proud as if she had accomplished a great feat. A minute ago, I had no idea there was a place in me for her; I feel as refreshed as after a spring shower. She's young, that one, she still believes it's worth it to refuse, she's like a plant seeking the sun. She is ripe for me.

Shortly after Marie replied to her governess, Madame Mort

hurriedly left the dining room. No one noticed her leaving, not even Bernard who, as impassive as ever, is looking at Marie. If I noticed that departure, it was in the periphery of Marie's face. Without seeing Théodora, I sense her shadow beside me, the cold shadow of Théodora.

The governess is now disfigured by pallor.

'Marie, leave the table right now.'

Marie looks at her governess and keeps her eyes riveted on her. The governess returns Marie's gaze, but her lips are quivering.

'No,' says Marie.

Someone, it's Madame Bois, says to her little girl, 'Don't look.'

It's the thing to say, the most perfect thing to say. But in vain, since Madame Bois continues to look, the little girl continues to look. It had to be said, however.

The face of the governess is open, as torn open as genitals in a rape. It falls apart before our eyes, and while that defeat is accomplished and becomes this dazzling perfection, Marie becomes shrouded in mystery. She refuses without deigning to explain herself. She refuses everything. She would have refused not only to eat the apple tart and to obey her governess, but everything anyone could have proposed to her. Once she was set on refusing, she would refuse everything. Théodora knows this. When I look at her, I know she knows this: she's laughing a laugh that is silent and endless, endless, endless.

The governess leaves. She rises, pushes her chair gently back, and leaves, followed by Odile. Bernard appears to hesitate. It seems to me he's looking to Marie for guidance about what attitude to take. But Marie appears to have no idea that Bernard is still there. She has begun playing with her napkin ring.

Then Bernard stands up, a little disappointed not to have been the real stake in the game. Marie stares at her hands playing with the napkin ring; no one can see her eyes anymore. She is alone at the table.

'Eat the tart now,' says Théodora. 'If I were you, I'd go ahead and eat it.'

Marie starts. Who spoke?

'Why?' says Marie. 'I no longer want it, otherwise I'd have eaten it just now.'

'Please excuse me,' says Théodora.

Marie leaves the dining room. She's quite flushed, she seems about to cry. She walks out somewhat unsteadily.

'Go comfort her,' says Théodora.

I leave. I look for Marie. If I have something to tell her it's right away. In a little while it will be too late. I find her sitting on a chaise longue in the courtyard, crying.

'Forgive Théodora, she didn't mean to hurt you. Perhaps she did so inadvertently?'

'If I refused to eat the apple tart,' says Marie, 'it's because I had my reasons, it's nobody else's business. I don't understand how she can . . .'

'I assure you, she realizes that perfectly: she wanted to say only what she said and nothing else. . . .'

'I don't know who you are. Whether she realizes it or not has nothing to do with this, it can't possibly mean anything to me. We don't know one another. . . .'

'What shall I tell her you said?'

'I don't understand,' says Marie.

'I came to apologize for her, and at her request. I don't know what to tell her when I return to the dining room.'

'But really,' says Marie, 'you are most extraordinary – I don't know her.'

'You cannot understand . . .'

'It's true that she's so beautiful,' says Marie dreamily. 'Did she seem amused by all that, do you think?'

'Everything amuses her. . . . What shall I tell her you said?'

* * *

'She's funny, that kid,' said Théodora.

She wanted to go up to the room right away. She lay down on the bed. She stretched out. She seemed to be tired.

'I do realize how idiotic this all is,' I said.

'There's no end to it,' said Théodora. 'You think I hurt her feelings?'

Silence of our room. Silence of our life. The shutters are open. Night has fallen. Night. Night.

'Don't think about it,' I said. 'I do realize how idiotic this all is. . . . You must have hurt her in a kind of way, but it's not important. . . .'

I asked Théodora to get undressed and go to bed. She did not answer. Théodora's stillness, eyes closed, lying on the bed. Outside, pitch black. In the mirror my face is pale, pale.

'There's no end to it,' says Théodora again.

First part: dining room – garden – flowers [offered] by T. to M. – the hero and Marie.

THE WAR
(ROUGH DRAFT)

FACING THE FIREPLACE. The telephone beside me. On the right, the door to the sitting room and the hall; at the end of the hall, the front door. He might come straight here, he'd ring the doorbell. 'Who is it?' 'It's me.' Or he might telephone as soon as he arrives at a transit center: 'I'm back, I'm at the {Hôtel} Lutétia, for the paperwork.' There would be no warning. He'd phone as soon as he arrived. Such things are possible. Some people are coming back, after all. He isn't a special case, there aren't any particular reasons why he shouldn't come back. There aren't any reasons why he should. He might come back. He'd ring the bell. 'Who is it?' 'It's me.' Lots of other things like that are happening. They finally crossed the Rhine. They finally broke through the major stalemate at Avranches.[1] I finally made it through the war. It wouldn't be an extraordinary thing if he came back. Careful: it would not be extraordinary. 'Hello?' 'Who is it?' 'It's me, Robert.' It would be normal and not extraordinary. Be very careful not to make it into something extraordinary: the Extraordinary is unexpected. Be reasonable. I am reasonable. I'm waiting for Robert, who should be coming back.

The telephone: 'Hello?' 'Hello! Heard any news?' Two beats. First one: phones do ring; waiting for it to ring is not a waste of time; phones are meant to ring. Second one: shit. Desire to rip someone's throat out. 'No news.' 'Nothing? No information?' 'None.' 'You know Belsen was liberated yesterday afternoon?' 'I know.' Silence. Am I going to ask yet again? That's it, too late, I'm asking: 'So what do you think? I'm beginning to get worried.' Silence. 'You must wait, and above all, hang on, don't get discouraged – you're not the only one, unfortunately. ... I know a mother with four children who . . .' Cut this off: 'I know. I'm sorry, I have to go out. Good-bye.' Done. I hang up the phone.

I'm still sitting here. Mustn't make too many movements, it's a waste of energy. Saving every bit of strength for the ordeal. She said: 'You know Belsen was liberated yesterday afternoon?' I hadn't known. Another camp liberated. She said: '[*illegible*] yesterday afternoon.' She didn't say so, but I know that the lists will arrive tomorrow. Go downstairs, pick up a paper, pay for the paper, read the list. No. I hear a throbbing in my temples, getting worse. No, I won't read that list. I'll ask someone to read it and let me know in case . . . First off, the system of lists – I've been using them for three weeks, and it's not the right way. Plus the more lists there are . . . No, no list: the more lists there are, the fewer . . . They'll keep appearing until . . . Until the end. He won't be . . . It's time to move. Stand up, take three steps, go to the window. The École de Médecine: still there, even if . . . Passersby in the streets; they'll still be walking . . . At the instant when I hear the news – still passersby . . . It happens. A notification of death. They're already informing . . . 'Who's there?' 'A social worker from the town hall.' The mother with four children was notified. If this pounding in my temples keeps up . . . Above all, I must get rid of this throbbing, it can be deadly. Death is inside me: it's pounding in my temples, no mistake about that; must stop the pounding, stop the heart, calm it down – it won't calm down on its own, it needs help; must keep reason from breaking down any more, draining away; I put on my coat. Landing. Staircase. 'Good afternoon, Madame Antelme.' Concierge. She didn't seem any different. The street either. Outside, April carries on as if nothing were wrong. In the street, I'm asleep, hands jammed into pockets, legs moving forward. Avoid newspaper stands. Avoid transit centers. The Allies are advancing along all fronts. Even a few days ago, that was important. Now, not at all. I no longer read the news bulletins. Why bother? They'll advance until the end. Daylight, broad

daylight on the Nazi mystery. April – it will have happened in
April. The Allied armies surge across Germany. Berlin in
flames. The Red Army continues its victorious advance in the
south. Past Dresden. The Allies are advancing on all fronts;
past the Rhine, that was bound to happen. The great day of
the war: Remagen.[2] It began after that. Ever since Eisenhower
was sickened by Buchenwald, three million women and
I don't give a fuck how the war turns out. In a ditch, face
turned toward the earth, legs folded, arms flung out, he's dying. I see. Everything. He starved to death. Through the skeletons of Buchenwald . . . his skeleton. Warm weather. Perhaps
he's beginning to rot. Along the road next to him pass the
Allied armies advancing on all fronts. He's been dead for three
weeks. That's it. I'm sure of it. The legs keep walking. Faster.
His mouth sags open. It's evening. He thought of me before
dying. The exquisite pleasure of pain. There are far too many
people in the streets. I'd like to move across a great plain and
be able to think freely. Just before dying he must have thought
my name. All along the road, along every German road, others
are lying more or less as he does. Thousands. Dozens, hundreds of thousands, and him. Him – one of the thousands of
others. Him – distinct from those thousands for me alone in
all the world, and completely distinct from them. I know
everything you can know when you know nothing. They
evacuated them, then at the last minute, they killed them. So.
Generalities. The war, generality. The war. The necessities of
war. The dead, necessities of war, generality.

He died saying my name. What other name would he have
said? The war: generality. I don't live on generalities. Those
who live on generalities have nothing in common with me.
No one has anything in common with me. The street. Some
people laugh, especially the young. I have only enemies. It's
evening, I'll have to go home. It's evening on the other side
as well. In the ditch darkness is taking over, covering his
mouth. Red sun over Paris. Six years of war are ending. Big

deal, big story, they'll be talking about it for twenty years. Nazi
Germany is crushed. The butchers, crushed. So is he, in the
ditch. I am broken. Something broken. Impossible for me to
stop walking. Dry as dry sand. Beside the ditch, the parapet of
the Pont des Arts. The Seine. Just to the right of the ditch.
Something separates them: darkness. The Pont des Arts. My
victory. Nothing in the world belongs to me except that
corpse in a ditch. Childhood, over. Innocence, over. It's evening. It's my end-of-the-world. Shit on everyone. My dying
isn't directed against anyone. The simplicity of my death. I will
have lived . . . I don't care about that, I don't care about the
moment of my death. In dying I don't rejoin him, I stop waiting for him. No fuss. I'll tell D.: 'I'd best die – what would
you do with me?' Craftily, I'll be dying while alive for him;
afterward death will bring only relief. I make this base calculation. Not strong enough to live for D. I have to go home. D.
is waiting for me. Eight thirty.

'Any news?' 'None.' No one asks how I am or says hello anymore, they say: 'Any news?' I say: 'None.' I go sit on the couch
near the telephone. I don't say anything. I know D. is uneasy.
When he's not looking at me he seems worried. It's already
been a week. I catch him puttering around. 'Say something,'
I tell D. Just last week he laughed and told me, 'You're nuts,
you haven't the right to worry like that.' Now he tells me,
'There's no reason . . . Be sensible. . . .' He doesn't laugh anymore but he smiles, and his face crinkles. And yet without D.
I don't think I could keep going. We turn on the light in the
sitting room. D. has already been here for an hour. It must be
nine o'clock. We haven't had dinner yet. We don't talk. D. is
sitting not far from me; I'm still sitting in the same place on
the couch. I stare fixedly out the black window. D. watches
me. Sometimes he says, 'Enough.' Then I look at him. He
smiles at me. Then I look at the window. Only last week he
was taking my hand, kissing me, telling me impulsively,

'Robert will come back, I promise.' Now I know he's wondering if hope is still worth it. Once in a while I say, 'I'm sorry.' He smiles. An hour later I say, 'How come we've had no news?' He tells me, 'There are still thousands of men in camps the Allies haven't reached yet.' 'The Allies have reached them all, there are Americans and British everywhere.' 'How do you expect him to get word to you?' 'They can write. The Bernards heard from their daughters.' This goes on for a long time, until I ask D. to assure me that Robert will come back. 'He'll come back,' D. tells me. Then he says we ought to eat something. I go to the kitchen, I put potatoes in a pot, water in the pot, I turn on the gas, I put the pot on the flame. Then I bow my head, lean my forehead against the edge of the stove, pushing harder and harder. I close my eyes. I don't move, leaning against the stove. Silence. D. doesn't make a sound in the apartment. The gas hums, that's all. Where? Where is he? Where can he be? Where, in the name of God where? The black ditch – dead for two weeks. His mouth sags open. Along the road, next to him, pass the Allied armies advancing on all fronts. Dead for two weeks. Two weeks of days and nights, abandoned in a ditch, the soles of his feet exposed. Rain on him, sun, the dust of the victorious armies. For two weeks. His hands open. Each hand dearer to me than life. Familiar to me. Familiar that way only to me. I shout: 'D!' Footsteps, very slow, in the sitting room. D. appears. He comes into the kitchen. Around my shoulders I feel two firm, gentle hands that pull me away from the stove. I huddle against D.

'It's awful,' I say. 'I know,' says D. 'No, you can't know.' 'I know,' says D. 'Just try. We can do anything. . . .' 'I can't do a thing anymore.' D.'s arms are around me. The tighter he holds me, the more comforting it is, much better than words. Sometimes, gripped by his arms, I might almost believe I feel better. Able to breathe for a minute. We sit down at the table. Two plates on the kitchen table. I get the bread from the cupboard. Three-day-old bread. Pause. 'The bread's three days old,' I tell D. 'Everything's closed at this hour. . . .' We look at each other. 'True enough,' says D. We're thinking the same thing about the bread. We start eating. We sit down again. The piece of bread in my hand . . . I look at it. I feel like vomiting. The dead bread. The bread he didn't eat. Not having bread is what killed him. My throat closes up – a needle couldn't get through. The bread, the taste of the bread he didn't eat. We didn't know until a month ago, and then the world was flooded with photographs: charnel houses. The light broke through onto mass graves of bones. We know their rations. While we were eating bread, they weren't. I'm not even going to discuss the Germans. Corpses thick on the ground, millions of corpses. Instead of wheat, crops of corpses: Take, eat, this is my body. There are still some who believe in that. In {the posh neighborhood of} Auteuil, they still believe in it. Class warfare. The corpse class. The only relief: dead people of the world, unite! And get that guy down off his cross. The Christians, the only ones who don't share the hatred. During the Liberation, when it was throat-cutting time, they were already preaching leniency and the forgiveness of sins. The little priest's bread: Take, eat, this is my body. The farm worker's bread. The maid's always-eaten-in-the-kitchen bread: 'We have a maid who constantly eats more than her ration card! Imagine, madame! Such people are simply appalling.' Hard-earned bread. Bakery bread bought by the capitalist papa for his dear little offspring who at this very moment is starting to take an interest in the war. The earthy bread of the Soviet partisan, all the trouble it cost him – in short the basic bread of the land of the Revolution. I look at the bread. 'I'm not hungry.' D. stops eating. 'If you don't eat, I don't eat.' I nibble so that D. will eat. Before leaving, D. says, 'Promise me to . . .' I promise. When D. said, 'I have to go home,' I wanted it to be over and done with, I wanted him already gone and then I wouldn't have to close the door behind him.

D. has left. The apartment creaks beneath my feet. One by

one, I turn off the lamps. I go to my room. I go very slowly. The important thing is to sleep. If I'm not careful I won't sleep. When I don't sleep at all things are much worse the next day. When I have slept, things aren't as bad in the morning for an hour. When I do fall asleep it's in the black ditch, near him lying dead.

Went to the center at the Gare d'Orsay. I had considerable trouble gaining admission for the Tracing Service of *Libres*.[3] They insisted that it wasn't an official service. The BCRA is already there and doesn't want to relinquish its place to anyone.[4] To begin with I got us set up on the sly, with forged papers. We have managed to collect a lot of information about the transfers and whereabouts of camp survivors, which has appeared in our paper. A great deal of personal news. 'You can tell the Such-and-such family that their son is alive; I saw him yesterday.' But my four comrades and I were thrown out. 'Everyone wants to be here, it's impossible. Only stalag secretariats are allowed here.' I protest, saying that 75,000 wives and relatives of prisoners and deportees read our paper. 'It's unfortunate, but regulations forbid the operation here of any unofficial services.' 'Our paper isn't like all the others, it's the only one that publishes special issues of lists. . . .' 'That's not a sufficient reason.' I'm talking to a senior official in the repatriation service of the Frenay ministry.[5] Apparently preoccupied, he's distant and worried. 'I'm sorry,' he says. I say, 'I won't go without a fight,' and I head for the main offices. 'Where are you going?' 'I'm going to try to stay.' I attempt to slip through a line of prisoners of war that's blocking the corridor. He looks at me and says, 'As you like, but be careful – those (he points at them) haven't been disinfected yet. In any case, if you're still here this evening, I'm sorry but I'll have to evict you.' We've [spotted] a small deal table that we place at the beginning of the 'circuit.' We question the prisoners. Many come to us. We gather hundreds of pieces of information. I work steadily, without looking up, without thinking of anything. Now and then, an officer (easily recognizable: young, starched khaki shirt, pouter-pigeon chest) comes over to ask who we are. 'Just what is this tracing service? Do you have a pass?' I present my forged passes. Next there's a woman from the repatriation service. 'What do you want with them?' 'We're asking for news of their comrades who are still in Germany.' 'And what do you do with that?' She's a perky young platinum blonde, navy blue suit, matching shoes, sheer stockings, manicured nails. 'We publish it in *Libres*, the newspaper for prisoners and deportees.' '*Libres*? You're not from the ministry?' 'No.' 'Do you have the authority to do this?' she says coolly. 'We're taking the authority. It's simple.' Off she goes. We keep asking our questions. Our task is made easier, unfortunately, by the two and a half hours it takes the prisoners to get to identity verification, the first office in the circuit. It will take the deportees even longer, since they have no papers. An officer comes over: forty-five, sweating in his jacket, very curt this time. 'What is all this?' We explain yet again. 'There is already a similar service in the circuit.' Boldly, I ask: 'How do you get the news to the families? We hear it will take at least three months before everyone will have been able to write. . . .' He looks at me and laughs haughtily. 'You don't understand. I'm talking about information on Nazi atrocities. We are compiling dossiers.' He moves away, then returns. 'How do you know they're telling you the truth? It's very dangerous, what you're doing. You must know . . . The militiamen . . .' I don't reply. He goes away. A half-hour later a general heads directly for our table, trailed by the first officer, the second officer, and the young woman. 'Your papers?' I present them. 'Unsatisfactory. You may work standing up, but I do not want to see this table again.' I object: it takes up hardly any room. 'The ministry has expressly forbidden the use of tables in the main hall.' They call two scouts over to remove the table. We work standing up.

The radio occasionally blasts music that varies between swing and patriotic tunes. The line of prisoners grows longer. Now and then I go to the ticket window at the far end of the room. 'Still no deportees?' 'No deportees.' Women in uniform. Repatriation service. They talk about the prisoners, referring to them only as 'the poor boys, the poor boys ...' They address one another as Mademoiselle de Thingummy, Madame de Butt-Hole. They're smiling. Their work is just so hard. It's suffocating in here. They're really very, very busy. Some officers come over occasionally to see them; they swap English cigarettes and idle banter. 'Indefatigable, Mademoiselle de [*illegible*]?' 'As you see, Captain. . . .' The main hall [rumbles] with footsteps. And they keep coming. Trucks stream in from Le Bourget. In groups of fifty, the prisoners arrive, and then – quick, {an army song on} the loudspeaker: '*C'est la route qui va, qui va, qui va* . . .' When it's a larger group, they put on the 'Marseillaise.' [Hiccups of silence] between the songs. The young men look around the main hall. All smiling. Repatriation officials herd them along: 'All right, my friends, line up.' They line up, still smiling. The first ones to get there say, 'Long wait,' but nicely, and still smiling. When asked for information, the men stop smiling and try to remember. The officers call them 'my friends'; the women, 'those poor boys,' or 'my friends' to their faces. At the Gare de l'Est, pointing to her stripes, one of these 'ladies' scolded a soldier from the Legion: 'So, my friend – we're not saluting? Can't you see I'm a captain?' The soldier looked at her. 'Me, when I see a skirt, I don't salute her, I fuck her.' A prolonged 'Ohhh!' greeted those words. 'How rude!' The lady beat a dignified retreat.

April. I went to see S., the head of the center, to sort things out. We are allowed to stay, but at the tail end of the circuit, over by the luggage checkroom. Really pleased. As long as there are no deportees I can handle it. (Some are turning up at the Lutétia, but only rarely at Orsay.) A few isolated cases. At which point I leave the circuit, my colleagues understand that. I return only after the deportees are gone. When I do return, my comrades signal across the room: 'Nothing.' I sit down again. In the evening I take the lists to the paper. And go home. Every evening: 'I'm not going back to Orsay tomorrow.'

But I do believe that tomorrow I won't be going back there. First convoy of deportees from Weimar. April 20. I receive a phone call at home that morning: they won't arrive until the afternoon. No courage. Whenever I pass by Orsay I run away. I run from newspapers. Outside the Orsay center the wives of prisoners of war clump into a compact mass. White barriers separate them from the prisoners. They call out, asking for news of this or that person. Occasionally the soldiers stop. A few of them know something. Women are there at seven in the morning. Some stay until three in the morning – and come back later that day. They're not allowed into the center. The prisoners arrive in an orderly way. At night they arrive in big trucks, and emerge into bright light. The women scream, clap; the men stop, dazed, speechless. Sometimes they reply, usually they go on inside.

At first I used to ask many of them, 'Do you know any political deportees?' No. Most of them knew STO workers.[6] No one knew any political deportees and they didn't really understand the difference. They'd seen some at the transit center 'in a terrible state.' I admire the women who stay and never stop asking {their questions}. I asked D. to come to the center to see the first deportees from Weimar. After breakfast, I feel like running away again. 'Antelme? Oh, yes. . . .' They won't tell me. They'll look at me in a way that . . . I'm working badly. All these names I add up, names of prisoners of war, are not his. Every five minutes I feel like packing it in, putting down the pencil, abandoning my questions, leaving the center. Each truck stopping out in the street: them. No. At around two thirty I get up; I'd like to know when they're arriving. I go looking in the main hall for someone to ask. Ten or so women are in a corner of the room listening to a tall woman, a general in a navy blue suit with the cross of Lorraine on the lapel. She has blue-rinsed white hair, curled with tongs. She gestures as she speaks; the girls watch. They seem spent, and afraid. Their bundles and suitcases are sitting around, and there's a small child lying on one bundle. Their dresses are filthy. But what's remarkable is that their faces are distorted – by fatigue, or fear? And they're quite dirty, young. Two or three of them have huge bellies, pregnant fit to burst. Standing nearby, another woman officer watches the general speak. 'What's going on?' She looks at me, lowers her eyes discreetly: '{STO} Volunteers.' The general tells them to stand up. They do, and follow her. They look frightened because people jeered at them outside the center. I heard some volunteers being booed one night; the men hadn't expected it and smiled at first, then gradually they understood and took on that same stricken look. The general now turns to the young woman in uniform: 'What should we do with them?' She points at the huddled group. 'I don't know,' says the other officer. The general must have informed them that they were scum. Some of them are crying. The pregnant ones are staring vacantly. They're all working girls, with big hands scarred by German machinery. Two of them may be prostitutes, but they, too, must have worked with machines. They're standing there, as the general had asked, looking at her. An officer comes up: 'What's all this?' 'Volunteers.' The general's voice is shrill: 'Sit down.' Obediently, they sit down again. That's not enough. 'And keep quiet,' says the general sternly. 'Understood? Don't think you're going to just walk away. . . .' The general has quite a refined voice. Her delicate hand with its red fingernails threatens and [condemns] the volunteers with their grease-stained hands. Machines. German machines. The volunteers don't reply. The man approaches the huddled group to study them with quiet curiosity. Casually, in front of the volunteers, he asks the general, 'Have you any orders?' 'No,' she says, 'do you?' 'I heard something about six months' detention.' The general nods her lovely curly head: 'It would serve them right.' The senior officer blows puffs of cigarette smoke over the bunch of volunteers following the conversation open-mouthed, watching with haggard eyes. 'Right!' says the senior officer, a horseman, pirouetting elegantly, Camel in hand, and off he goes. The volunteers watch everyone and look for some sign of the fate that awaits them. No sign. I snag the general as she's leaving: 'Do you know when the convoy from Weimar is arriving?' She looks me up and down. 'Three o'clock.' Another once-over and then, a delicate, threatening finger: 'But I warn you, it's not worth your getting in the way here, only generals and prefects will be coming.' I look at the general. 'Why? What about the others?' I wasn't being careful, my tone must not have been appropriate to use with a lady of such quality. She draws herself up: 'Oh-oh-oh. I detest that kind of attitude! Peddle your complaints elsewhere, missy.' She's so indignant that she reports this to a small group of women, also in uniform, who listen, take offense, and look my way. I approach one of them. I hear myself say: 'So she's not waiting for anyone, that woman?' I get a scandalized look: 'She has so much to do, her nerves are in a state.' I return to the Tracing Service at the end of the circuit.

Shortly afterward, I go back to the main hall. D. is waiting for me there with a forged pass.

Around three o'clock there's a rumor. 'They're here!' I leave the circuit to go stand at the entrance to a small corridor opposite the main hall. I wait. I know that Robert A. won't be among them. D. is beside me. His job is to find out from the deportees if they've seen Robert Antelme. He's pale. He pays no attention to me. There's a great hubbub in the main hall. The uniformed women are busy with the volunteers, making them sit on the floor somewhere out of the way. The main hall is empty. No prisoners of war are arriving at the moment. Some officers bustle about. I hear: 'The minister!' I recognize Frenay among the officers. I'm still in the same place, at the mouth of the little corridor. I watch the main entrance. I know Robert Antelme hasn't a chance of being among them.

Something's wrong: I'm shaking. I'm cold. I lean against the wall. Two scouts emerge abruptly from the entryway, carrying a man. His arms are wrapped around the scouts' necks. The scouts carry him with their arms crossed beneath his thighs. The man's {head} is shaved, he's in civilian clothes, and he seems in great pain. He's a strange color. He must be crying. You can't call him thin – it's something else: there's hardly anything left of him. And yet he's alive. He looks at nothing – not the minister, not the room, not anything. He grimaces. He's the first deportee from Weimar to arrive at the center. Without realizing it, I've moved forward, into the middle of the hall, with my back to the loudspeaker. Two more scouts appear, supporting an old man, who is followed by about ten other men. They are guided to garden benches that have been brought in. The minister goes over to them. The old man is weeping. He's very old, at least he must be – it's impossible to tell. Suddenly I see D. sitting next to the old man. I feel very cold. My teeth are chattering. Someone comes over to me: 'Don't stay there, it's making you sick, there's no point.' I know him, he's a guy from the center. I stay. D. has started talking to the old man. I go over everything rapidly: there's one chance in ten thousand that he knows Robert Antelme. But I've heard they have lists of the survivors of Buchenwald. So. Aside from the {skeletal deportee} and the weeping old man, the others don't seem too badly off. The minister is sitting with them, along with some senior officers. D. talks to the old man for quite a while. I look only at D.'s face. He seems to be taking too long. So I go toward the bench, into D.'s field of vision. He notices, looks at me, and shakes his head. I gather that he's saying, 'Doesn't know him.' I go away. I'm very tired. I feel like leaving the center and taking a rest. I'm sure that I could manage to sleep this afternoon. Now the uniformed women are bringing the deportees some mess tins. They eat, and while they eat, they answer {questions}. But what's striking is that they don't seem interested in what's said to them. The next day I'll read in the papers that the group included General Challe; his son Hubert Challe (who would die that night), a former cadet at Saint-Cyr; General Audibert; Ferrières, the head of the State Tobacco Department; Julien Cain, the director of the Bibliothèque Nationale; General Heurteaux; Professor Suard of the faculty of medicine in Angers; Professor Richet; Claude Bourdet, {a writer and journalist}; the father of Teitgen, the Minister of Information; Maurice Nègre, {an agricultural engineer}; Marcel Paul, {a union activist}, and others.

I go home toward five in the afternoon, walking along the Seine. It's lovely weather, a beautiful sunny day. Once I've left the embankment and turned onto the rue du Bac, I've left the center far behind. I'm going home, I'm eager to be home. Maybe he will return. I'm very tired. I'm very dirty, I spent part of the night at the center. I intend to take a bath when I get home. I must wash; not washing doesn't solve anything. But I'm cold. I don't feel like washing. It must be at least a week since I last washed. I think about myself: I've never met a woman more cowardly than I am.

I think about the wives and mothers I know who are waiting for deportees. None is as cowardly as that. Absolutely none. I am very tired. I know some who are quite brave. The fortitude of S., R.'s wife, I'd call simply extraordinary. Although I am a coward, I know it. My cowardice is so bad that no one dares discuss it around me. My colleagues in the service speak to me as if I were sick in the head. So do M. and A. Me, I know I'm not sick. I'm cowardly. D. tells me so sometimes: 'One never, ever, has the right to destroy oneself like that.' He often tells me: 'You're a sick woman, you're crazy.' When D. also says to me, 'Take a look at yourself: you don't look like anything anymore,' I can't understand. Not for one second do I grasp the need to have courage. Maybe being brave would be my way of being a coward. Why would I have courage? Suzy is brave for her little boy. Why would I husband my strength, for what? If he's dead, what good is courage? There's no battle out there for me to fight. The one I do fight is invisible. I struggle against a vision: the black ditch, the corpse stone-dead for two weeks. And it depends – there are moments when the vision takes over. I don't care to live if he's no longer alive. That's all. 'You must hold on,' Madame Cats tells me. 'Me, I hang on; you have to hang on, for him.' I feel sorry for Madame Cats. Why fight it? In the name of what? I have no dignity. My dignity – can go to hell. No shame at all anymore. My shame has been suspended. 'When you think back on it,' says D., 'you'll be ashamed.' There's just one [thing]: we're talking about me. People who wait with dignity – I despise them. My dignity is waiting too, like the rest, and there's no rush for its return. If he's dead, my dignity can't do a thing about it. What's my dignity compared to that?

People are out in the streets as usual. Lines in front of stores. There are already a few cherries. I buy a paper. The Russians are in Strausberg and perhaps even farther along, on the outskirts of Berlin. I'm waiting for the fall of Berlin too. Everyone, the whole world, is waiting for that. All governments agree. The heart of Germany, the papers say. And the wives of deportees: 'Now they'll see what's what.' And my concierge. When {the heart of Germany} stops beating, it will be all over. The streets are full of murderers. People dream the dreams of murderers. I dream about an ideal city, its burned ruins flooded with German blood. I think I smell this blood; it's redder than ox blood, more like pig blood and wouldn't coagulate but flow a long way, and on the banks of these rivers, there would be weeping women whose butts I would kick, sending them nose-diving into their own men's blood. People who at this moment, today, feel pity for Germany, or rather, feel no hatred for it, make me pity them in turn. Most especially the holier-than-thou bunch.

One of them recently brought a German child to the center, explaining with a smile: 'He's a little orphan.' So proud. Leading him by the hand. Of course, he wasn't wrong (the disgrace of people who are never wrong). Of course he had to take him in: this poor little child wasn't to blame. The holier-than-thou types always find an occasion for charity. His little German Good Deed. If I had that kid I'd probably take care of him, not kill him. But why remind us that there are still children in Germany? Why remind us of that now? I want my hatred complete and untouched. My black bread. Not long ago a girl said to me: 'Germans? There are eighty million of 'em. Well, eighty million bullets can't be hard to find, right?' Anyone who hasn't dreamed that bloodthirsty dream about Germany at least one night in his life, in this month of April 1945 (Christian era), is feebleminded. Between the volunteers impregnated by the Nazis and the priestling bringing back the German boy, I'm for the volunteers. First off, the little priest, he'll never be a volunteer, he was a war prisoner, and then, no question, the clerical life pays well enough so that he doesn't have to choose – and he can easily forgive every sin: he's never committed any, he's real careful about this. That he could believe he has the right to forgive – no.

More news: Monty has crossed the Elbe, it seems; Monty's aims aren't as clear as Patton's. Patton charges ahead, reaches Nuremberg. Monty's supposed to have reached Hamburg. Rousset's wife phoned me: 'They're in Hamburg. They won't say anything about the Hamburg Neuengamme camp for several days.'

She's been very worried lately, and rightly so. In these last days, the Germans are shooting people. Halle has been cleaned out, Chemnitz taken, and they've swept on toward Dresden. Patch is cleaning out Nuremberg. Georges Bidault is talking with President Truman and Stettinius about the San Francisco conference.[7] Who cares? I'm tired, tired. Under the heading 'Wurtemberg Occupied,' Michel [*illegible*] says in *Libération Soir*: 'We'll never hear of Vaihingen again. On every map the delicate green of forests will sweep all the way down to the Enz. ... The watchmaker died at Stalingrad. ... The barber served in Paris, the village idiot occupied Athens.' Now the main street is hopelessly empty, its cobblestones belly-up like dead fish. 'Regarding deportees: 140,000 prisoners of war have been repatriated, but so far, few deportees. ... Despite all the ministerial services' efforts, the question requires action on a grander scale. The prisoners wait hours in the Tuileries gardens.' {And:} 'Cinema Night will be a particularly brilliant affair this year.' I feel like holing up in my apartment. I'm tired. They say one in five hundred will come back. 600,000 political deportees. 350,000 Jews. So 6,000 will return. He might be among them. It's been a month; he could have sent word. It seems to me I've waited long enough. I'm tired. I don't know if it's the arrival of those deportees from Buchenwald – I can't wait anymore. This evening I'm not waiting for anything.

I'm very tired. An open bakery. Maybe I should buy some bread for D. It's not worth it anymore. I won't wash, I don't need to wash. It must be seven o'clock. D. won't come before eight thirty. I'll go home. Perhaps I shouldn't waste my {bread} coupons. I remember {the refrain}: 'It's criminal to waste food coupons these days.' Most people are waiting. But some aren't waiting for anything. Others have stopped waiting, because he came home, because they've received word, because he's dead. Two evenings ago, returning from the center, I went to the rue Bonaparte to alert a family. I rang, I delivered my message: 'I'm from the Orsay center. Your son

will return, he's in good health, we've seen one of his friends.'
[I'd hurried up] the stairs, I was out of breath. Holding the
door open with one hand, the lady heard me out. 'We knew
that,' she said. 'We had a letter from him five days ago. Thank
you anyway.' She invited me in. No. I went slowly downstairs.
D. was right there waiting for me at home. 'Well?' 'They
knew, he'd written. So, they can write.' D. didn't answer. That
was the day before yesterday. Two days ago. In a way, every
day I wait less. Here's my street. The dairy store is packed.
There's no point in going there. Every time I see my building,
every time, I tell myself: 'Maybe a letter came while I was out.'
If one had, my concierge would be waiting for me in front of
the door. Her lodge is dark. I knock anyway: 'Who is it?' 'Me.'
'There's nothing, Madame Antelme.' She opens her door
each time. This evening, she has a favor to ask. 'Listen, Madame Antelme? I wanted to tell you: you should go see Madame
Bordes, she's in a bad way over her sons, won't leave her bed
anymore.' Am I going to go there now? No. 'I'll go tomorrow
morning. Tell her there's no reason for her to worry herself
sick. Today it was Stalag VII-A that came back. It's too early
for III-A.' Madame Fossé puts on her cape: 'I'll go. Pitiful, she
is; nothing for it – won't leave her bed anymore. Doesn't read
the papers. Can't make head or tail of 'em.' I go upstairs. Madame Bordes is an old woman, the school concierge, a widow
who raised six children. I'll go tomorrow morning. This
whole business has hit Madame Fossé hard. I used to go see
her occasionally, the last time was only three weeks ago. 'Sit
yourself down, Madame Antelme.' I don't go there anymore.
Whenever I see her, though, I'm tempted – just a little – to
stop by. 'No need to say it, I know what it's like.' When I tell
her, 'I have no one to be there for,' she replies, 'How well
I know, Madame Antelme.' Madame Fossé had her first
husband taken prisoner of war in 1914–18. He died a prisoner.
'That day I just set out blindly with my two brats, wanted to
kill myself and them too. Walked like that with them all night,

and then the feeling passed. Told myself I shouldn't. I went back to the factory.' She has told me that story ten times but since Robert's arrest, tactfully, she hasn't mentioned it. I go home. I'm not expecting anything. I'm cold. I go wash my hands. The water is frigid. I go sit once more on the couch, near the phone. I'm cold. I hear the street bustling down below. It's the end of the war. I don't know if I'm tired. I believe I am. For some time now, I haven't truly slept. I wake up, and then I know I've been asleep. In a ditch for two weeks now, day and night. He said my name. I should do something. I stand up and go to the window, lean my forehead against the glass. Night falls. Below, the Saint-Bênoit is lit up. The Saint-Bênoit, literary café. The world eats, and always will. They have a secret menu for those who can {afford it}. 'Madame Bordes – won't leave her bed anymore.' Madame Bordes doesn't eat anymore. 350,000 men and women are waiting, and bread makes them feel like vomiting. Two weeks in that ditch. It isn't normal to wait like this. Women waiting behind closed doors for their lovers: 'If he's not here by eleven, it's because he has betrayed me. . . .' Mothers waiting for the child due home from school who is two hours late: 'He must have been run over' – and they clutch their bellies because the thought gives them shooting pains. But in the next few hours, these women will know. Madame Bordes has been waiting for almost three weeks now. If her sons don't return, she'll never know anything. I'll never know anything. I know that he was hungry for months and died without having eaten, that he didn't have a morsel of bread to ease his hunger before dying. Not even once. The last cravings of the dying.

Since April 7 we've had a choice. Perhaps he's among the two thousand shot dead in Belsen the day before the Americans arrived. At Mittel Glattbach they found fifteen hundred in a charnel house, 'rotting in the sunshine.' Everywhere, huge columns on all the roads, where they drop like flies. Today: 'The 20,000 survivors of Buchenwald salute the 51,000 dead of Buchenwald' (*Libres*, April 24, 1945). We have a choice. It's no ordinary wait. *They've* been waiting for months. Hunger ate into their hope. Their hope had become a fantasy. Shot the day before the Allies arrived. Hope had kept them alive, but it was useless: machine-gun fire on the very eve of their liberation. An hour later, the Allies arrived to find their bodies still warm. Why? The Germans shot them, and then left. The Germans are in their own country, you can't reach out to stay their hands and say, 'Don't shoot them, it's not worth it. . . .' Time is different for them: they're losing the war, fleeing. What can they do at the last moment? Bursts of machine-gun fire, the way you break dishes in a tantrum. I'm no longer angry at them, you can't call it that anymore. For a while I was able to feel anger toward them; now I cannot tell the difference between my love for him and my hatred for them.

It's a single image with two sides: on the one, him facing the German, a [bullet hole] in his chest, twelve months' hope drowning in his eyes at this very moment, in a moment; on the other, the eyes of the German aiming at him. That's the image – two sides between which I must choose: him crum-pling into the ditch; the German swinging the machine gun back onto his shoulder and walking off. I don't know whether I should concentrate on taking him in my arms and let the German run away (forever), saving his skin, or whether I should grab the German and with my fingers dig out those eyes that never looked into his – thus abandoning {Robert} to his ditch. Everything, every image, matches {that conun-drum}. I have only one head, I can't think of everything any-more. For three weeks, I've been thinking {the Germans} should be kept from killing them. No one has dealt with that. We could have sent teams of parachutists to 'secure' the camps for the twenty-four hours before the Allies' arrival. Jacques Auvray began trying to arrange that in August 1944. It wasn't possible, because Frenay didn't want any such initiative to come from a resistance movement. Yet he, the Minister for Prisoners of War and Deportees, had no way of doing it himself. It wasn't possible. That's what interests me, in the end. I don't understand why; I can't think of everything. It wasn't done, that's all. They'll be shot down to the last concentration camp. There's no way to prevent it. Sometimes, behind the German, I see Frenay, but it doesn't last.

I'm tired. The only thing that does me good is leaning my head against the gas stove, or the windowpane. I cannot carry my head around anymore. My arms and legs are heavy, but not as heavy as my head. It's no longer a head, it's an abscess. The cool windowpane. D. will be here in an hour. I close my eyes. If he did come back we'd go to the seaside. That's what he'd like best. I think I'm going to die anyway. If he comes back I'll still die. If he rang the bell: 'Who is it?' 'Me, Robert.' All I could do would be open the door and then die. If he comes back we'll go to the beach. It will be summer, the height of summer. Between the moment when I'll open the door and the one when we're at the beach, I'll have died. Surviving somehow, I see a green ocean, a pale orange beach; inside my head I feel the salt air; I don't know where he is while I'm looking at the sea but he's alive. Somewhere on this earth he is breathing; I can stretch out on the beach and relax. When he returns we'll go to the shore. That's what he'll like the best. He loves the sea. Plus it will do him good. He'll be standing on the beach looking at the sea, and it will be enough for me to look at him looking at the sea. I'm not asking anything for myself. As long as he's looking at the sea, so am I. My head against the windowpane. My cheeks become wet. I might well be crying. Out of the six hundred thousand, here's one who's crying. That's him by the sea. In Germany the nights were cold. There on the beach he'll be in shirtsleeves and he'll talk with D. I'll watch them from a distance. Absorbed in their conversation, they won't be thinking of me. Anyway, I'll be dead. Killed by his return. Impossible for it to be otherwise. That's my secret. D. doesn't know this. One way or another I will die, whether he returns or not. My health isn't good. Many times in my life I've had to wait as I'm waiting for him. But him – I've chosen to wait for him. That's my business.

I return to the couch, I lie down. D. will arrive. He rings the doorbell. 'Nothing?' 'Nothing.' He sits down next to the couch. I say: 'I don't think there's much hope left.' D. looks exasperated, he doesn't reply. I continue: 'Tomorrow is April 22. Twenty percent of the camps have been freed. I've seen Sorel at the center, he told me that about one in five hundred will come back.' I know that D. no longer has the strength to answer me, but I continue. The doorbell rings. D. looks at me: 'I'll get it.' I stay on the couch. I hear the door opening. It's Robert's brother-in-law. 'Well?' 'Nothing.' He sits down, he tries to smile, he looks at me, then he looks at D. 'Nothing? . . .' 'Nothing.' He nods, reflects, then says: 'If you ask me, it's a question of communication. They can't write.'

D.: 'Marguerite is crazy. Practically speaking – let's be practical – Robert isn't in Besançon, right? There's no normal mail service in Germany, right?'

Michel: 'The Americans have other things to do, unfortunately.'

Me: 'Well, we've definitely had news from people who were in Buchenwald. There's a chance he was in the August 17 convoy that reached Buchenwald.'

D.: 'And what tells you he stayed there?'

Me: 'If he left on a transport, there's not much hope.'

Michel: 'No one's told you that he left at the last minute; he might have been transferred elsewhere earlier in the year.'

D.: 'If Marguerite keeps this up, when Robert comes back . . .'

I'm tired. I'd like M. and D. to go. I lie down. I hear them talking, then after a while, the conversation flags, with some long pauses. I couldn't care less what they're talking about.

Whatever happens will happen. I'm tired. ... Suddenly D. grips my shoulder: 'What's the matter with you?' 'I don't know.' Michel is standing next to him: 'Why are you sleeping like that?' 'I'm tired, I'd like you to go.' They continue talking. I go back to sleep. Then D. again. 'What is it?' I ask where M. is. He's gone. D. fetches a thermometer. I've got a slight fever. 'It's fatigue, I wore myself out at the center.'

NOTES

1. During the Battle of Normandy, in Operation Cobra, the Americans ended several weeks of stalemate by breaking through the German defenses on the western flank of the Normandy beachhead. On July 30, 1944, the Fourth Armored Division seized the strategic prize of Avranches, and Patton's Third Army began pouring through the Avranches corridor to fan out through northwestern France.

2. On March 7, 1945, the U.S. Ninth Armored Division captured the Ludendorff Bridge at Remagen and established the first Allied bridgehead across the Rhine, a watershed event in the Allies' push eastward across Germany.

3. Marguerite Duras was a journalist at *Libres* (*Free*), a newspaper in which she passed on whatever relevant information she could glean to those waiting for their loved ones to return. *Libres* was the newspaper of the MNPGD (National Movement of Prisoners of War and Deportees), a Resistance movement founded by François Mitterrand.

4. In June 1940, General de Gaulle entrusted the creation of the London-based Bureau Central de Renseignement et d'Action (Central Bureau for Intelligence and Action) to André Dewavrin, alias Colonel Passy. The BCRA operated its own missions in France and coordinated intelligence from all the Resistance networks there, providing vital information about German military operations to the Allies.

5. Henri Frenay was a conservative Catholic army officer who turned in disillusionment from the Vichy regime to become one of the first and most important leaders of the Resistance. He was a founder of the movement Combat in 1941; in 1944 de Gaulle appointed him Minister for Prisoners, Deportees, and Refugees, and Frenay served in de Gaulle's first provisional government after the war.

6. By early 1942, Germany needed more foreign labor for its war effort. Many thousands of French workers were sent to Germany, mostly prisoners of war at first, then volunteers enticed by promises of good pay and decent food. By February 1943 the Germans had introduced the Service du Travail Obligatoire (Compulsory Labor Service), an organized deportation of French workers, with the complicity of the Vichy regime – the only European government that legally compelled its own citizens to serve the Nazi war machine. France was the second largest contributor of unskilled labor and the largest contributor of skilled labor to the German wartime economy.

7. The United Nations Conference on International Organization, known inform-
ally as the San Francisco Conference (April 25–June 26, 1945), was attended by
delegations from the nations that had signed the 1942 Declaration of the United
Nations (a statement of the Allies' objectives in World War II). The conference
concluded with the signing of the Charter of the United Nations.

U.S. secretary of state Edward Stettinius, Foreign Secretary Anthony Eden
of Great Britain, and French foreign minister Georges Bidault, an important
Resistance leader, headed their respective national delegations to the conference.

HUNDRED-PAGE
NOTEBOOK

INTRODUCTION

THE THIRD of the *Wartime Notebooks*, called the *Hundred-Page Notebook*, is a small exercise book of lined paper with a blue cover. Only the first thirty-two pages were filled and numbered by Marguerite Duras, probably at about the same time as the second notebook was written, somewhere around 1947. These thirty-two pages – in the second of the two 'notebooks in the blue armoires at Neauphle-le-Château' mentioned in the author's preface – contain the end of what will be the central text of *The War*.

Pages 239–42 were reused in the second fragment of 'Did Not Die Deported,' published in the second issue of the magazine *Sorcières* in 1976. In its published form, the text contains a series of chronological references: 'Saturday April 26'; 'Sunday 27'; 'Tuesday April 29.'

THE WAR
(ROUGH DRAFT)

SUNDAY, APRIL 22, 1945. Dionys slept in the sitting room. I wake up. Again, no one telephoned last night. I have to go see Madame Bordes. I make myself some strong coffee and take a corydrane tablet, {a combination of aspirin and amphetamine}. My head is spinning and I'm nauseated. I'll feel better; mornings, after the coffee and the corydrane, it passes. I go into the sitting room: 'It's Sunday, there's no mail.' D. asks me where I'm going. I'm going to see Madame Bordes. I make him some coffee, I take it to him in bed. He looks at me, giving me a sweet, sweet smile. 'Thanks, Marguerite darling.' I say 'No.' 'Come on, now.' I say 'No.' I can't bear hearing my name. After the corydrane, I perspire heavily and my temperature drops. I go downstairs. I buy the paper. Today I'm not going to the printer's. Another photo of Belsen: scrawny bodies lined up in a very long pit. The heart of Berlin, within three miles {of the front}. 'The Russian communiqué is unusually frank.' M. René Pleven announces: a reorganization of the wage scale, higher farm prices. Mr. Churchill says: 'We haven't long to wait now.' {The Russians and the Allies} may meet up today. Debû-Bridel rails against the elections that will take place without the deportees and prisoners of war. Page two of the *Front National*[1] says that a thousand deportees were burned alive in a barn on the morning of April 13, near Magdeburg. In *Art and War*, Frédéric Noël says: 'Some people imagine that war produces revolutions in the arts, while in reality wars affect other dimensions of life.' Simpson takes twenty thousand prisoners. Monty has linked up with Eisenhower. Berlin is in flames: 'From his command post, Stalin must see a wondrous and terrible sight.' 'There have been thirty-seven alerts in the past twenty-four hours.'

* * *

I arrive to visit Madame Bordes. Her {youngest} son is in the front hall: 'Mama won't leave her bed anymore.' The daughter is crying on a couch. The concierge's lodge is dirty and untidy. 'We're in a fix,' says the son. 'She won't leave her bed anymore.' I enter the bedroom where Madame Bordes is lying. In a loud voice I say, 'Well, Madame Bordes?' She looks at me with red eyes. 'So, there it is,' she says weakly. The son and daughter come into the room. The neck of her nightgown reveals how thin and wrinkled she is. Madame Bordes has had six children.

Her sleeves are rolled up, uncovering her dry, knobby elbows. She usually wears a small chignon; today her hair hangs loose. 'Making herself sick,' says the son. 'Can't taste anything now,' says Madame Bordes. 'They won't be coming back.' Then the tears brim over and run down her cheeks. She doesn't feel them. 'There's no reason to get yourself into a state,' I say. 'The III-A hasn't returned yet.' Madame Bordes slaps the sheet with her fist. 'You already told me that a week ago but Marcel, he saw some III-A at the center.' She knows two of her sons are in the III-A, but she doesn't know where the III-A is. Her young son spends his nights in the centers trying to find out. 'I'm not making this up,' I say. 'Read the paper and you'll see. . . .' 'The papers don't explain clearly,' says Madame Bordes. I tell her it won't do her any good to make herself ill. 'I can't go on,' she whimpers. 'Not knowing – that's the terrible thing. I can't go on.'

I sit down on the edge of her bed. She's stubborn, she won't look at me anymore, and weeps. 'That's the terrible part,' says the son. 'We don't know anything. . . .' Mewling, Madame Bordes tells me, 'You say he's just not back yet but that's all there is in the streets and none of them's mine! I can't go on.' I cannot think what to do. They know I work for the Tracing Service. If I handle this right, she'll be up and about for another three days – once again. I want to go home. It is rather worrisome, though, that they haven't written yet. I'm lying: the III-A must have been liberated two days ago. 'I just know I'll never see them again,' says Madame Bordes. She weeps in spasms, she's spent. Out there on the roads, in the columns: 'I can't go on.' He stops; machine-gun fire. Here, Madame Bordes 'won't leave her bed anymore.' Here, the closer we come to victory, the more Madame Bordes empties out, but she'll get up. She has to get up: there's no point in her staying in bed, no point at all. I also feel like leaving her on her own, it's her business. But her young son is looking at me. I take the paper and read the list of those coming back [*illegible*]. The three of them listen. I explain. I go back to the paper. I re-explain. Madame Bordes has stopped crying; she listens open mouthed. 'You see,' says the son. The daughter smiles: 'She's awful. ...' 'It's not that,' says Madame Bordes. 'But when you don't know ...' I leave them, go back upstairs. Before that, I go get some bread. A woman comes up to me. It's the dairy-store owner. 'Madame Antelme, please, have you heard anything about III-A?' 'No, but I could find out.' 'Because my mother ... She's beginning to wonder,' says Madame Gérard. 'She's falling apart.' I'll tell her this afternoon; yes, she can count on me. I get the bread, I go upstairs. D. is playing the piano. I sit down on the couch. D. is oblivious.

I don't dare tell him not to play the piano. It gives me a headache. Still, it's strange: no news. The troop movements in Germany ... They've got other things to do. Thousands of men are waiting; others advance toward the Russians. Berlin is on fire. A thousand cities razed. Thousands of civilians are fleeing. Fifty men take off every minute from the airfields. Fifty passengers, fifty prisoners. Not him, not yet. Here we're busy with local elections. We're also repatriating {prisoners of war}. There had been talk of commandeering civilian cars and apartments, but they didn't dare, for fear of causing offense. After all, they couldn't go that far. Still, it was the perfect occasion, the only one in centuries. De Gaulle isn't that keen on it. De Gaulle has never spoken of his political deportees save as a sideshow – his North African Front comes first. On April 3, de Gaulle said: 'The days of tears are over. The days of glory have returned.' He also said, 'Among all the places on earth where destiny has chosen to deliver its judgments, Paris has long been a symbol. It was so when the city of Saint Geneviève, with Attila in retreat, announced the victory of the Catalonic Fields.[2] It was so when Joan of Arc ... It was so when Henri IV ... It was so when the National Assembly of the Three Estates proclaimed the Declaration of the Rights of Man. It was so when the surrender of Paris in January 1871 sanctioned the triumph of Prussian Germany. ... It was so again during the famous days of September 1914. ... It was so in 1940 ...' (Speech of April 3, 1945.)

He skipped 1848, {the February Revolution that overthrew King Louis Philippe}. In 1871, {the year of the Paris Commune,} he saw only one thing: the consecration of Prussian Germany. And that's what we've got in power. France is caught in a reactionary Catholic grip. That's what *reaction* is: reacting against the people's impulsive belief in their own strength. De Gaulle bleeds the people of their strength. Popular uprisings nauseate him, offend his delicate sensibility. He believes in God, in his works and pomps and vanities. It pains him not to be able to speak openly of this in his speeches. The difference between de Gaulle and Hitler, it's that de Gaulle believes in transubstantiation. He speaks straight to the heart of Catholics. Hitler believes in power from above. De Gaulle believes in the Power Above. And that's what we've got in power. No difference, except in the nature of the founding myth. Beyond the Rhine, Aryanism. Here, the Good Lord. Fortunately, he didn't declare himself: 'After Saint Geneviève, after Joan of Arc, myself, Saint de Gaulle.' All he knew how to do was to send the people to be butchered. 'The days of tears are over. The days of glory have returned. . . .' He doesn't dare talk about the concentration camps and clearly recoils from mingling the people's tears with victory for fear of diminishing it, of weakening its meaning. He is the one who demands that local elections be held now. He is a regular army officer.

At this moment the people are paying. He doesn't notice. The people are made for paying. Berlin is burning. The German people are paying. That's normal. The people, a generality. The thousands of Frenchmen rotting in the sunshine: a generality. Discrimination takes place on high, not down below. Throughout history, the people have been the ones who pay. De Gaulle refuses to remind them of this. Glorifying the people's suffering is dangerous and risks reassuring and emboldening them (see 1871). Later he will say: 'The dictatorship of popular sovereignty entails risks that must be tempered by the responsibility of one man.' He loathes blood, it's against his temperament. Catholics cannot bear blood. De Gaulle is a Catholic general, meaning that his role is to spill blood but under orders. Popular uprisings make him upchuck. Speaking about the word 'revolution,' another damn idiot, the Reverend Father Panici, ventured to remark several days ago in Notre-Dame: 'Popular uprising, general strike, barricades, etc. All that would make a lovely film. . . . But is that more spectacle than revolution? Is there any real, profound, lasting change there? Look at 1789, 1830, 1848.[3] After a period of violence and some political upheaval . . . the people grow weary: they have to go back to work and earn a living. . . .' {One must} discourage the people. He also said: 'When it's a question of hierarchy, the Church does not hesitate: it approves.' De Gaulle has declared a day of national mourning for the death of Roosevelt. No national mourning for the five hundred thousand deportees shot and starved to death. We must treat America with tact and consideration. Roosevelt, he's not some generality, he's an officer, a leader. There's a protocol among leaders. Day of national mourning:

France in mourning for Roosevelt. We don't go into mourning for the people.

I can't go on. I tell myself: something's got to happen – it's just not possible. . . . I should describe this waiting by talking about myself in the third person. Compared to this waiting, I no longer exist. There are more images going through my head than there are along the roads of Germany. Every minute, bursts of machine-gun fire inside my head. But I'm still here, they're not fatal. Shot down along the way, shot, shot. Dead with an empty belly. Hunger, Hunger wheeling in his head like a vulture. Impossible to give him anything. I can hold bread out into the empty air. I don't even know anymore if he needs bread. If he's dead – useless. I bought some honey, sugar, rice, pasta. I tell myself, if he's dead, I'll burn it all; no one else . . . But nothing can diminish the way his hunger burns me. People die of cancer, a car accident. Of hunger, too: you're dying of hunger – and they finish you off. What hunger has done is capped off with a bullet through the heart. I'd like to be able to give him my life and I'm unable to give him a piece of bread. I can't go on – this isn't what anyone would call thinking. Everything is in suspended animation. Madame Bordes isn't thinking anymore. Madame Bordes is me. We're interchangeable. 'Every absurdity,' D. tells me, 'every bit of goddamned nonsense – you'll have spouted them all. . . .' Along with Madame Bordes. There are currently people who do think. 'We must think over what's happening.' D. tells me, 'You should try to read. . . . One should be able to read no matter what happens.' I tried to read. I don't understand a thing anymore. Words no longer form a logical chain. Sometimes I suspect that they do, but in a different experience of time. Sometimes, quite simply, I believe that they don't, that they never did. A different chain (my chain, I'm in chains) holds me fast: maybe he's been dead for two weeks, already crawling with vermin in that ditch; dead without having tasted

a morsel of bread, with a bullet – in the back of the neck?
Through the heart? A burst right in the eyes? His mouth pale
against the German earth ... and I'm still waiting because
nothing is certain, he might yet be alive, might die from one
moment to the next, from moment to moment every possibility comes and goes – he might be in the column, advancing
step by step, head bowed, so tired that perhaps he doesn't take
that next step, he stops. ... Was that two weeks ago? Six
months? A little while ago? A second ago? The second
afterward? There's no room in me for the first line of the best
book in the world. The most beautiful book is useless, it lags
far behind; me, I'm at the front lines of waiting. Madame
Bordes is at the front lines of a battle without weapons, blood-
shed, or glory. Behind Madame Bordes civilization lies in
ashes: thought, enlightenment, reason. The wisdom of
centuries, gathered from every corner of the world, would not
explode in a heartbeat the way her heart explodes with every
beat. Madame Bordes disdains all hypotheses, all consolation;
what she wants to know is whether the men of III-A have returned. Sometimes her heart and head are invaded by
upheavals, analyses, syntheses, wrenching turmoil, bright
hopes, crushed expectations, precipices around which
thought wanders shivering and dazed, unable to make sense of
anything. 'Every possible absurdity – you'll have spouted it
all.' That's our business. This is our business, and ours alone:
you who judge us, just go along home. If I were told, 'You'll
be fucked by ninety soldiers and he'll receive a piece of bread,'
I'd ask to be fucked by a hundred and eighty soldiers so he'd
get two pieces of bread. If someone told Madame Bordes, the
school concierge, 'Scream "Long live Hitler" in the middle
of the street at one in the morning and {your sons} will get a
piece of bread,' Madame Bordes would ask to do that every
night. To us, these aren't idiotic suppositions, and we're ready
to believe that, too. Calculations like those – I make them
three hundred times a day. A finger for a piece of bread; two

fingers for two pieces. Ten years of my life to give him two
more. Anything is always possible since we know nothing.
Alive or dead? Not only {is anything possible} at every second
of the day, but at every second of the day, *that question* arises,
and we have no idea how to answer it.

Still on the couch near the telephone. It's Sunday. Today
Berlin will fall. It's really the end. The papers are saying how
we'll know: the sirens will sound one last time. The last time
of the war. People are saying, I'm going to get roaring drunk,
or, I'll dance a jig, or, I'll stay out all night, but most of all they
say, I'm going to get plastered, and how. I don't go to the
center anymore, I'll never go again. They're arriving at the
Lutétia. They're arriving at the Gare de l'Est. The Gare du
Nord. It's over. Not only am I never going back to the center,
I'm not budging at all. I think so, but I thought so yesterday,
too, then at ten in the evening I went out and took the métro
to D.'s place. D. opened the door and wrapped his arms
around me. 'Anything new since a little while ago?' 'Nothing,
I can't stand it.' I left, I didn't even want to go in. I'd wanted
to see D.'s face, make sure nothing strange was showing there,
no fresh worry since that morning. So I left. I'd gone to see
him because at ten thirty that evening, I'd been stricken with
fear. Suddenly. Fear. 'But don't you see that he'll never come
back?' More than that. Ice in the heart. I found myself downstairs, driven out. Once outside, I told myself, 'I've got time
to get there and back before the last métro.' Panic. Flight:
that's what it is. Sweating all over. Something new in this waiting. I'd looked up abruptly and the apartment had changed
completely – even the lamplight wasn't the same. Something
was threatening. On all sides. Abruptly, I was sure, sure, sure.
He's dead. Dead. Dead. Dead. Today's the twenty-seventh of
April today's the twenty-seventh of April today's the twenty-
seventh of April. Dead Dead Dead. The silence. The silence.
Silence. New, there's something new. I stood up and went to

the middle of the room. It happened in an instant. What's happening to me? Black night at the windows is watching me. I draw the curtains. It's still watching me. What's happening to me. . . . The signs – the room is full of black and white signs, black and white. No more throbbing temples. It's not that anymore. I feel my face change, change, fall slowly apart. No one is there. I'm going to pieces, coming undone, changing. I'm scared. Shivers at the back of my neck. Where am I? Where? Where is she? What's happening to her? My head has stopped pounding. I don't feel my heart anymore. The horror rises slowly, like the sea. I'm drowning. A small part of me is left, a wafer: my head. I'm not waiting anymore. I'm afraid. It's over. Where are you? How can I find out? I don't know where he is. I'm with him. Where? With him. Where with him? I don't know, with him. Where? I don't know anymore. What's this place called? What *is* this place? In fact, just what is this whole business? What business? What's it about? Robert Antelme – who's he? You're waiting for a dead man, yes, of course you are, a dead man. No more pain. I am just about to understand: you and that man have nothing in common. He's dead, I mean, it's so obvious. . . . Might as well wait for someone else. You don't exist anymore. Once you no longer exist, why wait for Robert Antelme? Another would do just as well, anyone at all if you'd like. Nothing left in common between you and that man. Who is Robert Antelme? Has he ever existed? What makes him Robert and not someone else? In fact, talk about that a little. What are you waiting for like that? What makes you wait for him and no one else? Why the hell have you been beating your own brains out for two weeks? Who are you? What's going on in this room? Who *I* am? D. knows who I am. Where's D.? I can see him and ask him to explain. . . . I must see him. Because now there's something new.

Tuesday, April 24. The phone's ringing. It's dark. I turn on the light, check the alarm clock. Five thirty. I hear: 'Hello? What?' It's D., sleeping in the next room, who answers. This is it. This is it. I hear: 'What? What are you saying? Yes, this is the place, Robert Antelme, yes.' A pause. I'm next to Dionys, who's holding the phone. I try to grab the receiver. D. tries to hang on to it. There's more. . . . 'What news?' Silence. I try to wrestle the phone away. This is hard, impossible. 'And, so? Some friends?' D. turns from the receiver to me: 'It's friends of Robert's who've arrived at the Gaumont center.' I say: 'It's not true.' Then: 'And Robert?' D. listens to the receiver. I try to snatch the phone away. D. says nothing, he listens, he's got the phone. We're fighting over the receiver. 'You don't know anything more?' He turns to me: 'They left him two days ago.' I've stopped trying to get the receiver. I'm on the floor by the phone. Something has given way. He was alive two days ago. I give in to it. It's bursting, coming out my mouth, nose, eyes. It has to come out. D. has hung up the phone. 'Marguerite, Marguerite darling.' She doesn't answer. She's busy. Leave her alone. It's coming out everywhere as water. 'Alive, alive.' Someone replies: 'Marguerite, my dear, my dear.' Two days ago, as alive as you and me, oh yes. 'It isn't possible. . . .' Some- one replies: 'Marguerite darling, my dear.' 'Leave me alone, leave me alone.' It comes out in whimpers, too, it comes out any way it likes. It's coming out. She lets it happen. 'Oh, he's so incredible! I knew it. . . .' D. picks me up and says: 'All right, let's go there. They're at the Gaumont, they're waiting for us. Let's make ourselves some coffee.' D. said, let's make ourselves some coffee, but it was so that I'll have some coffee. D. under the electric ceiling light in the kitchen, laughing. D.'s extra- ordinary laughter. He keeps saying: 'Ha! You thought they'd get him! But he's sharp, Robert. . . . Probably hid at the last moment. . . . Us thinking he couldn't take care of himself because he seemed so . . .' D. is in the bathroom, washing. He says: 'Because he seemed so . . .' She's leaning against the kitchen cabinet door. 'Seemed so . . . he doesn't seem like

everyone else, it's true. He's so absentminded. He's a funny
one, really. He always seems so up in the clouds but he must
have been way ahead of them. . . . You can't let that fool you.'
She's still leaning against the kitchen cabinet. D. from the
bathroom: 'You're getting the coffee ready?' 'Yes.' She puts
the water over the gas flame. She grinds the coffee. D. repeats:
'We have to move fast. He'll be getting here in two days.' D.
comes in. The coffee's ready. The taste of hot coffee: he's alive.
I dress quickly. I've taken a corydrane tablet. Still some fever,
I'm dripping with perspiration. I'll have to deal with that. The
streets are empty. D. walks quickly. We get to the Gaumont
Cinéma, now a transit center. They'd told us to ask for Hélène
D. We ask for her. She comes over. She laughs. I laugh. But
I'm cold. Where are they? At the hotel. She takes us there.

The hotel is old. All lit up, bustling with assistants in white
and {deportees in} stripes. 'They've been arriving all night
long,' we're told. Here's the room. The woman leaves. I tell
D.: 'Knock.' My heart is pounding so, I won't be able to
go in. Just when D. is about to knock, I ask him to wait a moment. Then he knocks. Inside the room are two people at the
foot of a bed. A man and a woman. The woman's eyes are
red. They're both looking at the bed. They don't say anything.
They're relatives. Two 'zebras' are in the bed: one's asleep, he's
about twenty; the other smiles at me. I ask: 'You're Perrotti?'
'That's me.' 'I'm Antelme's wife.' He's quite pale. 'Well?' 'We
left him two days ago.' 'How was he?' Perrotti looks at D. 'In
better shape than lots of others.' The young man has
awakened: 'Antelme? Oh, yes. We were going to escape with
him.' I've sat down near the bed. They don't seem in any
hurry to talk. I say: 'They were shooting people?' The two
zebras look at each other, don't answer right away. 'Well,
they'd stopped shooting.' D. speaks up: 'You're sure?' Perrotti
says: 'The day we left, they hadn't shot anyone for two days.'
The {two deportees} talk to each other: the young man asks,
'How do you know?' 'The Russian kapo told me.' Me: 'What

did he tell you?' 'He told me offhand they'd been ordered to stop shooting.' The young guy: 'It depended on the day – there were days they shot people, others they didn't.' Perrotti looks at him, at me, at D., and smiles: 'Please forgive us, we're really tired.' D. is staring at Perrotti: 'How come Robert isn't with you?' 'We looked for him so we could escape together when the train left, but we couldn't find him.' 'We looked hard, though,' says the young guy. 'How come you didn't find him?' asks D. 'It was dark,' says Perrotti. 'And then there were still a lot of us in spite of . . .' I see: the train, the station in the middle of the night. They didn't find him because he'd been shot: 'You looked carefully for him?' 'Well, that is . . .' They look at each other. 'Oh, yes!' says the young guy. 'I mean, we even called his name, although it was dangerous.' 'He's a good comrade,' says Perrotti. 'We looked for him. He used to give talks about France. . . .' The young guy: 'Should've been there, he could really mesmerize an audience.' Me: 'If you didn't find him it's because he wasn't there anymore, because he'd been shot.' D. goes over to the bed, gesturing brusquely, almost as pale as Perrotti: 'When did you last see him?' They look at each other. I hear the woman's voice: 'They're tired. . . .' We're interrogating them as if they were criminals, not letting up for a moment. 'Anyway, me, I saw him,' says the young guy. 'I'm sure of it.' He stares vacantly and repeats: 'I'm sure of it.' But he isn't sure about anything. I hear D.: 'Try to remember when you saw him last.' Perrotti: 'I saw him in the column, you remember, on the right: it was still daylight, an hour before we reached the station.' The young guy: 'Were we ever exhausted! Me, in any case, I saw him after {his} escape, I'm sure about that at least, since we'd agreed to leave at the station. . . .' Me: 'What? His escape?' Perrotti: 'Yes. He tried to escape but they caught him. . . .' I repeat: 'What? Didn't they shoot people who ran away? You're not telling the truth.' Perrotti seems to lose heart. 'I mean, we've told you he'll come back, we saw him. . . .' D. breaks in, tells me: 'Be quiet.' Then he takes over: 'When did he escape?' They look at each other: 'Was it the day before?' 'I think so,' says the young guy. Me: 'How did they shoot the people?' 'Be quiet,' says D. Then: 'Make an effort, we're very sorry, but try to remember. ...' Perrotti smiles: 'I understand, sure. We're tired. ...' Silence for a minute. Then, the young guy: 'I'm certain I saw him in the column after he tried to escape. ... Now I'm certain of it.' Perrotti: 'When?' 'With Girard on the right, I'm sure of it.' I repeat: 'How did you know when they were shooting people?' Perrotti: 'Don't worry, we'd have found out – the SS did their shooting at the rear {of the column}, then pals would pass the news along, we always knew who ...' D.: 'What we'd like to figure out is why you didn't find him.' 'It was dark,' says Perrotti. 'Maybe he'd escaped,' says the young guy. 'In any case, you did see him after his escape.' 'Definitely,' says Perrotti. 'Absolutely,' says the young guy. 'What did they do to him?' 'Well, he got beaten. ... Philippe'll tell you better than I can, he was his pal.' Me: 'How come they didn't shoot him?' 'The Americans were so close, they hadn't time anymore.' 'Plus it depended,' says the young guy. 'Where did they go?' 'We don't know. But they wouldn't have had to go far. ...' 'Oh, no!' says the young guy. 'The Americans were all around.' Me: 'Was it before or after his escape that you agreed to escape together at the station?' Silence. They look at each other. D.: 'If you talked to him afterward, it's very important, you understand. That's a little more proof. ...' They don't know anymore. They no longer recall. They try their best: 'Don't remember.' We leave. 'I'm completely reassured,' says D. I say: 'I'm very worried.' D. insists that Robert will arrive. 'If he's not here in three days ...'

Another period of waiting begins.

April 24, eleven thirty {in the morning}. Another telephone call: 'It's François.[4] Philippe's back; he saw Robert ten days ago. Philippe escaped. Robert was all right.' I explain: 'I saw

Perrotti. It seems Robert escaped and was recaptured. What does Philippe know?' François: 'That's true, he did try to escape, he was caught by some children. . . .' Me: 'When did he last see him?' Silence. 'They escaped together. He was by the side of the road. . . . He was beaten. Philippe was far enough away, the Germans didn't see him. He waited. He didn't hear any shots.' Silence. 'He's sure?' 'He's sure.' 'That's not much. He didn't see him after that?' Silence. 'No, because he'd escaped.' Me: 'That was when?' (I know François has figured all this out.) 'It was the thirteenth.' Me: 'What should I think?' François: 'No question, he'll be back.' 'Were they shooting people in the column?' A pause. 'It depended. . . . Come to the printer's.' 'No. I'm tired. What does Philippe think?' Silence. 'There's no doubt, he should be here within forty-eight hours.' Me: 'How is he?' 'Exhausted. He says that Robert was still hanging on and in better shape than he was.' 'Does he have any idea where the train was going?' 'No, no idea.' 'You're not just trying to keep my spirits up?' 'No – come to the printer's.' 'No, I'm not coming. And if he doesn't arrive in forty-eight hours?' 'What do you want me to tell you?' 'Why in forty-eight hours?' 'Because by this time, they've been liberated. According to Philippe they were liberated between the fourteenth and the twenty-fifth, definitely. That's the only possible timetable.'

Perrotti escaped on the twelfth. He came back on the twenty-fourth. Philippe escaped on the thirteenth. He came back on the twenty-fourth. So it takes eleven to twelve days. Robert should be here the day after tomorrow. Perhaps tomorrow.

Wednesday 25
Thursday 26
Friday 27
Saturday 28
Sunday 29

Monday 30
Tuesday 1
Wednesday 2
Thursday 3

Wednesday 25. Nothing.

Thursday 26. Nothing. D. called the doctor. I have a temperature, it isn't serious. The flu, says the doctor. He gave me a sedative. Madame Cats and D. are sitting beside me. It's dark out. Ten in the evening. Riby phoned. I didn't know him. He asked for Robert. He was in the column, he escaped after Perrotti and got back before him.

Friday 27. Nothing during the night. D. brings me *Combat*.[5] The first session of the San Francisco conference: 'Molotov impassible, Bidault concerned, Eden a dreamer. . . . Much was said there about justice, to the great satisfaction of the lesser powers.' At the last minute, the Russians have captured a métro station {in Berlin}. Stettin and Brno have fallen.

The Americans are on the Danube. I tell D.: 'All Germany is in their hands.' D. is cautious. 'In theory, but practically speaking, it's difficult to occupy a country.' 'What can {the Germans} do with {their prisoners}? What did they do with them at the last minute?' I figure that those who've come back from the column are those who escaped. And the others? I don't dare ask D. anymore. We fight almost every day. D. gets angry. I'm harassing him. Sometimes he tries to 'change the subject.' That's not possible. He says: 'Still, what [days] these are. . . .' 'Yes,' I say. When Madame Cats is there, I don't dare say much; she's had no news of her daughter. She tells me: 'They'll come back, my dear.' I say: 'Yes.' She keeps me from smoking, so I smoke at night. She's adamant about my not smoking. It's funny. I go along with her. 'The doctor said so.' She's insistent, it's not normal, she's incredibly tenacious. Sometimes she says: 'I can feel myself becoming mean, pay no attention.' She's sixty, she's still quite strong but she has a bad heart. She makes me remain lying down and heats me up some American milk. Occasionally, after she's gone, I tell D.: 'Madame Cats is awful.' D. explains to me that it's the only thing that does her some good. If I were truly ill, I believe Madame Cats wouldn't think so much about her daughter. It's extraordinary. She arrives at nine in the morning and leaves in the evening. All day she stays by me while I'm lying down, and she won't let me smoke. It's been like that for three days. Sometimes she says: 'I'm an old woman, it's not important to me. You're the one who should be receiving news.' While she's heating the American milk, she shouts from the kitchen, 'If you smoke, I'll know it from the smell!' When D. is there, that's when he smokes and he gives me a puff. This morning she noticed; D. tried to joke about it but I thought she was going to cry. When we're alone in the afternoons we don't say anything to each other. Sometimes she puts her thumb and index finger up to her eyes and presses on them; that's when things have become too much for her. The rest of the time she tries to smile. She tells me: 'Don't think, try to sleep.' And sometimes she forgets all about me. Her eyes glaze over from staring outside; she nods, and speaks: 'I'll never see her again, never see her again.' Then she shakes her head for a long time. Her daughter was a cripple, she had a stiff leg. 'I know they killed cripples. How could she have walked, poor thing. . . .' (Madame Cats waited six months, from April to November. In November she learned that her daughter had been dead since March.) I don't talk about Robert with her. It's not worth it – all she does is say 'I'm sure they'll come back.' And then she says: 'I'm sure I'll never see her again.' It's not worth asking her anything at all. The days are long. Toward five o'clock there's some sunlight in the sitting room. Toward five o'clock. Sometimes a phone call. Madame Cats takes it. She says: 'No, nothing yet.' Then: 'She's resting.' Then she hangs up. She has given instructions at her place to phone her here, and she left a letter addressed to her daughter with the concierge of the building where the daughter lived, because 'she would go directly home – she doesn't know that I'm in France' (Madame Cats is Belgian). She has also left a letter with her own concierge, because 'if she were to arrive, she would need to know where to find me.' That letter says: 'I am at the home of Marguerite Antelme, the telephone number is . . .' She has also left letters at the train stations, the transit centers, at the homes of her cousins and her sister, because 'you never know: instead of going home, she might go straight there.' She has bought fifty cans of American milk, twenty pounds of sugar, twenty pounds of jam, some calcium, phosphates, alcohol, eau de cologne, rice, potatoes, a rubber doughnut cushion, and draw sheets. She says: 'All her underwear is washed, mended, ironed,' and also, 'I had her black suit lined and I fixed her coat pockets,' and, 'I'd put everything in a big trunk with mothballs, and the day before yesterday I aired everything, it's all ready,' and, 'I've had new taps put on her shoes and darned her stockings,' and, 'I don't think I've forgotten anything, it's all ready – except that I'll need to buy more sugar: they need lots of sugar for the heart, yes, they all have weak hearts.' And also, 'I won't see her again. With her stiff leg, they'll have gassed her.'

When the conversation turns to the Germans, Madame Cats says: 'I wish every last one of them were gone, even the children; I'd kill them myself if need be.' I saw Madame Cats about two weeks ago and she hadn't changed her mind. 'If one showed up at my office in Brussels,' she told me, 'I'd throw my paperweight in his face. I'm still strong – I'm sure I'd kill him.' Madame Cats says these things calmly; I believe she could do what she says. She's good and bad, without compromise. She says to me: 'How much sugar do you have?' I say: 'I have no sugar, I've got time.' 'That's not wise, Marguerite: at the last minute you won't be able to find any.' Then she returns to her thoughts. So do I. Perrotti, Philippe, Riby. He should have arrived today, though. He was beaten. Philippe didn't hear a shot. If he waited, it's because they usually shot them. Perhaps they shot him a bit farther off, and Philippe wouldn't have heard. Philippe is the last person to have seen him. Perrotti looked for him at the train: he says he saw him but that's not certain, he didn't seem so sure about it. Whereas Philippe is sure he saw him because they'd arranged to escape together. But Perrotti didn't see him. He looked for him at the station; he didn't find him. Yet he, too, is sure that he wasn't shot. I have to wait. I reconstruct – but there's a hole: between the moment when Philippe *didn't* hear a gunshot and the train station, what happened to him? I must be reasonable and try to understand. A black hole. I do my best; no light dawns.

April 27. I get up. Madame Cats has left. No one telephoned last night. He was still alive on the fourteenth, maybe the fifteenth. I get dressed, I stay close to the phone. D. insists that I go eat at the restaurant with him. Maybe he's at a transit center waiting to leave. The restaurant is full. But in that case, why doesn't he write? People are talking about the end of the war, about Berlin, teasing one another about the sirens. 'What if the last German planes bomb Paris?' I'm not hungry. He's back in that ditch. I'm not hungry. 'They will never pay enough for this,' people are saying about the German atrocities. Well, I've had enough. I want to die. No, I'm not hungry. Since he's dead, I want to die. The people talk, talk, and eat. It's not their fault: 'I know one of them who came back from Belsen. Horrible!' 'I know one who ...' Cut off from the world, even from D. If I don't get a letter this evening or a phone call this afternoon, then he's dead. D. looks at me. He can look at me all he wants. He's dead. I could tell D. a million times, he wouldn't believe me, but *I know.* I also feel a bit sorry for D. Everybody's reading the papers. The Red Army in the heart of Berlin, Stettin taken, Brno taken. *Pravda* writes: the bell has tolled for Germany. The ring of fire and steel tightens around Berlin. It's over. He won't be here for the peace. If he's

not here for the peace, what will I do? What can I do? I'm
not hungry. The Italian partisans have captured Mussolini at
Faenza. All northern Italy is in their hands. Mussolini has been
caught; that's all they know. The earth turns, the papers turn,
the German people are crushed to a pulp. Germany is pulp.
So is he. {The Communist daily} *L'Humanité* says that Pétain
is returning in a sleeping car, while the deportees are returning
in cattle cars. *Le Monde* is talking about the future and the
'Gaullist order.' The future. A future will emerge from this
adventure. Thorez[6] is also talking about the future, saying that
we'll have to work, that the refusal of sacrifice is more costly
than combat, and that a wait-and-see policy is a deadly poison.
Yes. *Le Monde* says we're lucky France didn't collapse into
anarchy in September 1944, when {Paris was liberated and up
for grabs, and} there was an obvious temptation to go for
broke. It says that 'reforms should be well thought out,' and
that only de Gaulle . . . It's true, we'll be voting. Thorez speaks
of the sovereignty of the people; *Le Monde*, of order. Nothing
about the people. When he returns I'll explain to him what
Le Monde is, what it represents for us at this point, what it
means to us – this future envisioned by *Le Monde*. He'll have
to know this. He won't figure it out on his own. As soon as
he's back, we'll lay it out for him, this temporizing role of *Le
Monde*: three-franc paper, mouthpiece of the governmental
'soul,' the {conservative} *Le Temps* reborn, the moment has
come to restore order – resurfacing intact after six years of
silence, with three times as much paper as *L'Humanité* at its
disposal BECAUSE *L'Humanité* made the mistake of selling
clandestinely at the cost of the people's blood. If he comes
back, we'll tell him. What a joy. To tell him that and everything else. I've saved all the papers for him. If he returns I'll
eat with him. Before, no. No. The moment has come to pay
up. Everyone's paying. I'm paying. I won't eat. In Germany,
the mother of the little sixteen-year-old German who lay dying on August 17, 1944, alone on a pile of stones on the Quai

des Arts, is paying as well. He must have been dumped in the river. We're paying for a 'criminal' waiting game. Our dark past. Our sad childhood. Our threatened future. De Gaulle is in power. Perhaps he saved our honor; people believed that for four years. Now that he's out in the daylight, there's something frightening about him. He begrudges the people any praise. The people are being stifled. He talks about the French as if he were Louis XVI, and the Gaullists have now revealed their true colors. What's terrible is that in April 1945 there are so many differences between me and the person next to me at the table. Unanimity doesn't exist. A few hundred thousand French lie rotting on German soil, but they don't rally anyone, they haven't tipped the Gaullist balance one inch. The elections will take place anyway, says de Gaulle, because I said so, because nothing can interfere with order: 'For as long as I'm here, the firm will soldier on.' De Gaulle will never get over the fact that after these six years of war, France still leans toward socialism. He's paying too, like us. Not once will he speak directly to those who are paying now; when he addresses 'his' French, his sheep, it's always to distract them from their pain – and this because the people's hope is rooted in their pain. At this moment, the person next to me reading *Le Monde* isn't waiting for anything. What a sad ending. Something broken in hatred – in anger – in joy. 'I'll get roaring drunk.' 'Me, I won't do a thing.' We are the only ones waiting for something: news. The rest of the world's phony expectation, waiting for peace. In France millions are waiting. Only the Americans know what has happened to their people. The French, the Germans, the Russians will never know. American communications are reliable. The American war machine moved to the continent with its news pipelines, tanks with transmitters, and all manner of links and channels. No American will have vanished, lost completely. The parents of the little gypsy children in Buchenwald will never learn if they were gassed, had their throats cut by the Official Slaughterers of Jewish Children (in German), were burned, or rotted out in the open. Millions of Soviet partisans have disappeared. I'm waiting. No news pipeline, simply the constantly yearning soul of this part of the world, where the dead pile up in a jackstraws heap of bones: Russians, Czechs, Frenchmen, Germans, Italians, Belgians, Dutchmen, Greeks. America has seen the giant crematoria smoking. The mother of the German sixteen-year-old will never, ever, know: I was the only one in the world to know and I can't help thinking of a gray-haired old woman who will wait, grieving, for the rest of her life. Perhaps someone saw {Robert} in that ditch, when his hands reached out for the last time and his eyes wept blood – someone who will never learn who he was, and whom I will never know. Only the American and British dead get identi-fication tags; that's the advantage of going abroad. Here at home, in our old Europe, we've shown less foresight. That's where the wind of Socialism swept through, and where the cancer of Fascism took root. Europe, the [fucking nuisance] of the world. The pride of belonging to that race, a pride I can't use for anything because there isn't *anything* I can use for anything, as long as I don't know whether he's alive or dead. And yet, there's a trace of pride in Madame Cats's pain and mine. We are of the same race as the people of the cremat-oria, the gassed of Majdenek. The egalitarian function of the crematoria of Buchenwald, and their hunger. The proletarian truth of the mass graves of Belsen. In those graves, we have our share of blood. We've never seen men so equal, so alike as the skeletons of Belsen, so amazingly identical. America can't take credit for a single one of those skeletons: they are all Euro-pean, and in the vanguard of this war. The four hundred thou-sand skeletons of German Communists who died in Dora between 1933 and 1938 are in the great European common grave; the extra-continental nations have no place there – only the peoples of Europe claim them. That is the sole foundation from which a European man can think. When the Americans tell us: 'There isn't one American now, be he a barber in Chicago or a dirt farmer in Kentucky, who doesn't know what happened in the German concentration camps,' they're trying *at the same time* to lavish consolation on us, to reassure us, and to dazzle us with the admirable workings of the American war machine. What I mean by that is their reassurance of the Kentucky farmer who hadn't really known why his son had been taken away and sent to the European front.

But when you tell him that Italian partisans executed Mussolini and parked him on some meat hooks so that all Milan could take a look, the American will not feel that intense joy, that fraternal satisfaction we take in this image. That the Italian people were capable of this gives us hope, one peculiar to us Europeans – even though it was these same Italians who bombed us during the exodus of 1940 – because we see there the beginnings of one of those characteristically European reversals.

April 28. Those waiting for peace aren't waiting, not really. I don't even think about the peace: I'd like to know where he is, to know *something*. No news since Riby. To me peace still seems like a distant payoff I don't dare believe is near. I live from hour to hour, I last from morning to afternoon. Still nothing. The waiting is settling in. I see peace as a twilight that will fall over the dead. Then there will be no more reasons not to have news, they'll all drop away. Peace: darkest night. As well as the beginning of forgetting. Paris is lit up at night. I found myself the other day on the Place Saint-Germain-des-Prés: it was completely illuminated, as if by a spotlight. Les Deux Magots was packed. Heads swam above the cigarette smoke inside. It was still too cold to sit out on the sidewalk. The street was deserted. Peace seemed possible to me, and I hurried home. I glimpsed a possible future taking shape. I'm a wreck, there's no place for me anywhere, I'm nowhere else, just with him – somewhere inaccessible to those who have no one over there. I'm left hanging in suspense over an unlikely outcome, and things affect me only as signs. The lamppost on the square is a sign. To me it has lost all other meaning. Nothing is real anymore, to those of us who wait. Everyone else grows impatient, on the contrary: soldiers, civilians – they want to go home. You hear this over and over: 'What are they waiting for to sign the peace?' And every time I hear that, I know the threat is growing.

Today we learn that Hitler is dying. Himmler said so on the German radio in a last appeal, while offering to surrender unconditionally. My concierge comes upstairs and says: 'Did you ever hear the like? We won't get to skin that bastard alive.' 'There's no justice.' 'It's too much, not to have his hide, it's too much.' 'We've been robbed.' That finishes spoiling the peace, rotting the harvest on the stalk. The one most responsible among all those responsible is escaping us. That completes as well the incredible sense of the dismemberment of Germany. Berlin is burning, defended only by the 'thirty suicide battalions,' and at its heart, Hitler puts a revolver bullet in his brain. Hitler is dead.

The news hasn't been confirmed. Some believe it, others don't. But uncertainty hovers. The entire world is thinking of Hitler.

'Still.'

'Still – what?'

'What he must have gone through! Have you thought about the last three hours of his life. . . . Never since the world began has any man ever led an event of such importance to its conclusion.'

'What do you imagine he was thinking of before he died?'

'Of himself, perhaps; of his life, for the first time.'

'Let's be rigorously objective about this.'

'No.'

April 28–29. Himmler declares in his message that 'Hitler is dying' and that 'he will not last forty-eight hours after the announcement of unconditional surrender.' That would be a mortal blow to him. The United States and Britain said they would accept the surrender only with the USSR. Himmler sent his offer of capitulation to the San Francisco Conference. At the last minute, *Combat* announces that the offer of surrender has been addressed to Russia as well. The Italians don't want to hand Mussolini over to the Allies. The press is unanimous in their opposition. The newspaper *Avanti* writes: 'The Italian people were Mussolini's first victim, and he should die by their hand.' {The Italian Fascist politician} Farinacci was judged by a people's tribunal and executed in a city square (unnamed) in the presence 'of a considerable crowd.' In San Francisco: difficult hours; Europe is in the minority there. Stettinius presides. 'Witnessing the behavior of the Great Powers, the lesser powers can hold their heads up once again' (*Combat*, April 28). Meaning France and Italy and . . .

Peace has not yet been secured, and already there is talk of the 'after-peace.' That's normal. *They* won't be here for it, or for the peace, either. There are so many of them, so very many, and you can't bring back the dead: there is no resurrection, just that single one in all of world history, and it's still an endless source of astonishment. Impossible: no matter what you say or do, you cannot make a German Communist who died in Dora in 1939 amid the rise of Fascism understand that he shares in this victory. Thälmann[7] did know this before he was shot. Much has been written about death. It's the chief inspiration for artistic endeavor. The face of death discovered in Germany, on the scale of eleven million human beings, confounds art. Everything comes up against this crime and struggles against this giant dimension no cross could bear. Something new has happened. Someone quoted to me a certain man of letters opining that he is very 'moved,' and has become melancholy, and has much 'food for thought.' I think of all our poets, of all the poets in the world, who are now waiting for peace so that they may sing of this crime. One problem. The people, more simply, confront this issue when it's time to eat bread, to work. For the poet who is able *not* to write, the issue becomes more difficult, a question of life and death. All thoughts, all beliefs are under attack and defend themselves. If this crime is not 'understood' collectively, then humanity will not be worthy of having lived through it. A man who died in Belsen was not entombed in 'the purple shroud wherein the dead gods sleep.' He knew why he died: to save a justice in its birth throes, and whatever his 'political position,' he died to throw off a yoke of servitude. He died all alone – save for that collective soul and class consciousness with which he removed a bolt from a railroad one night, somewhere in Europe, without any uniform, any witness, any leaders. He was on his own. He had no part in the immortal glory of soldiers. There are no more soldiers. A people is breaking free of nineteen centuries of bondage. There are no more soldiers or civilians: now they are one and the same.

NOTES

1. Created in May 1941, the Communist-led Front National de l'Indépendance de la France was a vital Resistance movement whose armed wing was the Francs-Tireurs et Partisans Français. The FN itself engaged in sabotage, provided logistical support to Resistance members, and published their own newspaper, *Front National*.

2. When the Huns threatened Paris in 451, Saint Geneviève rallied its citizens to save the city. Francs, Burgundians, Visigoths, Bretons, and Saxons were among those who fought in the decisive battle of the Catalonic Fields (between Troyes and Châlons-sur-Marne), where the Roman emperor Valentinian III defeated Attila the Hun.

3. In 1789 the French Revolution surprised King Louis XVI; in 1830 the July Revolution overthrew King Charles X; in 1848 the February Revolution overthrew King Louis-Philippe and established the Second Republic.

4. In her biography of Marguerite Duras, Laure Adler tells the 'legendary' story (with variations) of how François Mitterrand, whose nom de guerre was Morland, helped save the life of Robert Antelme, who was on the brink of death when finally found in Germany by his friends.

5. Founded in 1941 by Henri Frenay and Claude Bourdet, among others, the Resistance movement Combat published a clandestine newspaper of the same name. Georges Bidault was recruited by the great Resistance leader Jean Moulin to set up an underground press and organize this paper, on which Albert Camus served as editor in chief and editorial writer between 1944 and 1947.

6. Maurice Thorez was an important prewar French politician, a leading Communist, and a founder – along with Blum, Daladier, and others – of the left-wing Popular Front, which was distinguished by its interest in social reform. When the Communist Party was banned by the French government after the Nazi-Soviet pact of July 1939, Thorez fled to the Soviet Union. In the summer of 1944, in recognition of the Communists' contribution to the Liberation, de Gaulle allowed Thorez to return to France, where he later became deputy prime minister (1946–47).

7. Ernst Thälmann, a founding member and leader of the German Communist Party, ran against Hitler in the presidential election of 1932. Thälmann was imprisoned in March 1933, during the Nazi pogrom against left-wing opponents of the regime after the Reichstag fire. On August 18, 1944, he was executed in Buchenwald.

BEIGE NOTEBOOK

INTRODUCTION

THE WORK OF editing the *Wartime Notebooks* was most crucial by far in the preparation of this last of the four, which was probably written over a rather long period, between around 1946 and 1949. To this *Beige Notebook* – with a reinforced, clothbound cover – belong ninety-two pages of material, a few of which are partially or entirely filled with a child's drawings. Most of the pages have come loose from their binding, and some (the number is difficult to determine) have been lost. In addition, the composition is rather discontinuous and does not respect the order of the remaining bound pages. To facilitate their reading, and rather than seeking to recreate a hypothetical order of composition, we juxtaposed fragments linked to a particular theme or to the same published work. Certain fragments, quite short and difficult to decipher, were omitted.

The inspiration of the *Beige Notebook* is very largely autobiographical; at the same time, almost all of the texts it contains were later rewritten and published, most of the time as works of fiction. This notebook thus presents an unusual opportunity to observe the way in which Marguerite Duras, from the beginning of her writing career, drew on the stories of her own life as material for fiction.

Marguerite Duras excerpted several passages from the *Beige Notebook* for the {feminist} journal *Sorcières* (1976); three of these contributions are included here: 'The Thin Yellow Children' {'The children of the plain,' p. 266}, 'The Horror of Such Love,' and the first fragment of 'Did Not Die Deported.' Other, longer pieces would later be integrated within the novels or novellas of the early 1950s: *The Sea Wall*,

The Sailor from Gibraltar, Madame Dodin. Finally, the notebook contains writings that will not appear among her published works: autobiographical texts on the return of Robert Antelme; a vacation in Italy in the summer of 1946; her pregnancy and the birth of her son Jean; political commitment; reading; writing; daily life on the rue Saint-Benoît. That Marguerite Duras reread these pages is confirmed by many marginal annotations in her handwriting made with a red felt-tip pen, notes that refer to themes or titles of her works ('Deportation'; 'War'; 'Sea Wall'; 'Dodin'; 'Sailor'; 'Sorcières') or to the abandonment of the text in question ('not used').

THE SEA WALL
(ROUGH DRAFT)

WHEN HER children ate, she would hover in front of them and watch, following their every move; she would have liked Suzanne to grow some more and Joseph too, if possible.

'Have some of the wading bird, Suzanne. That condensed milk, that won't nourish you. . . .'

'Plus it rots your teeth,' said Joseph. 'Look at me – it rotted all my teeth, even left me with a goddamn lot of trouble.'

'When we have money, you'll get yourself a bridge and no one will notice a thing,' the mother said to Joseph. 'Take some of the wading bird, Suzanne dear.'

The mother became very gentle with them when she wanted to make them eat.

Suzanne was coaxed into taking a piece of the waterfowl. The mother prepared a coffee for Joseph, who was adjusting his acetylene lamp. After setting it down, he lighted it and went out onto the veranda to see if the angle of the beam was correct.

'Shit,' said Joseph, 'he's croaked.'

The mother and Suzanne went out to join Joseph. The acetylene lamp cast its beam on the embankment by the river, where the horse lay on its flank. Its nostrils almost touched the gray water; it must have simply collapsed in one go.

'You should take a closer look,' said the mother.

Suzanne went back inside. She couldn't bear to look at the dead horse. She huddled in one of the cane armchairs, tucked her legs up under her, and stared at the acetylene lamp.

'Poor beast,' said the mother. Then she called out, 'Well?'

'He's still breathing,' yelled Joseph from the yard.

'Could we do something?' said the mother. 'Suzanne, go fetch the old checked blanket from the car.'

Suzanne went beneath the bungalow to get the blanket.

'I'm not going down!' she shouted to Joseph. 'Come get it!'

Joseph returned, took the blanket, spread it over the horse, and went out to meet the arriving trackers.

'Poor beast,' continued the mother, 'it's terrible.'

There were many children on the plain. They perched on the buffaloes. They fished at the edges of the river's backwaters. There were always plenty of them playing in the river. When boats came down the *rac*, you saw them aboard those as well. As the sun went home to bed, so did the children, off to their corners in the straw huts, to lie on the bare floors of bamboo slats. Approaching hamlets up on the mountain, one also encountered children venturing outside their village: children, goats, and the first mango trees. There were lots of stray dogs as well, wandering from village to village, covering twelve or thirteen miles a day, searching through garbage for something to eat. Thin dogs, long in the leg, chicken thieves, whom the Malays drove off with stones or killed to eat them. These dogs were the children's natural companions. Wherever there were children, there were dogs: the children did not chase them away. Every woman had a child a year, so it was the same with the children as it was with the rice, the [*illegible*] and the tigers, and the rains, the floods, the epidemics. The children flourished on the big plain: there were crowds of them, herds. The women began bearing them in their bellies, carried them afterward on their backs, then launched them on their own, and never did a child prevent its mother from going to set out rice seedlings, sow the fall seeds, and walk the thirty-seven miles to Ram to buy the year's *pagnes*. When a child was quite young, the mother carried it on her back in a kind of hammock, tied at the waist and shoulders; the child rode from place to place on the mother and the mother, at mealtimes, would chew rice and stuff the child with the paste of chewed rice, mouth to mouth. And when this happened before a Westerner, the Westerner would turn away in disgust, and the mother would laugh because they'd been doing that on the plain for a thousand years, and disgust was beside the point. The plain was steeped in poverty; no one mourned children when they died, no one made them tombs, and they buried them right in the ground, in the plain: the children returned to the plain like the wild forest mangoes, like the fruits of the mangrove trees. Many of them died every year, a great many. They died of the cholera brought on by green mangoes, but how can one keep children from climbing mango trees? And every year there were hordes of them perched in the mango trees, and then a certain number would die, and the next year others would take their places beneath those same mango trees. And lots of them would drown; still others caught worms from the dogs, filling up with worms and dying suffocated. The [*illegible*] who came down from the mountain rubbed the children with saffron {to protect them from mosquitoes}, but still some of them died, in enormous numbers. Some of them had to die, after all. The plain gave only its quota of rice and fish and [*illegible*]. Supposing that the children hadn't died anymore, they would have become like a poison, the plain would have been invaded by children as if by locusts, and perhaps people would have been forced to kill them. When one asked a woman how many children she'd had, she counted on her fingers the dead children and those still alive, and every time there were many more dead than alive. All these children learned how to talk, to sing, to laugh, to swim, to fight, all on their own, among themselves, without help from the parents, and once they were grown they were like their parents, hardworking, cheerful, and brave.

The mother had always had a few of these children at the bungalow. She'd taken many of them under her wing. They were usually orphans or children who'd been given to her. A beggar

woman had given her a little girl who'd caught worms from
the dogs; that little girl died like the horse did, of the great
misery of the plain, of that fine and fatal equilibrium of this
plain. The mother and Suzanne had wept over that little girl.
And in Suzanne's life, that day had been a day of anger and
injustice.

What the mother would have liked would have been to build
great barriers against the flood tides that scorched the crops.
Not only for herself, but for the entire plain, to see the arable
land stretch far beyond its present limits; she would have liked
to see more villages spring up along both sides of the *rac*, and
see large paddy junks on that waterway sailing the open sea all
the way to Siam. The mother went to the city several times to
ask the Land Office to please come evaluate the state of the
plain. The land office representatives had come and then they
had left, and that had been three years ago. And the sea,
making itself at home, would come in and scorch the crops.
She didn't know what to do with herself in this country, the
mother, and she was burning herself out with impatience.

Joseph had met her at the movies. She had smoked American
cigarettes throughout the entire film and since she hadn't had
a light with her, Joseph had lit her cigarettes for her and
smoked the ones she'd offered him. They had left the theater
together. And from that day on, Joseph had left Carmen and
had not been back to see her at the Hôtel Moderne for eight
days and nights.

That's how the mother, who had finished what she'd
had to do, was forced to wait eight days for Joseph's return.
Neither the mother nor Suzanne could drive the car, and
they'd had to wait for Joseph to return and take them back to
the plain.

The first two days, the mother had not stopped crying, and she'd taken so many pills that she'd slept all day long. She had paid no attention to Suzanne, leaving her to her own devices. Suzanne had spent her mornings with Carmen, and the rest of the time in the {well-to-do white district called} the Hauts Quartiers.

Now she made a habit of going to the Hauts Quartiers. She never strolled there anymore. She would leave the hotel at around five o'clock and go directly to a movie theater. Then she would leave the first theater and head straight for another one. After which, she would come right back to the hotel. The mother had given her a little money, and with Carmen's contribution she had enough to buy a ticket in the orchestra seats where she would be less conspicuous. She was through with feeling ashamed. Suzanne thought a great deal about Joseph; she believed that Joseph was through with them, and she knew she didn't count for much in her brother's life. The mother was no help to her at all. Carmen was the only one who talked to her, asked her what she had done, and gave her money. Suzanne didn't like Carmen, but she accepted her money all the same. Every evening, Carmen would ask her if she had met anyone, and Suzanne would say no. The next day, Carmen would give her more money. Suzanne felt no gratitude toward Carmen. When she returned in the evening, Carmen would kiss her, take her to her own room and ask her if she had 'met anyone' or seen Joseph. Suzanne had not seen Joseph. Carmen wasn't the least bit distressed that Joseph had left her, but what she would have liked was to reassure the mother.

'She hasn't gotten up yet,' Carmen would say. 'What Joseph's doing, that had to happen, but she's like a young girl, she doesn't want to understand.'

Suzanne would leave Carmen and go see the mother.

Instead of a bed, Carmen's room had a divan covered with hand-painted cushions. There were Harlequins and Pierrots on the walls. On the vanity table with its triple mirrors, there was a pot of artificial flowers. Suzanne had a true horror of that room, because she knew that it was where everything with Joseph had begun.

Suzanne knew what it was all about. Joseph had told her it meant being completely naked with a completely naked woman and in the same bed. Suzanne saw Carmen completely naked and she did not understand Joseph. And now he was again completely naked lying with a completely naked woman. And that made a huge difference between herself and Joseph.

It was always the same thing. The mother, awake, lying on the bed in a chemise, would be waiting for Joseph in the dim light.

'So, you saw him?' the mother would ask.

'Didn't see him,' Suzanne would reply.

Since the mother was letting Suzanne go into the Hauts Quartiers in the hope that Joseph would turn up, she would then start crying and ask for a pill.

'You'd be better off coming down to dinner,' Suzanne would say, 'than taking your stupid pills.'

The mother insisted. She had never yet felt so afraid of having an epileptic fit and dying as at that moment. It was probably staying alone in her room all day that was giving her such ideas. Suzanne felt a dull, pent-up anger at her mother for waiting like that for Joseph. Suzanne repeated what Carmen kept saying.

'Sooner or later,' said Suzanne, 'it had to happen. That's no reason to make yourself sick.'

The mother said that she knew this, but that it was still terrible to lose Joseph that way, so suddenly.

Suzanne went to the window, sat down by the casement, and watched the river that spread its wide and shining waters in the distance, beyond the bustling city. The mother fell asleep. Suzanne thought about the movies she had seen.

It was at the hotel that she was supposed to meet the thread salesman from Calcutta. He was passing through, staying at the hotel. He was looking to get married and wanted the woman to be [young], French, and a virgin.

He had confided in Carmen, who told him immediately about Suzanne.

He was a man of about forty, who had traveled several times around the world.

THE HORROR OF SUCH LOVE
(ROUGH DRAFT)

I WAS TOLD: 'Your child is dead.' It was an hour after the delivery; I'd caught a glimpse of the child. The next day, I asked: 'What was he like?' I was told: 'He's blond, a bit sandy haired; he has your high brows, he looks like you.' 'Is he still there?' 'Yes, he'll be there until tomorrow.' 'Is he cold?' R. replied: 'I haven't touched him but he must be, he's very pale.' Then he hesitated. 'He's beautiful: that's because of death, too.' I asked to see him. R. told me no. I asked the mother superior. She told me: 'It's not worth it.' I did not insist. They had explained where he was: in a little room next to the delivery room, to the left as you go in. The next day I was alone with R. It was quite hot. I was lying on my back; my heart was very tired, I wasn't supposed to move. I wasn't moving. 'What's his mouth like?' 'He has your mouth,' R. said. And every hour: 'Is he still there?' 'I don't know.' I couldn't read. I looked at the open window, at the foliage of the acacias growing on the embankments of the railroad line encircling the city.

In the evening, Sister Marguerite came to see me. 'He's an angel, you should be content.' 'What will they do with him?' 'I don't know,' said Sister Marguerite. 'I want to know.' 'When they're that little we burn them.' 'Is he still there?' 'He's still there.' 'So they're burned?' 'Yes.' 'It's quick?' 'I don't know.' 'I don't want him to be burned.' 'There's nothing to be done about it.' The next day, the mother superior came: 'Do you want to give your flowers to the Holy Virgin?' I said: 'No.' The nun looked at me: she was seventy years old, withered by the daily work of running a clinic; she was terrifying, she had a belly I imagined as black and dried out, full of shriveled roots. She returned the following day. 'Do you want to take communion?' I said: 'No.' Then she looked at me. Her face was horrible, it was the face of wickedness, the devil's face. 'So: it doesn't want communion and it's feeling sorry for itself because its child is dead.' She left and slammed the door. People addressed her as 'Reverend Mother.' (She is one of the three or four people I've met whom I would have liked to gut. To gut. The word is staggering. To gut. The word was made for her, for her belly bloated with black ink.)

It was very hot. It was between the fifteenth and thirty-first of May. Summertime. I told R.: 'I don't want any more visits. Just you.' Lying down, still facing the acacias. I was so empty that the skin of my belly was sticking to my back. The child had come out. We were no longer together. He had died a separate death. An hour, a day, a week ago, a death apart, dead to a life we had lived nine months together and through a death he had just died separately. My belly had collapsed heavily, plop, into itself, like a worn-out cloth, a rag, a pall, a slab, a door, a void, that belly. It had gloriously carried in an adorable bulge that flourishing seed, a submarine fruit (a child is a green fruit that, like a green fruit, makes your mouth water) that had lived only in the dark, viscous, and velvety warmth of my flesh and had been killed by daylight, by the death blow of its solitude in space. So small and already so much, ever since he had died apart. 'Where is he?' I kept saying to R. 'Has he been burned?' 'I don't know.' People were saying: 'It's not so terrible at birth. Better that than to lose them at six months.' I didn't answer people. Was it terrible? I believe that it was. Precisely that coincidence between his 'coming into the world' and his death. Nothing. I had nothing left. That emptiness was terrible. I had not had a child, not even for an hour: forced to imagine everything. Motionless, I imagined.

This one, who is here now and sleeping, this one laughed a little while ago, he laughed at a giraffe someone had just given him. He laughed and that made a sound. It was windy, and a tiny bit of the sound of that tiny laugh reached me. Then

I raised the hood of his carriage a little more and gave him back his giraffe so he would laugh again. He laughed again and I plunged my head under the carriage hood to capture all the sound of the laugh. Of my child's laugh. I put my ear to this shell to hear the sound of the sea. The idea that this laughter was blowing away with the wind was unbearable. I caught it. I'm the one who got it. Sometimes when he yawns, I inhale his mouth, the breath of his yawn. I am not a crazy mother. I am not living only on that laughter, that breath. I need many other things, solitude, a man. No. I know what a child is worth. 'If he dies,' I thought, 'that laugh – I will have gotten it.' It's because I lost a child, it's because I know they can die that I'm like this. I measure the full horror of the possibility of such love. Motherhood mellows you, they say. Crap. Since having my child I've turned mean. At long last I'm certain about that horror, at last I've grasped it, at last people who believe in God have become complete strangers to me.

VACATION WITH D.

IT WAS A beautiful afternoon. It was August. Oh, that month, that terrible month you know is the hottest one, the heart of the year – that peak – that calvary of beauty – that Via Dolorosa, the month of August. The balcony of the studio apartment overlooked the valley, a gigantic valley over sixty miles long, almost twenty miles wide, and two-thirds of a mile deep spreading out forests, lakes, fields, and clearings beneath our balcony in a cosmic, aerial view for us, moving D. to say, 'Our Mother Earth is green.' On the balcony we'd feel the razor-sharp wind that almost never stopped whipping past, day and night, blowing, blowing. Enough to drive you crazy. I was telling D., 'In Carcassonne, in the seventeenth century, they used to adjourn trials after three days of wind. It influenced the juries.' That afternoon – a lull. (The calm before the crime, before death.) We were reading down in the garden, D. and I, on a mat, in front of the valley. Then, having had enough of reading, D. went to watch the ants at the base of the linden and I went to adjust the rubber hose on the cellar faucet and I began to water the garden path then I got undressed and I watered myself then said to D., 'Come and get watered.' D. didn't want to, then the grass, then the wall [...]

MEMORIES OF ITALY

HE WAS, however, separate from me. I loaned myself to him so that he could make himself. In my flesh bathed his, nascent, but distinct, with his youth, nervousness, freshness, independence, the anger of a sea creature struggling toward the surface. His independence was deep inside me, so naked, so striking, that I felt as if torn apart by the truth, stripped bare, like a woman screwing, his truth. That is how the virility of maternity feels. None of the most acknowledged aspects of virility can touch that one, if by virility one means the brutal exercise of a freedom. I brutally exercised my freedom in the face of that complete freedom rooting around deep inside me. I felt that freedom live, and my own, just as free, outside, containing it.

(Now when I reread those lines, he is here, outside of me, a few yards away, asleep. His freedom is no less complete, nor is mine. My life is linked to his, dependent on it down to the slightest details. If he dies, the beauty of the world dies and it will be pitch dark on my earth. In other words, if he dies, I die to the world. That's why I don't fear his death more than I do death. That's why, just when I am the most fettered, I am the most free. My revolt, my rebellious power, has never been as violent. Since such a love, such an amorous imprisonment, is within the realm of possibility, while at the same time this possibility contains the death of the object of that imprisonment, in this case I would want God to exist in order to embody this possibility, and so that I could curse him. Because the object of my love is more important to me than myself – not only in my own eyes but in itself, embedding itself more preciously in the world, with a greater value. I'm not the one who imparts that precious worth to him, but it's important to me that he live. People who have no children and who speak of death make me laugh. Like virgins and priests who imagine love. They have an imaginary experience of death. Alive, they imagine themselves struck down by death, whereas the dead cannot enjoy that death. With a child, though, one lives out that idea every day and if it should actually happen, you enjoy your death alive, you are among the living dead.)

And I became afraid that it was too late for anything at all, even for having that child. It was then that I thought of the evening between Pisa and Florence, of that evening and our stay in Bocca di Magra, because it was there, in the sun, in the luminous haze of the beach, beside the sea, in mid-August, that for the first time in my life the feeling of death inside me vanished. Just as if, amid that light and those colors, the slow fog of the idea of death that always darkens my life had suddenly ceased, and left me free. Then I felt, on my burning skin, the cool shivering of my blood and organs – I really felt that, because I had come out of the water and sat down in the sun and, profoundly refreshed by my dip, at the same time I felt that coolness pearling in my armpits in a very light sweat; I felt my flesh cooled by my swim and well protected by my skin, and even though that skin was burning, I wasn't hot. My sweat began to bead among the hairs in my armpits, and then – below my ribs, in a hollow still throbbing from my swim (looking down, I saw my heartbeat on the skin of my abdomen) – hunger struck. That was when my life was so precise, so well delineated, there, crushed beneath the sun yet fighting and demanding and carrying on, that the idea of death became acceptable, as a reality as implacable as my own. And then I told myself that as long as I could live such moments and feel myself so strongly, bathed in such a light, I could gladly grow old.

And then Ginetta called to me: 'Let's go take a sunbath.' We climbed up the dunes and went deep into the reeds, the two of us. The others – Elio, Robert, Dionys, Anne-Marie, Menta, Baptista, and the rest – stayed on the beach. The reeds were so dense that they muffled almost all sound. Ginetta spread her towel out in a nice snug bare spot, and took off her bathing suit. I did the same, placing my towel beside hers and shedding my suit. It was the first time I had seen Ginetta stark naked. I found her very beautiful. 'You're very beautiful, Ginetta.' She said, 'I don't know about that, but Elio tells me so.' She was very long, very long, the way certain animals are long: the antelope, the panther, certain breeds of dogs, long-legged bitches with hollow flanks and long necks, bred for hunting and racing. She had an almost flat belly, barely curved, and firm breasts, rather small for her body, and suspended in a unique way, with equal tension on all sides as if they had roots reaching all the way to the shoulders, down to the top of the abdomen, even into the armpits, widespread roots. When she lay on her towel, her arms behind her head, you saw almost nothing of her breasts except their brown tips. They barely made a bulge above her ribs. She told me that she found me beautiful, too, and then we fell silent. Above the reeds, the snowy flanks of the marble quarries of Carrara sparkled with whiteness. On the other side, we saw Monte Marcello, above the hill overlooking the mouth of the Magra River, Monte Marcello wrapped in its vines and fig trees, way atop its dark slopes of pines. Elio, Robert, Dionys, Baptista, and Gino were playing ball, and we heard their laughter along with the soft sound of the August sea, flattened by the heat. Listening to Elio like that, lying near Ginetta's naked body, I thought about their love, not through time, but in space, about how that love of Elio's had taken root in and was feeding every day on that woman. It was a terrifying love, which terrified us perhaps because it was always so present, every minute, so present and definitive that it was frightening the way the absolute is frightening, because it forced you to believe in love and because far from impoverishing you (since you, you were not living a great love like that), far from depressing you, it made you hope for more than you'd ever expected from love until then, and made you wonder (that's the word, I believe, wonder, meaning to stand bereft of reason before a marvel) at the fact that two beings, a man and a woman, could take in each other an interest so overwhelming, inexhaustible, and daily resurgent that each represented, for the other, the whole world. Not that Elio or Ginetta devoted all their time to loving each other – far from it, they're on the contrary people very busy with life, absorbed in various occupations, but each is for the other the springboard that launches them into every day, strengthened by that élan they find only in one another. You might tell me that it was a stroke of luck, witnessing such a love, in a setting like Bocca di Magra. I believe it was a stroke of luck.

Hearing Elio's voice, Ginetta smiled. 'He's like a child,' she said. Then shortly afterward she said: 'I'm forty-one years old.' She was brushing away flies with a hand she'd freed from beneath her head, a long brown hand with pale fingernails. Through the slits of her eyelids, you could see her pupils staring at the reeds. And since she was brown from the sun, those pupils seemed much greener than usual – exactly the color of the sea when the {southwest wind called the} *libeccio* blows. 'And Elio, he's thirty-eight,' she said. The sea breeze could not penetrate the reeds, and the heat was terrific. Ginetta and I felt the sweat gradually trickling from our pinned-up hair past our eyelids, and from the creases of our drawn-up knees, and beading on our upper lips, where it was cool and salty when we licked them. Ginetta sat up, reached into her bathing cap, pulled out two lemon halves, and handed one to me; she lay down again and we squeezed the lemons over our open mouths. 'It's very good,' said Ginetta. There was more to it than that, but I knew what she meant. I felt quite friendly toward her, for saying that. The sun was beating down on us almost unbearably, but it was such a violent way of feeling our physical being that this burning was a pleasant pain. We were thinking about the sea fifteen yards away and into which, running to avoid searing our feet on the sand, we would be jumping in a moment. But we could still wait, and bear a bit more broiling sunshine. It was a terrible burning and now and then, unable to endure it anymore in the same spot, we would turn over, passing our palms soothingly over our bellies and thighs. I knew that Ginetta was thinking about her approaching old age (worse than her death), the time when their love would lose some of its splendor, and I knew that at that moment, she accepted this, vanquished by the reality of the sun, of this August noon in which she lay, every bit as real. So powerful was this radiant reality that it forced a halt on the way to death. And if death was at the end of this reality, it was acceptable. That's what Ginetta was feeling, the same as I was feeling, at that moment. Drop by drop the lemon juice slipped down our throats to land on our raw hunger, reviving it, making us take the measure of its strength, its depth. After the taste of salt in our naked, sea-washed mouths, the lemon made our mouths water with saliva that seemed as cool as a spring in that heat, and the lemon was quite ideally the very fruit of that particular kind of sun, and that particular moment. These lemons of the Carrara plain are enormous, they have a thick peel that keeps them cool in the sun, they're as juicy as oranges, but they have a harsh flavor, a pure acidity, and they don't have that refreshing taste our lemons do.

The others kept playing, shouting when someone managed to catch the ball, or missed it, louder when someone missed it or took too much time returning it to his partner who, frozen in expectation, was searing the soles of his feet. Elio and Baptista were shouting the most. Dionys, somewhat less, and Robert hardly at all. Menta was also shouting with Anne-Marie; they were refereeing, cheering or booing the players. We had scrambled back into our suits – it wasn't possible to stay in that sun – and passed through the reeds to arrive at the top of the dune. Ginetta let out a hoarse, wild cry the way she always did when she had come over from her side of the Magra to ours in a boat (a dog, Gibraltar, came along). Elio turned around: 'Hey, Ginetta!' We ran into the sea. Ginetta swam a long way out. Me, I swam a few strokes, near the shore; I was one of the less-accomplished swimmers. The sea was blue, even there, right under our eyes, and there were no waves but a very gentle swell, the breathing of a deep sleep. The others left their game and huddled on their towels on the sand. I stopped swimming and looked at them, at Dionys and Robert. Robert was looking at me; he blinked behind his glasses, smiled at me and jerked his head upward in little nods, as if to say: 'And what about you? How's it going? You, you're so tiny in the sea, and look at you! Managing to swim and live – sometimes I forget to watch little old you and finding you again, that makes me happy.' And I was looking too, at him, and thinking, 'He's there because he didn't die in the concentration camp.' I knew he knew that I'd been thinking this, every day, for a year. And that at that moment I was thinking: 'There he is laughing away, he doesn't know a thing; me, I know.' When he weighed his eighty-four pounds and I used to take him in my arms and help him pee and go caca, when he had a fever of 105.8, and down at his coccyx, his backbone was showing, and when day and night, there were six of us waiting for a sign of hope, he had no idea what was going on.

He was curious about everything. Dionys would read him *L'Humanité*. He'd ask us if we were doing all right. He didn't know that he was dying. He was happy. He didn't feel the fever, he'd say, 'I feel stronger,' and it was the fever, he was just wasting away with fever, and when he tried to lift the little spoon to eat his gruel, his hand drooped from the weight. And he'd gotten to the point where the blanket felt too heavy and was hurting him. And now, there he is laughing on the beach in the sunshine. He's in Italy, that's right, taking sunbaths, playing ball, he's a Communist, he talks with Elio and Dionys about the Marxist justification of tourism in a revolutionary period. Yes indeed, he eats *pasta chuta* – {pasta with fresh tomatoes, black pepper, sea salt, and chives} – and drinks chianti, he climbs up to San Marcello like nobody's business. Only Dionys and I know these things, know what he does – the others don't, and he least of all. Dionys and I, watching him in action, we kept reviewing the past, and behind his back, we'd crack up. And even though things weren't going well between Dionys and me, on that point, we were in perfect complicity. We laughed ourselves silly, with looks that said, 'You believe it? We fooled him!'

It was the only thing we agreed on. On everything else, we didn't. It isn't time yet to say those things, anyway I couldn't say them clearly, because, besides the fact that I don't have clear ideas about anything, on that subject I had even fewer. What made the shadow that lay between Dionys and me at that time even worse was that he claimed to know perfectly why it was there, but said he wasn't going to explain it, he refused, accusing me of bad faith because I knew just as well as he did 'what was going on' but was pretending I didn't. I don't believe that this was really that important, that it seriously affected our memories of that trip. At the time, it wasn't a big deal, at least I don't think so; I don't know if Dionys agrees with me. We haven't talked about it, because shortly after our return, I was expecting the baby. It's his nature to have views on the subject, though; Dionys certainly has some, but I don't know what they are.

The baby came and temporarily swept everything away. This morning, as a matter of fact, in that harsh and implacable light, I felt that the baby was a solution. No, Dionys would say, there is no solution to a problem except the one that follows from the very conditions of the problem. And yet, this morning, I felt that the baby was a solution even for Dionys;

{I felt this} on his behalf and no matter what he thinks about it. I don't mean that this child will replace anything whatsoever, and in particular what is past, between us, the madness of the first months. No. It's a soothing solution. When a couple is breaking up, when everything falls apart, at one of life's moments of greatest doubt, when love is dying on itself and there's no way of telling how life will regain its savor, and when, after having four arms and legs you find yourself crippled by the amputation of the other – this flower grows in your womb. So you stop driving yourself goddamn crazy trying to find out if you exist. You exist because of this community. And then you feel free to leave each other, without this leaving the mortal taste of death in your mouths. More precisely, you are free. The past is not destroyed down to its roots. Free from the past. Even though it was all going badly at that point, Dionys carried the same weight, his life and death had the same meaning in me, and I could watch him swim with the emotion of four years earlier. With even greater emotion, probably, because I was not discovering it but rediscovering it, and he was swimming bathed for me in my knowledge of him, of all that I knew he'd done over these four years before going swimming that day.

One day, I thought he'd drowned. A terrible *libeccio* was blowing the way it does every August. Even in just over two feet of water, the waves would knock you down. The entire sea was rearing up, white, rugged with waves three times the height of a man. Everyone had decided we shouldn't swim; at most, we'd go to a large flat area sheltered by the jetty at the mouth of the Magra, to be splashed by the waves. Dionys had decided to go swimming. It's his nature to trust other people only moderately and simply to be nice, but never with conviction. Everyone had argued against it. Dionys had finally given in.

And after deciding that, he was furious about deciding that. He looked longingly at the sea. I knew what he was thinking:

that he'd let himself be persuaded, which was beneath him, and that I was the one who'd prevented him, I was the obstacle to his living as he pleased. The sea was alone in its uproar. In the brilliant sunshine, colors were bright after the previous night's storm and the air was cool: it was weather for going along the beach all the way to Marina di Carrara while looking at the sea. Robert, Anne-Marie, and I had decided to do that. After accompanying us for a little while, Dionys sat down on the sand, intending to stay there, he said, to look at the sea. This was halfway between Marina di Carrara and the jetty where the others were, Elio, Ginetta, Menta, and Baptista. And we knew that Dionys was planning to go swimming without any interference while we were gone. We had stopped in front of a line of rocks twenty yards out from the shore and against which the sea was breaking with all its strength. A veritable wall of spray shot up from the rocks and drained endlessly away with a mighty noise. At their base the sea struck muffled sounds like blows, then plumed up into the sun and evaporated. Dionys said he wanted to stay there to watch. 'You're not going to watch that for two hours,' Robert said. Dionys said that yes, indeed, he wanted to, that it was by watching the same spectacle, ceaselessly renewed, that one managed to pass from curiosity to interest, that seeing was precisely that. He said this, and lay down, determined to stay. We were standing around him, looking sometimes at the sea, sometimes at his body stretched out on the sand. And we saw his body in the sea. Just as completely as fire, the sea would have devoured him. It was quite simply unimaginable that he could make it out of there. Seeing how powerfully the waves were crashing against the rocks, we imagined that force attacking him head-on, at chest height, bowling him over and holding him down, implacably and with the weight of a massive slab of water, until he was dead, then releasing him, and then him coming back in the cresting tangle of frothing waves like a mat of crushed reeds. Because the sea that morning was inhumanly high and you might as well have bathed in flames in a huge oven, attacked a raging bull, a pack of ravening wolves, hurled yourself alone against an oncoming tank, pitting flesh against steel. And yet no one said anything. We could tell from the look in his eye that Dionys had reached that stubborn limit where he became completely unreasonable and would, if we opposed him even the least bit more, head without any hesitation straight for death. Tight-lipped, he stared at the rocks, disdaining us absolutely. At that moment we hated him, all the while measuring, as never before, what it would be like to lose him, and what that whole admirable valley of sunlight, fruits, and snowy marble, and our lives, would be like once the sea had swallowed him up. By staying, however, we would be displaying such unbearable, dishonorable, unforgivable tactlessness (just as if, by preventing him from satisfying his desire to go swimming that morning, we had kept him from making love with a woman for whom he'd felt an insane desire, and all because of some odious formalism, for example because the woman would have ruined him, just as if – in short – we had prevented him from living, by denying him the adventure of risking danger, claiming concern for his safety whereas, by not running the risk, he would find his life impossible to live, etc.) that without discussing it, or saying anything to him to let him know anyway what that silence meant, we went off to Marina. To tell the truth, we weren't sure he would go swimming. I said to Robert, 'You think he'll go swimming?' 'He's not crazy,' said Robert.

I don't remember Marina di Carrara very well. Before reaching it, we passed a holiday camp run by Alfa Romeo. All the little children were eating, standing up, near a long table. Marina was crisscrossed by clanging and crowded streetcars, hurtling beneath a torrid sun down the middle of dusty avenues lined with flowering oleanders in front of bombed-out houses. All I will say is, once again it looked like Africa, just like Sarzana on market day. Naked children white with dust surrounded stalls of watermelons and cotton goods; there wasn't one tree, one blade of grass on the dust-whitened square. It was noon. Large awnings of white canvas shaded cafeterias and their terraces sprinkled {with water to settle the dust}; a peddler thundered into a mic in praise of his rubber bands, while the little black-eyed Italian children with their skinny legs pinched one another, shrieked, or napped in the shade of the stalls, in the dust. Now and then a girl would come out of a house, and one of them came from the cafeteria where we were going to have lunch: she was fresh, pink and brown, dressed in black, dazzling and moist like a fruit of water and night pulled from the water still dripping with coolness and night. Or it was as if the dense darkness of the cool houses of Marina – while the sun outside was scorching colors, sounds, the very earth rising in a fiery white dust – had harbored a kind of equatorial undersea vegetation, the mere sight of which flooded you with coolness and desire in the burning sun, and made you feel the value of that sunshine in which bloomed a darkness so rich, so heavy, so fertile, so brimming with beauty. And when we entered the restaurant, the girl's eyes gleamed in silence, black and wet; she stood in the shade of the awnings, her mouth half-opened on her teeth, her mouth like the virgin interior of an oyster, moistened, her lips like the edges of a fresh wound ready to bleed, and they would have made, those lips alone, the manhood of every fellow who saw them parting in a smile rise up naked and deadly, while she simply stood there, completely, as completely as a plant, unself-conscious, her hand resting on the white table laden with a heavy dish of tomatoes shining with oil and as red as the girl's lips, red with the cold fire of dark shadows after the sun.

I was saying that Marina resembled Sarzana, and as I said it I believed that Dionys was already cold and dead, floating on the crest of the waves. I felt the sun on my life but the whole inside of my body was drenched in an icy stream. Robert bought a bottle of chianti. He seemed reassured. Anne-Marie bought some chocolate. We were on the main avenue of Marina. Streetcars were still going by. I went to have a coffee in a bar, under a sun umbrella. The coffee was quite good and it was nice on that terrace. Anne-Marie and Robert came to join me carrying the chianti and the chocolate, and I said to myself it wasn't worth the bother because Dionys was dead. They ordered a Cinzano and I, another coffee, and they told me what they'd seen and what they should have bought in the grocery store. They were so emphatic about it all that I realized they were trying to reassure me about Dionys, to prove to me that if they'd been really worried, they wouldn't have been thinking about such things. But I told myself: 'If they've bought the chianti, it's to reassure me,' and I didn't believe in it anymore. We took the streetcar back and at the last stop, by the edge of a pine forest, we returned to the beach. To the right, we walked past a wood of olive trees for a while; they were very old, with squat, twisted trunks, gnarled and distorted, but their foliage was light, young. Afterward we came to the thick stand of reeds. There was no wind; the sun was directly over the plain, and all the villages in the Carrara Mountains – when we turned around, which we couldn't help doing – stood out whitely in the valleys against the mountainsides. I was waiting for the moment when we'd reach the wall of rocks. The sea was still terrifying, whipped up by a vain and bitter fury. Anne-Marie and Robert were talking about Marina and the bombings of the coast, especially around Marina. Strewn all over the beach, little mollusks were dying, torn from the sea; they were drying out in the sun and collapsing in small sticky puddles of bright green. Death was everywhere. The air smelled of death; the scent of pines, iodine, rain – it was the smell of death. I looked at the jetty in the distance and thought that my life extended that far, after which, I would not be able to return to the hotel. We reached the wall of rocks; Dionys wasn't there. On the beach, there was the imprint of his body lying down. 'He'll have gone back to the hotel,' said Robert.

But afterward, Anne-Marie and he didn't chat anymore and they looked off into the distance, on the beach. I had ceased to exist. Everyone has experienced that, has seen an empty beach when they were expecting to find someone there. We've all seen that, the empty beach and the empty sea and that's all, the sun overhead, and in the distance, mountains, villages bright and bustling in the sunshine, orchards as far as the eye can see, laden with fruit. Who hasn't seen that? The empty sea, the empty beach, the sun and *all* the rest. Empty. There where you expected to find someone, nothing, only the imprint of a body on the sand, and beside it, the sea. Beside it, the sea. Unfathomable. As far as the eye can see, the sea. You make the connection between the sea and the imprint of the body on the sand, and it's horror. The insuperable thing. To go on living with the idea of that precious body lost in the sea of inhuman scale, of mathematical, diabolical proportions, buffeted by the whims of the water, in the depths of the night. The body you've touched, loved, felt beneath your fingers. A second death, that.

So Dionys wasn't where we'd left him, but a little farther on, near the jetty. He had dug himself a hole in the sand and was waiting quietly for us, he said, but actually somewhat impatiently, because we'd taken so long. And I – I didn't say one word more than the others. 'Hello,' we said, and Dionys stood up; we went along the beach and then returned to the hotel via the path leading through the Jews' Camp (more about that later). I was quite calm, and I was discovering that, listening to Dionys talk and knowing he was there, walking beside me, I asked for nothing more, nothing. He was still cross with me because of my attitude that morning and he directed a few pointed remarks at me, but it was as if he were speaking a million miles away or in ancient times. Besides, I listened only to the sound of his voice, and if he'd cursed me I would have heard only the tone of his voice, I would have felt only the contours, the weight, the sound of it in the sun.

I was a cave to receive that voice, nothing more – I was no longer of this earth, not that I would have been any happier, but I was experiencing a kind of cosmic moment, a sort of ascesis, if you will, in which nothing of life could reach me anymore save the very idea of life, and not its earthly manifestations. Dionys was pictured, so to speak, and nothing would ever disfigure [that image] again.

That's how I knew, once I'd had that experience because of him, that I was attached to him, at my core. Not that I loved him, for the experience was no proof of love, because passion adjusts to death, which it subordinates to itself. No: that I was attached to him. And that it was important. I remained in that state all day and through a strange contagion, Robert was, in my eyes, possessed of the same eternity as Dionys. And at noon, al fresco, I let them drink all the Cinzano they wanted, and they were astonished. They were astonished and I smiled at their astonishment; they were little children and I was like a believer before the heathen, or someone who believes in eternal life before some children oblivious to everything, except their games.

It was like that for months after Robert returned from Germany. I would look at him and be fulfilled. He would eat a lamb chop and then suck the bone, eyes lowered, entirely absorbed in finding every scrap of meat. After which he'd eat a second chop and then a third, without looking up. He was sitting near a window in the drawing room, all surrounded with cushions, in his slippers, his cane by his side, his legs as scrawny as crutches in his trousers, and when the sun shone, you could see through his hands. He'd come back from far, far away, a place from which one almost never returns. You know, behind him there was an abyss of pain: death was behind him, he was coming back from it, you could see this, he was clawing his way out of death, hauling himself along by clinging to his chop bone like a drowning man clutching a wreck he didn't dare let go of yet, not yet, in those first days, when he didn't waste one crumb of bread. Me, I used to watch him, everyone did, a stranger would have watched him too because that was an unforgettable sight, the spectacle of blind life. Of life scorned, crushed, humiliated, spat upon, beaten, a life supposedly mortally wounded at its root, and then there in the deepest density of the body, a trickle of life still ran, the withered tree isn't dead: at its foot, a bud. And it gets going again. And the sign of its new start is hunger, more than hunger, blind, stubborn devouring, the gulping of a newborn at the breast. After careful thought, I do not believe that anything in the realm of strength and beauty has ever stunned me like the sight of Robert eating for the first time three weeks after his return. The doctor kept him on gruel for three weeks when he was gripped by fever, not knowing what he had.

All food simply raced through him, without nourishing him, and he used to choke on a teaspoon of gruel: after swallowing it he would sit up straight in his bed, supported by us, gasping for air. After three weeks, the doctor said we had to give him everything to eat, to put him in front of food. And then he began to be hungry: as soon as he'd eaten and his hunger could feed on itself, it became gigantic, frightening. We'd leave him with the food, *alone, in the dim light of the drawing room*, and in silence, in a silence more pious and sacred than that of any religious service, he would eat. We avoided distracting or speaking to him at such moments, and walked on tiptoe. We would set the dish down in front of him and leave him and he would function. During that initial period he had no marked preferences for any dish, he was a chasm of hunger: an enormous call came from his wasted entrails, such a powerful, rumbling voice, an order that he obeyed, humble, servile, just as blind as a plant. Once he feels hungry, the doctor said, it means life is picking up again. I watched him. I watched Dionys sleep, warm and breathing, tanned, alive,

beneath the arbors of muscat grapes, on that afternoon following his death within me. For a month I watched Robert,
unable to get used to it, or tired of it. When the dishes didn't
arrive quickly enough he would sob, he'd say that no one
understood him. 'Is he hungry?' the doctor would ask. We'd
laugh. And when he sobbed with hunger, we'd hide to laugh
our fill. All those things left their mark on me and this morning, when I awoke, they weighed on me, not that I'd thought
about them specifically but they were there, they furnished me
– the way my furniture furnishes my bedroom without me
seeing it all every instant: these things are there, profoundly
there. I don't think they're not there; they are there. It's my
life, it's what I cannot share or remove. These things *were* in
the rumbling of the garbage bin on the sidewalk, in the light
beaming through the foundations of the {new} École de
Médecine as well, and had a part in the meaning of a man's
footsteps as he walked alone in a silent street. Ever since I saw
Robert eat after his return, since that deathly fear, next to
which all vanity, ambitions, all plans were literally swept
away [. . .].

Among all cities I love these, the ones that resemble Sarzana,
Marina di Cararra, Aden, and certain Corsican cities, Bonifa-
cio, Pontevecchio, Toulon as well, the treeless cities (Florence,
too, the most striking thing is that there isn't a single tree in
Florence) with the torrid squares that, from noon until three,
empty out, close up, are completely dead. Such cities are
usually dirty, smelling of onion, horse manure, and since
they're by the sea, fish. The houses there are old, badly constructed, poor, crowded; the entryways and halls smell musty,
there are no gardens, and on the square a fountain dispenses a
trickle of water. Shop displays are rare, and set in windows:
there are slippers, turnovers, caramels, postcards, work
smocks. Everything's crumbling in these cities; the pavement

is potholed, the street sweeper naps from one to three o'clock, there's only one sweeper for the whole city because the municipality is poor, and there's garbage in the gutters. These cities are swept by the sea wind that rises toward three in the afternoon, and then, on those empty squares, dust flies up in clouds; the dust of these cities is fine, salty, smelling of urine, and it's everywhere, covering the box trees in the priest's garden (the only plants in the city), powdering the little children's feet.

When it rains at the end of August, these cities smell like no other: the dust of five months of summer and all sorts of rotting rubbish swells and exhales its odors of wet hides. These cities weren't made to please, they're markets that provision the surrounding countryside. On their outskirts camp traveling picture-shows, funfairs. To me these cities are the most erotic in the world. Cities of shadow, of sunlight. Contrasting shadow. Shadow is erotic.

It's of these cities, I tell myself, that Gaston the sweeper is dreaming.

DID NOT DIE DEPORTED

YOU HAD TO see him eat. That man ate like no man ever eats. Or beast, either. Or anything, any species, not even the tiger, or the shark that goes miles and miles with its mouth open and, through a maddening excess of hydrochloric acid in its stomach, swallows twelve times its own volume in food. No, he ate with patience and passion.

At first he could not eat like that. I mean right after his return, because his stomach was so shrunken that the weight of the food would have torn it open, or if it hadn't burst, it would have pressed against his heart, which on the contrary, in the cavern of his emaciation, was now dilated and pumping so fast you could have counted its pulsations, unable to say that it was beating in the proper sense of the word, for it trembled like a hunted animal consumed by terror. No, he could not have eaten without dying of it. Yet, he had to eat: he could no longer go without eating without dying of that.

That was the problem. He was hungry. When he arrived, he embraced his friends. He went all around his apartment. He was smiling. In other words, his cheeks puckered and unstuck themselves a little from his jawbone. Then he sat down in the drawing room. That's when he started looking at the {cherry} clafoutis sitting on a console table. Then he stopped smiling. 'What's that?' 'It's a clafoutis.' Then, 'Can I have some?' 'Let's wait for the doctor.' But in a moment, 'I really can't have any?' Then he asked us about what had happened while he was gone. But it was over: now he had eyes only for the clafoutis. When the doctor entered the drawing room, Robert was on the couch. The doctor stopped short and stood with his hand on the doorknob, turning pale. But he did come into the room and go up to Robert, he didn't leave, as we might have feared he would.

The doctor did not allow him any clafoutis. But he told the rest of us that if Robert was craving some clafoutis, that probably meant there was still a little hope. We removed the clafoutis without him noticing it. Then the struggle began. Against death. We had to tackle death gently, with delicacy, tact, finesse. It surrounded him on all sides, but, but, nevertheless, there was still a way to reach him – it wasn't large, this opening for communication with him, but life was in him after all, barely a scrap (but a scrap of life, it's got color and a name after all: life). Death attacked. 103.1 degrees the first day. Then 104. Then 105.8. Death was getting winded. 105.8. The heart was quivering like a violin string. Still 105.8. But it was quivering. The heart, we thought – the heart will stop. Still 105.8. Death was striking staggering blows. But the heart was deaf. It isn't possible, the heart will stop. No.

Gruel, the doctor had said, by teaspoons. But one teaspoon of gruel choked him – he would cling to our hands, sucking air, and fall back onto his bed. Yet he'd swallow it.

Six or seven times a day we gave him gruel. Six or seven times a day he asked to make caca. We'd lift him by grasping him under his knees and arms. He must have weighed about eighty-three pounds: skin, bones, heart, liver, intestines, brain, lungs, everything. Eighty-three pounds on a frame just under five feet ten inches tall. We'd set him down on a commode pan, its edges covered with a small cushion so he wouldn't wound himself, because at his joints, where there was nothing over the bare bone but skin, this skin was damaged and raw. (The elbows of the seventeen-year-old Jewish girl from the Faubourg du Temple were sticking through the skin of her arms and the joint was outside instead of inside, no doubt because she was young, with delicate skin. She wasn't in pain; the thing had happened gradually, without suffering: the joint stuck out, naked, clean, and the skin had hardened around the edges without forming a wound. There was no pain in her abdomen, either, where they had cut out, one by one, at lengthy intervals, all her reproductive organs, the better to study the ensuing premature aging.) Once seated on his commode, Robert would release his shit in a single spurt, in an enormous, unexpected, disproportionate gurgling. What the heart could keep from doing, the anus could not, and it let go all at once. Everything was letting go, even the fingers couldn't hold on to their nails, letting them go as well; only the heart held on to its contents. The heart. And the head, haggard but sublime, alone, it rose from this charnel house, it emerged, remembered, recounted, related, recognized, demanded. It was attached to the body by the neck as heads usually are, but this neck was so wasted (the fingers of a single hand could encircle it), so withered, that you'd wonder how life got through there, *how*, when even a teaspoon of gruel could barely squeeze through, blocking the passage. (At the base, the beginning of the neck, there was a right angle, and on top, below the head and jaws, he was choking. Through his skin you could see the vertebrae, carotid arteries, nerves, pharynx, as on anatomy models, beneath that skin now like cigarette paper, still covering everything after so long. Yet blood did pass through this neck.)

So he would make his shit. It was a gummy shit, dark green, and it bubbled. No one had ever seen the like before. Sometimes, when he'd done it and we were putting him back to bed, eyes closed, prostrate from the exhaustion following the ejection of shit like that, I used to lean my forehead against the closed blinds of his room (when I'd been waiting for his return, it was on the gas stove that I'd pressed my forehead to try not to think about anything anymore) in an effort to suppress the despair filling me at the sight of that unbelievable shit coming out of his body. For seventeen days, that shit looked the same. That shit and the way he made it were inhuman. That's what separated him from us more than the fever, more than the thinness, the fingers without nails, the marks of blows. Even though we gave him only gruel, the shit stayed dark green. That clear, golden-yellow gruel, a gruel for pink-lipped infants – it came back out of him dark green and bubbling like marsh slime. Have you ever seen shit that seethed? That shit did. When the commode was closed, you could hear the rising bubbles bursting at the surface. That shit was as phlegmy and viscous as a big gob of spit. And as soon as it came out of him, the room filled with the odor of sludge, an odor not like that of putrefaction, of corpses (was there still enough matter in his body to make a corpse?), but more like the smell of a vegetal humus, of dead leaves in overgrown underbrush. It was indeed a dark odor, dense, like the reflection of that dense night from which he was emerging – one we would never know. (I'd lean against the blinds and the street, before my eyes, would carry on. And since they didn't know what was going on in the bedroom, I felt like telling them that in this room above them a man was shitting like that, a shit so different from the one they knew, that it would change them forever.) Obviously, he had grubbed through garbage cans, eaten dandelions, water from machines, but that didn't explain it. We looked for other reasons. Maybe he was eating himself, while we watched; perhaps he was digesting his liver, his spleen. How could we tell? How could we tell what that belly still contained of pain, of the unknown?

I repeat, seventeen days without that shit becoming one bit more human, resembling something familiar. Each of the seven times he went daily we would inhale it, we'd look at it, but without recognizing it. We carefully hid it from him to avoid horrifying him. Same thing with his legs, his body, which we shielded from his own eyes and which we *could not* get used to, and which was unbelievable, unbelievable because he was *still alive* (that was the unbelievable thing). When people entered his room for the first time and saw his form under the sheet, they *could* not bear the sight, they looked away.

All that to tell you how he was.

After seventeen days death got tired. The shit stopped bubbling, became liquid, remained green, but had a more human smell, the smell of a man's shit (more delightful to us than the perfumes of spring, that shit smell we finally recognized).

And one day the fever dropped. After he'd received twelve liters of saline solution, one morning, the fever dropped. Lying on his nine pillows (one for the head, two for the forearms, two for the hands, two for the upper arms, two for the feet, because all that could no longer support itself, carry its own weight, which had to be cushioned by the duvet), motionless, he listened to the fever leaving him. The fever returned but fell again, returned again, a bit lower, but fell again and lower still, and one morning – 'I'm hungry,' he said.

We witnessed this mystery.

And one day the doctor told us: 'Try to give him food. Let's start. Everything, give him everything.'

Perhaps it was some of his spleen that was coming out of his body, or some of his heart. Because after all what was it? Those who wince at this very moment, reading this, those whom it nauseates – I shit on them, I hope one day they encounter a man whose body will empty out like that through its anus, and I hope that man is the most beautiful and beloved and desirable thing they have. Their lover. I wish that kind of devastation on them.

THE SAILOR FROM GIBRALTAR
(ROUGH DRAFT)

SPENDING A few days here in Rocca, I knew old Eolo. I was afraid of finding myself alone. I wanted to stay in a place where I'd know somebody, even one man. I know what I'm like – I would have fled a place where I knew no one, after two days I would have gone back to Paris. In Rocca, I already knew old Eolo.

'She knows you're going to leave her?' asked the girl softly.

I found it natural to be telling her my story. It was a very ordinary story, quite simple, one anybody could hear and understand.

'I told her, but she doesn't believe it.'

What made me believe that I had reached a decision was the cautious way I was handling it, my constant wariness.

'Maybe you've often told her, without having the courage to do it.'

'I'd never told her. I've been thinking about it for four years [*illegible*]. This is the first time I've told her.'

'Maybe you aren't [*illegible*] going to do it. If it hasn't happened yet, you can't tell until the last minute whether you'll do it.'

She was quite serious. We were talking like friends and not like a man with a woman.

'I will do it,' I said. 'It's very simple. I don't even have to actually do anything. She'll pack her bags, she'll take the train. Me, I'll stay here. For what I want to do, I don't even need to lift a finger.'

'And if she cries? If she begs you to come with her on the train?'

'She's a brave woman,' I said. 'She won't cry.'

The girl thought for a moment.

'I see,' she said, 'what kind of person she is.'

'And if she cries I won't go away with her, I'll stay in the sea, three days if I have to, so I don't have to see her. For me, it's a very important decision.'

The girl looked at me with great friendliness.

'Shall we dance? It will do you good.'

Around here, the girls had breasts like [marble].

'And you?' I asked. 'What do you do?'

'I'm a servant,' she said, 'in a writer's house. I'm married to a sailor. It was all over between us a long time ago but we can't get divorced. So I take life as it comes.'

The look she gave me told me that if I wanted to, she'd be glad to sleep with me. Not to please me but because she liked that.

She chose the place herself.

'What's your name?' I asked.

'Candida,' she replied with a laugh. As if the name were only for me.

'Why? You have lots of lovers. . . .'

Her face clouded over for just an instant.

'I'll be a servant all my life,' she said, 'and all my life I'll be married to that sailor. A divorce costs lots of money. So what else is there for me to do?'

'And when there's one you like better than the others, you keep him?'

'I keep him, of course, and I do everything I can to keep him.'

'And when you can't manage it, you beg, you cry?'

'I beg, I cry, every time,' she said laughingly, 'and that [keeps me busy] for at least two months. Until I meet another one. I always have to have another one.'

* * *

The next day I rose early and went to the beach. It was just as hot as in Florence but that wasn't important anymore here, in Rocca. Quite on the contrary.

After lunch, which I had with Jacqueline, I went off by myself to take a dip in the Magra. Jacqueline left for the beach. I swam for a long time, until one o'clock. Eolo had loaned me his boat and I used it as a diving platform. I swam along the opposite shore, and I saw the dance hall and the place where we had been together, Candida and I. I was pleased to have met her. Not many houses sat along the banks of the Magra, but there were large and very well-kept orchards that each included a small private dock. As the morning wore on, the traffic on the river increased. Boats were going in all directions. They were covered with tarps that concealed their cargo. Peaches and lemons, probably.

I was greatly enjoying my swim. The evening I had spent with Candida had done me good, somewhat in the way my encounters with the driver of the van and Eolo had. While I swam I thought about her again, about Candida, and I told myself that I must try getting to know other people like her and the driver. And then, for the first time since that driver had told me about her, I felt like seeing that Americana. It was obviously a slight feeling, very slight, not insurmountable, and it left me completely free. But there were no reasons not to indulge that feeling. I had recovered my curiosity about people, and that's why I felt like seeing what that Americana everyone was talking about was made of.

'I'll go out to the beach,' I thought. 'That's where everybody will be at this hour.'

I returned the boat to Eolo and left for the beach. As I arrived I could tell right away she wasn't there. Since everyone said she was extraordinarily beautiful, it was easy to see she wasn't there.

I looked at her one last time. In her eyes, beneath her [*illegible*], I saw concern; it was true that I hadn't touched her since Florence. 'Hello,' she said. 'Hello.' She walked away without {another} word to me. I closed my eyes halfway. I'll have to explain things to her, I thought, but I couldn't say anything. I had given her enough explanations that very morning. Then it was suddenly so hot that I forgot about her.

I was refreshed by my swim in the Magra. I had walked in the heat to get to the beach, but that coolness still lingered. The sand and the sea – everything was shining around me as brightly as gold dust. My eyelids were still at half-mast. The sun-drenched colors stung my eyes whenever I opened them. I [did] that several times: I closed my eyes for a long minute and opened them abruptly: the images were so strong that they slammed into my brain. In closing my eyes, I was bringing the sea into my head and it filled me up for several seconds. The feeling of defeat that had been bothering me until the previous evening disappeared. I had no qualms about my decision to leave the Registry Office and Jacqueline, and I did not understand why it had cost me such effort for so many days.

Beneath that sun, bathed in those colors turning me inside-out like a glove, I felt myself to be quite precisely of no importance whatsoever.

I was beginning to perspire, to feel the sweat pearling in my armpits.

I was well aware that one could not allow oneself to just drift along. But at the same time, I thought that in a pinch, one could be content with that. One could be content with anything beneath that sun, accept anything, even dying. I had always been quite frightened of diseases, germs, death. At the ministry, whenever I completed a death certificate with a final line where, at the heading 'deceased,' I would put a date, I would go wash my hands. Even if the guy had died in Guinea, I'd go wash my hands. To wash his death off me. I recalled that mania and began to smile. I was a jerk but I found myself likable. Suddenly I tapped my thigh. . . . Fraternity. This moment deserved a celebration. I must offer a treat, I thought, to this likable jerk that I am.

I had a craving for something. For what, exactly?

I thought about it; my stomach was always gurgling. I had an excellent stomach. I was in excellent health.

I realized all at once what I was craving. An apéritif. Something that would take hold of my stomach and exasperate that liberating gurgling. I thought – and that required all my strength – about which apéritif I craved.

I considered the lot of them. I wavered between a pastis and a Cinzano.

I was seized with an insane hope. I had never liked Pernod. I'd sampled it two or three times, but without pleasure. On the other hand I did enjoy Cinzano. And then all of a sudden, I understood pastis, the incomparable delight of drinking a pastis, and without needing to taste it I began to love it. I sat up: Now I've gone and gotten too much sun, I thought, trying to find an explanation for this new craving and my exaggerated joy over it.

I swiveled my head all around and clamped my hands to my temples. How can you tell if you're suffering from sunstroke? Aside from my craving, I felt quite normal. I didn't hurt anywhere.

'Just calm down,' I told myself. 'Trying to understand what's happening to you – that's what will screw you up.'

I gave up and stretched out motionless again, prostrated by my craving for Pernod.

Jacqueline came over to me.

'What's the matter?'

'Nothing,' I said. 'It's the sun.'

*   *   *

Her face with its closed eyes bespoke time the way others do freshness and innocence. Until that moment only the faces of certain men had made that same impression on me. And, I repeat, certain landscapes, certain cities.

It wasn't just her beauty. Otherwise it was impossible. This beauty that really was immense, truly distinctive, must have helped her acquire a great knowledge of the world. She was said to be quite rich, and certainly wealth must have flowed to her as do rivers to the sea. But, and I was sure of this from the first minute, she had once been poor. She must never have forgotten it. Money did not cloud her view of the world in any way.

I was convinced that she accepted being rich with a certain sorrow. Wealth had demanded of her an increased watchfulness. But now that had become part of her, like a phantom consciousness, and gave her entire being a kind of rare gravity. People born to wealth, I had noticed, all had something in common: the neglect of detail, and thus of nuance. They had all somewhat given me the impression of having more or less begun to die. I had always [found] the living face of a rich man deader than the face of a dead workman.

She was a sort of landscape, that woman. Hers was not a natural beauty. She must have formed herself with the passage of time and history. Everyone had a history, no doubt, but she, because of her beauty, must have had an exceptional one. That was definitely it. She had about her, not only in her face but in her long, naked body as well, a kind of wakeful peace that, while not essentially different from the serenity of women, resembled the equanimity of men of wisdom and experience.

RUE SAINT-BENOÎT:
MADAME DODIN
(ROUGH DRAFT)

WHEN I AWOKE, I did not immediately look at the alarm clock. I did not open my eyes. But my window was open and I heard someone coming along the street, walking with a quick, even step. Then, when this someone had reached the end of the block, someone else turned into the street. As the first person's footsteps were fading, those of the second one grew louder until they passed my window, resounding sharply in the empty street, for by then the first person was gone.

So I understood that morning had arrived and that people were already leaving for work.

Saint-Germain-des-Prés pealed six times. I opened my eyes. There was a pale gray light. I don't know from which direction the sun rises, but it must be behind the {new} École de Médecine. Light was coming through the reinforced concrete foundations {of the construction work there}. It was neither a color, nor daylight; it was light. You could have said that it was gray, gray through the concrete columns. Everything else was in shadow, and in my bed, I myself was in dense shadow at the far end of my bedroom, and I saw the medical school standing out like a screen. I could not go back to sleep, or keep my eyes closed. Sometimes you wake up like that, for no reason, and can't fall asleep again. I looked at the medical school and while I looked at it, I was listening. Footsteps were relaying one another in the street. They hammered at the silence, they filled it completely: they completely filled the resonant space from the boulevard Saint-Germain to the rue Jacob. I also heard a clear, bright sound, of rushing water. It was a gutter draining. Rain was falling. Not a hard rain, but steady, settled in. I realized that those people going by were walking in the rain. I raised my head from the pillow and turned toward the open window. That way I was able to hear the rain. It was a very faint rustling: soft, diffuse. As I was listening, I was looking: it was a soft rustling, in the gray light. People were still passing by.

I could not go back to sleep. Suddenly, I couldn't. I was more awake than at any other moment of the day. I remembered being awakened like that, at dawn, and it was always an exceptional awakening, clear, gliding through the motionless body washed by sleep and unconcerned with rising, and you think and you feel, you listen and you see into yourself and outside as if through a windowpane.

The concierge dragged the big garbage bin from the small inner courtyard of the apartment building out to the street. The noise of the garbage bin on the flagstones of the entryway was a dull rumbling, quite loud: in the street it became sharp and metallic, with a pause when the concierge slid the bin over the step between the entryway and the sidewalk. The sound was metallic and gray in the gray light.

I then thought quite intensely about Madame Fossé, my concierge. I very often hear her take out the garbage bin, not every morning, but still, perhaps once a week. It's a chore she detests. When I heard her at it, I imagined her grumpy face straining with the effort. She says it's taxing work, beyond her strength now – she's sixty-nine – and that if the tenants emptied their garbage cans every day the way they're supposed to, the one in the courtyard wouldn't be so heavy, but that they don't give a damn, and don't empty them until they can't stuff another thing inside. I remembered that the concierge had told me this quite often, and I'd reply that in the long run, it must come to the same thing, given that all the tenants didn't empty their garbage cans every day. But my concierge cannot understand this, or doesn't want to. She says that the garbage bin is heavy, too heavy for her. If you ask me, I believe it's a moral question with her. What she finds unbearable is having in the courtyard, so close to her lodge, a bin filling up with several-days-old garbage that stinks, and having to drag it, and smelling its stench while she's dragging it. She says that when you look at those tenants, so well dressed, and so rich (when you consider the rent they pay), you would never believe they'd be disgusting enough to put up with rotting garbage in their homes and for several days, too. And so each morning, when she drags out the garbage bin, my concierge once again bitterly ponders – or rather, relives, in the sense of 'revives' – an aspect of human nature she feels she alone understands, one that makes her all the more bitter in that she alone perceives it and cannot share it with anyone. And because of her station in life (which requires her to endure the performance of that disgusting chore or lose her job), finding herself forced in the end to empty that garbage, which stinks because it suits the tenants to empty it when they damn well please, makes her reexperience each morning the horror of her station in life. She has been dragging out that bin now for four years and for four years she's been complaining about the way she's treated by the tenants, whom she has never managed to convince of the real horror she feels at the thought that they despise her enough not to make an effort she claims is trifling: taking their garbage out every day.

When I heard her this morning and imagined her face distorted by effort and disgust, a face she must avert from the bin as she drags it along, I thought that this was the deeply moving face of a fierce and impregnable dignity. For, I repeat, she has never managed to get used to the task. And in this gray light, in this tenacious rain, this morning, that was quite obvious to me. It was a violent hour, and that's still not the right word; 'a strong hour' would be better, I believe: an hour that has strength, because it is virgin, dawning, the hour when the sun has not yet risen but soon will, when that immense event is imminent. That is where the hour's strength lies, for the hour is one of hope and possesses all its features, containing more promises than the nascent day will keep, since as the day goes by, this hope will sink once more into the following night, but while the day is yet unborn, this hope is intact and filled with the mystery of the coming day, which keeps the flame of life alight in man.

One ought to be able to say these things, and say them so well, so adequately, that attempting to repeat that feat would be useless, and although what I'm saying here is colossally absurd – for it's like saying that there can be a success compared to which all others, be they ever so much more valid, would collapse of their own accord, constrained by the first one – I have learned to look at things, to listen to them, and to assign myself in this business only the importance of 'the other.' That lone man walking briskly who inhabits the street more completely and evocatively, with more real and impressive presence, than a tragic hero upon the stage – I listen to him, the representative of a community. I am listening, in my selfhood, to an entire city, wide awake and restless, for that man concerns me not as a particular individual with specific experiences and sensibilities, but as a member of that community to which we both belong, on the same footing. What is extraordinary is that this man walking along is anyone at all; I am anyone at all, listening to {someone} walking; and this anonymity exists with a great strength, filling me with joy, with love, with hope.

Nothing has happened but this: a man passes on the sidewalk and I awaken at that moment, cleansed by sleep, new, receptive, and then – his steps pass over my body, marking it and filling the conch shell I am with their resonance. This happens regularly, just like the rumbling of the garbage bin. And even though I know Madame Fossé, I now rediscover her, apart from the specific relationship we may have: she is any elderly woman at all, dragging out a garbage bin at six in the morning, cursing, embittered, terrible; her wrinkled old face is savage and indignant, and she bends to her task so that she can eat until she dies, after sixty years of toil. After sixty years of service, she found herself once more dragging her garbage bin out into the rain this morning, alone, anonymous, and bottling inside herself what she'd like to scream in the world's face: that it horrifies her. One ought to be able to describe that: a man walking alone in an empty street, at dawn, when you have just awakened, when daylight is barely filtering through concrete construction work, while at the same time an elderly concierge drags, from her courtyard to the street, a bin full of reeking garbage, and you hear the sound of the bin and the man's footsteps, while you are in your bed, relaxed, warm, at peace.

[. . .] existence so perfect it might be lived instead of your own: sometimes I would wish this, and that afterward men would abandon the vanity of writing. I know what Dionys will say: that I've been reading too much Hemingway lately. I'll show him my text and he'll say: 'You've been reading Hemingway again, haven't you?' And he'll walk off, leaving me in despair. I'll tell him: 'It's true that I read *Green Hills of Africa*. But you know, what I've written here . . . Do you think I wouldn't have been able to write it just as well, one day?' Besides, the story about the garbage bin – if there is a story there – belongs to me: it's a slow and static story, one that brings me a joy and sadness that have nothing to do with the blazing emotions of Hemingway's heroes. The day will come when I give Dionys a definitive reply. I've been trying to come up with one for four years now, without success. Dionys is always the one who produces the definitive pronouncement about me. I'd have to go into this at considerable length, and explain that although I believe in his definitive statements, and his alone, Dionys doesn't believe in mine. I've never said anything definitive to him about someone we know, because I don't believe anything definitive can be said about something that by virtue of its fluid nature can disprove your affirmation at any moment. Robert, however, is a constant temptation, one Dionys himself cannot resist. Because in his life, with his slightest actions, words, and deepest thoughts as well as the way he strolls down a street, Robert embodies such harmony that you must inevitably search for his secret. The other day, I said that Robert operated through tropisms, and I'm not displeased with that turn of phrase. Dionys says that it's not enough, though; he's on the hunt as well. Regarding Robert, it's irresistible. You ought to be able to keep quiet, but instinctively you seek to express how you feel watching him eat, shave, or simply sleep.

In the summer, Madame Fossé, my concierge, takes out, as she does every morning, her big garbage bin. But at that hour in the summer, it's daylight, and the proprietress of L'Abbaye, the residential hotel across the street from my apartment building, is standing on her doorstep. So they chat. And at that hour, the street is so quiet that from my bed, when I am awake, I hear their words distinctly. It's always my concierge who begins: she doesn't say good morning, she complains about the garbage cans. 'After all, the tenants really go too far,' she says. And Mademoiselle Ginsbourg invariably replies that indeed they do. Because of Mademoiselle Ginsbourg's presence, in the summertime, Madame Fossé's suffering is more bearable, since at the most critical moment she finds an echo in Mademoiselle Ginsbourg. After she has complained, her voice softens, and she usually talks about what kind of day it will be. She says: 'That sky's overcast, going to be stormy.' Or else, 'That's sky's clear, going to be nice.' Mademoiselle Ginsbourg agrees or adds a few touches, saying, 'It'll clear up around noon,' or else, 'Won't necessarily be nice, sky's clouded up over there. . . .' She must point in the direction she means, but I don't know which one.

Sometimes, when the man who sweeps the streets has started doing the rue Saint-Benoît a little earlier than usual, or when Madame Fossé is running a bit late, he happens to be sweeping in front of number 5 while Madame Fossé and Mademoiselle Ginsbourg are talking on their doorsteps, so he joins in the conversation, at the urging of Madame Fossé. Then the conversation takes a more general and philosophical turn, dealing with their respective jobs, the advantages and disadvantages entailed. The sweeper says his profession is a difficult one in the winter, especially when it snows. More briefly, Madame Fossé says his profession, street sweeping, is a profession, whereas hers is not.

She tells him that when he has finished his work, he has finished his work, that outside of his work hours he can do as he likes, but that she, on the contrary, never finishes here, that even at night, she's still a concierge, that she's constantly awakened by the front door bell, that she cannot take any vacation because even if she managed to find someone to sit in her lodge, no one, on the other hand, would take over emptying the garbage bin in her place, that it looks easy, being a concierge, but that it's a rotten job, especially concerning the garbage cans, etc. She's a concierge at night, during the day, every minute of her life. She doesn't explain what she means very well. She doesn't do a lot of work, but she's in the position of concierge day and night. She monitors the footsteps on the stairs day and night. It's a position so tightly superimposed on her own human condition that if you think about it, it's nightmarish, it coincides so perfectly that it's dehumanizing. The obsession. The horror. The sticky glue of nightmares. No escape.

She never explains herself at length on this subject. Mademoiselle Ginsbourg rarely joins any conversation with the sweeper, whose political opinions she does not share. Since they all speak from where they are standing, i.e. at their front doors and in the middle of the street, they raise their voices, which reach me loud and clear. In the summer, when the pink and saffron-yellow sunlight peeks through the scaffolding around the École de Médecine, these voices arrive – mingling with the resonant footsteps of passers-by on the concrete sidewalks – and depending on the day, sink me more groggily into sleep, or pierce me like arrows of light, flooding me with such intense clarity that I cannot go back to sleep.

When Madame Fossé talks about the coming day's weather, before opening my eyes I know the color of the sky, I know that morning has dawned, and I find that moment conjured up by Madame Fossé's voice strictly irreplaceable. Madame Fossé calls things as she sees them, she says them succinctly, and her voice, more strident, more prophetic than the crowing of the cock, announces the advent of the day. The cock crows every morning, indiscriminately, metaphysically. Madame Fossé, though, stirs me to my soul, because she announces humanly, and by virtue of maturely digested human experience, the destiny of a day in the life of men, which will be what it will be, but the broad outlines of which she cannot change.

Last year, in the back of her hotel garden, Mademoiselle Ginsbourg raised a rooster, and I heard it many a time. That was how I came to compare the reverberation of its message with that of Madame Fossé. The sweeper sometimes gives his opinion on the coming day's weather, but he offers it in an offhand way, without the solemnity of the concierge. Despite his youth, this sweeper has turned this idea of the day's weather into an inescapable misfortune. Good weather or bad, his schedule never changes: he sweeps the rue Saint-Benoît, the entire length of the rue Jacob and, I believe, the rue Bonaparte. It's different for Madame Fossé, especially in the summer.

When it's nice out, she parks herself in a chair in front of her door and for two whole hours, after lunch, she unravels old sweaters, which she then patiently reknits, stopping anyone she knows who lives on the street for a chat. We have had conversations about the sweeper. For a while, I was impressed by his confident stride, his handsome, intelligent expression, and something noble in his bearing. We exchanged greetings every day. Planted in the middle of the street, his cap tipped over his left ear, {the Communist daily} *L'Humanité* sticking prominently from his pocket, he did his work with both sovereign efficiency and supreme casualness, using broad, even movements of his large broom, never stepping aside even for the passage of large trucks, which were obliged to drive around him. One day I asked Madame Fossé if the sweeper belonged to the Communist Party. She told me she didn't know, but that one might think so from the way he talked. I don't remember on what occasion I approached this sweeper and deftly asked my question. He told me that he was a Communist in his feelings but that he hadn't joined the party, because politics disgusted him and he would never join any party, he was much too independent for that. He told me all this with some embarrassment, and I was so surprised that I didn't know what to say. I walked away disappointed. Since then, we shake hands, but never address the question of whether he has changed his mind. He retains his nobility in my eyes, but I believe less in his freewheeling ways now that I know they reflect not the clear-sighted, principled consciousness of a self-aware worker, but the unself-consciousness of a naïve and disillusioned man who fancies himself an individualist, who rejects all constraint save that of his work, work he endures without enjoyment, which embitters him more with each passing day, without allowing him to raise this {dissatisfaction} to the level of a revolutionary stance and find his salvation. I tried to explain this to Madame Fossé, telling her that a man like the sweeper, in the prime of his life, should either become a militant Communist if he remained a sweeper, or try to change jobs, to do something else. Madame Fossé told me that this was indeed too bad, without any further explanation, but she spoke sincerely; she felt that it was too bad that he didn't belong to the Communist Party, but she did not seem truly convinced of it to me.

And, well, she and the sweeper are friends, and while I was speaking to her, she was wondering, I could tell, if my words did not reflect a certain disparagement of him. It's also true that she knows nothing about the Communist Party, and that she must have gathered that I had reservations about the Communist sympathies of her friend. He chops her wood, and when she's sick, he drags out her garbage bin, in return for which she occasionally gives him a pack of cigarettes. Even if he did nothing for her, as long as he listens to her when she complains about the tenants, she considers him a true and understanding friend. I told her one day that complaining like that to the sweeper, and

Mademoiselle Ginsbourg, and me, would get her nowhere, and that she needed to join the Union of the Concierges of the Sixth Arrondissement, that only there would she find recognition of her grievances, and that afterward, if many others did as she had, the union would certainly find a way to deal with the tenants. She took her time about it but she did join, and ever since has been one of the Union's most faithful members. Her morale has improved now that she is sharing her concerns with other concierges and they are pooling their anger and indignation.

This morning, I heard neither Mademoiselle Ginsbourg nor the sweeper, only the noise of the garbage bin on the flagstones and the sidewalk. For it's still winter, and Madame Fossé has no one to talk to. I imagined her standing for a moment on her step, watching the rain fall, hoping the sweeper would arrive. Then she must have gone back inside. I could not fall asleep again. After I'd listened to the garbage bin, I did try to go back to sleep, but my eyelids were opening by themselves. The light was growing more distinct through the scaffolding around the medical school and the church of Saint-Germain-des-Prés and of . . . I heard the bells for the first Mass. I thought about what I would do that day, aside from the ordinary obligations of my work and household chores. I'd have to make up my mind about putting curtains on the sitting room windows and moving the round table from Robert's room, replacing it with the bridge table from the dining room. I wanted Robert to have a quiet room, so nicely set up that he could work there comfortably. I was thinking that I would have liked to see R. happy and D. as well, those two in particular. And then for everybody to be happy. It seemed to me that if Robert had that square table in his room, he would be comfortable working there, and that having worked well all day long, he would be happy in the evening. I felt kind and prepared to put myself out for the happiness of others, especially for Robert and Dionys. People were still going by in the street.

* * *

One evening, not too long ago, a man and a woman went by beneath my windows. It was the middle of the night. They were singing a particular song, I don't know which one, but I felt that I'd heard it before, once, only once in my life, perhaps in a moment of happiness. It was a tune with a strong beat, with the tone and tempo of an old ditty. So it was the middle of the night and at that hour, meant for sleep, two people were singing that song. Alone in the world, they were singing, in quiet, careful voices; they weren't braying like drunks, they were listening to themselves sing. Only two people in love, who were still in the quick of a nascent love affair, could sing like that, in the middle of the night, alone; at that hour when the human race, weighed down by oblivion, feeds on sleep, they had spared time to devote to singing. In the middle of the empty night, where the two slopes of the night meet, arose that song: it was a red flower blooming suddenly from a night of stone. A song against death, to make you move mountains. All my flesh began to cry out and I wanted a man; the couple were long gone and I still couldn't sleep for wanting a man. I was alone. I imagined that a man could have come in. A stranger. Above all, a stranger, as unknown as the street. Why? Probably from a concern for purity. To prevent sentiment from intruding upon this moment when I was fulfilled by the love of others, of those who had just passed by. The stranger would have entered me completely and stayed silent and motionless, and I, in the same way, would have remained motionless and satisfied, filled with what I was empty of – a man's sex, as full as a glass of wine – and linked to others, to the world by that penis lodged inside me, rooting me to the ground.

We are immobility and what we aspire to is that immobility.

Two passed by together, and they were talking as they walked quickly through the rain. I told myself that if everyone could listen to the street this way for a certain time each morning, they would find themselves changed. Not too long ago, I took the métro at six in the morning; everyone reads *L'Humanité* in the métro. There's a coincidence there between the worker's lot in life and his adherence to the Communist Party, and if people were to observe this coincidence, becoming aware of it as if it were a fact, as real and indisputable as a purely material fact and as material as the realization of the great social laws that govern our society, many people would reflect and lose heart just enough to tire of imagining reality instead of seeing it, and would be disposed to accept this reality, naturally and without preconceived ideas. That's what I told myself, and also that I would have to say that simply and well, but it's very difficult. I was listening to the street, the footsteps, and I'd heard the sinister rumbling of the garbage bin that – through the workings of class destiny – Madame Fossé found herself forced to drag out every morning (and that morning in particular, so alone in the rain), and I felt I was at the heart of a living reality that claimed all things, claimed my body as well as my thoughts, which were clear and distinct like things.

And then the child I am carrying moved inside me. He moved while those workers were passing, in the precise reality of the street. I had not forgotten my child, while he kept still, deep in my womb, for can one forget one is alive? But in the moment of his movement, he added himself harmoniously to the surrounding reality. It was when, tired of trying to fall back asleep, I had deliberately turned onto my back, with my ears well clear of my pillow, that he made his move. He began to wriggle just a bit above my pubis, and then I placed my hands flat on that part of my belly, to feel him. He lifted up my hands and rummaged around in there, so merrily and in such an early-morning way that I had to smile. I wondered if he was sleeping, because there were moments of stillness and moments of movement, impatience, fidgeting. With my hands I tried to feel the parts of his body but could feel only its contour, especially the height, from just beneath my navel down to my pubic bone.

He was deep inside me, almost against my back, and in this warm basin he frolicked comfortably, living inside me and bumping me around as he pleased, growing bigger and more robust every day, sucking a little of my blood every day, flexing muscles growing stronger every day until the day when, a fait accompli, he would solemnly become still to traverse that passage of my flesh still separating him from daylight. I have already had one child, and I know that this moment is terrifying when, head down, he will push at my uterus until it widens enough to let the whole of him out. At that point he will stop moving, and his heart will be pounding from his efforts. I know, for I've already had a child, that it's a terrible ordeal, and it awaits me in three months. This morning, when I felt him stir beneath my hands in the darkness of my womb, barely separated from me by that supple wall of my skin, I thought about the birth, that passage he would be making, that exit, and I could not imagine it: my womb was so closed, and my child was so peaceful there, so blissfully contained. It's an extraordinary thing. Of course, it has been experienced and said and described, but nonetheless, it is still extraordinary.

This morning, however, no matter how extraordinary giving birth seemed to me, it took its place in that totality of the dawn, and I found it no less extraordinary to hear the footsteps of the first workers along the sidewalk, the muffled noise of the garbage bin, the slow and steady pouring of the rain, to know that the day was coming imperceptibly on and would tuck all that away into its diversity, among its many aspects. But for the moment, a few of its facets – the solitary morning workman walking briskly along the sidewalk; the horror of Madame Fossé's unchosen lot in life rearing its grumbling head; my child in my womb – were isolated, promoting so strongly in me what Paulhan calls 'the illusion of the wholeness of the world' that I felt as if I were touching it, feeling an abstraction beneath my fingertips. While my hands were on my belly, the worker walked and moved along in the steady clatter of his footsteps, audible in the silence broken by the rumbling garbage bin of the oppressed proletariat.

I would like to portray the joy of that hour. It isn't an exaltation or excitation of the mind. The joy came not from the day dawning on these things, but rather from these things arising in the dawn, just as if there existed a visible morning of things. While children are being formed, while the disgust of the oppressed proletariat grows stronger, men go to work in factories and prepare for liberation. It was an hour opening onto the future in every way. This morning, I saw that, and interpreted things in a certain way, and not because I am a Communist. (I don't think so, at least; how can one tell?) I feel that this morning, anyone else would have seen the rain, heard the footsteps, the rumbling of the garbage bin, and felt her child move within her womb all in the same way, and would have found a fundamental bond that linked together these various expressions of the world.

But perhaps it is because I am a Communist that I believe that anyone at all would have perceived these things in the same way. Dionys would tell me that people don't say this, that it's false to say it. That one doesn't announce it. I belong to the Communist Party, which doesn't mean that I'm a Communist: that's what I would say. Between Pisa and Florence, I was sitting beside the driver of a delivery truck, and I announced it to him. I told him half in English, half in Italian. After arriving in Florence, I informed Dionys that I'd told him; that time, he said I was right. We went off to have a glass of Chianti in a cafeteria: Dionys, Robert, the driver, a mason, and I. We'd been 'recognized' in Pisa by the mason, who was also a comrade. We were waiting for the bus, and so was he (he was on a team of workmen helping to rebuild Pisa, and every Saturday they went home to Florence). When the delivery truck drove up, the mason went to tell the driver that we were French 'comrades' and that he should give us a lift, because the Saturday evening bus from Viareggio was always full. And so, while I was talking with the driver, Dionys and Robert were getting to know the mason, whom they told that they, too, were comrades. It was the end of August. The driver got going on the subject of Gasperi.[1] Whenever he said 'Gasperi,' he let go of the wheel, brandished his fists, then pounded them on the wheel while the truck swerved wildly and the tarps over the back flapped in the wind. He was from Tuscany, the driver, twenty-five, quite handsome. He told me that he was an internationalist, and that he didn't make any distinction 'between you and one of my comrades in Florence.' When we went through villages, he drove very slowly to let me read the slogans chalked on the walls of houses: 'Viva il Partito Comunista,' 'Viva la Republica,' and the upside-down 'V' in front of 'Il Re.' I read everything carefully, and told him that it was the same in France, that we used the same methods. He talked about Gasperi and I spoke of de Gaulle, and the way we'd gotten rid of him. He was happy, thrilled at each resemblance between our two countries.

The sky was red when we entered the Arno Valley, above the river; cypresses stood out against the Tuscan hills, the only hills in the world inhabited in a way that makes them unimaginable without this human presence, and here and there, among the villages, there were long, low monasteries with arched doors, flattened by their wide-angled roofs. 'Are you from Florence?' I asked the driver, who replied, 'Not from Florence itself, but I'm a Tuscan, from these parts.' I looked around; between its dark banks, the Arno was green, moss green. The vehicle sped along the road, still without headlights. It was cool, the heat of the day had passed; the coolness had come as we'd entered the Arno Valley, as if this coolness were rising from the river, a freshness made iridescent by forests of olive trees and the Arno's high banks of moss-covered rocks. Florence was waiting for us at the end of the road. I couldn't wait to see Florence. Every ten minutes the driver kept telling me, 'Another quarter of an hour, twenty minutes – and you'll see, the hills of Fiesole, too. Right now we're just above the *Città*!'

I don't know why I'm talking about that driver, and the evening we saw Florence for the first time. Why wouldn't I talk about it? That hour, beside that Italian comrade, was as pellucid as this morning. It did not have the same meaning, of course, but I thought of it again this morning, and of our stay in Bocca di Magra. I thought of it because after listening to the rain and, hands upon my belly, feeling the unexpected movements of my child, I thought of my death, or rather, of my age. I'm thirty-two years old and this morning, since everything was so clear, the number 'thirty-two' followed by the word 'years' popped into my mind, and stuck to me. Lightning bolt. It was a number that concerned me. I had lived thirty-two years. I know those moments. Useless to describe them.

Whenever I hear it, I experience it as essentially quotidian. It's every day that it happens, every morning of every day, every day of the year. As for me, I hear it only rarely and when I do, I feel that I don't hear it every day but that it happens every day; I hear and understand it as such: quotidian. I would like to succeed in expressing this perfectly. In the abstract maelstrom of noise from a locomotive passing close by (the only noise that annihilates you, empties you out, you're a bug beneath that noise), all locomotives pass by and you feel that there are thousands of them in the world, locomotives that exist and that you don't hear, and you place yourself, in a blinding flash of consciousness, in the world of the locomotives of the world, in your world full of locomotives that – in every direction – shriek and race by, hauling swarms of cars filled with your traveling contemporaries. In the same way – but in time, not space – the garbage bin makes me feel the world of garbage bins in my world, those bins full of peelings and empty tin cans from my contemporaries who eat, eat again, chew and chew again to hang on, to keep themselves alive, who digest, absorb, digest again, keep themselves going, in an astonishing effort of perseverance, of such breadth and regularity that in itself it is more conclusive proof of man's desire to endure than the most famous cathedrals, which – although offered as examples – are mere record accumulations of perseverance that astonish with their gratuitousness, astonishing only those who do not hear the enormous din of chewing, the rumination daily repeated by man. That rumbling, that rumbling taken up and echoed by the garbage bins – it's the most perfect noise possible to place you among your contemporaries, in your historicity: it's the cry of fraternity, because everyone eats and, refusing to resemble your enemies in any way whatsoever, you do as they do, you endure. Through this great [effort], from this soil, spring other [endeavors].

Soon she came back out, and in exactly the same way, stared again at the door to number 5 like an idiot. Leaning slightly from my window, I saw that Madame F.'s shutters were not yet open, and that Mademoiselle G. was looking straight at those shutters, but without making the slightest gesture or move toward them. Have I mentioned that Mademoiselle G. was for me the very embodiment of stupidity? Mademoiselle G. is forty and a virgin. Anyone seeing her manage her residential hotel so carefully, so conscientiously, in the most perfect contentment and obvious satisfaction, anyone witnessing her happiness at the economy of her existence, the happiness of self-sufficiency, of providing that certainty for herself, would understand that Mademoiselle G. is a superlatively obvious target for crime, and the idea that her murderer might be punished for such a crime could lead to the direst conclusions regarding justice itself. Mademoiselle G. is a plaything in the hands of Madame F. And one can say that Madame F. is for Mademoiselle G. the only outlet in her life toward folly, passion, irrationality.

Through what admirable subterfuge has Madame F. arranged for Mademoiselle G. to practically feed her for free, and obtained an incontestable right to her share of the most delicious and exceptional dishes that Mademoiselle G. whips up for herself alone? I don't know. But it's an established fact that now Mademoiselle G. can hardly ever resist sharing her treats with Madame F. Each day at noon and seven in the evening, Mademoiselle G.'s maid crosses the street, bearing to Madame F. – carefully wrapped in a spotless cloth – her rightful portion of Mademoiselle G.'s lunch and dinner.

'Not bad, your leg of lamb, but a touch underdone, you ask me,' says Madame F.

'Ah!' says Mademoiselle G. 'You think so?'

'Well that's what I said,' replies Madame F., 'and I don't usually talk to hear myself speak.'

So I believe that Mademoiselle G. can no longer do without this kind of authority. Thus, having through mindless virtue escaped the supremacy of a male, Mademoiselle G. does not escape that of Madame F., in which she daily seeks brutal and arbitrary condemnation, exercised not only with regard to the dishes she sends her, but apropos of her slightest initiatives and actions.

The street sweeper is too gloomy. The street sweeper has been brooding over something big for two days now. It's getting bigger, bigger. And (Madame F. admitted this to me the other day, in secret, but without giving me any explanations) he is drinking. When he's been drinking, she can tell from way off. If she's standing on our front step as he turns into the rue Saint-Benoît, she studies him immediately from fifty yards away, hands on her hips, and shakes her head. 'Been drinking.' She goes back into her lodge, gets her largest pot, fills it with water, and places it on her table. And she gets on with her work without betraying her intentions in any way, except perhaps through her quickened pace. When the sweeper is close to the building, she opens her shutters, and waits motionless by the window, holding the pot of water. The sweeper, who is used to this, begins to chuckle, but softly. And to whistle. He only whistles when he's drunk. He's still lucid enough to sweep the street, and to provoke Madame F. by whistling quietly in front of number 5. He's sweeping: that is, he's sweeping the way one must sweep in a dream: dancing in the sunlight, without really sweeping anything, in a street from a dream. So he's whistling in front of number 5, laughing softly to himself, while keeping his eyes fixed on Madame F.'s barred window. Once directly before the window, he becomes motionless in turn, stops whistling, and says, 'Let 'er rip.' Madame F. dumps the whole pot of water on his head. And then the sweeper starts laughing boisterously. 'Pig,' says Madame F. Her rage is at its peak. But the sweeper's laughter has attracted Mademoiselle Ginsbourg and the waiter at the Restaurant Saint-Benoît, however. They laugh along with the sweeper. Madame F. comes out into the street as well. 'That'll teach you,' says Madame F. And then she joins in with her magnificent, throaty, velvety laughter that never comes completely out into the open, the loveliest laugh I have ever heard. 'That'll teach me what?' hiccups the sweeper. 'That'll teach you not to drink anymore,' says Madame F. 'Next time I'll use my wash basin.' They laugh together for a long while until Madame F. withdraws into her lodge and thinks about this sorrow dogging the street sweeper.

Madame F. and the sweeper share an obvious complicity. I shouldn't like to put a name to it and I don't think I could. It's clear that if Madame F. were only twenty years younger, she would inevitably have slept with the sweeper. She knows this, and has certainly thought about it. He knows this, and has certainly thought about it. And she knows that he knows this, and he knows that she knows this. In short, they like each other perfectly, they suit each other. They 'hit it off.' But she's sixty and he's thirty.

*　*　*

[. . .] This drama that turns short, turns in circles, in defiance of the most sacred and consecrated laws of drama, is one of the most moving and unsettling moments imaginable. For if Madame F. struggles against the sweeper's unfortunate inclination to drink, she is struggling not only to save him, but to save herself from the fate that threatens her. Because if he continues to drink, she must be convinced that it will end badly for her, and that a day will come when he will kill her. He knows it. She knows that he knows it. Which is why she dumps her pot of water on him, and why they laugh it off together.

The murderer takes aim at his victim, but his revolver jams, and would you believe it, victim and murderer burst out laughing at how seriously the murderer took aim, at how ridiculous a murderer – no matter how accomplished – sometimes winds up looking before even the most defenseless victim, and so they 'make up' at the expense of all mankind, which was expecting the bang of a bullet through the heart, and not the blowup of this monumentally aborted tragedy. Victim and murderer 'switch places.' The victim becomes the murderer of the murderer, by challenging the latter's status as a murderer (a murderer whose revolver jams in front of the victim is as ridiculous as a head of state taking a pratfall before his subjects) and dominating the murderer by laughing, literally diluting all his gravity – and what gravity! – with laughter.

One day, my venerable mother, revered and forbidding, tumbled, before my eyes, all the way down the stairs of a métro entrance. And on her derrière, too, while I, seeing her venerability going unexpectedly ass over teakettle, burst into uncontrollable laughter. And my mother yells at me, hollering for me to help her get up. And people are outraged that a daughter is laughing at her mother like that. And finally my mother, who shared the same gift of laughter with me, laughs with me in turn, against the crowd.

Saint-Germain-des-Prés: the Church
Rue Saint-Benoît: rue Sainte-Eulalie: rue du Père, rue du Fils
Mademoiselle G.: Mademoiselle Marie
Madame F.: Madame Dodin

1. Do not involve myself.
2. Avoid damning descriptions of Madame D.
3. It's not a simple psychological portrait but a story, a *novel*.
4. Return of the garbage bin *necessary*.
5. Use short chapters?

- Main theme.
- [Drinking]
- The street?
- *Royalty* of Madame D.
- Surprise and mother on her ass
- *We* instead of *I*
- Difficulty of writing about one's mother? about Madame D.?

- The theft of the butter
- The theft of the baby blanket
- Mention the fear Madame D. and the sweeper inspire in the neighborhood, and the *respect*
- Return to the garbage bin, unheard on that particular morning
- Madame D.'s funeral
- Madame D.'s son, and her daughter
- Conversation with Mademoiselle G., who informs me of the existence of 24,000 francs
- The street sweeper

* * *

And ever since, he's been claiming he would need an equivalent sum to go off to the Midi – to change his life – to enable him to abandon his shameful profession – change his life – to be happy. In short the game goes on. It's an exceptional game, in which the players themselves don't know what's at stake. He knows she won't give him her savings. She knows he knows that. That she'll never give them up. Not only because they're six years' worth of savings (all her former savings were abandoned, twice, to her husbands) – for if the sweeper's health required it, she would certainly give them to him – but also to keep him from, as she puts it, 'going under,' drifting off toward a kind of seaside happiness, quite suspect, made of laziness, sunshine, refusal. For – instinctively – Madame Dodin does not like happy people. There would be a lot to say on that subject; she denounces her tenants' adulteries, and carefully takes advantage of every opportunity to stir up trouble between couples.

That's what Madame D. and the sweeper have come to. In addition to stealing, Madame D. has lately taken to writing anonymous letters. She's just getting started. She has sent anonymous threatening letters to a tenant – the very same one from whom she was stealing butter. [Since] she is more or less illiterate, it's Gaston the sweeper who writes them.

'If I write anonymous letters, it's because I like to, and who's to say anything against that?'

And so all the tenants find themselves challenged in their right, implicit until now, to have a garbage can, and therefore, to live.

Some of them, doubtless ill prepared for a war of contestations, thus find themselves treated with that same lack of consideration. But these tenants, naïve enough to become indignant, are the ones whom Madame D. hounds with the best results.

Because – setting aside, perhaps, the institution of the garbage bin – nothing will ever assuage Madame D.'s dissatisfaction; nothing will ever temper what might be called her fundamental skepticism. The great nobility of Madame D. is just that: she is impervious to charity. When the nuns of the parish of Saint-Germain-des-Prés bring her the 'roast meat for the elderly of the Sixth Arrondissement' at Christmastime, she looks at them and laughs.

'I'm still not going to Mass, I'm warning you,' she tells them. 'Not my style.'

And when the sweeper, [to whom she turns for confirmation], stands there laughing along with her, she tells him, 'What business is it of theirs? I mean they should all get buns in the oven, those bitches, that'd teach them not to stick their noses so much in other people's affairs.'

And in the same way, aside from her bosom buddy and sole accomplice, Gaston the sweeper, Madame D. will refuse all compromise with humanity, be it even through the medium of Mademoiselle G.'s kindness toward her. And as I was saying, Mademoiselle G. is nothing more for both her and the sweeper but the frightened witness of their complicity, a plaything, and so to speak, their victim. That's why, when Gaston shows up whistling fifty yards from the apartment building, and he's been drinking [. . .].

[. . .] and above all that even the last act, Gaston's murder of Madame D., does not change profoundly. For although Madame D. worries about the sweeper, to keep him from ending up as her murderer, it's true nonetheless that she esteems him nonetheless, and that to be worthy of his friendship, to hold up her end of their daily competition, she finally gives in to her deepest nature and to her hitherto repressed truth: what is

commonly called vulgarity. On the whole, Madame D. blos-
soms along with the sweeper. She winds up writing anonymous
letters and stealing. Stealing – the way I don't know anyone else
her age can steal: purely. And so, even while she's deploring
Gaston's propensity to drink, she encourages him in his
gradual downfall. They compete with each other in saying the
most blasphemous things, flouting the most sacred values,
the most recognized authorities, in accomplishing the most
audacious feats. In short, Madame D. wishes to be worthy of
Gaston's crime.

The things they say make the entire neighborhood shudder,
which gives them great pleasure.

'Wars,' says [Gaston].

To which Madame D. replies:

'The Germans [. . .].'

And although Madame D.'s thefts are known only to a few
[*illegible*], the two of them tend, ever so slowly, to make them
public, they try to commit them more and more carelessly.

Along the entire range of private ecstasies, there is only the last
act, the liquidation: the flowers in the gutter.[2] In other words,
there was a time when Gaston believed that [*illegible*] his profession could satisfy his great curiosity. He no doubt believed that
he could also be the sweeper of souls, of consciences; that he
could gather in the inadmissible confessions one admits only
to the sweeper. But alas, when he asks Mademoiselle G., 'And
your eye, how is it doing?' – she replies that it's doing just
beautifully. And he knows this is not so, that Mademoiselle G.'s
eye is getting worse every day, but that she's hiding this from
him because she fears (perhaps without fully realizing it) that
one fine evening, when Gaston is drunk and when he knows
her eye is bad enough not to recognize him, he might venture
into her respectable residential hotel bent on a very, really
very frightening purpose – because of his political convictions.

So, the sweeper hears false news, even about Mademoiselle G.'s eye. As a result, naturally, he strongly feels he belongs on the side of murderers, outlaws. He overdoes it in that department.

'Pierrot is dead,' he announces, referring to Pierrot le Fou,[3] or else he must know everyone's name by heart [*illegible*].

'A fine crime: for a sweeper, that's the best thing that can happen to him. There's not a single crime they don't check with the sweepers. That's the sweeper's only entertainment.'

Madame D. and Mademoiselle G. look at him, and after he's gone, Mademoiselle G. announces hypocritically, 'For some time now, he's been saying things that . . .'

And Madame D., who is on the sweeper's side, after all, replies, 'A man like that, it's not everyone can understand him.'

As soon as Gaston arrives, the conversation takes a more general, more philosophical turn. It's a question of their respective jobs and the advantages and disadvantages involved.

'That's a profession, at least, street sweeper,' begins Madame D.

'Shouldn't ever talk about what you don't know,' says Gaston. 'Otherwise you're talking without saying anything.'

For Gaston, too, has a certain horror of his profession. But a philosophical attitude toward it as well.

'We both,' says the sweeper, 'have unappreciated professions.'

'You certainly know what you're talking about,' says Madame D.

At dawn, when the Club Saint-Germain closes its doors, along comes the sweeper.

'I always arrive too late,' he says. 'It's closed, music's over. In the pretty girl department, seems it's full of 'em, but not for me. All I get to see is that there's some serious pissing on the club walls. You should go take a look. The walls are black, it's even rather astonishing.'

''Course people got to piss,' says Madame D., 'seeing as they drink all night.'

'The piss, that's for Gaston the street sweeper. Gaston's promoted to these gentlemen's piss.'

Madame D. looks at Gaston with love and pride. Gaston and she have the same way with words. Mademoiselle G. lowers her eyes. Everything Gaston says seems to her tainted with secret and unsavory intentions.

'If you're judging from the piss,' continues Gaston, 'they must drink nonstop.'

'They piss, therefore they drink,' says Madame D.

'That reminds me of something,' says Gaston the sweeper. 'What you just said there. A philosopher must have said the same thing: I think therefore I am, he came up with that. Descartes.'

'Been better off if he'd kept quiet,' says Madame D. 'Anyone could say that. Day carts of what?' she [ventures]. 'Day carts of piss–all? And besides, how come you know that?'

'I like to read,' says Gaston. 'I've got an arrangement with a guy on the garbage truck: he slips me the old books, I hand over the cigarette butts.'

'In the meantime,' says Gaston, 'it doesn't get us anywhere.'

'As to that,' says Madame D., 'I really don't know what would get us anywhere. And anyway we got a writer in the building, he's the worst of the lot.'

'Don't mean a thing,' says the sweeper.

'Mustn't generalize,' says Mademoiselle G. timidly.

'You, with your de Gaulle,' says Madame D., 'you [get right on my nerves].'

* * *

Although Madame D.'s colorfulness might possibly come close to ordinary picturesqueness through its regularity, its monotony, its repetitiveness – it would be a shame to assign her merely the standard picturesque quality, which is always dumb by definition.

Madame D. cannot share our enthusiasm for life. Were she to let herself accept, even once, a disgraceful compromise, she would be siding with her natural enemy: the tenant.

With great style, Madame D. refuses to knuckle under.

For Madame D. has a very distinctive idea of Providence (quotation) and a no less distinctive conception of the future of socialism (quotation). Still, Madame D. does throw into doubt, in its very principle, one of the most commonly accepted institutions, the most innocent, absurd, hidden violence in bourgeois society: the institution of the garbage can. Sending the letter,[4] giving her cause for satisfaction in her particular case, would make Madame D. (although I have my doubts) a replete, sovereign, contented concierge who would no longer send rampaging through number 5 rue Saint-Benoît one of those rages that truly ought to exist. All the tenants, whatever their merits, are lumped together and treated with equality, even perfect equality, of which I see no other instance in everyday life. And I really don't believe it's a bad thing that some of them should be challenged {politically like that}, even in what they feel is their right to fast on Fridays.

[. . .] every day her refusal is as complete as on the first day, as untouched as possible by any submission, any acceptance whatsoever. Madame F. could die for the cause: the suppression of the institution of the garbage can. Not a day goes by without her justifying her disgust in some way or another to [one of the] tenants. Her reasons are numerous, rooted in the most flagrant bad faith, and that's quite normal. Her passion blinds her, and she cannot put it into words when she is calm. The tenant {who catches it} is usually the last one to empty a garbage can. This has become one of the particular little obligations of the building. To get yelled at because of emptying a garbage can. A can you emptied because you had one to empty, which you had because you eat, and because as long as you live you'll have one to empty. And that's how the many tenants unprepared for this kind of thing have learned that someone could contest their hitherto accepted legal right to have garbage cans, and how those who are the most convinced of their [rights] have seen themselves treated with such [. . .]

The most unexpected consequence of her friendship with Gaston is that he has alienated her from her children, especially her youngest son. She no longer wants to see him: he bores her. She raised him very well and has made uncommon sacrifices for him. Her husband used to drink up her salary and she, to [raise her] children, she worked in a factory for fifteen years. After the factory, in the evenings, she took in laundry. Her daughter is a post-office employee. She lives in a distant *département* and rarely sees her mother.

'On that score, I've no worries.'

But her son is a truck farmer in Chatou. He comes to see her on New Year's Day, Bastille Day, and Easter, when she invariably welcomes him by saying, 'I did so much for them that I'm tired of them. All I want from them is just to stop bothering me.'

Her son and daughter often ask her to come 'live out her days' with them.

'Even if I'd be living like a queen with you, I'd rather croak in an old-age home.'

*   *   *

Sometimes Madame D.'s son comes to see her. For Madame D. has two children. He comes to see her on New Year's Day, the anniversary of the Liberation, and Easter. Just as she has constant grievances against her tenants, Madame D. has some against her son: just as vague, just as terrible.

'Children, they're all lousy bastards, and even the best ones,' begins Madame D., 'no exceptions.'

The son sits down in her lodge.

'And she's off,' says Madame D.'s son.

'If you can't handle hearing a few home truths,' says Madame D., 'just you go right back where you came from.'

'It's not that he's bad,' Madame D. tells the tenants, 'but it's only normal, he's waiting for me to croak. So naturally he's the one I've the least to say to.'

And she invariably adds, 'Don't like macaronis.'

This seemingly benign, gratuitous remark is aimed at her daughter-in-law, who is Italian.

'Really like to know what it is you got against me,' says the son.

Seeking lady with child-care experience and excellent references (preferably around forty years old) mornings nine to
noon for housework and four to six p.m. to take the baby out,
except Sundays.

    In return:

        furnished maid's room with electricity

        4,000 francs

        breakfast

        and midday meal.

We cannot sleep anymore.

The opening of the Club Saint-Germain-des-Prés has turned the rue Saint-Benoît upside down. All night long, nothing but engines revving, horns blowing, car doors slamming. It's practically impossible to close your eyes until three in the morning. Let's note that on the rue Saint-Benoît, almost opposite the Club Saint-Germain-des-Prés, there's an old-age home. Let's note, for example, that in number 5 alone there are eleven children. And we've learned that another Tabou[5] will be opening on the impasse des Deux-Anges. That will make three nightclubs on one narrow street and [*illegible*]. Couldn't the rue Saint-Benoît be made a one-way street? And the [*illegible*] be situated on the Place Saint-Germain, where parking will be available? And where the noise, given the size of the square, would be less unbearable?

The Socialist Party has come out against cantonal elections. It shuns universal suffrage, the suffrage of workers, housewives, the middle classes. It is afraid. And with reason. And wishing to hide its fear, it betrays, it sells, it plays the informer. During the parliamentary session devoted to the cantonal elections, it 'gave up' the Madagascan parliamentarians.

And to fool its people, here's what it did: although the elections were the only subject under discussion, the party hijacked the question, starting off with a motion to suspend proceedings against the Madagascan parliamentarians. Two deputies – [Violette], the Democratic and Socialist Union of the Resistance, and [*illegible*], an independent – {then} rise to announce that the Parliament cannot block a judicial [*illegible*]. And as if struck by this fact, the socialists immediately withdraw their motion and abstain. And because of their disgraceful action, the motion is withdrawn.

And then the Socialist Party, believing it has honorably redeemed itself in advance through an [*illegible*] initiative, having sold out the Madagascan parliamentarians to the reactionaries, [votes] against the cantonal elections and for a uninominal ballot – {voting for a single member only} – in two rounds in March 1949.

After that fresh disgrace, on the heels of a struggle that had already gone on too long, five socialist deputies and Paul Rivet, director of the Museum of Natural History and city councilor from our arrondissement, tendered their resignations. For which we congratulate them. We see a connection between their action, the creation last Sunday of the Unitarian Socialist Party, and the 'fed-up' socialists, whose numbers increase by the day. And let us hope that the voice of the masses will be increasingly heard 'from the bottom up' against their leaders.

It's uncomfortable sitting at a round table: your elbows aren't resting on anything and you can't lean on them to rest from writing, and while you're writing they're sticking out into nowhere, and if you don't notice that right away you tell yourself, 'I don't know what's wrong with me, I'm tired,' and it's because your elbows aren't resting on the table.

NOTES

1. The distinguished Italian statesman and politician Alcide De Gasperi, cofounder of the Italian Popular Party and prime mover of the Christian Democratic Party, was an anti-fascist and a staunch supporter of the idea of a European community.

2. In her novella *Madame Dodin*, Marguerite Duras writes that Gaston has become blasé because 'he has lived too much [. . . .] He has witnessed every event, public or private, that happens in the streets he sweeps.' And so, his 'personal philosophy,' which is perhaps that of the true street sweeper,' is that all human events, 'first communions, marriages, deaths, invariably finish, according to him, in the same way, with flowers tossed into the gutter and guided by him downstream to their final destination, the sewer.'

3. 'Pierrot the Madman,' alias Pierre Loutrel, was a criminal who came into his own during the Occupation, a 'Gestapiste' and cold-blooded murderer. When the tide turned, he and his gang switched sides, shielding their pimping, racketeering, robberies, and assassinations in the Resistance. When he died in 1946 after a botched holdup, Pierrot le Fou was France's public enemy number one.

4. This enigmatic letter is not one of the 'anonymous threatening letters' mentioned earlier in the text, but – as explained in *Madame Dodin* – a letter the narrator has considered sending to the other tenants on the concierge's behalf concerning her complaints about the garbage situation. But such a letter, reflects the narrator, if successful, might do the concierge 'more harm than good. If her tenants become irreproachable, won't she experience painful nostalgia for her enemies?' So the narrator decides not to send such a letter.

5. The famous 1950s nightclub Tabou, at 33 rue Dauphine, was frequented by the likes of Boris Vian, Juliette Greco, Miles Davis, and Sartre.

★

The editors wish to thank Yann Andréa and Jean Mascolo first of all, for their authorization and encouragement of the publication of these notebooks; Jean Vallier, who assisted us in providing dates and biographical background for the various works; and all those at IMEC who collaborated with us in this endeavor.

PRACTICALITIES

MARGUERITE DURAS SPEAKS
TO JÉRÔME BEAUJOUR

TRANSLATED BY BARBARA BRAY

CONTENTS

This book helped us pass the time. From the beginning of autumn to the end of winter. All the pieces in it, with very few exceptions, were spoken aloud to Jérôme Beaujour. Then the spoken texts were transcribed, we read them over and appraised them, I made corrections, and Jérôme Beaujour read the result. It was difficult at first. We soon abandoned questions and answers. We tried a subject-by-subject approach, but gave that up too. The last phase of the work consisted of my shortening and lightening the texts and toning them down. It was all done by common consent. As a result of the method we evolved, none of the pieces deals with a topic exhaustively. And none reflects my general views about a particular subject: I don't have general views about anything, except social injustice. At most the book represents what I think sometimes, some days, about some things. So it does incidentally represent what I think. But I don't drag the millstone of totalitarian, i.e. inflexible, thought around with me. That's one plague I've managed to avoid.

The book has no beginning or end, and it hasn't got a middle either. If it's true that every book must have a raison d'être, this isn't a book at all. Nor is it a journal, or journalism – it doesn't concern itself with ordinary events. Let's just say it's a book intended to be read. Very different from a novel, though its writing was closer to that of a novel – strangely enough, seeing it started out orally – than to the composing of an editorial. I had doubts about publishing it in this form, but no previous or current genre could have accommodated such a free kind of writing, these return journeys between you and me, and between myself and myself, in the time we went through together.

MARGUERITE DURAS

THE SMELL OF CHEMICALS

IN 1986 I'LL have been in Trouville from the middle of June until the middle of October – longer than the summer. Whenever I'm away from Trouville I feel I've lost the light. Not only the direct bright light of the sun but also the diffused white light of overcast skies and the dark grey light of storms. If I'm away at the end of summer I miss the skies, those long-haul travellers of skies, that come up from beneath the Atlantic. If I'm away in the autumn I miss the haze of high tide, the wind, the oily miasmas of Le Havre, the smell of chemicals. If you get up early you can see a perfect projection of the Black Rocks slanting slightly to the north over the empty beach. Then as the hours go by the shadow shortens and finally disappears.

For years I've moved back and forth between the three houses, at Neauphle-le-Château, Trouville and Paris. For ten years, not wanting to leave Neauphle, I didn't go to Trouville. I even let the place there for a few summers to cover the high running costs. All those years I lived on my own at Neauphle-le-Château, which is why for a long time I didn't get to know anyone at the Black Rocks Hotel. If I spent the summer in any one place it was usually Neauphle, where I knew the whole village.

I've never been anywhere where I felt comfortable. I've always been hanging about looking for somewhere or for something to do; I've never been where I wanted to be, except perhaps some summers at Neauphle, in a sort of happy woe. The enclosed garden in *The Atlantic Man*, the despair of loving him – it all happened in that now untended garden. I can still see myself there, closed in on myself, trapped in the ice of the deserted grounds.

I'm the sort of person who's never on time for meals,

appointments, the cinema, the theatre, aeroplanes – I always arrive at the last minute. Because I don't trust myself I've taken to getting to the theatre an hour early. I'm delighted when I see other people rush in afraid of being late. I've always turned up on the beach just as everyone else is leaving. I've never acquired a tan because I loathe sunbathing and having sand on my skin and in my hair. I have got brown, though, driving the car or walking in Spain or Italy.

Yet for a considerable part of my life I longed to be able to sunbathe. It went on for ages. I used to work out systems for doing the same as everyone else. That's how, much to my chagrin, I used to be always late. I did what everyone else did, I went on the beach – but in the evening. I did things by halves, just in order to have done them at all, and it didn't work. I very much regret having been like that – obeying the rules but never getting any satisfaction out of it. At the end of the summer I'd feel like an idiot who doesn't know what's been happening, and only knows it's too late to find out. But there is one thing I'm good at, and that's looking at the sea. Not many people have written about the sea as I did in *Summer 1980*. But that's the point: the sea in *Summer 1980* is something I never experienced myself. It's something that happened to me but that I never experienced, something I put into a book precisely because I couldn't have lived it. Always, all my life, that thing about time passing. All my whole life long.

I could have gone on after *Summer 1980*. Just doing that. Keeping a journal of time and the sea – of the rain, the tides, the wind, the rough wind that blows away beach umbrellas and awnings and swirls round the bodies of children in hollows on the beach, and inside the walls of hotels. With time at a standstill in front of me, and the great barrier of the cold, the Arctic winter. But *Summer 1980* remains the only journal I have ever kept. Telling how I was shipwrecked, near to the sea but on land, in the bleak summer of 1980.

THE LADIES OF
THE BLACK ROCKS

EVERY AFTERNOON HERE during the summer a number of ladies already getting on in years meet on the terrace of the Black Rocks Hotel and talk. We call them the Ladies of the Black Rocks. Every day, every afternoon of all the summer. But of course you can talk about your life your whole life long; a life is no small matter. The ladies talk on the terrace overlooking the sea until dusk, when it starts to get cool. Other people, passing by, often stop to listen. Sometimes the ladies ask them to stay and join them. The ladies tell about things that have happened to them in their lives, and about things that have happened to other people in other lives, and they are marvellous at it. They've been there for forty years, perched on the débris of the war, talking about central Europe. Some people come every year to this big hotel on the Channel coast. Just to talk.

The ladies would have been between twenty and thirty-five in 1940. Some of them live in Passy. Ladies – the word has no meaning unless you know the ladies of the *département* called 'the Channel', the Ladies of the Black Rocks.

In summer they rebuild Europe out of their networks of friendships, acquaintances, and social and diplomatic connections; out of balls in Vienna and Paris; out of people who died in Auschwitz; out of exile.

Proust used to come to this hotel sometimes. Some of the ladies must have met him. He had Room 111, overlooking the sea. It's as if Swann were still here in the corridors. And it's when the ladies are little girls again that Swann walks.

THE MOTORWAY OF THE WORD

IN THIS sort-of-a-book which isn't really a book at all I'd have liked to talk about this and that, as one does all the time on an ordinary day just like any other. To drive along the motorway of the word, slowing down or stopping as I felt inclined, for no particular reason. But it's impossible – you can't get away from the road itself and the way it's going; you can't not go anywhere; you can't just talk without starting out from a particular point of knowledge or ignorance, and arrive somewhere at random amid the welter of other words. You can't simultaneously know and not know. And so this book, which I'd have liked to resemble a motorway going in all directions at once, will merely be a book that tries to go everywhere but goes to just one place at a time; which turns back and sets out again the same as everyone else, the same as every other book. The only alternative is to say nothing. But that can't be written down.

THE THEATRE

I HOPE TO be able to get out of the house this winter and produce some theatre that's read, not acted. Acting doesn't bring
anything to a text. On the contrary, it detracts from it – lessens
its immediacy and depth, weakens its muscles and dilutes its
blood. That's what I think today. But I think it often. Deep
down, that's how I really see the theatre. However, as that kind
of theatre doesn't exist, I've tended to forget and go back to
thinking about the usual kind. But since the experiment at the
Théâtre du Rond-Point in January 1985, I've thought what
I'm saying now. Absolutely; once and for all.

An actor reading a book aloud, as in *Blue Eyes Black Hair*,
has nothing else to do but be still and bring the text out of the
book by means of the voice alone. No need to gesticulate to
show how the body is suffering because of the words being
uttered: the whole drama resides in the words themselves and
the body remains unmoved. I don't know of any theatrical
utterance as powerful as that of the officiants at the various
kinds of mass. The Pope's people speak and sing in a curious
flat language in which every syllable is given equal weight,
without tonic or any other accent; and yet there's nothing to
compare with it in either theatre or opera. In the recitatives in
the St John and St Matthew Passions, and in Stravinsky's *Noces*
and *Symphony of Psalms* there are similar acoustic dimensions,
seemingly newly created, in which the full resonance of the
words is heard as it never is in ordinary life. That's what
I believe in. Only that. In Gruber's *Bérénice*, which was almost
without movement, I didn't like the rudiments of motion that
remained – they distanced the words. Bérénice's laments, even
conveyed by a great actress like Ludmilla Michaël, didn't have
the acoustic dimension they deserved. Why do people still

fool themselves about it? Bérénice and Titus are narrators; Racine is the director; the audience is humanity. Why play it in a drawing room or a boudoir? I don't care what anyone thinks about what I've been saying. Give me a theatre to have *Bérénice* read in, and they'll see. The beginnings of what I'm saying now lie in the conversation between the young lovers in *Savannah Bay*, what I've called the 'reported voices'. Something strange happened when the play was done in The Hague – something never achieved by my own two dear actresses. They held the whole theatre with their eyes, they just gazed at the audience, yet they showed what *can* happen in the theatre when the story of the lovers is merely related.

No play by a woman had been performed at the Comédie Française since 1900, nor at Vilar's TNP, nor at the Odéon, nor at Villeurbanne, nor at the Schaubuhne, nor at Strehler's Piccolo Teatro. Not one woman playwright or one woman director. And then Sarraute and I began to be performed by the Barraults. George Sand's plays were produced in Paris, but for seventy, eighty, ninety years no play by a woman had been performed there or perhaps in the whole of Europe. I found that out for myself. No one ever told me. And yet it was there for all to see. And then one day I got a letter from Jean-Louis Barrault asking if I'd adapt my long short story, *Days in the Trees*, for the stage. I agreed. The adaptation was rejected by the censors. The play wasn't performed until 1965. It was a great success. But none of the critics pointed out that it was the first play by a woman to be performed in France for nearly a century.

THE LAST CUSTOMER AT NIGHT

THE ROAD WENT through the Auvergne – the Cantal area. We'd set out from Saint-Tropez in the afternoon and driven through part of the night. I can't quite remember what year it was, but it was in the summer. I'd known him since the beginning of the year. I'd met him at a dance I'd gone to on my own. But that's another story. He insisted on stopping before dawn in Aurillac. The telegram had been delayed – sent to Paris, then on from there to Saint-Tropez. The funeral was to take place late the next afternoon. We made love in the hotel in Aurillac, then made love again. And again the next morning. I think it was then, on that journey, that that particular desire emerged clearly in my mind. Because of him, I think. But I'm not quite sure. But yes, it probably was because of him, because he had it too, the same desire. But it could have been anyone. At random, like the last customer at night. We'd had hardly any sleep, but we set out again very early. It was a lovely drive, but terribly long, with bends every hundred yards. Yes, it was on that journey. It's never happened to me again. The place was ready. On the body. In the hotel rooms. On the sandy banks of the river. At night. It was in the châteaux, too, in their walls. In the cruelty of the chase. And of men. In fear. In the forest. In the wilderness of the rides through the forest, the lakes, the sky. We took a room by the river. We made love again. We couldn't speak to one another any more. We drank. He struck me, in cold blood. In the face. And parts of the body. We couldn't be near one another now without fear and trembling. He drove me through the grounds and left me at the entrance to the château. The people from the undertaker's were there, and the wardens of the château, and my mother's housekeeper and my elder brother. My

mother hadn't been put in her coffin yet. They were all waiting for me. My mother. I kissed the cold forehead. My brother
was crying. There were only three of us at the church in
Ozain, the wardens of the château had stayed behind.
I thought about the man waiting for me in the hotel by the
river. I didn't feel any grief for the dead woman, or for the
man who was weeping, her son. I've never felt any since.
Afterwards there was the meeting with the solicitor. I agreed
to everything it said in my mother's will; I disinherited myself.

He was waiting for me in the grounds. We slept in the hotel
by the Loire. We lingered on by the river for a few days.
We used to stay in our room till late afternoon. We drank. We
went out and drank. Then came back to the room. Then went
out again at night. Looking for cafés that were still open. It
was madness. We couldn't tear ourselves away from the place,
from the river. We didn't speak of what was in our minds.
Sometimes we were afraid. We were overwhelmed with grief.
We wept. But the word was never spoken. We were sorry we
didn't love one another. We couldn't remember anything.
That's what we said. We knew it would never happen to us
again, but we never referred to it, nor to the fact that we were
both faced with the same strange desire. The madness lasted
the whole winter. After that it became less important – just a
love affair. And after that again, I wrote *Moderato Cantabile*.

ALCOHOL

I'VE SPENT WHOLE summers at Neauphle alone except for drink. People used to come at the weekends. But during the week I was alone in that huge house, and that was how alcohol took on its full significance. It lends resonance to loneliness, and ends up making you prefer it to everything else. Drinking isn't necessarily the same as wanting to die. But you can't drink without thinking you're killing yourself. Living with alcohol is living with death close at hand. What stops you killing yourself when you're intoxicated out of your mind is the thought that once you're dead you won't be able to drink any more. I started drinking at parties and political meetings – glasses of wine at first, then whisky. And then, when I was forty-one, I met someone who really loved alcohol and drank every day, though sensibly. I soon outstripped him. That went on for ten years, until I got cirrhosis of the liver and started vomiting blood. Then I gave up drinking for ten years. That was the first time. Then I started again, and gave it up again, I forget why. Then I stopped smoking, but I could only do that by drinking again. This is the third time I've given it up. I've never smoked opium or hash. I 'doped' myself with aspirin every day for fifteen years, but I've never taken drugs. At first I drank whisky and Calvados – what I call the pale kinds of alcohol. And beer, and vervain from Velay – they say that's the worst for the liver. Lastly I started to drink wine, and I never stopped.

I became an alcoholic as soon as I started to drink. I drank like one straight away, and left everyone else behind. I began by drinking in the evening, then at midday, then in the morning, and then I began to drink at night. First once a night, then every two hours. I've never drugged myself any other way. I've

always known that if I took to heroin it would soon get out of
control. I've always drunk with men. Alcohol is linked to the
memory of sexual violence – it makes it glow, it's inseparable
from it. But only in the mind. Alcohol is a substitute for pleasure though it doesn't replace it. People obsessed with sex
aren't usually alcoholics. Alcoholics, even those in the gutter,
tend to be intellectuals. The proletariat, a class far more intellectual now than the bourgeoisie, has a propensity for alcohol,
as can be seen all over the world. Of all human occupations,
manual work is probably the kind that leads most directly to
thought, and therefore to drink. Just look at the history of
ideas. Alcohol makes people talk. It's spirituality carried to the
point where logic becomes lunacy; it's reason going mad trying to understand why this kind of society, this Reign of
Injustice, exists. And it always ends in despair. A drunk is often
coarse, but rarely obscene. Sometimes he loses his temper and
kills. When you've had too much to drink you're back at the
start of the infernal cycle of life. People talk about happiness,
and say it's impossible. But they know what the word means.

What they lack is a god. The void you discover one day in
your teens – nothing can ever undo that discovery. But alcohol
was invented to help us bear the void in the universe – the
motion of the planets, their imperturbable wheeling through
space, their silent indifference to the place of our pain. A man
who drinks is interplanetary. He moves through interstellar
space. It's from there he looks down. Alcohol doesn't console,
it doesn't fill up anyone's psychological gaps, all it replaces is
the lack of God. It doesn't comfort man. On the contrary, it
encourages him in his folly, it transports him to the supreme
regions where he is master of his own destiny. No other
human being, no woman, no poem or music, book or painting
can replace alcohol in its power to give man the illusion of real
creation. Alcohol's job is to replace creation. And that's what
it does do for a lot of people who ought to have believed in
God and don't any more. But alcohol is barren. The words a

man speaks in the night of drunkenness fade like the darkness itself at the coming of day. Drunkenness doesn't create any- thing, it doesn't enter into the words, it dims and slackens the mind instead of stimulating it. I've spoken under its influence. The illusion's perfect: you're sure what you're saying has never been said before. But alcohol can't produce anything that lasts. It's just wind. I've written under its influence too – I had the knack of keeping tipsiness at bay, probably because I have such a horror of it. I never drank in order to get drunk. I never drank fast. I drank all the time and I was never drunk. I was withdrawn from the world – inaccessible but not intoxicated.

When a woman drinks it's as if an animal were drinking, or a child. Alcoholism is scandalous in a woman, and a female alcoholic is rare, a serious matter. It's a slur on the divine in our nature. I realized the scandal I was causing around me. But in my day, in order to have the strength to confront it publicly – for example, to go into a bar on one's own at night – you needed to have had something to drink already.

It's always too late when people tell someone they drink too much. 'You drink too much.' But it's a shocking thing to say whenever you say it. You never know yourself that you're an alcoholic. In a hundred per cent of cases it's taken as an insult. The person concerned says, 'You're only saying that to get at me.' In my own case the disease had already taken hold by the time I was told about it. We live in a world paralysed with principles. We just let other people die. I don't think this kind of thing happens with drugs. Drugs cut the addict off completely from the rest of humanity. But they don't throw him to the winds or into the street; they don't turn him into a vagabond. But alcohol means the gutter, the dosshouse, other alcoholics. With drugs it's very quick: death comes fast – speechlessness, darkness, closed shutters, helplessness. Nor is there any consolation for stopping drinking. Since I've stopped I feel for the alcoholic I once was. I really did drink a lot. Then help came – but now I'm telling my own story instead of talking about alcohol in general. It's incredibly simple – for real alcoholics there's probably the simplest possible explanation. They're in a place where suffering can't hurt them. *Clochards* aren't unhappy, it's silly to say that when they're drunk from morn till night, twenty-four hours a day. They couldn't lead the life they lead anywhere else but in the street. During the winter of 1986–7 they preferred to risk dying of cold rather than go into a hostel and give up their litre of *rouge*. Everyone tried to work out why they wouldn't go into the dosshouse. That was the reason.

The night hours aren't the worst. But of course that's the most dangerous time if you suffer from insomnia. You mustn't have a drop of alcohol in the house. I'm one of those alcoholics who can be set off again by drinking just one glass of wine. I don't know the medical term for it.

An alcoholic's body is like a telephone exchange, like a set of different compartments all linked together. It's the brain that's affected first. The mind. First comes happiness through the mind. Then through the body. It's lapped around, saturated, then borne along – yes, that's the word for it, borne along. And after a time you have the choice – whether to keep drinking until you're senseless and lose your identity, or to go no further than the beginnings of happiness. To die, so to speak, every day, or to go on living.

THE PLEASURES OF
THE 6th ARRONDISSEMENT

I'VE MISSED OUT on the pleasures of the 6th arrondissement which people talk about all over the world.

I may have been to the Tabou once – perhaps twice, but I don't think so. I've cast an eye at the Deux Magots and the Flore, but not very often. As soon as I'd made *Hiroshima* and people started recognizing me, that was it – I steered clear of those fearful terraces. (I used to go to Lipp's because of Fernandez. And I have been to the Quatre Saisons.)

Why?

Pride. I was too short to go to places where the women were tall. I wore the same clothes every day. I had just the one dress, black and all-purpose, dating from the war. I was self-conscious, as young people often are, at not being 'in the swim'. All in all, for various reasons, my whole life's been overcast by that sort of shame.

It's soon too late in life to go to the Tabou or the Deux Magots. It was soon all over – public places, dancing. In my day. For women, I mean.

VINH LONG

THERE WAS Vinh Long, and there was Hanoi. I've talked about Vinh Long already, but never about Hanoi. As I've said before, Vinh Long was an outpost in Cochin China. You're already on the Plain of Birds there, the biggest irrigated land-scape in the world, I should think. I was between eight and ten years old when it happened. Like a thunderbolt, or faith. It affected my whole life. I'm seventy-two now, but it's still as though it were yesterday: the paths there in the afternoon when everyone was asleep, the White quarter, the empty streets with their rows of flame-trees. The sleeping river. And her going by in her black limousine. Her name is almost Anne-Marie Stretter. Her name is Striedter. The governor's wife. They've got two children. They came here from Laos; she had a young lover there. He's just killed himself because she went away. It's all there, as in *India Song*. The young man stayed on in Laos, the post where they'd met, away up north on the Mekong. He killed himself there. In Luang Prabang.

First there was Vinh Long, through which the river linking the lovers flowed, a thousand kilometres farther downstream. I can remember what my childish body felt: as if some know-ledge had been vouchsafed to it that was still forbidden. The world was huge and complex yet very clear. One would have to invent a word for it – for the way I managed to act as if I didn't understand what was there to be understood. I couldn't talk about it to anyone, not even my mother – I knew she lied to us children about such things. I had to keep the knowledge entirely to myself. From then on Anne-Marie Stretter was my secret.

HANOI

AND THERE WAS Hanoi too, which I've never talked about,
I don't know why. Before Vinh Long, six years before, there
was Hanoi. In the house my mother had bought on the Little
Lake. At that time my mother took in paying guests. Vietnamese and Laotian boys aged about twelve or thirteen. One
afternoon one of them asked me to go with him to a 'hidey-
hole'. I wasn't afraid, so I went. The place was on the edge
of the lake, between a couple of wooden huts that must have
belonged to the house. I can remember a kind of narrow passage between walls made of planks. This was where the
defloration in the book took place: among the bathing huts.
The lake became the sea, but the pleasure was there even then,
its nature already essentially foreshadowed. And also unforgettable even then, in the body of a child light-years away from
understanding what it was, but already receiving the signal,
even then. The next day my mother sent the Vietnamese boy
packing – I'd thought it my duty to tell her everything, confess
everything. I can remember it all quite plainly. It is as if I was
dishonoured by having been touched. I was four years old. He
was eleven and a half – not yet pubescent. His prick was still
limp and soft. He told me what to do. I took hold of it, he put
his hand on mine, and our two hands stroked it more and more
strongly. Then he stopped. I've never forgotten the feel of its
shape in my hand, or its warmth. Or the child's face, eyes shut,
martyr-like, waiting for, straining towards, a pleasure still out
of reach.

I never mentioned it to my mother again. For the rest of
her life she thought I'd forgotten. She'd said, 'You must never
think about it again. Never, ever.' For a long while I did think
about it, though, as about something terrible. I only spoke of

it much later, to men in France. But I knew my mother had
never forgotten those childish pranks.

The scene shifted of its own accord. It grew up with me,
in fact, and has never left me.

THE BLACK BLOCK

WHEN YOU'RE WRITING, a kind of instinct comes into play. What you're going to write is already there in the darkness. It's as if writing were something outside you, in a tangle of tenses: between writing and having written, having written and having to go on writing; between knowing and not knowing what it's all about; starting from complete meaning, being submerged by it, and ending up in meaninglessness. The image of a black block in the middle of the world isn't far out.

It isn't the transition Aristotle speaks of, from potential to actual being. It isn't a translation. It's not a matter of passing from one state to another. It's a matter of deciphering something already there, something you've already done in the sleep of your life, in its organic rumination, unbeknown to you. It isn't something 'transferred' – that's not it. It might be that the instinct I referred to is the power of reading before it's written something that's still illegible to everyone else. I could put it differently. I could say it's the ability to read your own writing, the first stage of your own writing, while it's still indecipherable to others. It's as if you have to regress, condescend towards other people's writing for the book to become legible to them. This could be said in other words again, but it would still amount to the same thing. You have in front of you a mass suspended between life and death and entirely dependent upon you. I've often had this feeling, of a confrontation between something that was already there and something that was about to take its place. I'm in the middle, and I seize the mass that's already there, move it about, smash it up – it's almost a question of muscles, of physical dexterity. You have to move faster than the non-writing part of you, which is always up there on the plane of thought, always threatening to fade out, to disappear into limbo as far as the future story is concerned; the part which will never descend to the level of writing; which refuses all drudgery. But you have the feeling that sometimes the non-writing part of you is asleep, and thereby yields itself up and enters completely into the ordinary aspect of writing that will constitute the book. But between these two states there are many intermediate ones, of differing degrees of felicity. Sometimes you could almost use the word happiness. When I was writing *The Lover* I felt I was *discovering* something: it was there before me, before everything, and would still be there after I'd come to think things were otherwise – that it was mine, that it was there for me. It was more or less as I've described, and the process of writing it down was so smooth it reminded you of the way you speak when you're drunk, when what you say always seems so simple and clear. Then all of a sudden it would start to resist. When that happens you feel as if you're in a sort of carapace – nothing can get through from yourself to yourself, or from yourself to anyone else. How can I convey it, how can I describe the experience, the sense of an almost tragic refusal to go on writing, as if it were impossible. Then, after ten minutes or so, perhaps after I'd interrelated a couple of words, some more lines would begin to emerge.

Writing isn't just telling stories. It's exactly the opposite. It's telling everything at once. It's the telling of a story, and the absence of the story. It's telling a story through its absence. Lol V. Stein is destroyed by the dance at S. Thala. Lol V. Stein is created by the dance at S. Thala.

The Ravishing of Lol V. Stein is a book apart, the only one of a kind. It separates the readers-cum-writers who've identified with L. V. Stein's madness from those who have not.

I'd like to draw a distinction between what I've said, and

said several times, and what I haven't said about the book. Here's what I think I've said: during the actual dance at S. Thala, Lol V. Stein is so carried away by the sight of her fiancé and the stranger in black that she forgets to suffer. She doesn't suffer at having been forgotten and betrayed. It's because her suffering is suppressed that she later goes mad. You could put it differently and say that she realizes her fiancé is being drawn towards another woman, and she completely identifies with this decision, although it's against herself; and it's because of this that she loses her reason. It's a kind of oblivion. Like a phenomenon related to the freezing of water. Water turns to ice at zero degrees, but sometimes, when the weather's very cold, the air is so still that the water *forgets* to freeze. It can descend to minus five degrees and freeze only then.

What I haven't said is that all the women in my books, whatever their age, derive from Lol V. Stein. Derive, that is, from a kind of self-forgetting. They all see quite clearly and lucidly. But they're imprudent, improvident. They all ruin their own lives. They're very timid, they're afraid of streets and public places, they don't expect to be happy. The women in all these books and films are alike, the whole procession of them, from *The Woman from the Ganges* to the last version of Lol V. Stein in the script that got lost. Where did I get the idea for that script from? I forget. It was just like one of the hallucinations I used to get after I had the drying-out treatment.

It took place in a town. The casino was lit up, and the same dance was in progress, as if it had been going on for twenty years. Yes, I think that was it. It's a repetition of the dance at S. Thala, but treated dramatically. You don't get to know any more about Lol V. Stein – that's all over and done with. Now she's going to die. She's stopped haunting me, she lets me alone, I kill her, I kill her so that she'll stop getting in my way, lying down in front of my houses, my books, sleeping on the beaches in all weathers, in the wind and the cold, waiting, waiting for this – for me to look at her again for the last time. Her madness is famous; she's old; she's carried out of the casino in a chair; she's Chinese now. The chair is carried by porters – on their shoulders, like a coffin. She's heavily made up. She doesn't know what's going on. She looks at the people, the town. Her hair is dyed, she's painted like a whore, she's utterly destroyed – or, as you might say, born. She has become the most beautiful sentence I ever wrote: 'It's S. Thala here as far as the river, and beyond the river it's S. Thala still.'

Thala's the word that's cried out on the top floor of the Black Rocks Hotel by the young stranger with blue eyes, black hair.

A few days ago a friend of mine just back from Rio de Janeiro said to me: 'Would you believe it? Lol V. Stein, that book of ours that's so difficult – the first thing I saw there was "O Deslumbramento 5 Ediçāo" all lit up in the windows of the airport bookshops.'

Lol V. Stein.
    Mad.
    Brought to a halt at the dance at S. Thala. She stops there. It's the dance that grows, making concentric circles round her, bigger and bigger. Now the dance, the sound of the dance, has reached as far as New York. Now, of all the characters in my books, Lol V. Stein comes top of the list. It's a funny thing. She's the one who 'sells' the best. My little madwoman.

BONNARD

NO, IT WASN'T a Monet or a Manet. It was a Bonnard. It was at the house of some people in Berne who were great art collectors. They had a painting by Bonnard: a boat, with the wife's family in it. Bonnard always wanted to alter the sail, and because he kept on about it they let him have the painting back. When he returned it he said he considered it finished now. But the sail had swallowed up everything, dwarfing the sea, the people in the boat and the sky. That can happen with a book: you can start a new sentence and change the whole subject. You don't notice anything; you look up at the window and it's evening. And the next morning you find you've sat down to a different book. The making of pictures and books isn't something completely conscious. And you can never, never find words for it.

THE BLUE OF THE SCARF

I'M THE ONLY one who knows what kind of blue the girl in the book's scarf is. That doesn't matter – but there are other inadequacies that do. For example, I'm also the only one who can see her smile and the look in her eyes. But I know I shall never be able to describe them to you. Make you – or anyone else, ever – see them too.

And some things remain unknown even to the author. In my case, some of the things Lol V. Stein does, some of the risks she takes, at the party she gives where Tatiana Karl and others play billiards. A distant violin is heard somewhere in the house. It's Lol's husband playing. Her attitude – the secret understanding between her and Jacques Hold during dinner, which changed the book's ending – I can't translate it or convey its meaning because I'm completely with Lol V. Stein and she herself doesn't quite know what she's doing or why. Blanchot has criticized me for using someone like Jacques Hold as an intermediary, in order to get close to her. He'd have preferred there to be no intermediary. But I can only get to grips with her when she's engaged in some action with another character; when I can see her and hear her. She's never hand-to-hand with me, like the Vice-Consul. A piece of writing is a whole that proceeds as a whole – it never presents itself as a matter of choice. Even if I find at the end of a book that one of the characters really loved a certain other character and not the one I've indicated, I don't alter the book's past, which is already written – I alter its future. When I myself notice the love isn't what I thought, I'm with the new love, I start off again with it. I don't say the love that's abandoned was wrong; I say it's dead. After the dinner at LVS's the colours remain the same, the colours of the walls and those in the garden. No one knows yet what is just about to change.

I've talked a lot about writing. But I don't know what it is.

MEN

IF YOU HAVE a mind to generalize you might say *The Malady of Death* is a preliminary version of *Blue Eyes Black Hair*. But *The Malady of Death* is an indictment, and there's nothing at all like that in the longer book.

Other people, from Peter Handke to Maurice Blanchot, have seen *The Malady of Death* as being against men in their relationship with women. If you like. But I say if men have taken such an interest in the book it's because they've sensed there's something more to it than that – something of particular concern to them. It's extraordinary that they should have seen it. But it's also extraordinary that some of them haven't seen that in *The Malady of Death*, as well as a man in relation to women, and seen through that, there's a man in relation to men.

The men are homosexuals. All men are potentially homosexuals – all that's missing is awareness of the fact, an incident or revelation that will bring it home to them. Homosexuals themselves know this and say so. And women who've known homosexuals and really loved them know it and say so too.

The covert queer – loud, intrusive, delightful, a favourite everywhere – bears witness at the very centre of both his body and his mind to the death of the organic, fraternal contradiction between men and women; to the absolute disappearance of woman as a secondary element.

The book is not so much the result of an actual experience as an intuition, a kind of blinding perception of what really goes on among men. It isn't due to a personal knowledge of men and of their general condition – it's self-evident. But I don't apply words to it any more. Now that I know it I no longer have the words to say it. It's just there, and it can't be named any more. You can proceed from a distance, using metaphor to get closer if you like. But I don't say now what I said before, in *The Malady of Death*. What I say now is this: it's a difference residing in one word, but no one knows which; residing in the depth of a shadow over a word, in the way it's said. All of a sudden a colour that's ordinary, a blue that's ugly. Only a slight difference, but conclusive. Or perhaps, on the other hand though equally likely, the absence of a shadow – everywhere, on land and sea. And in the eyes the gentle glaze that comes from lack of love.

It's between men and women that imagination is at its strong-est. And it's there that they're separated by a frigidity which women increasingly invoke and which paralyses the men who desire them. The woman herself usually doesn't know what the malady is that's depriving her of desire. Much oftener than is generally supposed she doesn't know what desire is, how it manifests itself in women. She thinks there are things she has to do in order to feel it as other women do. There's nothing to be said about this, except that wherever you think imagina-tion is absent, that's where it's at its most powerful. In frigidity. Frigidity is desire imagined by a woman who doesn't desire the man offering himself to her. It's the desire of a woman for a man who hasn't yet come to her, whom she doesn't yet know. She's faithful to this stranger even before she belongs to him. Frigidity is the non-desire for whatever is not him. And the end of frigidity is something unpredictable and infi-nite – a man can't altogether keep up with it. It's the desire a woman feels for her lover alone. Whatever he's like, whatever social class he belongs to, he will become her lover if it's him she desires. This inescapable vocation for just one being in the whole world is a feminine characteristic. It can happen with heterosexual lovers that desire attaches to just the one person for both of them, and the man, like the woman, becomes frigid or impotent if they change partners. But it happens much less often with men. Even if these notions are rather sweeping and depressing, they're the ones that come closest to the truth.

Heterosexuality is dangerous. It tempts you to aim at a perfect duality of desire.

In heterosexual love there's no solution. Man and woman are irreconcilable, and it's the doomed attempt to do the impossible, repeated in each new affair, that lends heterosexual love its grandeur.

But in homosexual love the passion is homosexuality itself. What a homosexual loves, as if it were his lover, his country, his art, his land, is homosexuality.

Desire for our lover hits us in the vaginal cavity, which reverberates like an echo chamber within our bodies. A place from which our lover's penis is absent. We can't deceive ourselves – can't imagine another penis in the place meant for just one man, the one who's our lover. If another man touches us we cry out in disgust. We possess our lover just as he possesses us. We possess each other. And the site of the possession is one of absolute subjectivity. It's there our lover deals us the strongest blows, which we implore him to deal so that they may echo all through our body and through our emptying mind. It's there that we want to die.

A writer who hasn't known women, has never touched a woman's body and perhaps never read any books or poems written by women, and yet thinks he's been involved in literature, is mistaken. You can't be ignorant of such essential data and still be an intellectual leader, even just for your peers. Although I felt quite friendly towards Roland Barthes I could never admire him. He always struck me as very careful and professorial, and strictly partisan. After the 'Mythologies' series I couldn't read him any more. I tried after he died to read his book on photography, but again I couldn't get on with it, except for a very fine chapter about his mother. The much revered mother who had been his companion, and the only heroine in the wilderness of his life. Then I tried to read *A Lover's Discourse: Fragments*, but I couldn't. Obviously it's very clever. Jottings on love – yes, on love, but in making them he managed in fact not to love at all, as far as I can see. A charming man, really charming, of course. And a writer, of course. That's the point. A writer of writing that's stiff and regular.

Even if they belong to some religious sect, people need to open up to the unknown – let it come in and stir things up! We also need to open up the law and leave it open, so that something can come in and upset the usual mechanisms of liberty. We need to open up to what's impious and what's forbidden, so that the unknown element in things may enter and be seen. Roland Barthes must have gone straight from childhood to adulthood without ever passing through the dangers of adolescence.

Men often interpret the sexual passages in my books as due to prejudice on my part. They pick over everything they read, everything we do. And laugh at any sexuality not their own.

Some men have been repelled by the couple in *The Lover* – the little white girl and the Chinese lover. They skip some pages, they say, or shut their eyes. Shut their eyes while they're reading! To them *The Lover*'s just the crazy family, the drives, the ferry, Saigon by night and the whole colonial caboodle. But not the little White and her Chinese lover. On the other hand, the couple in *The Lover* fills most men with a strange desire – one that rises up from the mists of time and the depths of humanity: the desire of incest and rape. For me that little girl walking through the town as if she were on her way to high school, but really, as she goes along the vast boulevard full of trams, through streets and markets crowded with people,

making her way towards the man, towards her slavish obligation towards her lover – she has a freedom I myself have lost.

I can remember the feeling of hands on bodies, and the coolness of the water out of the jars. I can remember the heat, such
heat it's unimaginable now. I'm the one who lets herself be
washed; he doesn't dry my body; he carries me, still wet, over
to the camp bed – the wood smooth as silk, and cool – and
switches on the fan. He devours me with a strength and
gentleness that shatter me.

The skin. My little brother's skin. It's the same. And the
hand. The same.

I think men's behaviour to women is generally brutal and
high-handed. But that doesn't necessarily mean men are brutal and high-handed – only that men are like that in the context of the heterosexual couple. Because they are uneasy in
that relationship. They act a part, because they're bored. In a
heterosexual couple the man is biding his time – his own time.
He doesn't know he's doing it. The number of men in heterosexual couples (or in drawing rooms or on beaches or in the
streets) who are just waiting, all alone, with no language in
common between them and their partners, and don't know it
– if you take all the countries in the world it must run into
millions and millions. But such men come out of themselves
when they drop the role they play in a heterosexual couple.
The equivalent of intimate conversation between women is
something men experience only with other men. Talking
means talking about sex. And talking about sex is part of sex
itself. Not at all the same as talking about sport or the office.

It's women who upset the applecart. Between themselves they
talk only about the practicalities of life. They're not supposed
to enter the realm of the mind. Very few of them are aware of
it. A lot of them still haven't found out. For centuries women

have been informed about themselves by men, and men tell them they're inferior. But speech is freer in that situation of deprivation and oppression just because it doesn't go beyond the practicalities of life. It's much more ancient, too. For centuries women were merely the vehicles of a more or less inevitable suffering – until it came to light in the first book written about women. It's not men, it's women who are young and fresh. But in the past they didn't know.

The thing that's between us is fascination, and the fascination resides in our being alike. Whether you're a man or a woman, the fascination resides in finding out that we're alike.

If you're a man your favourite company – that of your heart, your flesh and your sex – is the company of men. And it's in this context that you approach women. It's the other man, man number two inside you, who lives with your wife and has sexual relations with her – ordinary sexual relations which may be utilitarian, gastronomical, vital, amorous, or even passionate, and which also produce children and families. But the chief man inside you, man number one, has real relationships with men, his brothers. You listen to your wives' restful conversations as a whole, not in detail, as if they were just old refrains. One doesn't listen to women, doesn't pay any attention to what they say. But we're not blaming you for that. Women do tend to be boring still, and a lot of them haven't the nerve to step out of line. Nor would you want them to. The French bourgeoisie would like women to go on being treated as minors. But now women know what's what. And they're quitting, they're leaving men; and they're much happier than they used to be. Each one used to be acting a part with her man. Though much less so in the case of homosexuals, even then.

A man's transition from heterosexuality to homosexuality involves a very severe crisis. No change could possibly be greater. The man doesn't know himself any more. It's as if he were being born. In most cases he can't control or understand the crisis. He doesn't recognize what's happening, for a start, because of course he rejects the possibility that he might be a homosexual. As for his wife, she knows, whether she finds out from him or from others, including women friends. She begins to 'realize' everything. She sees all he's done or said in the past in a new light. She says, 'It must have been there all the time and he didn't see it. And he, together with everyone else, has suddenly found out.'

It will be the greatest disaster ever. At first it will only be below the surface. A slight fall in the population. People won't work any more. There'll be massive immigration to ensure that things get done. And then no one will know what to do. Perhaps everyone will just wait for the population to dwindle away. They'd sleep all the time. The death of the last man would pass unnoticed. But maybe some more heterosexuals would turn up and begin the game all over again.

Yes, it really is difficult to talk about sex. Before they're plumbers or writers or taxi drivers or unemployed or journalists, before everything else, men are men. Whether heterosexual or homosexual. The only difference is that some of them remind you of it as soon as you meet them, and others wait for a little while. You have to be very fond of men. Very, very fond. You have to be very fond of them to love them. Otherwise they're simply unbearable.

HOUSE AND HOME

A HOUSE MEANS a family house, a place specially meant for putting children and men in so as to restrict their waywardness and distract them from the longing for adventure and escape they've had since time began. The most difficult thing in tackling this subject is to get down to the basic and utterly manageable terms in which women see the fantastic challenge a house represents: how to provide a centre for children and men at one and the same time.

The house a woman creates is a Utopia. She can't help it – can't help trying to interest her nearest and dearest not in happiness itself but in the search for it. As if the search were the point of the whole thing, not something to be rejected out of hand because it's too general. She says you must both understand and be chary of this strange preoccupation with happiness. She thinks this attitude will help the children later on. For that's what a woman, a mother wants – to teach her children to take an interest in life. She knows it's safer for them to be interested in other people's happiness than to believe in their own.

At Neauphle I often used to cook in the early afternoon. That was when no one else was there – when the others were at work, or out for a walk, or asleep in their rooms. Then I had all the ground floor of the house and the garden to myself. It was then I saw most clearly that I loved them and wished them well. I can recall the kind of silence there was after they went out. To enter that silence was like entering the sea. At once a happiness and a very precise state of abandonment to an evolving idea. A way of thinking or perhaps of not thinking – the two things are not so far apart. And also of writing.

Slowly and carefully, so as to make it last, I'd cook, those afternoons, for the people who weren't there. I'd make some soup so that it would be ready for them if they came in very hungry. If no soup was ready there wasn't anything. If nothing was ready it was because there wasn't anything; nobody was there. Often the ingredients were there, bought that morning, and all I had to do was prepare the vegetables, put the soup on, and write.

I thought for a long while about buying a house. I never imagined I could ever own a new one. The house at Neauphle used to be a couple of farms built a little while before the Revolution. It must be just over two hundred years old. I've often thought about it. It was there in 1789 and 1870. It's where the forests of Rambouillet and Versailles meet. And in 1958 it belonged to me. I thought about it some nights till it almost hurt. I saw it lived in by the women. I saw myself as preceded by them, in the same bedrooms, the same twilights. There'd been nine generations of women before me within those walls; dozens of people gathered around the fires – children, farm workers, cow girls. All over the house there were surfaces rubbed smooth where grown-ups, children and dogs, had gone in and out of the doors.

The thing women brood on for years – it's the bed their thoughts flow along while the children are still small – is how to keep them safe from harm. They usually brood in vain.

Some women can never manage it – they can't handle their houses, they overload them, clutter them up, never create an opening towards the world outside. They can't help it, but they get it all wrong and make the house unbearable, so that the children run away as soon as they're fifteen, the same as we did. We ran away because the only adventure left to us was one all worked out by our mothers.

Lots of women never solve the problem of disorder – of the house being overrun by the chaos families produce. They know they'll never be able to overcome the incredible difficulties of keeping a house in order. Though anyhow there's nothing to be done about it. That sort of woman simply shifts disorder from one room to another; moves it about or hides it in cellars, disused rooms, trunks or cupboards. Women like that have locked doors in their own houses that they daren't open, even in front of the family, for fear of being put to shame. Many are willing enough but naïve – they think you can solve the problem of disorder by putting the tidying-up off until later, not realizing their 'later' doesn't exist and never will. And that even if it did come it would be too late. They don't realize that disorder, or in other words the accumulation of possessions, can only be dealt with in a way that's extremely painful. Namely by parting with them. Some families with big houses keep everything for three hundred years – dresses, toys, and anything to do with the children, the squire or the mayor.

I've thrown things away, and regretted it. Sooner or later you always regret having thrown things away at some time or other. But if you don't part with anything, if you try to hold back time, you can spend your whole life tidying life up and documenting it. Women often keep gas and electricity bills for twenty years, for no other reason than to record time and their own virtues. The time they once had, but of which nothing remains.

I say it again. It bears a lot of repetition. A woman's work, from the time she gets up to the time she goes to bed, is as hard as a day at war, worse than a man's working day. Because she has to make her time-table conform to those of other people – her own family and the various organizations it's connected with.

In a morning five hours long, she gets the children's breakfasts, washes and dresses them, does the housework, makes the beds, washes and dresses herself, does the shopping, does the

cooking, lays the table. In twenty minutes she gives the children their lunch, yelling at them the while, then takes them
back to school, does the dishes, does the washing, and so on
and so on. Maybe, at about half-past three, she gets to read the
paper for half an hour.

From the man's point of view a woman is a good mother when
she turns this discontinuity into a silent and unobtrusive
continuity.

This silent continuity used to be regarded as life itself, not
just one of its aspects, the same as work. And now we've got
to the root of the matter or the bottom of the mine.

The silent continuity seemed so natural and lasted so long
that in the end, for the people around the woman who prac-
tised it, it no longer existed at all. To men, women's work was
like the rain-bringing clouds, or the rain itself. The task
involved was carried out every day as regularly as sleep. So
men were happy – men in the Middle Ages, men at the time
of the Revolution, and men in 1986: everything in the garden
was lovely.

I've forgotten to say one thing that women ought to get into
their heads. Don't let anyone tell you different: the sons are
no different from the fathers. They treat women just the same
way. Cry the same way when one of them dies. Say nothing
can ever take her place.

That's how it used to be in the past. In the past, wherever
I turn, to whatever point in the history of the world, I see
women in an extreme and intolerable situation. Doing a balancing act over death.

Now, whichever way I turn in my own time I see the star-
lets of the media, tourism and banking, each one the bright
girl of the class, spruce and indefatigable, equally knowledge-
able about everything. And doing a balancing act over death.

So, you see, I write to no purpose. I write as it seems to me one has to write. For nothing. I don't even write for women. I write about women in order to write about myself, about myself alone through the ages.

I've read Virginia Woolf's *A Room of One's Own*, and Michelet's *The Witch*.

But I don't have books any more. I've got rid of them, and of any idea of having them. It's all over. With those two books it was as if I'd opened up my own body and mind and were reading an account of my own life in the Middle Ages, in the forests, and in the factories of the nineteenth century. But I couldn't find one man who'd read the Woolf book. We're cut off from one another, as M.D. says in her novels.

The mental house and the physical house.

My first school was my mother herself. How she ran her houses. How she did the work. It was she who taught me cleanliness – the thoroughgoing, morbid, superstitious cleanliness of a mother with three young children in Indochina in 1915.

What my mother wanted was to make sure that we, her children, whatever happened, however serious, even war – that we'd never in all our lives be caught unawares. As long as we had a house and our mother, we'd never be abandoned or swept away or taken by surprise. There could be wars, droughts, we might be cut off by floods; but we'd always have a house, a mother, and something to eat and drink. I believe that right up to the end of her life she made jam in preparation for a third war. She stockpiled sugar and pasta. Hers was a kind of gloomy arithmetic derived from a fundamental pessimism which I've inherited in its entirety.

Over the episode of the dykes my mother had been swindled

and abandoned by everyone. She brought us up completely unaided. She told us she'd been swindled and abandoned because our father was dead and she was defenceless. One thing she was certain of, and that was that we were all abandoned.

I have this deep desire to run a house. I've had it all my life. There's still something of it left. Even now I still have to know all the time what there is to eat in the cupboards, if there's everything that's needed in order to hold out, live, survive. I too still hanker after a sort of shipboard self-sufficiency on the voyage of life for the people I love and for my child.

I often think of the houses my mother had, the ones that went with her various posts. Seven hours' trek along unmade roads from the nearest white settlement and the nearest doctor. The cupboards were always full of food and medicine – gruel, soft soap, alum, acids, vinegars, quinine, disinfectants, Emetine, Peptofer, Pulmoserum, Hepatrol, charcoal. I mean, she wasn't just my mother – she was a kind of institution. The natives used to come to her too, for treatment. A house is that too – it overflows. That was how it was with us. We were conscious of it very early on, and were very grateful to our mother for it. Home was simultaneously her and the house – the house around her and her inside the house. And she extended beyond herself with predictions of bad weather and years of disaster. She lived through two wars – nine years of it altogether – and she expected there to be a third. I think she expected it right up to her death, just as everyone else expects the next season. I think she only read the paper for that – to try to read between the lines whether war was getting closer. I don't remember her ever saying it was getting further away.

Sometimes, when we were children, she played at war to show us what it was like. She'd get hold of a stick about the same length as a gun, put it over her shoulder, and march up and down in front of us singing *Sambre et Meuse*. Then she'd burst into tears, and we'd try to console her. Yes, my mother liked the wars of men.

I believe that always, or almost always, in all childhoods and in all the lives that follow them, the mother represents madness. Our mothers always remain the strangest, craziest people we've ever met. Lots of people say, 'My mother was insane – I say it and I mean it. Insane.' People laugh a lot at the memory of their mothers. I suppose it is funny.

In the house in the country, at Neauphle-le-Château, I made a list of all the things that ought to be always in the house. There were a few dozen of them. We kept the list – it's still there – because it was I who'd written it down. It still includes everything.

Here at Trouville it's different – it's only an apartment. I wouldn't think of doing such a thing for here. But at Neauphle there have always been stocks of things. Here's the list:

table salt	butter	lavatory paper
pepper	tea	light bulbs
sugar	flour	kitchen soap
coffee	eggs	Scotchbrite
wine	tinned tomatoes	eau de Javel
potatoes	kitchen salt	washing powder
pasta	Nescafé	(hand)
rice	nuoc mam	Spontex
oil	bread	Ajax
vinegar	cheeses	steel wool
onions	yoghourt	coffee filters
garlic	window cleaner	fuses
milk		insulating tape

The list's still there, on the wall. We haven't added anything.

We haven't taken to using any of the hundreds of new articles that have been invented in the twenty years since it was written.

Outer and inner order in a house. The outer order is the visible running of the house, and the inner order is that of the ideas, emotional phases and endless feelings connected with the children. A house as my mother conceived it was in fact *for* us. I don't think she'd have done it for a man or a lover. It's an activity that has nothing to do with men. They can build houses, but they can't make homes. As a general rule, men don't do anything for children. Nothing practical. They might take them to the cinema or out for a walk. But I think that's about all. The child is put into their arms when they get home from work – clean, changed, ready to go to bed. Happy. That makes a mountain of difference between men and women.

I seriously believe that to all intents and purposes the position of women hasn't changed. The woman is still responsible for everything in the house even if she has help, even if she's much more aware, much more intelligent, much bolder than before. Even if she has much more self-confidence. Even if she writes much more, a woman is just the same as she was before in relation to men. Her main ambition is still to watch over and look after the family. And even if she has changed socially, everything she does is done *on top of* that change. But have men changed? Almost not at all. Perhaps they don't shout so much. And they talk less. Yes. I can't see anything else. They can sometimes keep quiet. Be reduced to silence. Naturally. As a rest from the sound of their own voice.

The woman is the home. That's where she used to be, and that's where she is still. You might ask me, What if a man tries to be part of the home – will the woman let him? I answer yes. Because then he becomes one of the children.

Men's needs have to be met just the same as children's. And

women take the same pleasure in meeting them. Men think they're heroes – again just like children. Men love war, hunting, fishing, motorbikes, cars, just like children. When they're sleepy you can see it. And women like men to be like that. We mustn't fool ourselves. We like men to be innocent and cruel; we like hunters and warriors; we like children.

It's been going on for a long time. Ever since my son was a little boy I've brought the food from the kitchen and put it on the table. And when one course was finished and the next one was due, I'd go and fetch it without thinking, quite happily. Lots of women do it. Just like that, like me. They do it when the children are less than twelve years old, and they go on doing it afterwards. With the Italians, for example, you see women of eighty serving children of sixty. I've seen it myself in Sicily.

With a house – might as well admit it – it's rather as if you'd been given a boat, a yacht. And it's a very demanding job, running a house – the building itself and its human and other contents. It's only women who are not really quite women at all, frivolous women who have no idea, who neglect repairs. Now I've got where I wanted to get to – the repairs. I'd love to go into all the details, but perhaps the reader wouldn't understand why. Anyhow, here's what I have to say. Women who wait until there are three electric plugs that don't work, and the vacuum cleaner is unusable, and the taps drip, before they phone the plumber or buy some new plugs – these women have got it all wrong. As a rule it's women who've been neglected themselves who let things go like that – women who hope their husbands will notice and deduce that they're making their wives unhappy. Such women don't realize men never notice anything in a house run by their womenfolk: it's something they take for granted, something they got used to in their childhood with the woman who happened to be their mother. They can see very well that the plugs don't work, but what do they say? They say: 'Good heavens, the plugs don't work,' and go on with what they were doing. If the vacuum cleaner's broken they won't even notice. They simply don't see that sort of thing. Just like children – they don't notice anything. So women's behaviour is incomprehensible to men. If a woman omits to do something – forgets, or gets her own back by not buying new plugs – the men just won't take it in. Or they'll think she has reasons of her own for not buying new plugs or not getting the vacuum cleaner mended, and it would be tactless to ask what those reasons are. They're probably afraid they might suddenly be confronted by the women's despair, afraid they might be overwhelmed by despair themselves. People say men are 'adapting' now. It's hard to know what's really going on. Men try to 'adapt' themselves as regards practical things – one can accept that. But I don't really know what to think. I have a man friend who does the cooking and the housework. His wife doesn't do anything. She loathes housework, and doesn't know the first thing about cooking. And so my friend brings up the children and does the cooking; he washes the floors, does the shopping, makes the beds, sees to all the chores. And on top of all that he works to provide for them all. His wife wanted to be out of all the turmoil and have lovers whenever she felt like it. So she's taken a little house next door to the one her husband lives in with the two children, and he accepts this in order to keep her. Because she's the mother of his children. He accepts everything. He doesn't even suffer any more. What can you say to that? I personally feel slightly repelled by a man with such a strong sense of duty.

I'm told men often do the rough work and that you often see them in the household section of department stores. I don't even answer that sort of thing. Rough work is fun for men. To cut down trees after a day at the office isn't work – it's a kind of game. Of course, if you tell a man of ordinary build and average strength what needs doing, he does it. Wash up a couple of plates – he does it. Do the shopping – he does it. But he has a terrible tendency to think he's a hero if he goes out and buys some potatoes. Still, never mind.

People tell me I exaggerate. They say it all the time. Do you think exaggeration is the word? You talk of idealization, say I idealize women. Perhaps. Who's to say? Women could do with being idealized a bit.

You can think what you like about what I've just said. I must sound incomprehensible to you, talking about women's work. The main thing is to talk about them and their houses and their surroundings, and the way they manage other people's good.

Men and women are different, after all. Being a mother isn't the same as being a father. Motherhood means that a woman gives her body over to her child, her children; they're on her as they might be on a hill, in a garden; they devour her, hit her, sleep on her; and she lets herself be devoured, and sometimes she sleeps because they are on her body. Nothing like that happens with fathers.

But perhaps women secrete their own despair in the process of being mothers and wives. Perhaps, their whole lives long, they lose their rightful kingdom in the despair of every day. Perhaps their youthful aspirations, their strength, their love, all leak away through wounds given and received completely legally. Perhaps that's what it is – that women and martyrdom go together. And that women who are completely fulfilled by showing off their competence, their skill at games, their cooking and their virtue are two a penny.

Some women throw things away. I do it a lot.

For fifteen years I threw my manuscripts away as soon as the books came out. If I ask myself why, I think it was to wipe out the crime, to make it seem less important in my own eyes. It was so that I could 'pass' better in my own circle; to tone down the indecency of writing, if you were a woman, about forty years ago. I used to keep bits of sewing material and left-overs from the kitchen, but not manuscripts. So for all those years I burned them. And then one day someone said, 'Keep them for your son later on – you never know.'

The deed used to be done in the fireplace in the living room at Neauphle. It was total destruction. So did I know so early in my life that I was a writer? Probably. I can remember the days that followed the burnings. Everything became neat and virginal again. The house seemed lighter, the tables were free again – smooth and empty and without a trace.

In the past, women used to keep a lot of things. They kept children's toys, their homework, their first essays. They kept photographs from their own youth. Dark, blurred photographs that filled them with wonder. They kept the frocks they wore when they were girls, their wedding dresses, the orange blossom bouquets – but above all the photographs. Photographs of a world their children had never seen. Photographs with a meaning only for themselves.

One reason, perhaps the chief reason, why houses are flooded with material possessions is the longstanding ritual by which Paris is regularly submerged by sales, super-sales and final reductions. White sales, sales of left-overs from summer in the autumn and from autumn in the winter – women buy as some people take drugs, not because they need the things but because they're cheap. Then, when they get them home, as often as not they just throw them away. 'I don't know what came over me,' they say. As they might say if they spent a night in a hotel with a stranger.

In previous centuries most women would own two or three caracos or under-blouses, a camisole and a couple of petti-coats. In the winter they used to wear them all, and in the sum-mer they kept them tied up in a square of cotton. They took them along when they went away to work or to get married.

Now women must own two hundred and fifty times as many clothes as they had a couple of centuries ago. But women's existence in the house has remained the same. A life that seems, even to the woman herself, to have been written down and described already. It's a sort of role in the usual sense of the word, but a part she seems to play to herself inevitably and almost unconsciously. And so women journey on through the theatre of profound loneliness that has constituted their lives for centuries. Their voyage hasn't been to the wars or the crusades; it's taken place in the house and in the forest and in their heads, riddled with beliefs and often crippled or ill. It was then that she was promoted to the rank of witch, like you, like me, and burned. But some summers, some winters, at certain times in certain centuries, what with the passage of time, the light, the noises, the wild animals ferreting about in the bushes and the cries of the birds, the women just took themselves off. Men haven't known about these departures. They can't know about that sort of thing. They're busy in one of the services or professions; they have a responsibility that preoccupies them all the time and prevents them from knowing anything about women or women's freedom. Very early on in history men lost their freedom. For a very long time the only men really close to women were the farm labourers, ill-used, helpless, often simple-minded, but cheerful. They stayed at home among the women and made them laugh, and the women hid them and saved them from death. At certain hours of the day, in those times, a solitary bird would cry out in the luminous dark before night fell. Even then night fell fast or slowly according to the day and the season or the state of the sky, or whether the pain in someone's heart was terrible or only slight.

The cottages in the forest had to be strong, to keep out both wolves and men. Let's suppose, for example, it's 1350. She's twenty, or thirty, or forty – not more. She seldom lives longer than that, yet. In the towns, plague is rampant. She's always hungry. Always afraid. But it's the loneliness around this scrawny figure, not the hunger and fear, that supports things as they are. Michelet can't bear to think about us, we're so thin and rickety. We produce ten children in order to keep one. Our husbands are far away.

When shall we tire of it, that forest of our despair? That Siam? And of man, who first set light to the pyre?

Forgive us for talking about it so often.

We're here. Where the story of our lives takes place. Nowhere else. We have no lovers but those in our sleep. We have no human desires. All we know is the faces of animals, the form and beauty of the forests. We're afraid of ourselves. Our bodies are cold. We are made up of cold and fear and desire. They used to burn us. They kill us still in Kuwait and the wilder parts of Arabia.

There are also houses that are too well made, too well thought out, completely without surprises, devised in advance by experts. By surprise I mean the unpredictable element produced by the way a house is used. Dining rooms are large because that's where guests are entertained, but kitchens are small – and getting smaller and smaller. Yet everyone squeezes in there to eat. When one person leaves the kitchen the others have to stand up to make way. But the habit persists.

Efforts are made to break it, but it's in the kitchen that everybody congregates at the end of the day. It's warm there, and you can be with Mother and hear her talk while she gets on with the cooking. Pantries and linen rooms don't exist any more either, yet they're really irreplaceable. Like big kitchens. And yards.

*   *   *

Nowadays you can't design your own house any more. It's frowned on. 'That was all very well in the past,' they tell you, 'but now there are experts and they can do it much better than you.'

This kind of attitude is increasingly common, and I dislike it intensely. In most modern houses there are none of the rooms you need to supplement the basics of kitchen and bed-rooms. I mean rooms to keep things in. How can you do with-out them, and where are you supposed to do the ironing and the sewing and store things like nuts and apples and cheese and machines and tools and toys and so on?

And modern houses don't have passages, either, for chil-dren to play and run about in, and for dogs, umbrellas, coats and satchels. And don't forget that passages and corridors are where the young ones curl up and go to sleep when they're tired, and where you go and collect them to put them to bed. That's where they go when they're four years old and have had enough of the grown-ups and their philosophy. That's where, when they're unsure of themselves, they go and have a quiet cry.

Houses never have enough room for children, not even if they're castles. Children don't actually look at houses, but they know them and all their nooks and crannies better than their mothers do. They rummage about. They snoop around. They don't consciously look at houses any more than they look at the walls of flesh that enclose them before they can see any-thing at all – but they know them. It's when they leave the house that they look at it.

I'd like to talk about water, and cleanliness in houses. A dirty house is a terrible thing – the only people who can live in it are a dirty woman and a dirty husband and children. You can't live in it if you're not one of the dirty family. But a dirty house signifies something else to me, too – that the woman is in a dangerous state, a state of blindness. She's forgotten other people can see what she's done or left undone; and she's dirty herself without realizing it. Piles of washing up, grease everywhere, all the saucepans dirty. I've known people who waited until the dishes were crawling with maggots before they washed them up.

Some kitchens are frightening and fill one with despair. The worst of it is that children brought up amid dirt remain dirty for the rest of their lives. Dirty babies are the dirtiest things in the world.

In the colonies dirt was fatal. Dirt brought rats, and rats brought the plague. In the same way as piastres – piastre notes – brought leprosy.

So for me cleanliness is also a kind of superstition. Even now, when a person's mentioned to me I always ask if they're clean, just as I might ask if they're intelligent or sincere or honest.

I hesitated about keeping the passage on cleanliness in *The Lover*, I don't quite know why. As children, in the colonies, we were always in the water. We bathed in the rivers, we took showers morning and evening using water stored in jars, we went barefoot except in the street. But it was when the house was sluiced through with great buckets of water that the close fraternity between the children of the houseboys and the children of the Whites was celebrated. On those days my mother used to laugh with delight. I can't think of my childhood without thinking of water. The country where I was born is a land of water. The water of the lakes, the mountain torrents and the rice-fields. The muddy water of the rivers on the plain, in which people took shelter during storms. The rain came down so heavily it hurt. In ten minutes the garden was submerged. Who can ever describe the smell of the warm earth, steaming after a storm? Or of certain flowers. Of a jasmine in a garden. I'll never have been back to the country where I was born. Probably because the climate there, and Nature, seemed made for children. Once you're grown up it becomes external to you. You can't take such memories with you – you have to leave them where they came into being. I wasn't born anywhere.

Recently we had to break up the kitchen floor – here in France, at Neauphle – to put in an extra stair. The house is sinking. It's a very old place close to a pond: the soil's soft and very damp, and the house is gradually sinking. So the first tread on the stairs had become too high, too much effort. The mason had to dig a hole to get to the ballasting, then he found he couldn't get to the bottom of it. He dug deeper, and it still went on down further and further. But to what? What had the house been built on? He gave up digging and trying to find out. He filled in the hole. Cemented it over. And put in the new step.

CABOURG

IT WAS AT the end of the long promenade at Cabourg, near the harbour where the yachts are. There was a child on the beach flying a Chinese kite, as in *Summer 1980*. He didn't move from the spot where he was standing. All around him other children were playing football. I was quite a long way away, on the terrace. It was windy, and it would soon be dark. But the child didn't move, and his not moving became first irksome and then actually painful. Then by dint of peering hard at him, really concentrating, I saw what was the matter. Both his legs, which were as thin as sticks, were paralysed. Someone would no doubt be coming to take him home. Some of the other children were already leaving. He went on playing with the kite. Sometimes you say I'm going to kill myself, and then you go on with the book. Someone must have come and taken the child home before it got dark. The kite in the sky showed where he was. There couldn't be any mistake.

ANIMALS

I'D LOVE TO have lots of animals, lots of different ones. But you can't have a cow in Paris any more than you can go out of your mind. A cow tied up outside a block of flats in Paris means the lunatic asylum next morning for both the cow and its owner. Last week on television I saw a big she-bear come out from under the Arctic ice. She poked her head out and looked around. Then she hoisted herself out of her hole, and she was so weak she fell down. That big she-bear had had three cubs during the winter of 1986, and she hadn't moved or had anything to eat for three months. Her three cubs were very sturdy and well-nourished with her milk. But she herself was exhausted. She stayed out for one minute the first day, ten minutes the second day, and so on. After a week she rolled over and over down to the sea. As she swam about she watched the hole: the cubs weren't supposed to come out. But she didn't stay away long. She ate half a small seal and took the other half back to the cubs. She was as tall as General de Gaulle; she reminded me of him. Very lofty. A hundred yards away from her hole a male bear stood looking at her. She stopped in her tracks and looked back at him. He fled in terror.

TROUVILLE

THE HOUSE AT Trouville is where I live now. It's superseded Neauphle and Paris. It was there I met Yann. He came into the courtyard all lanky and thin. Walking very fast. He was going through a depressive spell then. He was very pale. Scared at first. Then it passed. I showed him the sea. It's a great luxury, being able to see it from the balcony. When cities are bombed there are always ruins and corpses left. But you can drop an atomic bomb in the sea and ten minutes later it's back as it was before. You can't change the shape of water. While I'm writing that Yann came to my house in 1980, he's speaking on the telephone. He spends ten hours a day doing that – he's going through a telephonic spell now. The bill came to four thousand five hundred and fifty francs for the month of August. He phones up people he doesn't know. And people he's met only once in his life. And people in Austria or Germany or Italy that he hasn't seen for ten years. Every time he calls someone up he howls with laughter. It makes it very difficult to work. Afterwards he goes out for walks in the hills. Sometimes he'll phone someone three days running and then give up on them altogether. Often because of something they've said. Such as: 'Where would I be without my wife?' The humble remark of all the great men of this century, from Dumézil to de Gaulle.

THE STAR

DEATH, the fact of death coming towards you, is also a memory. Like the present. It's completely here, like the memory of what has already happened and the thought of what is still to come. Like the accumulated springs of years gone by, and like the spring that's coming now, a leaf at a time, on the brink of being here. And death is like the explosion of a star, which occurred seventy-four million years ago and yet is visible from the earth one night in February 1987. A time as precise as the moment when a leaf bursts forth. Death is that present too. And the thought that you might never have known about it.

THE M.D. UNIFORM

MADELEINE RENAUD is dressed by Yves Saint-Laurent: he makes her some dresses, someone puts them on her, and lo and behold she goes about in them. You wonder if she knows that the dress she's wearing is new. These days Madeleine doesn't know so much as she used to. But we're very fond of one another, and I think she still knows that. I often think she and I are the only two women who don't care about the clothes we wear. But it's more complicated than that. For fifteen years I've had a uniform – the M.D. uniform. It apparently created a 'Duras look', which was taken over by a fashion designer last year: black cardigan, straight skirt, polo-neck sweater and short boots in winter. I said I didn't care about clothes, but that's wrong. A uniform is an attempt to reconcile form and content, to match what you think you look like with what you'd like to look like, what you think you are with what you want to suggest. You find this match without really looking for it. And once it's found it's permanent. And eventually it comes to define you. This is what's happened to me, and it's a help. I'm very short. This has meant I've never been able to wear most of the clothes the majority of women wear. My whole life has been affected by this difficulty, and the need to avoid wearing anything that might call attention to my size. The solution was to stop people thinking about it by always wearing the same clothes. So that people would notice the sameness of the uniform rather than the reason why it was adopted. I don't carry a handbag any more, either. It's changed my life. But even before I started wearing a cardigan, it was already a kind of different sameness.

I didn't need to dress up, because I was a writer. And the argument applies even before you start writing. Men like women who write. Even though they don't say so. A writer is a foreign country.

So now you know everything.

WRITERS' BODIES

WRITERS' BODIES are involved in their writing. Writers invite sexuality. Like kings and other people in power. As regards men, it's as if they'd slept with our minds, penetrated our minds at the same time as our bodies. There haven't been any exceptions as far as I'm concerned. The same kind of fascination operated even with lovers who weren't intellectuals. And for a worker a woman who writes books – that's something he'll never have. It's like that all over the world, for all writers, men and women alike. They're sex objects *par excellence*. When I was still very young I was attracted to elderly men because they were writers. I've never been able to imagine sex without intelligence, or intelligence without a kind of absence from oneself. Lots of intellectuals are clumsy lovers – unadventurous, apprehensive and absent-minded. It was all the same to me as long as when they weren't with me they were, as writers, just as absent about their own bodies. I've noticed that writers who are superb at making love are much more rarely great writers than those who are scared and not so good at it. Talent and genius evoke rape, just as they evoke death. Sham writers don't have these problems. They're sound and healthy and you can go with them quite safely. When both members of a couple are writers the wife says: 'My husband's a writer.' The husband says: 'My wife writes too.' The children say: 'My father writes books, and so does my mother, sometimes.'

ALAIN VEINSTEIN

THIS IS a bad period for me. It's the end of a book, and there's a kind of loneliness, as if the closed book were going on still somewhere else, inside me. And that again I can't get hold of it properly. I can't talk about it. Throughout the whole broadcast with Alain Veinstein last night (25 November, on France Culture – it lasted two hours), I couldn't utter a sentence. It was as if I'd been struck speechless. It was very strange. Veinstein would just wait, and I always managed to say something in the end. Then I'd stop again. I wondered what had happened to me, what sort of nightmare had struck me. I don't really know what the answer is. Of course, there was that affair. The affair that started when I was sixty-five, with Y.A., who's a homosexual. That's probably the most unexpected thing that's happened to me in the latter part of my life – the most terrifying and the most important. It's like what happens in *The War*. But in this case the man is here, I'm not waiting for him, he isn't in the camps, he's here, guarding me against death. That's what he's doing, though he tries to ignore it. He thinks he doesn't know. But one thing's clear, and that's that neither he nor I can bear the idea of going on living after the other one dies. We know we love one another. But we don't say anything. It's unapproachable, even by us. There wasn't only the affair, there was also the backbreaking book, and Yann blocking its way, like a lunatic, throwing himself on it as if to stop it from being written, and only making sure that it was.

In the American Hospital, while I was in a coma, I had lucid intervals in which I saw he was with me. These moments were very rare and very brief, but I could see he desired me. I asked him about it. I said, 'When I was in a coma and you didn't

know whether I was going to survive, you desired me.' He
said: 'Yes, I did.' We spoke, but came to no conclusion.
I couldn't speak any more, or write. I couldn't even hold a
spoon – I dribbled and spilt things everywhere. I'd forgotten
how to walk. I got mixed up. I fell down. And that was the
woman Y.A. desired and loved.

RACINE'S FORESTS

WHEN I'M at Trouville I can't imagine going back to Paris. I can't think what I'd do there now. I see very few people these days. But it's much worse than that. Much worse. I *can't* live in Paris any more. You get yourself into that sort of situation, without thinking, and there you are. I can't see even a couple of days ahead in my life. Either with this man or without him – it's the same as in quite different affairs from ours. It's true – to confirm what I said to Veinstein – it's not a question of suffering. It's a ratification of an original despair, dating you might almost say from childhood, as if all of a sudden you experienced the same sense of impossibility as you felt when you were eight years old. A sense of impossibility when you looked at things, people, the sea, life, the limited nature of your own body; or the trees in the forest, which you couldn't get to without risking death; or the sailing of liners, which seemed to be going away for ever and ever; or my mother, mourning my dead father with a grief we knew to be childish but which might take her away from us. That must be the great thing about old age. I haven't reached it yet, but I'm getting closer. That's the obvious thing people get wrong when they don't establish their own personal way of behaving. My mother always cried in the appropriate situations, and she always laughed as one's supposed to do, after a dinner party, at the coarse jokes made by the men. Sometimes we used to feel it so terribly when she acted just like everyone else that when she came home we almost had to forgive her. We were very distant. When she came home from parties where she'd pretended to be amused, we knew she hadn't been amused at all, she'd nearly died of boredom. She did all the right things to be like other people, but it never worked with us. We knew she'd been somewhere else, unknowingly, in some sacred state outside which we couldn't bear to see her. There was something sacred about her, and we were the only ones who knew it. If anyone knows there's something sacred about Van Gogh, and Matisse, Nicolas de Staël and Monet, it's because they've had that sort of childhood, spent in the same kind of unwearying scrutiny of unfathomable depth that we directed upon our mother. I want to bring Van Gogh and the rest into the business with Yann because it too has something sacred about it. Music is sacred too. I've found you have to look a long while for the sacred in writing: but the wind of the sacred does blow through the great forests of Racine. Through the tops of the trees in the great Racinian forest. That's Racine. Not in detail, not as he's read and thought about. It's his music. It's music speaking. Yes, that's what it is, though people often get it wrong. That's Mozart, and Racine. It shouts at you.

THE TRAIN FROM BORDEAUX

I WAS SIXTEEN years old. I still looked like a child. It was when we'd come back from Saigon, after the Chinese lover. It was on a night train, the train from Bordeaux, in about 1930. I was with my family – my two brothers and my mother. We were in a third-class compartment with eight seats in it, and I think there were two or three other people besides us. There was also a young man sitting opposite me and looking at me. He must have been about thirty. It must have been in the summer. I was still wearing the sort of light-coloured dress I used to wear in the colonies, with sandals and no stockings. The man asked me about my family, and I told him about what it was like living in the colonies: the rains, the heat, the veranda, how different it was from France, the walks in the forest, and the *baccalauréat* exam I was going to take that year. That sort of thing – the usual kind of conversation you have in a train when you pour out your own and your family's life history. And then all of a sudden we noticed everyone else was asleep. My mother and brothers had dropped off soon after we left Bordeaux. I spoke quietly so as not to wake them. If they'd heard me telling someone else all our business their yells and threats would soon have put a stop to it. And our whispered conversation had sent the other three or four passengers to sleep too. So the man and I were the only two still awake. And that was how it started, suddenly, at exactly the same moment, and with a single look. In those days people didn't speak about such things, especially in circumstances like that. All at once we couldn't go on talking. We couldn't go on looking at one another either; we felt weak, shattered. I was the one who said we ought to get some sleep so as not to be too tired when we got to Paris in the morning. He was sitting near the door so he switched out the light. There was an empty seat between us. I curled up on it and closed my eyes. I heard him open the door. He went out and came back with a blanket and spread it over me. I opened my eyes to smile and say thank you. He said: 'They turn off the heating at night and it gets cold towards morning.' I went to sleep. I was wakened by his warm soft hand on my legs; very slowly it straightened them out and tried to move up towards my body. I opened my eyes just a fraction. I could see he was looking at the other people in the carriage, watching them; he was afraid. I very slowly moved my body towards him and put my feet against him. I gave them to him. He took them. With my eyes shut, I followed all his movements. They were slow even at first, then more and more slow and controlled until the final paroxysm of pleasure, as upsetting as if he'd cried out.

For a long while there was nothing except the noise of the train. It was going faster and the noise was deafening. Then it became bearable again. He put his hand on me. Distraught, still warm, afraid. I held it in mine for a moment, then let it go, let it do as it liked.

The noise of the train came back again. The hand went away, stayed away for some time. I don't remember how long – I must have drowsed off.

Then it came back.

It stroked me all over first, then my breasts, stomach and hips, in a kind of overall gentleness disturbed every so often by new stirrings of desire. Sometimes it would stop. It halted over my sex, trembling, about to take the bait, burning hot again. Then it moved on. Finally it resigned itself, quietened down, became kind in order to bid the child goodbye. All around the hand was the noise of the train. All around the train, the darkness. The silence of the corridors within the noise of the train. The stops, waking people up. He got off into the darkness. When I opened my eyes in Paris his seat was empty.

THE BOOK

THE BOOK is about two people who love one another. But who love one another unawares. It happens outside the book. What I'm saying now is something I didn't want to say in the book but which I mustn't forget to say now, even though it's hard to find the words. The essence of this love is that it can't be written. It's a love that writing hasn't yet reached. It's too strong, stronger than the people themselves. It's not at all organized. It happens at night, mostly while they're asleep. Loves are usually organized to start with, even if only around a central inhibition. A love creates habits and customs for itself. The people eat, sleep, lay one another, quarrel, make up, attempt suicide, are fond of one another sometimes. Sometimes they part and come back together again. Sometimes they talk about other things – they don't weep all the time. But in this case they don't do anything. They don't make love, they just wait in the dark; sometimes he wants to kill her. Personally I think he ought to have killed her, he was bound to have felt like it, but it struck me as rather a forced and premature solution. I'm tempted to say it's an absurd love, without real subjects, like the smile without a face in *Alice*; but that would be abstract and wrong. No, I come back to what I was saying, that it's a love that loves even now, which invades everything, and which is immune from anything anyone may say about it, for reasons that might be called religious. For it resembles a need to suffer, an obscure need to suffer in order to recall an absence without an image, without a face, without a voice. But which, like music, sweeps the whole body towards the emotion that goes with deliverance from some formal burden.

*   *   *

Yes, the book is about an unavowed love between people prevented by an unknown force from saying they love one
another. And who do love one another. It's not clear. It can't
be stated. It's elusive, helpless. And yet it exists. In a confusion
which they share, which is peculiar to them, and which arises
from the similarity of their feelings. Are they conscious of any
of what passes between them and binds them together? I don't
know. They know more than other people do about the
silence that should be kept about love; but they don't know
how to deal with the experience. Instead, they have another
affair, as if they were different people. When one says people
love one another one usually means they love each other with
physical passion. These are people who don't know how to
love one another and yet do have a love affair. But the word
to express it never crosses their lips, nor does desire come to
their sex, to express it and vent it and then be able to chat and
have a drink. Nothing but tears.

I know the people in the book, but I don't know their story,
just as I don't know my own. I have no story, just as I have no
life. My story is pulverized every day, every second of every
day, by the immediacy of life, and it's impossible for me to
see clearly what's usually called one's life. Only the thought
of death puts me back together again, and the love of this man
and of my child. I've always lived as if it were impossible for
me to resemble any model existence, any given pattern.
I wonder in what terms other people tell their life histories.
Accounts based on chronology or external facts seemed to be
the most popular. You start at the beginning of your life, then
trundle along towards the present on the rails of public events,
wars, changes of address, marriages, etc.

Some books are perfect as they stand: *Summer 1980*, *The Atlantic Man*, the Vice-Consul crying out in the Shalimar Gardens,
the beggar woman, the smell of leprosy, *M.D.*, *Lol V. Stein*,

The Lover, The War, The War, The War and *The Lover*, Hélène Lagonelle, the dormitories, the light from the river. *The Sea Wall* became perfect in that sense too: the camouflage, the replacement of some personal elements by others less apt to pique the reader's curiosity and thus less likely to distract him from the story I wanted him to read – everything was integrated into the original story, which itself disappeared. This went on right up to *The Lover*. So there are, in my life, two little girls and me. The one in *The Sea Wall*. The one in *The Lover*. And the one in the family photographs. I can't see what happened while I was writing this last book, during the terrible summer of 1986. In that story, which actually happened although it is transposed, it's difficult to find the untruth, the point where the book lies, and on what level, in which adverb. It may lie in just one word. I don't think it lies about desire. It must always happen like that when the man is repelled by your body. And yet the book does tell a story that actually happened. I've just made a special and not a general case of it. Perhaps the time for writing it had gone by; I had to remember having suffered. The suffering was still there, but it was more even. The same with the emotion. In *The Lover* and *The War* the emotion is still warm and pulsating. It echoes through the slightest breath in those two books; I can hear the voices too. But here, no; I can't see or hear anything. I've merged into the characters, and what I'm doing is telling of an impossible just as I'd tell of a possible affair between a woman and a homosexual, whereas what I really want to tell of is a love affair which is always possible even though it seems impossible to people unfamiliar with writing. For writing isn't supposed to concern itself with that kind of possibility or impossibility. It may be that I was trying, unsuccessfully, to say the same thing as I'm saying now – i.e., it wasn't a love affair that took place between the characters: it was just love. Perhaps what I wanted to say was that once, one night, on the confines of their relationship, love appeared like a shaft of light in the darkness.

That once, at a certain moment, the affair became love.

If it upsets me so much to write untruthfully, even slightly, it must be because it doesn't often happen. But I'm probably still too much affected by writing the book to know. I must get to feel better disposed towards it again; I need to stop treating it as some hostile and dangerous object, a weapon directed against myself. What happened? It's as if I were being told that not everything comes within the reach of writing; that whether you like it or not, writing stops short at closed doors. Whereas I believe the opposite – that it gets through everything, doors that are closed included, no matter why they're closed. But there's a sort of latent didacticism *à la* Barthes in the book: I have ideas, and I display them, so that the novel is sometimes *explained* like the sort that wins prizes. In other words I didn't bring it off. I put the sea and a river in the middle of the story, but that wasn't enough to untame the characters and their love. I was too involved. It remained too far away.

I don't know what I ought to have done. What took place every day was not what happened every day. Sometimes what didn't take place was the most important thing that happened. It was when nothing took place that it was most interesting. I ought to have entered into the book myself, with all my paraphernalia – my ravaged face, my age, my profession, my roughness, my insanity; and you ought to have stayed in the book too, with all your paraphernalia – your smooth face, your age, your idleness, your terrible roughness, your insanity, and your fabulous angelicness. And even that wouldn't have been enough.

We snapped our fingers at all compromises, all the usual 'arrangements'. We confronted the impossibility of that love without flinching or trying to escape. It was a mysterious love, impossible to imagine. It was so strange we used to laugh at it. We couldn't recognize it, and we took it as it came – impossible – without doing anything to suffer less, without running away, not trying to kill it, not going away. And it wasn't enough.

All the time before I gave in the manuscript, right up to the last minute, I thought I might still avoid handing it over to be printed. But I was the only one to think that, and it was too late, and in the end they were right to publish it.

QUILLEBEUF

I TOLD YOU Quillebeuf triggered off the desire to write. In fact it was the other way round. It was because I already wanted to write that the Quillebeuf story stuck in my mind as it did. But I'm talking to you from the outside about a book that isn't yet written. Let me explain: the book that grew in my mind out of Quillebeuf was supposed to come before a third book, the one I've just finished. And I'd have been writing the Quillebeuf book now if I hadn't lost the manuscript. But I had to make another trip to Trouville to look for it.

Time went by.

The ten lost pages were found among the drafts of the book that's already been published.

The new book was finished in March 1987 and delivered to the publisher six months after *Blue Eyes*.

It's a long time since I've liked a book as much as I like that one.

THE MAN WHO WAS A LIE

I RECENTLY tried to write a book that was going to be called *The Man Who Was a Lie*. It was about a man who lied. He lied all the time, to everyone and about everything that had ever happened to him. Deception crossed his lips even before the words to express it. He didn't feel himself doing it. He didn't lie about Baudelaire or Joyce, or to blow his own trumpet or boast about his amorous adventures. Nothing like that. He lied about the price of a pullover, or a journey he'd made on the métro. Or about the time a film began at the cinema, a meeting with a friend, a conversation, a menu, all the details of a trip he'd been on, including the names of the towns he'd visited. About his family, his mother, his nephews. It was completely uninteresting. At first it was maddening too. But after a month or two you got used to it.

He was a marvellously talented writer. Very shrewd, very funny, very very charming. He was also an extraordinarily gifted talker. Born into the middle class, but courteous as a prince. He'd been brought up like a king by his mother, but that never affected his naturalness or his charm.

If I make him out to be so irresistible it's because he was a born lover, a born lover of women. At a glance he could see them, make out the very essence of their desire. And be overwhelmed by it in a way I've never seen in anyone else. It's that aspect of him I want to talk about – the gift he had for taking women into himself and loving them even before he'd experienced their beauty or the sound of their voice.

Women were the main concern of his life, and many of them knew it as soon as they saw him; as soon as they saw the look in his eyes. He had only to look at a woman and he was her lover.

He was a violent lover, with a roughness at once controlled and wild, at once terrifying and polite.

I've tried several times to write about him, but at every attempt his deceitfulness hid everything from me, including his face and his eyes. Now, suddenly, for the first time, I can do it.

He rented an apartment just for himself. He went there to escape the scrutiny of friends and family alike. He saw himself as young and eternally attractive; he wanted to live like a young man, lunching off a snack, dining in a restaurant, and having all the women at his disposal – Frenchwomen in the winter and English girls in the spring. In the summer he went to Saint-Tropez. He used to follow women around. That's how it was in 1950. He'd made up his mind to follow his passion for women through, even if it meant suffering and danger, and no matter how old he lived to be. He wanted to be overwhelmed by them, not to let any of his subjection go to waste. To turn his desire into something creative. Even if he'd seduced them only once, through a glance in the street, the essence of his sex never forgot them. Once obsessed by desire for a woman he'd set his heart on, he lived only for that passion. Other women ceased to exist. These periods of love for one woman had the intensity of a religious devotion. He never planned anything in such cases. He could neither plan his desire for a woman, nor decide to behave carefully and with moderation in the matter. All he could do was die of wanting her.

He was a magnificent and excellent fellow in every way, but worn out with always expiring without ever actually dying of it, and hoping for death as much as for passion. His only knowledge of himself came via women. They plunged him into a tragic and irresistible emotion. I've seen him, at night, in bars, go suddenly pale at the sight of certain women and look as if he were about to faint. While he was looking at one of them he completely forgot all the others. Each seemed to him the last and only one. And that went on until he died.

Death struck first one spring day at Etretat. But he didn't die of that – the awful inability to have anything to do with a woman for two years. Not allowed to smoke. Not allowed to love. Not allowed to make love. His life did go on, however, like that. But it had been a very bad coronary, and he died of it ten years later.

It was during those two years that he went on with a book he'd started some years before. A man's book. Very long; about the fifties. He won the biggest of the French prizes, the Médicis, with it. That made him happy.

Once – I think not long before he died – he told a friend we had in common that once in his life he'd loved a woman on a long-term basis. That for several years he wasn't unfaithful to her. But without having planned it. Why? He didn't know. Once in his life he'd managed to achieve a love that was exclusive and lasting. Why he'd reached that degree of intensity with her rather than another, he didn't know.

He thought it was probably because of her rather than himself. That it must always be like that. It was always the woman, the woman's desire, that kept lovers together. Love, the course taken by an affair, everything, depended on the permanence of the woman's desire. When the woman's desire ended, so did the man's – or, if it didn't, he became wretched, humiliated, mortally wounded, lonely.

He thought men and women were as fundamentally different in their flesh, their desire and their shape as if they belonged to two different orders of creation.

He died in a one-night hotel room. The hotel is very close to where I live. I've been told she was very young and beautiful, with auburn hair and green eyes like the woman in his novel. She was newly married and until that evening had always refused him.

She had to wait for him. He was late. He took his time and smoked a cigarette. He'd started smoking again a year before. He wanted her very much. For months he'd been asking her to go with him just once to a hotel. Finally she gave in. He was very pale. Unable to conceal his emotion. Since his coronary he was afraid every time he made love to a woman. His death took only a second. A sudden death. He didn't have time to see it coming. She told about it. Suddenly she knew he was dead by the weight of his body – he was already inside her. She realized instantly. She rushed out of the hotel, telling the reception desk as she went by that someone was dead in such and such a room and they'd better call the police.

My memory of him is very clear: he's striding along the street, very well-dressed. I can still see the colours: English shoes with metal tips on the soles, loose mustard-coloured pullover, light-brown corduroy trousers. He has very long legs and a graceful and remarkably even walk; instead of holding him back, his body is so slight it impels him forward. He looks about him as he walks along. His eyes have the blankness of someone half-asleep, and yet he looks about him. If anyone speaks his name it's the same: he looks around and hides behind his own gaze. He's watching out for women in Chanel suits, bored by winter afternoons.

One day a very young woman asked if I would see her and talk about him. Not the one in the hotel. His death had been a tragedy for her, and she still hadn't quite got over it. She was looking for someone who could talk adequately about him, about all that intelligence, profundity and purity. I said almost nothing.

*　　*　　*

We'd met at a party one evening at Christmas. I'd gone there on my own to find a lover. We left together, but I changed my mind and insisted on going home. We had a friend in common – everyone knew everyone else in Paris then, just as they do now – and he phoned this friend – the same one as before – and asked him to tell me he'd be waiting for me in a certain café. For five or six hours every day he sat and waited for me in that café, looking out at the street – every day for a week. But I held out. I went out every day, but not in that direction. And all the time I was dying for a new love affair. On the eighth day I went into the café as if I were mounting to the scaffold.

PHOTOGRAPHS

IT'S WHEN PEOPLE move that photos get lost. My mother moved between twenty and twenty-five times in the course of her life, and that's how our family photos got lost. They fall down and get stuck behind drawers, and if you're lucky you find them the next time you move. After a hundred years they're as brittle as glass. Have I told you this before? One day, in the fifties, underneath the drawer of a wardrobe that we'd bought in Indochina, I found a postcard dated 1905 and addressed to someone then living in the rue Saint-Benôit, where I live now. Photographs – one can't live without them – already existed when I was young. For my mother, a photograph of a young child was sacred. To see a child again as it used to be when it was young, you looked at a photograph. People still do. It's very mysterious. The only photos of Yann that I like are the ones taken ten years ago, before I knew him. They have in them what I look for in him now – the innocence of not knowing anything yet, not knowing what would happen to us in September 1980, for better or worse.

In the late nineteenth century people used to go and have their photographs taken by the village photographer in order to exist more convincingly, like the people of Vinh Long in *The Lover*.

There aren't any photographs of one's great-grandmother. You can search the whole world over and you won't find any. When you think of it, the absence of photographs leaves a serious gap; it even presents a problem. How did they live without photos? There's nothing left of anyone's face or body after they die. No record of their smile. And if you'd told people there'd be such a thing as photography one day, they'd have been shattered and appalled. But contrary to what they'd have thought and to what people still think today, I believe photographs promote forgetting. That's how it tends to work now. The fixed, flat, easily available countenance of a dead person or an infant in a photograph is only one image as against the million other images that exist in the mind. And the sequence made up by the million images I will never alter. It's a confirmation of death. I don't know what use photography was put to in its early days, in the first half of the nineteenth century. I don't know what it meant to the individual in the midst of his solitude – whether he valued it because it enabled him to see the dead again or because it allowed him to see himself. The second, I'm sure. One's always embarrassed or delighted by one's own photograph, but in either case also surprised. You're always more unreal to yourself than other people are. In life, even if you include the false perspective of the mirror, you're the person you see the least; and the best, composite image of yourself, the one you want to keep, is the specially prepared face that you try to summon up when you pose for your photograph.

THE CUTTER-OFF OF WATER

IT HAPPENED ON a summer's day in a village in eastern France, perhaps three or four years ago, in the afternoon. A man from the water board came to cut off the water in the house of some people who were slightly special, slightly different from most. Backward, you might say. The local authorities let them live in a disused railway station. The high-speed train now ran through that part of the country. The man did odd jobs in the village. And they must have had some help from the town hall. They had two children, one four years old and the other a year and a half.

The high-speed train ran close by where they lived. They were very poor, and couldn't pay their gas and electricity or water bills. And one day a man came to cut the water off. He saw the woman, who didn't say anything. The husband wasn't there. Just the rather backward wife, the child of four and the baby of eighteen months. The man looked just like other men. I named him the Cutter-off of Water. He realized it was the middle of summer. He knew, because he was experiencing it too, that it was a very hot summer. He saw the eighteen-month-old baby. But he'd been told to cut off the water, so that's what he did. He did his job and cut the water off. And left the woman without any water to bath the children; without any water to give them to drink.

That evening the woman and her husband took the two children and went and lay down on the rails of the high-speed train that ran past the disused station. They all died together. Just a hundred yards to go. Lie down. Keep the children quiet. Sing them to sleep perhaps.

People say the train stopped.

Well, that's the story.

*   *   *

The man from the water board said he went and cut off the water. He didn't say he'd seen the child, that the child was there with its mother. He said she didn't argue, didn't ask him not to cut the water off.

That's what we know.

I take the story I've just told and all of a sudden I hear my own voice. She didn't do anything, she didn't argue. That's how it was. We find out through the man from the water board. There was no reason why he shouldn't do what he did, because she didn't ask him not to. Is that what we're supposed to understand? The whole thing is enough to drive you mad.

So I go on. I try to see. She didn't tell the man about the two children because he could see them; she didn't say anything about the hot summer because he was there in it. She let the Cutter-off of Water go. She stayed there alone with the children for a moment, then she went into the village. She went into a café she knew. We don't know what she said to the woman who owned it. I don't know what she said. I don't know if the owner of the café said anything. What we do know is that the woman didn't say anything about death. She might have told the other woman what had happened, but she didn't say she meant to kill herself, to kill her two children and her husband and herself.

As the reporters didn't know what she'd said to the owner of the café they didn't mention the incident. By incident I mean what happened when she went out with the two children after she'd decided the whole family must die. When she went off for some reason we don't know, to do or say something she had to do or say before she died.

Now I restore the silence in the story between the time the water was cut off and the time when she got back from the café. In other words, I restore the profound silence of literature. That's what helps me forward, helps me get inside the story. Without it I'd have to remain outside. She could just have waited for her husband and told him she'd decided they must die. But instead she went into the village and into the café.

If she had explained herself she wouldn't have interested me. I'm passionately interested in Christine Villemin because she can't put two sentences together; because like the other woman she is full of unfathomable violence. There's an instinctive behaviour in their two cases that one can try to explore, that one can give back to silence. It's much more difficult, much less appropriate, to give men's behaviour back to silence because silence isn't a masculine thing. From the most ancient times, silence has been the attribute of women. So literature is women too. Whether it speaks of them or they actually write it, it's them.

And so that woman, who people thought wouldn't have spoken because she never did – she must have spoken. Not of her decision. No. She must have said something that took the place of her decision; something that was equivalent to it for her and that would be equivalent to it for all the people who heard the story. Perhaps it was something about the heat. The words ought to be held sacred.

It's at times like this that language attains its ultimate power. Whatever she said to the owner of the café, her words said everything. Those three words, the last before the implemen-tation of death, were the equivalent of those people's silence all their lives. But no one has remembered what those words were.

In life that happens all the time, when someone goes away, or dies, or when there's a suicide no one ever anticipated. People forget what was said, what went before and should have warned them.

* * *

All four of them went and lay down on the rails of the high-speed train near the station. The man and the woman held a child each in their arms, and waited for the train. The Cutter-off of Water didn't have an enemy in the world.

I add to the story of the Cutter-off of Water the fact that the woman, who everyone said was retarded, knew something for certain anyhow: she knew she couldn't count, now any more than ever, on anyone's helping her and her family out. She knew she was abandoned by everyone, by the whole of society, and that the only thing left for her to do was die. She knew that. It's a terrible, fundamental, awful knowledge. So the question of her backwardness ought to be reconsidered, if anyone ever talked about her again. Which they won't.

This is probably the last time she'll ever be remembered. I was going to mention her name, but I don't know what it was.

The case has been closed.

What stays in the mind is a child's unslaked thirst in a sweltering summer a few hours before it died, and a young retarded mother wandering about until it was time.

FIGON, GEORGES

MY FRIEND Georges Figon was thirty-five when he was granted a remission. Between the ages of eighteen and thirty-five he'd spent fourteen years and seven months in prison. There's something I shall never accept about his story: its end, his death. I'm talking about it here in order to put it on record. Figon was happy for a few weeks after he was let out. Then suddenly it all went wrong. One day depression descended upon him, and wherever he went after that he could never throw it off. Nothing would help. And it lasted right up to his death. For that's what he died of, that's why he got killed by the police. Figon died of despair, because he realized that the story of his imprisonment was useless outside jail – it couldn't be told to people who'd never been to prison themselves. He realized that together with all the other things prison meant, it meant above all this dispossession. Once he'd left Fresnes he descended into solitude once and for all. We listened to him for hours, days, nights. But as soon as our emotion wore off, the story that obsessed Figon himself began to seem more distant to us, and he knew it. Why? Probably because the person who has experienced the thing he tells about and the person who listens to it need to have some ordinary things in common – work, profession, morals, political persuasion and so on. If Figon had written a book, it ought to have been for inmates of the prisons he'd been in. Between prison and freedom however relative there is nothing in common, not the remotest similarity. Even reading and sleeping are different. If Figon was ever happy it was in prison, when he was acting as librarian and hatching a book about prison in the same way as he might have plotted a robbery. He thought his book would change society. But he didn't bring it off, and that killed him.

He died because he couldn't convey what he knew about prison to anyone else. He described day-to-day life inside with astonishing accuracy. He knew the staff of all the prisons he'd been in individually, and the CVs of all the lawyers from examining magistrate to public prosecutor. But it didn't do him any good. Probably part of the trouble was his own purity, his desire to reproduce faithfully what had happened. He got bogged down in verisimilitude, lost in the swamp of fact. If he'd forgotten everything and then reinvented it, above all if he'd depersonalized his experience, he might not have died in despair. He ought to have cheated, recast for others what he had undergone himself. His life out of prison consisted of going over and over his life in prison. He was afraid of forgetting. No doubt imprisonment is a kind of initiation completely different from any ordeal we 'respectable' people encounter. I can remember some of the details. Even the most trivial request would only be granted after bawling and threatening and a good deal of waiting. This was all thirty years ago, and there was no television or radio in prisons then. I think cigarettes were the only thing you could barter.

I've re-read the above. When I say Figon was never as happy as when he was in prison, I ought to add that I'm speaking of the happiness he got from looking forward to the happiness he'd enjoy when he was free. The only freedom he knew was inside the prison at Fresnes, and without prison around him to help him savour the happiness of freedom, the happiness vanished. It's probably always like that.

WALESA'S WIFE

I SEE JOURNALISTS as the manual workers, the labourers of the word. Journalism can only be literature when it is passionate. Cournot's articles have become part of a marvellous book on the theatre. And sometimes in a paper you suddenly come across a real text, especially in the law reports and the odd news items. And Serge Daney, especially perhaps on tennis, is in the process of becoming a writer. Serge July's a writer too, especially when he writes fast. And André Fontaine.

Godard once went on 'Seven out of Seven' on TV and said what he thought of television journalists. It was after Walesa won the Nobel Prize. His wife went to receive the prize for him because the Polish government wouldn't let him go to Stockholm himself. And Godard said to the journalists: 'When Walesa's wife went up to receive the prize she was centre of attention, and for the first time for ages, quite unexpectedly, you had a chance to shoot pictures of a beautiful woman. But you didn't attempt to get her in close-up. Why not? You don't even know. I think it may have been just because she *was* beautiful.' And he added: 'And because she wasn't a model or an actress, whose profession it is to be seen.'

Godard said something that needed saying.

It was marvellous, the idea of that young Polish woman going to get the prize in her husband's stead. But in actual fact it was deathly boring. Throughout the whole ceremony you waited to see her from close to, and you never did. It was very strange. As if certain shots and angles weren't allowed. As if the TV coverage was doomed to failure because it could only convey the principle of Walesa's wife's presence and not actually show her beauty.

A real news programme would have shown her because she was more than Walesa himself – she was the woman he loved. That day she was the map that enabled you to find the way to the whole, to the entirety to which she was linked. Just as a forest is linked to someone passing through it on the way to their death. Or like someone's dress, or hair, or a letter, or a footprint in a cave, or a voice on the telephone. A real news item is both physical and subjective. An image shown, written or spoken. But always indirect.

Sometimes I think polemical journalism, reviled as it is, is the best. At least it reinstates ignorance and makes people doubt what they're being asked to believe. You read it in order to correct it. You can adapt it to your own purposes. It's sad, all the trouble they went to, to make a mess of Stockholm and the little Polish pony, Walesa's wife.

THE TELLY AND DEATH

IT STARTED WHEN Michel Foucault died. The day after his death there was a piece about him on television, showing him giving a lecture at the Collège de France. Practically all you could hear was a sort of crackling in the background. His voice was there, but drowned by the voice of the commentator saying this was the voice of Michel Foucault delivering one of his lectures at the Collège de France. Soon after that Orson Welles died, and the same thing happened. You heard a very clear voice saying that the very faint and inaudible voice you could scarcely hear at all was that of Orson Welles, who had just died. It's come to be the rule whenever anyone well known dies – the aural image of the deceased is swamped by that of the journalist telling you that what you're listening to is of course the voice of so-and-so who's just passed on. Some editor no doubt discovered that if the presenter and the deceased both spoke at once it would save a minute's transmission time, and they could go on all the sooner to sport or some other more interesting and amusing subject.

In France we have no way of getting in touch with television journalists and telling them they shouldn't switch too fast from the mournful smile they wear to talk about the hostages to the grin they use for the weather forecast. It won't do. There are other ways. For instance they might just pause without any particular expression at all. And even if that's what they're told to do, they shouldn't act as if every news item is something extraordinary. And they shouldn't always try to look cheerful. You ought to modify your expression when you announce an earthquake, or a bomb attack in Lebanon, or a coach crash, or the death of a celebrity. But you're in such a hurry to get to the laughs you're already in fits over the coach crash. And if you do that you're in trouble. You start having sleepless nights. You don't know what you're saying any more. The television news bulletins are a riot from start to finish, and you have a nervous breakdown.

But on the whole, apart from the occasional major event such as the deaths of the famous, the Nobel Prize and votes in Parliament, nothing ever happens on television. No one ever speaks, really speaks, on it. I mean no one ever takes some minor news item like a dog accident as his starting point and uses it to trigger off the human imagination, our power to interpret the universe creatively; to awaken the strange genius so many of us have by means of a dog that got run over. Real talking has nothing to do with what happens on television. Though admittedly we customers, who buy TV sets and pay a tax for the privilege, look forward to slips of the tongue and suchlike, whether made by members of the government or journalists earning ten million francs a month. At the opening of the 1984 Book Fair, Chirac said he read poetry because as it's short it's the most convenient form of reading for someone who has to do a lot of flying. I once heard someone refer to *Hiroshima mon amour* as the famous film by Alain René and Jacqueline Duval. I've also heard someone talk about '*L'Amante anglaise*, with the celebrated actress Madeleine Barrault'. Admittedly, this was a shy little girl who'd only just been taken on.

But perhaps if we heard real language being spoken on TV, by people who instead of play-acting were simply talking about current events between themselves, we shouldn't care for it at all. The news wouldn't be sufficiently odd or far-out; it would be too true. People sit in front of the television because it lies, of necessity, about both form and content. If journalists ever say exactly what we want them to, as they did during the miraculous students' strike in December 1986, we're afraid for them. We feel like kissing them and writing to them. Their contribution became part of the strike – and that's something that almost never happens. But it did happen in France in December 1986. Everyone in Paris was talking as much about that as about the strike itself. Those news bulletins were a real joy, until Pasqua and Pandraud unleashed their bloodhounds.

A WAY WITH WORDS

MY MOTHER WAS scared of people in office – civil servants, income tax inspectors, customs men, bailiffs, customs officers, anyone whose job it was to enforce the law. She always felt in the wrong – the typical, incurable attitude of the poor. She never entirely got over it. But I did, through oral exams. Every time I passed one I felt I'd made some progress against the poverty endemic to our family. A way with words. It was like a physical confrontation between me and society, there to try to destroy me. Singers and actors must go through the same experience with the audience. The people who pay to hear you sing or speak are enemies you have to get the better of in order to survive. But when you've done it once, after you've once mastered the words and carried the audience with you, it happens to you all the time. You pretend it's up to you not to disappoint the people who've gone to the trouble of coming to hear you. But there's more to it than that. Something that verges on wanting to kill the person who's come to sit in judgement on you.

THE GREEN STEAK

NO, I'VE NEVER been afraid of offending them. Everybody else I see around me seems afraid of it, of letting them down, but on the contrary, I want to offend them so that they'll know we're not all at their mercy. When you go to buy a steak and they keep showing you the 'good side', the red side, I say, 'I'd like to see the other side, please.' They always answer, 'I'll show you the other side of *this* one – they're both from the same cut.' And they put the first bit to one side, with the surface you're not supposed to see facing down. One day when I came out of hospital – another of my attacks of emphysema – I asked Yann to buy me a piece of steak. I felt like eating some meat. But Yann never likes to say anything to people in shops – he'd rather put up with anything, even food poisoning. So that day he came back with a steak that was green through being kept too long. I picked it up and showed it to him and said: 'Didn't you say anything?' And he said, 'No, I didn't like to.' I started to cry. I couldn't help it. I said: 'Listen, this is my first meal after I come out of hospital. You could have thrown it away and bought me another.' He said: 'I didn't think of it.' I didn't cry any more. I got hold of the steak and threw it in the dustbin. I was purple with rage. The steak was green and I was purple. When he came back for dinner I took the steak out of the dustbin beforehand and put it on his plate. He took one look at it, gave a yell of horror, and threw it in the dustbin for good. It was never seen on a table again.

I've got another fad too, since we're on the subject. I always talk to the people sitting next to me, especially when I'm flying. I do it to make them say something back. If they answer it's because they feel safe, and that makes me feel safe too. I talk

about the landscape or about travel in general, including fly-
ing. On the train I talk for talking's sake to complete strangers.
I talk about what we can see, the countryside, the weather.
I often feel like talking very fast and very loud.

Once, on a plane, I was sitting next to a man who wouldn't
answer. Whatever I said to him, it wasn't any good. So I gave
up. I thought he just didn't like the look of me. It didn't occur
to me that he didn't know me. And as we were leaving he said,
'Goodbye, Marguerite Duras.' So I'd been right. He just
didn't want to talk to me.

WON'T YOU?

TO GO BACK to what I was saying about the sexual desires aroused by writers, including even women novelists seventy years old, I wanted to tell you about this. About two or three years ago I received a letter from a man, the sort of letter that says, 'I'm coming to make love to you on Monday, 23 January, and I'll ring at the door at nine in the morning.' A lunatic, you think, and forget all about it. And on Monday, 23 January, at nine o'clock in the morning, there's a ring at the door. 'Who is it?' 'Me.' I say, 'You must be joking.' The other person says, 'Won't you?' I say, 'No, I won't.' He didn't say any more. He just lay down by the door. He stayed there all the morning. I phoned the people in the other flats; we're all very neighbourly and they know I'm sometimes in a spot. So they came and said to the young man, 'We know her(!) – she's never going to open the door, you know.' He said something charming, like: 'I'm all right where I am. At least I'm close to her.' I couldn't go out till early afternoon. He left without saying goodbye.

I'll tell you all: if anyone else had written *Lol V. Stein*, I don't know that I'd have accepted it very easily. The same with *The Vice-Consul* and *The War*. And *The Atlantic Man*. I'd either have given up writing or I'd have done a Rinaldi. Who knows?

What do I think about Sartre? I don't think anything about him most of the time. When I do I can't help comparing him with Solzhenitsyn. The Solzhenitsyn of a country without a Gulag. I see him as all alone in a wilderness created by himself.

A kind of exile. I wish Conrad were still alive. How marvellous it would be to have a new Conrad novel every year.

My great craze in recent years hasn't been Proust, it's been Musil, especially *The Man without Qualities*, the last volume. If today, 20 September, I had to name the authors I've read with passion in the last few years, I'd say they were Ségalen and Musil. But, also on 20 September, the finest and most shattering thing I've read for years is Matisse on the Barnes Foundation ballet, in the collection *Ecrits et Propos sur l'Art* [Observations, written and spoken, on art], edited by the poet Dominique Fourcade and published by Hermann. I'm reading Renan at the moment – *The Life of Jesus* – and the Bible, and between whiles the marvellous dialogue in *The Mother and the Whore* by Jean Eustache. Are my books difficult? – is that what you want to know? Yes, they are difficult. And easy too. *The Lover* is very difficult. *The Malady of Death* is difficult, very difficult. *The Atlantic Man* is very difficult, but it's so fine it isn't difficult. Even if you don't understand it. You can't understand these books anyway. That's not the right word. It's a matter of a private relationship between the book and the reader. They weep and grieve together.

THE WATCHTOWERS AT POISSY

WHEN I'M IN Paris, writing, I miss the outside world, I miss being able to go out. None of the people round me have any idea how much. I can't write outside, but I need places not to write just as much as places to write. In Paris it's difficult for me to get out. I can't go out on my own − it's impossible. I can't walk far outside. I can't breathe properly. I *can* breathe and walk all right in the dark, empty corridors of the Black Rocks Hotel. For twenty years they've been telling me that what's wrong with me is emphysema. Sometimes, often, I believe it, but sometimes I don't. The attacks always happen when I leave my apartment − on the very landing. When I leave the building itself it's different again − it's as if I were entering an outside that's cut off from inside by a knife. As if I were entering *into* the street, a street that's harshly lit and like a huge cage, at once the outside and something that closes you in. It reminds me of the spaces lit up by the watchtowers of prisons, in particular those of the old prison at Poissy, which I've often driven past. The ground is evenly lit up all over without any shadow; there's nowhere for a body to be. I'm quite prepared to believe what's wrong with me is emphysema. As soon as I get into my car and shut the door, I'm saved. From what? From you, the people I write for, who recognize me wherever I go, even in the street. I can't get over the terror that seizes me when I enter that open, sunny place of public execution. When I'm submerged in it. I mean the street, the pedestrian crossings, the squares, the city. Just going out, as most people do, to stroll about and look at what's going on − for years and years that's been a thing of the past for me. I'll never be like those people, like you, again. But I have found the solution of the car. So long as I've got the car I can go on.

So long as I can drive around and look at the Seine, look at Normandy, I can go on. After that, I don't know. When no one wants to come out for a drive with me any more, I don't know what I'll do. This October I went to Paris and came back the next day all on my own. It isn't that driving tires me, but I find it difficult driving for a long time on my own. I can't manage to talk to myself, even once in five hundred kilometres. So I'd rather be shut up in the apartment than drive long distances alone. Another thing is that I can't go down into the underground garage to fetch the car or put it away. I'm terrified of underground garages. In the same way, I can't drive if anyone looks at me or recognizes me. It's the alcohol. And the terrible cure. 'Sometimes you'll have experiences you'll recognize, as if you'd been drinking again. But it'll pass,' the doctor said. And he was right.

Once out on the road I feel safe, and I can drive well and fast.

My son's here at Trouville, and he just said, 'You've taken up all the tables in the apartment again.' It's quite true. And when they don't want to come for drives with me any more, when they won't let me take up all the tables in the apartment any more, I don't know what I'll do. I know the time will come; it's inevitable. It's probably already there, already begun.

At Trouville the sea's always there. Night and day, even if you can't see it, the thought of it's there. In Paris only windy and stormy days link us to the sea. Otherwise we're bereft of it.

Here we're part of the same landscape.

Beyond every hill there's that great emptiness in the distance. Over every hill the sky is different, hollower, lighter. More resonant, you might say. And it's true the gulls make less noise in the city than they do over the water, over the beaches.

I can bear to live in Trouville. But not in Paris, I must admit. Because of the threatening spaces, the open streets, and the people who come ringing at the door, from a long way away, from Germany – often from Germany, actually. They ring at the door and they come just so as to have seen me.

'What is it, please?'

'We'd like to see Madame Duras.'

They want to talk to me, and about me, as if my time belonged to them, as if it was my job to talk to them about myself. Those people are you, whom I love and for whom I write.

It's you that frighten me, you who are sometimes just as terrifying as gangsters.

THE VASTY DEEP

IN MY STREET they're currently demolishing a big printing press that was built in the nineteenth century. The press where they printed the *Journal Officiel*. As the outside is listed, they're just knocking down the inner walls. I apologize for the noise you can hear in the book – the sound of pneumatic drills, and above all the crash of the great blocks of stone on chains that they use to knock the inside walls down with. And the shouts of the Arab workmen clearing everyone out before the chains go into action. It's going to be a three-star hotel. The name's wrong: 'Latitudes', as if it were on the Mediterranean. All the printing workers have gone. Never again shall we know the magnificent throb, strong yet gentle and harmless, of the great rotary presses that we used to hear every morning, and sometimes at night too when there was a special session of Parliament. They're going to add two extra floors. The press itself didn't come up as far as our floor; it stopped at the second. From Yann's room you could look through a courtyard and see the time on the clock of Saint-Germain-des-Prés. But that's all over. Since Friday, 18 December 1986 the view of the clock has been hidden by a breeze-block wall. The hotel will take up half the block between the rue Saint-Benôit and the rue Bonaparte. The style of the façade is reminiscent of the department stores on downtown Broadway. Fluted bronze columns and charming angels. The hotel opens in the spring of 1987. Three hundred bedrooms. Three stars. And called 'Latitudes'. Why not 'The Vasty Deep'? It gives you an idea of the philistinism of the property promoters. They're in the middle of the 6th arrondissement and they name their hotel as if it were some cheap modern place in the Languedoc. It's Bouygues' doing. It's both unpronounceable and meaningless. You might think it has a meaning, but it hasn't. For fifty years he made cement-mixers, and now all of a sudden he builds a hotel. You can't help feeling sorry for him.

PARIS

HERE THE SEA is a protection against asphyxiation, against being buried in the town. Here Paris seems a blunder, the kind of city that shouldn't be allowed to exist. Paris is where you find the market in death, the market in sex and drugs. It's there that old ladies get murdered. It's there that people set fire to immigrants' hostels – six in two years. It's there that there's a special race of motorists who don't know how to behave, who are coarse and insulting and use their cars to kill with. The *nouveaux riches* of the financial world, the managing directors of death, zooming about in Volvos and BMWs. They used to be the sort of cars that stood for elegance in other things as well – elegant shoes and perfume, elegant voices with a courteous word for everyone. Snobbery, but in a discreet form. Now you wouldn't want to buy that sort of car any more. Paris has become a kind of medina. You get lost in it. An ideal place for protecting, covering up and absorbing crime – a monster molecule made up of twelve million inhabitants. A crime like the murder of Georges Besse the other day is unimaginable anywhere but in Paris, inside the protecting walls of human concrete. Its disorder has become its ramparts. Disorder sets its seals on the suburbs one concentric circle after another. It's all happened in twenty years. The disorder is crossed and served by networks of motorways which lead to the international airports. There aren't any road maps for the suburbs any more; it's impossible to keep up to date with any but the main arteries. The wooded areas in and around Paris have a bad reputation. The Bois de Boulogne belongs to prostitutes and the police at night, and in the daytime to drug dealers. So what's left for us 'respectable' people? It's in Paris that foreigners come off the worst. The food is worse there than anywhere else in France. The 6th arrondissement, a ravishingly beautiful centre of French culture visited by intellectuals from all over the world, is notorious as one of the places where it's hardest to find a good restaurant. The food in most of them, as in all tourist haunts, is mass-produced; the two or three exceptions include the Brasserie Lipp and Le Petit Saint-Benôit. Don't let's even speak of the Asian restaurants and their moggy pâté. The poor little Asian cats! Paris is also the place with the most dogs, but that doesn't matter, seeing we don't eat *them*. Something has happened to this city. What? Is it the motorcar? I'm inclined to think so. Or else it's that slacking at school has been carried over into real life long enough to affect several generations. Perhaps through neglecting their studies people got to understand less and less, until finally they didn't understand anything at all. And afterwards they didn't know how to live. And then they ran away. We didn't believe in school, at any level. We behaved badly. We forgot all we'd learned, all our politeness, all our subtlety, all our wit. And all that's left is business know-how.

About ten years ago the suburbs of Paris had twelve million inhabitants. It's a long time now since I saw any official figures. Perhaps they've lost count of the number of people who live there. Perhaps it's a floating population that lives in hiding places rather than homes. What with drugs and robbery and terrorism, the suburbs must support about as many people as a provincial town. The largest section consists of people without any occupation, without work or home, family or papers; no one will take responsibility for them for fear of their past; they're abandoned, lost, like the street children in Mexico. All the food they get is what they can steal from supermarkets. The only way they can get clothes or shoes is by theft. The only way they can get a coffee or a cigarette is from one another. They've already developed a mixed colour from never mind what racial ingredients. Frizzy black curls, black

eyes. They're tall and handsome, and they'll be the front run-
ners in the unemployment crises foretold in *Green Eyes*. There
they are. Stagnating. Doing nothing. Except be alive. And
watch. You can see them hanging about in the television
stores, the métros, the railway stations and the shopping malls
of Créteil-Soleil.

Paris can't move any more, can't expand at a normal rate. And
it has lost the significance it once had. But people still come
here in the hope of getting closer to meaning, to what they
expect to find in a capital city, which is made up of the essence
of every kind of knowledge, from the arts of building, writing
and painting to that of politics. If you ask someone who lives
in the suburbs he'll say: 'I used to live in Chartres or Rambouillet, but in the end I got bored and came to Paris to be nearer.'
Just for that. But he can't say nearer to what. Yet this inability,
which is usually permanent, is perhaps what really gets closest
to the meaning of life, in every sense of the word. People come
to Paris, to the capital, to give their lives a sense of belonging,
of an almost mythical participation in society. Once outside
the northern gates of Paris you come to the windswept settle-
ments that stretch from Saint-Denis to La Courneuve and on
to Sarcelles. To the south, thanks to the miraculous enclave
formed by the Château of Versailles, you reach the fields
sooner – the forests, the byeways, the village squares. But the
real meaning of it all, the most important, is Paris.

No one can ever describe the beauty of Paris all the year round
– from Sundays in summer to winter nights when the streets
become primitive again, like roads. No other city in the world
is constructed like Paris, with its incredible wealth of open
spaces. Part of it rivals Versailles in the number of its great public buildings. It's in summer that the river emerges in all its
beauty, with its shady trees, its gardens, the great avenues lin-
ing or radiating from it, the gentle slopes overlooking it on all

sides, from the Etoile and from Montparnasse, Montmartre and Belleville. The only flat parts are around Concorde and the Louvre, and on the islands.

THE RED SOFA

I MOVED INTO this apartment in April 1942 and it's now February 1987, so I shall soon have lived here for forty-five years. In that time I've slept in three out of the five rooms. When my son was small I let him have what is now my bedroom so that he'd have more space. Once, in the bedroom overlooking the courtyard – the room where we kept coal when it was rationed during the war – I made a discovery. In broad daylight, though. And I was alone. It was inside a cupboard built directly on to the wooden floor. The strips of wood were coming apart, so I pushed them back together, but one of them wouldn't lie flat, and underneath I found some real tortoise-shell hairpins and a hand-made louse-comb of chalk-white bone. The teeth of the comb were as fine as linen threads, and at the base of some of them were tiny shadows – nits, perhaps, or lice, that had got caught. Apart from that, nothing. The apartment has stayed the same as when I first rented it, standing here stable and unchanging in the rue Saint-Benôit. But it did change once in all these years – one fortnight after my drying-out treatment. It seemed to me it had twisted round on a central axis. The windows had moved, and the walls went in different directions. It was no longer quite the same apartment, or rather it was the same apartment only turned round on itself. But the strangest thing about it was the logic, the mathematical rigour of the shift. All the windows and doors had moved through just the number of degrees necessary for everything to remain the same in itself but different in relation to the central axis. Not one detail had moved too much or too little. Nothing had been forgotten or left out; the change had been carried out with the accuracy of an architect's drawing. Even the right angle where the bathroom walls meet had become slightly acute. The same thing was repeated exactly outside. All that I could see out of the windows overlooking the courtyard was similarly displaced. But it was difficult to see everything. There were balconies now along the roofs.

There were some new pieces of furniture too – some that I'd known years ago and thought I'd forgotten, and others I'd never seen before. There were also some people I'd never seen before – the people who'd bought my apartment. They were merchants from Judaea dressed in gallabiyas, and they were sitting on a red sofa which really had existed in the past. But now it was in the wrong place, in front of my bedroom fireplace, waiting, as I believed, to be moved to a better position. I had to find out what that position was.

These things didn't all disappear in one night. The first one to go was the red sofa. It belonged to a friend of mine, Georgette de Cormis, who'd left it with me to look after during the war. She lived in Aix-en-Provence, and had taken it back again some time between 1950 and 1955.

THE ROUND STONES

ONE DAY I found a round stone with some straight grooves marked on it – a triangle with a line through. It had been left on top of the dustbin by some Portuguese workmen who'd come to repair the walls of the cellar. I found out afterwards that they'd put it there purposely in case anyone might be interested in it. I carried it up and put it on my kitchen table, then went downstairs again because I thought I'd seen another one. And sure enough there was another round stone, with more definite marks this time: it had a hole through the middle and a notch on one side, both obviously made by hand. Parallel to the notch was a grooved slot, probably to take a now vanished wooden tongue. The first stone was in its original form except for a small patch that had been polished to take the signature. The second had been completely reshaped. It fitted exactly over the other stone, and then they would both revolve. I sat looking at them all night. They were from the cellars of the abbey of Saint-Laurent, which used to stretch down as far as the banks of the Seine. One day I showed them to Michel Leiris, but he didn't know what they could have been for either. He thought they might have been for crushing grain or fruit to extract oil; the oil would have run out through the opening at the side. But it wasn't certain. I remembered the plague, and washed them, to be on the safe side.

THE CHEST OF DRAWERS

IT WAS A rustic Louis Quinze chest of drawers I'd got from an antique shop in the 6th arrondissement – I must have been about thirty-five or forty at the time, and I probably bought it with the money I got for *The Sea Wall*. I'd had it for about ten years or so when one night I was tidying my things, as lots of women do, and for some reason I don't remember now I took the middle drawer out and put it on the floor. And a piece of material that had been caught between the drawer and the back of the commode fell out of the shadows. It was a slightly yellowish white, but bright, crumpled like a screwed-up piece of paper, and flecked with pale pink stains. It was a caraco, a woman's loose under-blouse, gathered at the neck and with a narrow lace trimming round the edge. It was made of lawn. It had been there since the days of the chest of drawers' first owners. No one had ever taken the drawers out, even when moving house. '1720,' I said aloud. The pink marks were like those made by the light-coloured blood of the last days of menstruation. The caraco must have been put away after it had been washed: it was spotlessly clean apart from the marks, which would only come out in the big annual wash. The pink of the marks was the colour blood leaves on cloth after it has been rinsed. The caraco itself had taken on the smell of polished wood. The drawer must have been too full, and the under-blouse, on top, must have got caught and dragged by the drawer above until it disappeared down the back of the commode. And there it stayed for two hundred years. It was covered with months and years of darns – with darns which had been darned themselves, as beautiful as embroidery. The first thing you think when you realize what it is, is: 'She must have hunted for it all over the place.' For days and nights. She couldn't think where it could have got to.

WASTING TIME

IT'S VERY mysterious, what a woman does with her time at the distance I am from my youth. It's very frightening as well. Your own case is always the worst. Life is only lived full-time by women with children. Children give them certainty. They're overwhelmed by the demands children make – their bodies, their beauty, the care you have to lavish on them, the undivided love each one of them requires and without which they die. Women with their children is the only thing you can look at without feeling depressed. Apart from that, at the distance I am from you, just as at the distance you all are from one another, all lives seem completely meaningless and without *raison d'être*. Every life is an insoluble problem. All the people piled up on top of one another in blocks of flats – you ask yourself how it's possible, and yet you're one of the layers.

The best way to fill time is to waste it.

It's not so painful even to contemplate all the young people hanging around outside churches and public places, in TV stores or around the Forum des Halles, waiting for something to happen, as it is to look at the workers, piled up in layers in the giant housing schemes on the outskirts of Paris, woken up by the alarm on a winter's morning while it's still dark. To go to work just so as to stay alive.

THE CHIMNEYS OF *INDIA SONG*

ONE DAY, if I live to be very old, I'll stop writing. And no doubt it will seem to me unreal, impossible, absurd.

One day I thought it had happened – that I'd never write again. It was during that drying-out treatment. I remember it well. It was in the American Hospital. I was standing at the window, leaning on Yann's arm. I was looking at the red roofs opposite, and at the fair-haired woman with blue eyes who was sticking up out of the chimney. Her husband, the captain in *India Song*, was looking distractedly at the sky. He was emerging from another chimney. Suddenly I started to cry. It was quite clear to me: as I told Yann, I'd probably never write anything any more. It was all over. I really believed it, and I can still remember the terrible grief I felt. But it didn't get rid of the apparitions in the chimneys. They just watched me grieving.

When I came home from the American Hospital I tried straight away to write something in my engagement book. Physically, I mean – I just tried to hold the pen and write. At first I couldn't form the letters, and then it all came back. But where did this new, temporary writing come from? It was like the hole underneath the house when they heightened the step. It was the writing of a five-year-old child – irregular, smudged. Like the writing of a criminal, why not.

I'd like to write a book the way I'm writing at this moment, the way I'm talking to you at this moment. I'm scarcely conscious of the words coming out of me. Nothing seems to be being said but the almost nothing there is in all words.

You never know, in life, when things are there. You can't grasp them. You were saying the other day that life often seems as if it were dubbed. That's exactly what I feel: my life is a film that's been dubbed – badly cut, badly acted, badly put together. In short, a mistake. A whodunnit without either murders or cops or victims; without a subject; pointless. It could have been a real film, but no, it's a sham. But who's to say what one would have had to do for it to be otherwise? I suppose I should have just stood there in front of the camera without saying or doing anything; just being looked at, without thinking about anything in particular. Yes, that's it.

It's only late in life that you start drawing conclusions from your experience. You'll see. I mean, that you dare to say or write them. So it's afterwards you realize that the feeling of happiness you had with a man didn't necessarily prove that you loved him. Now I find evidence of love in memories less strong and less articulate. It was the men I deceived the most that I loved the most.

There's a comedy of love that sometimes – often – perhaps usually – applies to every couple. I've changed my mind about this, too. A great deal. Most people stay together because together they're not so frightened. Or because it's easier to live on two salaries than on one. Or because of the children. Or for lots of other reasons that they never really go into but which show that a choice has been made, even if it's an irrational one, and a definite position taken up, even if it's difficult or impossible to put into words. 'You couldn't understand,' they say. Or, 'I don't know myself what makes me stay, but I can't do anything else.' These aren't people who love one another, but it is love that's between them just the same. Loving someone for this reason or that, out of practical considerations or convenience, is still love. People don't usually talk about it – they may not even be aware of it – but it is love. It's the kind of love that's revealed by death. Sometimes one's horrified by certain couples: the man's brutish and coarse, and the woman tells anyone who cares to listen that she's going through hell. But one can be wrong about such people. Theirs is a kind of play-acting love, but it's often a mistake to think it has nothing to do with the real thing. When Bernard Pivot asked me what made me stay with the Chinese lover, I said: 'Money.' But I might also have said it was the fabulous luxury of the car, which was more like a salon. The chauffeur. Having the car and the chauffeur at my disposal. The sexual smell of the silk tussore, and of his, the lover's, skin. They conditioned me to love, if you like. I really started to love him after I'd left him, probably just when I heard of the suicide of the young man who was lost at sea. I must have found out then, in the middle of the voyage. I think love always goes with love: you can't just love by yourself – I don't believe in that. I don't believe in hopeless love affairs concerning only one person. He loved me so much I had to love him; he desired me so much I had to desire him. But it's not possible to love someone who doesn't see anything attractive in you at all, who finds you completely boring. I don't believe in that, either.

THE VOICE IN *NAVIRE NIGHT*

IN *Navire Night* it's the voice that acts, that produces desire and emotion. The voice is stronger than physical presence. It's as important as the face, the eyes, the smile. A real letter is moving because it's spoken, written with the spoken voice. I get letters that make me fall in love with the people who wrote them. But of course one can't reply.

I did reply to Yann. I began by seeing him, when *India Song* was shown in Caen. A group of us went to a café afterwards. At first, to Yann, I was the person who'd written *India Song*, who'd made Anne-Marie Stretter speak about the boredom in India. Michael Richardson, Lol V. Stein, the beggar woman – to begin with I was all these people to Yann, and it was because of them that he came to Trouville. After he began reading the books he'd come under a sort of spell and written to me. As in the other cases, I hadn't replied. And then one day I did. I remember that day very clearly. The only thing I wanted to do was to write to the young student I'd met in Caen and tell him how difficult I was finding it to go on living. I told him I drank a lot, that I'd been in hospital because of it, and that I didn't know why I drank so much.

It happened in January 1980. I was seventy. You, Jérôme Beaujour, were there when it happened. I had very high blood pressure and had been prescribed anti-depressants, but I hadn't told the doctor I was an alcoholic. As a result I had several blackouts a day for three days. I was taken to hospital in Saint-Germain-en-Laye in the middle of the night. And so on. It was after I came out that I wrote to Yann, a man I didn't know, because of the letters he'd written to me. I've kept them; they're wonderful. And then one day, seven months later, he phoned and asked if he could come. It was summer. Just listening to the sound of his voice I knew it was madness. But I told him to come. He left his home and his job. And he stayed. That was six years ago now.

EATING AT NIGHT

I BUY HIM cheese and yoghourt and butter in Trouville, because when he comes in late at night he devours that sort of thing. And he buys me the things I like best – buns and fruit. He buys them not so much to give me pleasure as to feed me up. He has this childlike idea of making me eat so that I don't die. He doesn't want me to die. But he doesn't want me to get fat either. It's hard to reconcile the two. I don't want to die, either. That's what our affection is like; our love. In the evening and at night, talking, we sometimes throw caution to the winds. In these conversations we tell the truth however terrible, and we laugh as we used to do when we still drank and could only talk to one another in the afternoon.

OCTOBER 1982

INSTEAD OF drinking coffee when I woke up, during the last few months I started straight away on whisky or wine. I was often sick after the wine – the pituitary vomiting typical of alcoholics. I'd vomit the wine I'd just drunk, and start drinking some more right away. Usually the vomiting stopped after the second try, and I'd be glad. Yann used to drink in the morning too, but less than me, I think. No, he didn't drink as much as I did.

He drank the evening he came to Trouville in August 1980, and he went on drinking until I went into the American Hospital. He'd put on weight too. I don't know why he drank with me; at the same time as I did. I don't think he saw I was dying. I seem to remember it was someone else who told him – Michèle Manceau, perhaps: 'You don't see it, but she's dying.'

She called in a friend of hers, a Jew from Moldavia – love and greetings, Daniel – but I think some time still went by after that. He wanted me to make my own decision and state it quite clearly.

Every day Yann asked me to fix the date, and one day I did. I said: 'October.' The beginning of October 1982.

They phoned and booked a room.

It still frightens me to write the words: October, the beginning of October.

Daniel had warned me. He'd said: 'I must tell you – it'll be very tough. But you have no choice. You'll never lick this on your own, you know.' I knew.

So I'd been warned the cure would be tough. But I really had nothing to judge by, as I realize now. If you could know in advance what the American cure called 'cold turkey' is really like, you could never bring yourself to undergo it, you'd never coolly choose a date for it. No, you'd run away.

It was when we were in the taxi and I saw Daniel hurry away, weeping, that I realized I'd let myself in for something from which there was no turning back. I'd drunk a lot that day. It had all been rather vague up till then, and I'd laughed at the others for their apprehensions. But there in the taxi I could see Yann's fear growing and becoming tense and terrible. My legs had suddenly swelled up too, and that had frightened us, though we didn't know why.

At eight o'clock in the evening I found myself alone in a room in the American Hospital. They'd asked Yann not to stay. I'm writing very fast – I'm sorry. I don't know if you can follow the order of events. Never mind.

There's one thing that has stayed with me, the most important one – the fear of doing it again. The cure, I mean. I know it only hangs by a hair – one sip of alcohol, a sweet flavoured with rum. Just before Yann came to Trouville I'd noticed in passing, not thinking anything of it, that there was still a drop of vermouth left in a bottle in the hall cupboard which I'd thought was empty. I thought about it a couple of days later, and then every evening of every day for a week or ten days. And then I drank it. After that Yann came and I told him to buy some wine; and that was it. That was the third time I'd started again. Now I'm in my third non-drinking period. As I've already told you.

The evening I went into the American Hospital I was relying on pills to make me sleep, but at four o'clock in the morning I was still awake. And suddenly I thought, There isn't any drink in the room. And I was frightened. I hastily thought of a plan to forestall the coma I knew was inevitable: I'd phone for a taxi and go to the Porte Maillot, ask the taxi to wait while I bought a bottle of red wine in a bar, and bring it back to the hospital without anyone being any the wiser. I got up and dressed quietly. Then suddenly there stood a nurse, who'd come in without my hearing her. I shouted at her: 'You know I could fall into a coma!' She said: 'But there's some wine here, Madame. I'll give you a glass.' They'd expected this to happen. That was my last drink. October 1982.

You must always see to it that you don't have anything dangerous within reach. I know the least thing could start me off again.

A DANGEROUS STATE

AT PRESENT I blame myself for writing: it's always like this after I've finished a book. And if it means falling into my present state afterwards, writing isn't worth the candle. If I can't do it without being in danger of drinking again, it's just not worth while. That's what I say to myself sometimes, as if I could help it. That's a dangerous state too.

Don't take any notice of what I said the last time about the cure. One could start again, cure or no cure. This evening. Just like that. For no other reason than that one's an alcoholic.

LETTERS

I MYSELF wrote letters once, as Yann did to me – for two years, to someone I'd never met. Then Yann came. He took the place of the letters. It's impossible to do without love altogether. Even if words are all that's left, it's still real. The worst is not to love at all. I don't think that's possible.

THE PEOPLE OF THE NIGHT

I HANDED *The Lover* in to the Editions de Minuit in June 1984. Then I made the film, then I cut it, and then I wrote *The War.* Then I fell ill. The day *The War* came out, I was in hospital. Yann brought me the article by Poirot-Delpech, but I was on artificial respiration. Again I was out of my mind for a week; as also in April 1985. I nearly killed a young nurse. The whole scenario was very clear. On the one hand that evening there was Yann, who'd gone home and to whom I'd given my rings. On the other hand there was a young night nurse, who'd advised me to give the rings to Yann so that they wouldn't get stolen. I'd told her I'd taken her advice, and that Yann had taken the rings back to my place, where he lived. At midnight the nurse, who was supposed to come in and see to me, still hadn't come. I waited for her till three or four in the morning. And then madness struck, with the irrefutable explanation: the nurse, with some of her so-called colleagues, had gone to the rue Saint-Benôit to kill Yann and take my rings.

When it got light I opened the window of my room and shouted out that I was going to be murdered and someone must come. Nothing happened, though I was told later that people had heard me. I yelled again. Implored. Nothing.

In the morning, when the nurse came back, I was hiding under a sheet with a knife I'd brought from home. She shouted for help. I shouted again too – I said my life was in danger, I was being murdered. A nursing auxiliary came. He was horrified. He leapt on me and took away the knife – wounding me in the process.

I think that was how I 'knew' I'd been kidnapped by the so-called 'doctors' at the hospital. For hours, apparently, I kept telling them how they could get a ransom. I told them whom to phone and how much to ask. I suggested quite a low figure. About what I thought I was worth on the murder market.

I've forgotten all those ravings, but what impresses me still is the logic, the cogency of the argument about the murder and the rings. It was so obvious that I was convinced it must be true.

This is what happens when you have a bad attack of emphysema: your brain doesn't get enough oxygen and your mind goes. The week before me they'd had a young man who refereed an imaginary football match for a whole afternoon. Then they put him on an oxygen machine and it was all over. The doctors found this sort of thing very amusing. But it still terrifies me. It's frightening when people tell you about things you've said or done that you don't remember. I remember practically nothing about the alcoholic delusions I had during the cure. I was in a kind of coma when I had them, and I only emerged occasionally, for a few seconds. On the other hand I can remember quite clearly the things I saw after the cure. They started while I was still in the American Hospital.

India Song had become a boat. I've told you this before, but never mind. The captain's wife lived on the roof opposite, sticking up out of a funnel or chimney. She was fair and pink, with blue eyes. Only her head emerged from the funnel. The captain was a couple of yards away in the same position as his wife: stuck in a funnel or chimney. One day it was very windy, and the wife's head shattered as if it had been made of glass. I was scandalized. *Exactly* ten thousand tortoises were arranged round the roof like books on shelves. When it got dark they went back under the eaves. All these images were brighter than reality, as if lit up from within. It took the tortoises several hours to huddle together and settle down for the night. I was shocked that nature should be so inefficient. They took so long to sort themselves out that a lot of them just had to stay where they were.

Among these 'memories' there's a kind of Asian mandarin all dressed up in blue and gold brocade. He used to roam about the hospital corridors, impassive, taciturn, and very frightening. I'm not sure if it was at Laennec or the American Hospital. No one else seemed to see him. Perhaps he didn't exist. In the American Hospital I could see Michael Richardson through the closed, uncurtained windows of the house in *India Song*. He was surrounded by plants and creepers. He smiled and wept at the same time, imprisoned in the story. Very handsome. The famous black Abyssinian cow, all skin and bones, was leaning against the wall by the front door. Beside her stood a big red and gold chair. Both were like the sort of thing you see chucked out and abandoned on the pavement in Neuilly. And some evenings Michael Lonsdale would be there, sitting in a corner dressed as a Bedouin and smiling at me.

After I'd gone home the most amazing delusions used to occur at night. The sound of singing, solo and in chorus, would rise up from the inner courtyard under my windows. And when I looked out I would see crowds of people who I was sure had come to save me from death. Some of them carried pikes with shrivelled heads on top. They talked about someone, a child apparently, whom they referred to as 'little Gauthier'. I remember someone on the stairs in the middle of the night, calling out softly and with unforgettable tenderness: 'If they hurt little Gauthier I shall die.'

There were a number of us living in the apartment then. In the bathroom there was a woman behind the toilet, holding a dead child wrapped up in white bandages. She was there so patently that in the end I stopped taking any notice. There were men too, five of them, who used to come into Yann's room at night. These were *real* men, who walked and talked. Their bodies were stuffed with crumpled newspaper. There were animals under my table, and the famous dwarfs with pig's tails, that we called 'lamias'. There was also a bust of a woman in painted terracotta – the French Republic – on a little shelf by my desk.

Above all there was the terrifying man who lived near Yann's room and spied on me. I was deafened all the time by telephone calls. I'd discovered that the exchange was in a maid's room, used by my enemies, on the sixth floor on the other side of the courtyard. My neighbour opposite had stolen my line. I knew it and I could prove it. The ringings formed a circle round my bedroom, and that didn't seem normal. But strangest of all were the scenes that took place every day inside the apartment. The dead dog hung up behind my radiator, for example. Though I wasn't sure if it wasn't at the same time a bird. A blue duck. I was under the impression I didn't sleep for days. But I didn't feel tired. In a way I never woke up.

It started with rats and other animals. The place was suddenly overrun with them in the middle of one night. Yann heard the commotion: I had my shoes on and was chasing the rats with an umbrella. That's how it began. Oh, and I was forgetting – all this went on to the accompaniment of music from Wagner's operas. And yelling from the German police. And then there were the things Yann described in *M.D.* – the scenes where the Jews were being shot outside my windows. And then there were the Black women in the sitting room . . . But I can't catalogue the whole horde of them. To give you a general idea: while the Jews and the Blacks were voluntarily swearing allegiance to the Nazis in the sitting room, my Moldavian doctor's friends were sitting in my bedroom on the red sofa – it hadn't been there the day before – preparing to buy the apartment, which the doctor himself must therefore have stolen. All day long, in the middle of this chaos, cats that only I could see prowled back and forth through the flat.

Reality returned quite suddenly. I can remember clearly a purée flavoured with nutmeg that Michèle Manceau had made for me. I devoured it. It was after that that the intruders gradually went away. The German police left the neighbouring balconies; the paper men disappeared from Yann's room. The man in my son's room was still there – the one with curly grey hair, a floury white face and staring wild blue eyes. There were a few cats left too. I think the last to go was Marianne – perhaps the most incredible and ridiculous thing of all, with her Lorraine cap. A shameful, patriotic object – God knows what she thought she was doing on the little shelf in my bedroom. Except that a week ago – we're now the beginning of April 1987 – I saw the same bust of Marianne in an apartment in the rue Bonaparte which overlooks the same courtyard as we do. I thought I'd never seen the bust before. But I recognized it as the one in the hallucination. It was now standing on a mantelpiece, and framed by an open window. The doctor said I'd remember everything in time. He said all the things in my delirium were real memories, things I'd seen or experienced. But so far I've traced only one. Sometimes, at night, I'm still afraid they might come back. It's impossible to imagine that you can see something when there's nothing there. But you can – right down to reality's last detail. The colour of someone's eyes, their hair, their skin. I recognized music by Wagner that I didn't even know. I told Yann, 'If this goes on for a couple of weeks I'll kill myself, I shan't be able to help it.' But why was it so unbearable? So unbearable that as the days went by it took away every reason for going on living? I think it must be because you're the only person who sees what you see, and all you're used to is being the only one who thinks what you think. Suddenly your brain lights up and becomes visible. You can see your own thoughts written up in large letters on a screen. But you know no one believes you. Even about the cats, which I tried to smuggle through by referring to them as if their presence was quite natural. And then you realize that it's soon going to be unbearable for the people who love you, and that they're going to have to part from you. The doctor had said I needed to have a lot of people around me all the time, people I didn't know too. But sooner or later I always had to go back alone into my room, to switch on the light and find the animals had got there again before me, the little pigs under the table and Marianne on the bookshelf. The doctor hadn't prescribed any tranquillizers; I found that rather strange, and so did my friends. All those creatures were supposed to leave me of their own accord. Not only were they not being kept out – they weren't even being urged to go.

I forgot to tell you that when I asked Yann to take the dead dog, the one the Nazis had killed, down from behind the radiator, I told him to throw it down hard out of the window on to the passers-by, so that they'd know some Jews had been murdered. I listened to what he was doing. It didn't seem to have taken him very long to unhook the dog and throw it out of the window, but that didn't make me doubt that the dead dog was real. What did make me doubt was Michèle Porte, one day. I was in the kitchen and she hung her coat up as she came in. We chatted for a while, and I told her about how I'd been seeing things. She listened, but didn't say anything. I said, 'I believe in them myself, but I can't convince anyone else.' Then I said, 'Turn round and look at your right-hand coat pocket. Do you see the little new-born puppy crawling out of it, all pink? Well, the others say I'm wrong and it's not really there.' She had a good look, then turned back to me. She gazed at me for some time, then said quite seriously, without a trace of a smile: 'Marguerite, I swear to you by all I hold dear that I don't see anything.' But she didn't say it wasn't there; she only said she couldn't see it. Perhaps that incident shows that even in madness there's a certain amount of reason.

And then one night I called Yann to throw out the man with the curly hair and the talcum-powdered face, who was now in the hall, only a couple of yards from my room. I heard a furious yell and then along came Yann, beside himself with anger and fatigue. Every night I was attacked by the 'people' lurking in the apartment and woke him up. 'Get it into your head that I can't see anything,' he yelled. 'Do you hear?

There's nothing there! Nothing! Nothing!' I hid behind my bedroom door, because while Yann was yelling I'd seen the man with curly hair come up beside him, and I implored Yann to send him away. Then Yann didn't say any more.

The man – he was wearing a black overcoat – didn't understand what was going on. He moved a few steps closer to Yann. Then stopped. He was looking at me all the time. It was me he was interested in – and so passionately that it turned him absolutely and horribly pale. He looked at me with a kind of pained indignation: how was it *I* didn't look at *him*, but only wept and tried to get away from him? He didn't understand how I didn't understand what he wanted. It was as if he were someone I ought to recognize, but didn't. Even as I write this, three years later, I'm still worried about him. Either he wanted to take me away somewhere, not necessarily to death. Or else he was there to remind me of some immemorial connection which had been severed, but which had been my *raison d'être* ever since I was born. He was either a Jew or my father. Or something else. Someone else, indefinitely. But he himself was definite enough. He'd been here for a fortnight without changing. He lived here. For the last fortnight he'd been living in the little room overlooking the street. He had small very blue eyes, and very curly hair partly black and partly white, from another world, from another age. Yes, he knew something about me that I couldn't know. Not something I'd forgotten – something I ought to know. He was there then, mingled with the other apparitions, but central to them all. It was around him, the master apparition, that the other apparitions turned. And turned around my life. He didn't understand why I was afraid of him. He could see I was afraid, but he didn't know it was him I was afraid of; he didn't know what it was. I went on shouting at Yann to send him away, send him away. Then I discovered something terrible: he didn't understand French. He didn't understand what I was saying to Yann. His lips were slightly mauve, and sealed. He never spoke; he hadn't said a word for a fortnight. He must have thought he didn't have to tell me why he'd been there all those days and nights. He must have thought I knew why he was waiting for me. If I didn't understand it was because I didn't want to. He thought it was impossible for me not to know. But I couldn't know. The look in his eyes was frank and open right to the end: I must understand. But I couldn't.

Yann went to the front door. I went back into my room so as not to see. He opened the front door and then shut it again. He said, 'You can come out – he's gone.' And he had gone. Yann put his arms round me, and I wept for a long time.

I've never told anyone about this until now. It's as if something happened between that vision and me, something that lasted only a few seconds but was like the beginning of a shared knowledge. I can remember quite clearly the remote feeling of guilt that came to me after he'd gone, when Yann and I were alone again. As if I ought to have spoken to him. Ought to have explained that I couldn't act any differently because I didn't understand what he wanted of me.

This book is set in BEMBO which was cut
by the punch-cutter Francesco Griffo
for the Venetian printer-publisher
Aldus Manutius in early 1495
and first used in a pamphlet
by a young scholar
named Pietro
Bembo.